DAVID ISAAK

Shock and Awe

PAN BOOKS

First published 2007 by Macmillan New Writing

This edition published 2008 by Pan Books
an imprint of Pan Macmillan Ltd
Pan Macmillan, 20 New Wharf Road, London N1 9RR
Basingstoke and Oxford
Associated companies throughout the world
www.panmacmillan.com

ISBN 978-0-230-70004-8

3 5 7 9 8 6 4 2

A CIP catalogue record for this book is available
from the British Library.

Typeset by Intype Libra Ltd, London
Printed and bound in the UK by
CPI Mackays, Chatham ME5 8TD

Visit www.panmacmillan.com to read more about all our books
and to buy them. You will also find features, author interviews and
news of any author events, and you can sign up for e-newsletters
so that you're always first to hear about our new releases.

Shock and Awe

David Isaak holds a BSc in physics and a PhD in resource systems, and has worked as an energy consultant in more than thirty countries, including many Middle Eastern nations. He lives in Huntington Beach, California.

For Pamela Blake

And Moses and Aaron did so, as the Lord commanded, and he lifted up the rod and smote the waters that were in the river, in the sight of Pharaoh, and in the sight of his servants, and all the waters that were in the river were turned to blood.

– *Exodus* 7:20

The blood-dimmed tide is loosed, and everywhere
The ceremony of innocence is drowned;
The best lack all conviction, while the worst
Are full of passionate intensity.

– *W. B. Yeats, 'The Second Coming'*

I

Carla

Phil ran a classy place – the cleanest, most spacious porn shop in downtown Portland, Oregon – but you didn't see many unaccompanied ladies there, so when the woman pushed through the frosted-glass door, jangling the overhead bell, he stood up behind the register and put on what he hoped was an open, non-judgemental expression, the face you'd want your doctor to wear.

She was bundled into a massive Gore-Tex jacket with the hood pulled up, as though she'd come in from mushing huskies rather than a wet Northwest evening. He didn't get a clear glimpse of her shadowed features before she turned and shambled across the store. In the middle of the shop she paused at the Valentine's Day display of lingerie, the dangling scraps of red and pink lace insubstantial as mist beside her shapeless olive-green coat.

There'd been a time, a brief time, back in the early 1990s, when as many women as men had visited the shop, the ladies usually arriving in giddy twos and threes. They seldom bought anything on the first visit, but they'd slip back to the store a day or two later, solo, and snap up the goodies they'd been embarrassed to buy in front of their friends. He'd liked it, women in the place; it made the whole enterprise feel happier, goofier, less, well, *dirty* . . . but the Internet had put an end to all that. Sure, women were buying more sex toys and more porn, if you could believe the surveys, but they were doing it on the sly with a click and a credit-card number, delivery in UPS brown; which left Phil with the raincoat crowd, and squirrels like the trio of frat boys who were sniggering their way through the video section in the front of the store.

He settled back onto the high stool behind the counter and picked up his book of crossword puzzles.

The woman was across the room now, her back to him, studying the wall that displayed vibrators and dildos in all their latex and glitter-jelly glory. She tossed back her hood and he saw short blonde hair. Short, but not dykey-short.

Phil was chewing his lip over the clue *Source of Nobel's fortune* when a burst of strangled laughter from the guys in the video section jerked his head upright.

All three were talking in loud whispers, looking towards the woman in the rear of the store. The biggest guy, the one with the mullet haircut – a mullet, for Chrissakes – said, 'Psst! Wanna save some money?' His friends giggled.

The woman ignored them, but Phil slid off the stool and onto his feet. 'Hey.'

Only one of the trio, a boy in an orange windbreaker, looked over at him. 'Cool it, Jake,' the kid said to the guy in the mullet.

'Yo.' Jake leaned back, still watching the woman, and

clasped his hand over his crotch, hefting. 'Yo, *Eskimo Pie*. Got the real thing here, no batteries required . . .'

The woman turned and looked over at the boys. Something about her stance made Phil stare. She hadn't recoiled, hadn't backed away; she stood with her legs braced, her face hidden from him by the thrown-back hood.

After a long moment she went back to her browsing, and one of the boys giggled again.

Phil roused himself and slapped the counter. 'Hey, goddammit!' This time the whole trio looked at him. 'Out.' He gestured at the door with his thumb. 'Now.'

Jake swayed, and Phil realized the boy was drunk. 'Look, man,' Jake said, 'it's a free country . . .' He started towards the counter. Another boy, the one in camo fatigues, put a restraining hand on his arm, but Jake shook it off and kept coming. 'Why doncha mind your own fuckin' business, huh?'

Phil held up the receiver of the phone. 'See the phone?' He held up his other hand, index finger raised. 'See the finger? Want to see it dial 9–1–1?'

'Wanta see that phone shoved up your ass?' Jake stumbled into a rack of discount videos, but kept coming, his fists shaking.

Phil dropped the receiver into its cradle and hoisted the twelve-gauge from beneath the counter. 'Want a couple pounds of lead up *your* ass?' He didn't point it, just held it in one hand like a sceptre, letting the boys see it. He tilted his head at the door. 'Out.'

Jake raised his hands, palms forward and even with his shoulders, somewhere between *slow down* and *I surrender*, but he didn't move until his pals crossed the room and led

3

him out the front door. As he stepped out into the night his courage revived enough for him to kick the doorframe and shout, 'And fuck you, man!' over his shoulder.

The bell ding-a-linged as the door shut.

The woman had gone back to her browsing. 'I'm really sorry about that,' Phil said. She shrugged without turning. 'Seriously. We're –' he searched for words, '– grateful for your business.' Grateful for your business. Christ. What a putz he was.

He sat down, realized he was still holding the shotgun, and stowed it back under the counter. It wasn't until he let loose of the gun that his hands started trembling, and for some reason it seemed that the thing to do was sit on them, palms down on the stool, the pressure of his weight strangely calming.

He sat like that until the woman headed towards the door. As she passed the counter, he stood again. 'I really do want to apologize . . .'

She stopped and regarded him with an indifferent frown, as though he were an unfamiliar television show: a little puzzling, but not of any real consequence. He guessed she was about thirty; a good face, strong bones, but one with red-rimmed, bloodshot eyes and skin that turned sallow under the shop's fluorescent lights. He smelled the alcohol on her – not the smell on her breath, though that was there, too, but the stale odour that emanates from the pores after a few days of hard drinking.

'We don't—' he began, and swallowed. 'Things like that don't happen here much.' She continued to stare. 'Maybe I

4

should call the police anyway, huh? Or, m̲ ̲ ̲ ̲ ̲ ̲
you a cab?'

It could have turned into a shrug, but she o̲ ̲ ̲ ̲
shoulder forward a half-inch before she turne̲ ̲ ̲ ̲ and
pulled the door open.

Out on the darkened sidewalk Carla tilted her head back,
eyes closed, letting the cold stroke her face. She should have
taken off the jacket when she was inside, but it'd seemed like
too much trouble, and besides, it was so damn bulky she'd
have knocked things over. She straightened up and unzipped
it halfway, shivering with relief as the chilly night air searched
out the perspiration on her blouse.

She checked her watch. A little after 10.30. Maybe time
for one more vodka-tonic before catching the 11.02 bus
across the river to the East Side. She headed north, wishing,
not for the first time, that she still had a car. And, hell, as long
as she was wishing, a licence, too.

The store was well south of Burnside, below the restaurant district, and at night cars passed infrequently, their tyres
making the sound of ripping paper as they rolled by on the
wet asphalt. Typical Portland weather: you had to look at
the puddles to tell whether it was raining or just misting. The
streets, sidewalks and buildings glistened like hard candies
beneath the streetlights.

The slapping sound of footsteps came from a dozen yards
behind her. She glanced back, and saw, without much surprise, the boys from the porn shop. 'Need some company?'
one of them yelled.

She kept walking, but unzipped her jacket and pulled it

5

..anging it over her right shoulder by hooking her thumb .n the hood. A catcall from the rear, and then a voice urging her to take it all off.

Her eyes scanned the sidewalk ahead. No open businesses, and nothing handy in the way of bricks or clubs.

Another voice: 'Guys, this is *not* cool.' She stopped and glanced back. The kid in the orange windbreaker backed away and headed across the empty street, putting distance between himself and the other two.

Jake and the kid in camo stopped for a moment. Then Jake made a gesture of acquiescence, tilting his head and revolving his thumbs outwards – hey, what can I say? – and the two of them turned into an alley on their right and vanished.

She didn't believe it, not for a minute.

Sure, it might be the adrenaline talking, but when adrenaline talked, Carla paid attention.

She shifted the jacket to her left shoulder as she walked, tried to get out of her head and into her body. Too much to drink. One drink, that could actually loosen you up, speed your reflexes, but she'd been knocking them back since, what, noon? She drifted to the left, towards the kerb; if they came back it would have to be from the right, and the main thing with males was to keep them from getting a grip, prevent them from using that unfair upper-body strength.

She reached the corner, glanced around it, crossed the street. Her face was wet from the continual drifting drizzle. Seemed sometimes like she'd been damp her whole life: Oregon, Georgia, and then, when she thought she'd left water behind for a while, even in the Middle East. Who would have thought it: a godforsaken *humid* desert. Jeddah, Dhahran, Bahrain, Abu Dhabi, even stinking Karachi. Wet, but barren.

Arizona. I'm going to move to Arizona. Air so dry your skin cracks.

They stepped out from a building ten feet ahead of her. How the hell had they got there without her seeing them?

Because you're drunk, you silly bitch.

The two boys stood there, hands on their hips, fingers forward, lords of the universe. Girls could put their hands on their hips in either direction, thumbs forward or thumbs back, but there was something wrong with boys, they always did it thumbs back. She kept walking towards them.

A hunnert men and a hunnert women, Jill had said, *take a hunnert men and a hunnert women, and pick the hunnert strongest out of the whole bunch, and you know what you get, girls? Three women and ninety-fucking-seven men. Ninety-fucking-seven.*

Jill slapped her hands down on her hips, thumbs backward, like a boy. *You girls think you're strong? You let him get aholda you and your average outta-shape fat-ass heart-attack banker will wrestle you down and pin you in a fair fight. Never close with a man. Never. Use our secret weapon. And you know what our secret is? Anybody?*

Jolene had piped up from the back row. *We're smarter than they are, Lieutenant.*

Chuckles.

Jill smiled, sweat glistening on her face in the Georgia sunshine, but shook her head. *Since when's that a secret?* Laughter. *Anybody?*

7

Silence.

Killer Jill grinned. *The secret is, we're meaner than they are. Way meaner. So you do this: hurt 'em bad and hurt 'em fast, before they get aholda you.*

Before.

Where was Killer now? Probably a fucking general. And here was Carla, out of shape and out of work and plastered, stumbling down the sidewalks . . .

Jake had said something, but Carla hadn't heard it, and now he was only a few feet away, and he said, *Hey, come on, we've got a room, we'll show you what a real one feels like, no charge for the first thirty minutes,* and he reached out a hand and snatched at her arm and Carla grabbed his thumb with her right hand and torqued with her whole upper body and there was a crack and he screamed, but she twisted harder and the pain hurled him to the ground and as soon as Jake hit the pavement she whipped her jacket over Camo-boy's head.

She booted Jake in the face with her imitation Doc Martens, not combat boots but damn near as heavy, and when Camo-boy finally threw the jacket from his head he left a beautiful opening, his arms upstretched and his neck tilted back, and she punched him in the throat, hard – not a killing blow, well, probably not, but his hands scrabbled at his neck as he choked. She took the time to glance at Jake, who clutched his hands to his bleeding face, before she stomped down hard, her full hundred and thirty pounds, on Camo-boy's instep, which brought him crashing to the sidewalk alongside his pal.

Carla waited, knees slightly bent, poised on the balls of

8

her feet, deciding what to do next, tuning out the sounds the boys were making. Breathe. Don't use energy you don't need. Scan the body. Relax the face. Shake it out of the shoulders and let 'em hang. The perineum, those complex, subtle layers of muscles between the anus and the genitals, let them go, you don't need them.

Unclench. Unclench everywhere. Breathe.

She turned her head away, almost ready to leave, shivering with the post-adrenaline let-down, but looked back. Camo-boy was still fighting for breath. Jake's hands covered his face, his broken thumb out at a cockeyed angle, and he might have been crying.

For a moment she felt a quiver of guilt, as though someone had plucked a tendon in her body like a guitar string; but then she pulled in a breath and thought about what Jake might have done if she were helpless, if he were the one making the decisions.

She shook her head to clear it, centred her balance on her booze-addled left leg. She kicked him in the knee with all the force and precision she could muster, and drove his kneecap out of its socket and up onto his thigh.

Carla was contemplating whether that was enough when the patrol car pulled up.

She worried that Lydia might still be out, but Lyddie picked up on the fourth ring, her voice filled with sleep. 'Yeah?'

'Lydia, it's Carla. I need a favour.'

A long pause. 'What is it this time?'

'I'm downtown. In County. I need to swing bail somehow. It's too late for tonight, but in the morning—'

A deep exhale across the phone line. 'Why didn't you call in the morning, then?'

'Wanted to be sure I got you.' Carla glanced at the deputy waiting stolidly by the door, a big woman whose broad hips were exaggerated by a belt carrying a half-ton of cop crap. 'I—' She stopped. 'Look, they're charging me with Assault –' she heard Lydia's intake of breath and hurried to forestall her, '– wasn't my fault, it wasn't, these guys jumped me, and I have a witness who'll tell 'em how they were hassling me, and probably the DA will just drop the whole thing, but that's what the police have booked me for right now, and—'

'How much, Carla?'

'It's . . . they tell me it's three thousand dollars.' She braced herself for the explosion, but there was a long silence. 'Look, I know I already owe you some back rent, and I know I been fucking up a lot lately—'

'That's not it.' Lydia's voice was mild. 'Hon, short of mortgaging this house, there's no way I can lay my hands on that kind of cash. Can't you go to one of those bail-bond guys or something?'

'They don't have those in Oregon. Besides, what could I give them as collateral?' The after-booze headache announced its arrival in her skull, strolling right in without knocking and making itself at home. 'Lyddie – I'm going to get a job real soon, I really am. I'll pay you back, with interest.'

'You're not getting it, are you? It's not that I don't want to help you, it's that I can't, okay? I can't.' The sounds of a cigarette being lit came across the phone, and Carla pictured smoke rolling out of Lydia's lips as she added, 'And I don't think you're going to get a job anyway. That LRI company that keeps calling—'

'Lyddie, they won't let me take a job as a rent-a-cop.'

'. . . And you just brush 'em off. Is that how you act if you really want a job?'

'Lyddie, it's not a matter of *want*. They can't bond me.'

'Well, the guy who owns that company was by here just before dinner – in person – and he seemed pretty anxious to meet you, and I tell you, he looked like he had serious money. Maybe he'd offer you some other kind of job, something else with his company.'

'Yeah, what? You think I know how to type?' The visiting headache, having spent some time lolling on the couch up in the frontal lobes, found the stereo hidden in Carla's brainstem and cranked the volume so high that all you could hear was the pulse of the rhythm section. She pushed the heel of her free hand against her temple. It's got a beat, you can dance to it.

'—but you're not even interested in trying, are you?'

'I'm trying.' Right now she needed aspirin more than she needed a get-out-of-jail-free card. 'I'm trying. But I need help.'

'Carla. Pay attention. By the time I could raise that much cash, you'd already have had your first court thingie. And if you're as innocent as they say, they'll turn you loose, right? And . . .' Lydia hesitated, and Carla heard her take a drag on her cigarette. 'And, hon? I know this is gonna piss you off, but it wouldn't hurt you none to stay there and dry out for a couple of days.'

The night could have been worse. Being booked on a violent felony kicked her to a cell of her own, skipping right past the drunk tank, and once she'd begged a couple of Excedrin from the deputy, she lay on her mattress and covered her eyes with one arm, trying to calm the throbbing in her head.

There was no thinking, not even any dreaming, before the door to the cell buzzed open. 'Smukowski?'

'Huh?' Carla uncovered her eyes and struggled to sit up.

A fat black woman stood in the doorway, ready to explode right out of her Multnomah-County-deputy costume. She checked her clipboard. 'You Carla Smukowski, right?'

'Yeah, sure.' Carla's stomach rumbled. 'Breakfast already?'

'Uh-uh. Morning. But no breakfast for you. Your bail's posted and you on your way out.'

Lyddie, God bless her. She'd found a way.

It took an hour to get through the formalities and climb back into civvies. When she finally walked out into the lobby of the Justice Centre, Lydia was nowhere to be seen. She glanced around the room, turning slowly with the big coat draped over her arm, but all she saw were streams of what seemed to be lawyers, heading to and from the elevators.

'Ms Smukowski?' The man's voice was southern but elegant, and the figure she saw when she turned matched the voice perfectly – a tall, slender man whose grey suit made his hair shine silver by contrast. His hand was outstretched to shake hers, and as she took it he said, 'Lamont Richter, LRI Security. You're a mighty difficult woman to find.'

She realized he was done shaking hands and that she ought to release her grip. 'Where's Lydia?'

'Your landlady? When I called on her this morning, she was kind enough to let me know where you were. I was hoping you'd have a little breakfast with me.' His eyebrows lifted and he gave the slightest sweep of his hand towards the entrance.

'You stood my bail?'

'Might have been hard for me to join you for breakfast if I hadn't. Short of getting myself arrested.'

He began ambling towards the doors, and Carla found herself keeping pace. 'I've told your office before, Mr . . .?' *Ricktah*? Was that what he'd said?

'Rich*ter*. Like the way they measure earthquakes.' He opened the glass door and ushered her through.

'I've told your office before, there's no bonding agency that'll cover me on a security gig . . .'

He swished the problem away with a languid toss of his long fingers and headed down towards the sidewalk. In the south-east a break in the ceiling of clouds let through the weak glow of the February sun, and up and down the street Oregonians craned their necks, seeking the source of this unexpected light. Richter stopped at the kerb and raised a hand as if hailing a cab. 'Truth be told, Carla – you don't mind if I call you Carla, do you? – truth be told, we're not in quite the line of work you might think.'

No, she didn't mind being called *Cahlah*, but she doubted that he really understood the situation. 'I just don't want you spending money thinking that—'

'Don't you worry about it. Either way, I assure you, I'll write it off on my taxes.'

A hulking blue-green Mercedes pulled up in the street,

and the chauffeur jumped out and ran round the car to open the doors. No, not a chauffeur, Carla decided, assessing his build and watching his moves. Bodyguard.

Once they were settled into the back seat, Richter asked where they should go for breakfast, and Carla protested that it was up to him. 'I don't know my way around this town,' he said. 'It's your breakfast. Pick anywhere you like.'

'Let's go to Sam's then.' The driver glanced back. 'Over in Hollywood?' Richter and the driver both blinked in that out-of-towner way that said the only Hollywood they knew about was in LA. 'Across the river, over by where I live. Just head for my place – you were just over there, right? – and I'll give directions when we get close.'

After profuse apologies, Richter immersed himself in a series of cellphone calls, discussing some sort of contract in terms that were meaningless to Carla. The Mercedes ran smooth but heavy, and it wallowed a little on corners, like an oil tanker changing course. Armoured. Had to be. She reached up and rapped the window with a knuckle, then swivelled her hand and tapped with a fingernail. Sure as hell not glass. Probably one of the new Lexan derivatives.

The driver caught her assessing the car and grinned.

Sam's Billiards was a venerable neighbourhood institution, one that was open to all kinds, but once the two of them were seated at a table, she regretted her choice. She watched Richter's eyes wander to the scarred L-shaped bar to the right of the door, and then back across the rows of pool tables on the left, tables that queued up far behind where they were seated. It was 9.30, too late for the weekday breakfast crush and too early for the lunch crowd. Far in the rear, a pair of hardcore pool pros practised, and the sharp cracks and the rumble of balls running down the throats of the pockets provided the only background noise. Sam's must have been there since the forties, and even with the windows that had recently been punched into the front wall, it felt dark and smoky inside, as though the ghosts of hustlers long dead still controlled the lighting.

The old guy behind the bar came out to take their order – poached eggs on toast with coffee for Richter, two over easy, bacon, hash browns, wheat toast and a Bloody Mary for Carla. In the silence after the waiter left, Carla said, 'Probably not your kind of place, huh?'

'It's –' Richter managed a small, graceful smile, '– colourful.' He leaned forward onto his elbows and clasped his hands. 'So. That *rara avis* in the flesh, a female Ranger.'

Carla snorted. 'Ain't any women in the Rangers. Never will be, either.'

He elevated his fingers and unclasped them, dismissing her words, and then interwove them again. 'A quibble. Same sort of training . . .'

'Not really. There were a couple of squads. My bunch got a lot of diplomatic training. K-Force.'

'Ah, yes, Special K.'

Carla put her palms flat on the table and studied him. 'Where'd you hear that?' Their drinks came, and Richter went through an elaborate ritual with his cream and sugar. Carla lifted her Bloody Mary, careful not to seem too anxious, and took a long swallow, letting her eyes close as the heat moved into her core and then radiated out. It was all she could do

15

not to give a sigh of relief, the same sweet outlet of breath that came to your lips when you emptied a painfully full bladder.

He watched her as she sat the glass down and doctored it with pepper. 'Why the Army?'

'Family tradition. Plus, hey, I grew up in Eastern Oregon. Short of swimming down the Columbia, military's about the only road out of there.' She made a sound she intended as a laugh. 'And here I am back in Oregon. Least I'm still on this side of the mountains.' She took a long drink and then sniffled as the pepper oils raced up the back of her nostrils. Her hand moved to set the glass down, but, on reflection, she lifted it again and drained it first instead. The clack of the tumbler on the table had the intended effect: the bartender looked over and she tapped the rim.

'Perhaps you'd be so kind as to give me a little background on your time in the Forces? An informal résumé, as it were?'

'Why? You seem to know everything.' She wasn't sure why she was being obstreperous; something about the man made her want to disrupt his smooth manner.

He smiled. 'Maybe I'd just like to hear *your* perspective on things.'

Carla's tongue sought out one of the cracked fillings in an upper molar while she considered. Why not?

K-Force had been a product of typical Army thinking: unless you want to fuck them, women are invisible.

Damned if the jackasses weren't right. Women bodyguards, women security forces, women counter-terrorist squads – it's like they weren't there. Has the target got anybody with him? Nah – just some girls.

There'd been some turf battles with the Marines at first –
the Marines had always supplied the security for US
embassies, and they didn't see why they should hand over
security details for travelling politicos to some newfangled
pussy parade – but after 9/11 there'd been more unofficial
diplomatic visits than ever before, and if you needed to stay
beneath the radar of the press, and sometimes beneath the
radar of your so-called allies, then a Marine escort wasn't
a buttload of help in staying inconspicuous.

Carla'd been in the right place at the right time; she'd
already been through two years of weapons training, hand-
to-hand, explosives and clandestine ops; they'd already had
three years to load her down with Arabic – though she had
a hard time making her accent understood west of Suez – plus
good Urdu, decent Hindi and even enough Pashto to negoti-
ate a surrender or order roast lamb. Once the Twin Towers
hit the ground, and low-key envoys – the ones the American
public never knew about – started slithering around the
Middle East and Pakistan, Carla was hot property.

Her second Bloody Mary came. 'You probably know
what happened after that.' She tossed the celery stalk onto
the table and shook pepper into the glass until less red than
black showed on the surface.

Richter sipped his coffee, his pinkie finger extended as
though he were at an afternoon tea party. He set the cup
down in the saucer and raised his eyebrows politely.

She exhaled. 'Okay. It's like a month after Bush Junior
goes into Iraq. We were in Amman, in Jordan, when we
weren't supposed to be, at least according to the official
Washington rap. We came in on tourist visas – yeah, right,

tourists in Jordan, in the middle of Gulf War Two, the sequel – and we don't even drop through our embassy. My guy is set up there for a few weeks to talk to the Palestinians, off the record, without the Israelis knowing. Or maybe Mossad was supposed to know – maybe the whole point was that they were supposed to find out. Who effing knows, right?'

Sometimes a drink before breakfast can go straight to your head. She looked at Richter to see if he was following. He nodded, so she went on. 'So we're there in this half-assed Jordanian international hotel, typical overpriced boring fucking Arab hotel, when some raghead sonofabitch slams a car-bomb into an Army checkpoint in Iraq. One of the first attacks, right after Baghdad goes down. And . . .' Carla lifted the glass, took a long drink, and then blinked, tears rushing to her eyes as the pepper rushed to her sinuses. 'My brother Kevin. Three other guys.'

He reached across the table and settled his fingers on her free hand, but she shook them off. 'Don't,' she said. 'Army was decent about it. Promised to fly me home right away, just as soon as they could rotate one of my cohort in, couple or three days at the most, a month's compassionate leave. Month's leave. I woulda rather they sent me into Iraq with an M60 and unlimited ammo belts, but, hey, they were being decent. And it all woulda worked out, except the next morning there's these fuckers, these fuckers right on the front steps of my hotel, *celebrating*, celebrating the fucking car-bomb that killed Kev, waving around this fucking poster of Osama, and worst of all I can understand what the fuckers are shouting, and . . . Shit. No excuses. I lost it. Totally effing lost it. Completely fucked the dog.' A sad smile. 'Course, the weasel-dick with the poster turns out to be the son of the Saudi ambassador . . . but you knew all that, didn't you?'

'Not the part about your brother.'

'Hmmph.' She took a big swallow of her drink and put the tumbler down, put it down so hard that even though it was only half-full the drink nearly sloshed out. 'So the brass had to waste me to keep the Saudis happy; but they couldn't totally fuck me without drawing attention to the whole Special K, which is low-profile city. So they double-dissed me – dishon discharge. And here's Smukowski, back in the grey and the green.'

He waited for a moment. 'Tell me, Carla. You sorry now you did it?'

She started to answer, but their breakfast orders arrived, and she sat silent until the waiter left. 'Sorry I fucked up the guys out on the steps? No. Sorry I got kicked out of the service? Of course. Why wouldn't I be?'

'I surely don't know.' He picked up his knife and fork and used the knife to slice through the yolks of his poached eggs, letting the startling gold liquid spill out across the whites. 'Exactly how *do* you feel about those fellows who were out on the steps?'

Carla tried to drop her shoulders and relax. Breathe. Out of your head and into your body. Unclench it. 'How do I feel? About them?' Part of her said *this is no way to get a job, babes*, but a bigger part of her said *just say it, just for once in your fucking life really say it*. 'Fuck 'em, that's how I feel. I'm sorry they're still fucking alive.' She tried to relax, just let it ride, but it felt too damn good to say it right out loud. 'In fact, you wanta know the truth, I'd like to see toe-tags on all of 'em, men, women and children, from Afgagisburg all the way over to fucking Morocco. Fuck 'em. They hate *us*? Fine. I hate them, too.' She sat back and folded her arms, staring at him.

'Well.' His voice was mild. He had sliced off a piece of yolk-saturated toast, and he forked it into his mouth. He chewed, swallowed and dabbed his lips with a napkin before he asked, 'And what about Nigeria? Or Is-rai-el?'

Carla's arms tightened. 'Fuck them, too. And Somalia. And Sudan.'

'Hmm. You know . . .' He folded the flimsy paper napkin as though it were top-class linen before he put it down beside his plate. 'You know, I might be able to offer you a position you'd appreciate. One that uses your real skills.' He flagged the bartender as the man passed. 'I believe the young lady needs another one of your fine cocktails.'

Carla unfolded her arms and leaned forward. 'What do you mean?'

'I think – just think, mind you – that I'm prepared to offer you a job. A job, I might add, that seems to mesh almost perfectly with your . . . attitudes.' He pointed with his fork. 'Your eggs are getting cold.'

She killed the last of her second drink, and then forked up a mass of egg and hash browns. The tastes in her mouth – greasy starch, fatty yolk, rubbery proteins – coaxed forth a rush of saliva, and in its train followed a low, demanding hunger that she hadn't felt in ages. She began to eat in earnest, chasing sloppy, egg-drenched potatoes with crunchy bites of toast, until her third Bloody Mary arrived.

She peppered it and raised it to her lips, but before she

sipped it, Richter said, 'You savour that one, okay, Carla? Because that's likely the last drink you're going to have in quite some time.' He stared at her.

She took a sip, rolled it on her tongue and then swallowed.

It felt good to be hungry again.

2

Atwater

He ran an empire of discount superstores that stretched coast-to-coast; he slipped in and out of the market with a legendary timing that left him grinning no matter which way Wall Street moved. He had the home phone numbers of half the Senate, from both sides of the aisle, and he owned a ranch in Montana larger than some European countries. Rex Atwater was one of the richest and most powerful men on the planet, but he had a reputation as one of the world's unluckiest fishermen.

It was a reputation he was happy to cultivate, and he smiled as he headed up the path from the stream, his rod over his shoulder, his catchbag empty again. The truth was, 90 per cent of the time he never even bothered to bait a hook or tie on a fly. The whole point of fishing, in his view, was to get outdoors, alone, and do nothing. He'd have been just as happy out hiking, or sitting on a rock and thinking, but heading out for the woods alone for the purpose of contemplation was the first step on the road to being labelled Eccentric, Reclusive Billionaire; while wandering outdoors with the stated intent of killing something, no matter how unsuccessful the venture, ensured that the press couldn't manage an article about him without proclaiming him a Rugged Individualist.

It was mid-April, too early for the trout to be rising in this tributary of the Truckee River, and only about nine in the morning, still too damn cold to be outdoors on the east side of the Sierras, so at first Atwater was grateful for the long uphill climb to his lodge.

Halfway up he had to pause, leaning his back against a ponderosa pine. Altitude. The lodge stood at little more than six thousand feet, but he only came here a half-dozen times most years. At sixty-eight he despised doddering old men; he'd stayed clear-eyed, trim, and kept a confident step. None of that was a defence against lack of oxygen. He let the tree prop him up, and looked up the slope to where the Institute perched, the varnish on the wrap-around wooden deck glowing in the morning sun.

The lodge, all twenty six thousand square feet of it, was known as the Tahoe Institute even though, to be truthful, Tahoe was still a good drive to the west. By the time he arrived at the back staircase, his internal thermostat ought to be set back on high and all of the guests should have finished breakfast.

Of all his tax-deductible expenditures, the Tahoe Institute was his favourite. Four times a year he organized weekend seminars. He chose the speakers; he invited the guests. Attendance was typically limited to fewer than thirty, every attendee hand-picked by Atwater himself – mostly CEOs and politicians, but accompanied by a smattering of lesser luminaries he wanted there for his own reasons. Invitations were a source of pride to the recipients – it was exclusive; Atwater kept a gourmet table and a top-flight bar; and the participants had the virtuous feeling of being movers and shakers, gathered together to discuss issues of social consequence.

He paused again when he arrived at the base of the stairway, and leaned on the handrail, breathing. His chest felt tight. Three hundred and fifty-three steps up to the kitchen. Perhaps he should stop at the two landings, and then pause again a little short of the top, and regain his breath before heading in and trying to mingle. This weekend the theme was 'Islam and the West', and it had stirred more controversy than any previous conference. The participants would be overstimulated, like half-dressed teenagers yanked from the back seat of a car. Everybody would want to talk to him. Maybe he'd stop and hide out in the kitchen.

Not in the mood to chat or argue, no, not a bit, especially if he had to stop and suck in a deep breath halfway through his sentence. Christ! Why hadn't anybody warned him getting old would be like this? He couldn't let this happen to himself, not yet. There were still too many things he needed to do.

Coffee, that was the solution – coffee, and a long rest in the kitchen before the morning session started up. Today it wasn't just chatter. Today there was someone he needed to watch.

Professor Richard Hollingsworth had a good Oxbridge accent and a lanky, pinched build that, in Atwater's mind, suggested a relationship to the Royal Family; he didn't so much stand beside the podium as drape himself upon it. 'To sum up: we none of us enjoy taking responsibility for our situations in the world – excepting, of course, those times when all is going swimmingly . . .'

Atwater listened with admiration from the back of the faux-rustic Great Hall. The man knew his field, but it was the accent plus that supercilious attitude that made it work. Hollingsworth had some of the most powerful people in America hanging on his words.

Every head was turned forward, with none of the usual clandestine checking of PalmPilots or pagers, so Atwater couldn't watch Boyce Hammond's face. He already had a huge dossier on the man, but he wanted a chance to size him up before making a final decision.

Hollingsworth had a wealth of synonyms for *in conclusion*, and he spent them freely over ten more minutes before he came to a genuine end. Warm applause filled the room, but hands were raised before the clapping had finished – first a few, and then the audience sprouted a cornfield of arms. A remarkable sight, really, Atwater thought; CEOs of major corporations waving their hands in the air like first-graders seeking the teacher's attention. Hollingsworth pointed a finger, selecting a question.

Atwater strolled down the left aisle of the auditorium, along the vast windows that looked back towards the Donner Pass. He shut his ears to the questions and answers, and studied the profile of Hammond's seated figure across the room.

He liked what he saw in the man's body language: someone in his mid-thirties, good-looking in a boyish way, with a shock of hair that fell across his forehead like a Beatle, circa '64. Torso leaned a bit forward, with hands palm-down lightly on thighs – attentive, reserved and without any strong reactions. Hammond had to be something of a nutcase to be in a group like the Ethan Allen Brigade, but he showed none of the fist-clenching opposition or open-handed approval that Atwater associated with zealots.

The sunlight outside called to him, and he let his mind drift down the hill to the trout stream, to the shaded tree roots where packs of January snow still hid . . .

A stir in the room brought his attention back to the discussion. Fawzy Sayeed, a Palestinian-American with a major presence in Silicon Valley, was on his feet, and Hollingsworth was answering a question Atwater had missed hearing.

'It's the *culture* of Islam, and not the Koran, that's at issue here. Some here today –' Hollingsworth glanced at Lee Velacott of American Way, '– seem to characterize the US as a Christian country. Yet, after 9/11, I don't recall hearing many calls to turn the other cheek . . . though it's hard for me to see how Christ could have been any more explicit on the subject.'

This resulted in some turmoil in the audience; a number of the participants found this statement offensive somehow, though when they had a chance to speak their minds, most of them were shockingly inarticulate. Hollingsworth, for his part, had begun to let a puzzled expression show, an expression that Atwater read as *My God, these are the people who are running the world's most powerful economy* . . . Atwater decided this had gone on long enough. He headed towards the dais, planning on thanking the speaker, calling for applause and then announcing lunch, when he realized that Hollingsworth had called on Boyce Hammond. Atwater stopped in mid-stride a few steps short of the platform and watched.

'I have a question about force – about military force.' Hammond brushed back his hair with one hand, but it fell back into the same pattern. Compared to the power brokers in the room, he looked like a kid. 'I was in Desert Storm. Before we went in, all we heard about was the *elite* Republican Guard, newscasters couldn't say *Republican Guard* without saying *elite* first. Once we hit 'em, they just crumbled. So I was just wondering . . . well, suppose Islam got hit just as hard. Maybe they'd change their minds, too?' Hammond glanced around the room, and sat down.

Hollingsworth smiled at Hammond like a fond uncle. 'It's a good point, but you can't compare a religion to a country – and Iraq was never an Islamist state in any case.' He leaned on his elbows and tented his fingertips. 'For fundamentalists of any stripe, Christian to Hindu to Muslim, victory proves God is on their side, and defeat proves God is testing them.'

Atwater climbed the three steps up to the dais, as Hollingsworth continued. 'It's the nature of faith to be nearly impervious to information. I doubt that any show of force or any catastrophe could make the slightest dent in the armour of the Faithful. Short, of course –' Atwater was ready to call the session to a close, but the image that Hollingsworth added stopped him – 'short of a meteor reducing Mecca to a smoking ruin. It might be that even the truest of believers wouldn't care to pray to a hole in the ground.'

The Top Floor was a glass gazebo, perched atop the Tahoe Institute Lodge like a diminutive cap on a swollen head. The view was a dizzying three-sixty, and, this high above the pollution, at night the stars shone down through the hexagonal glass roof in all the detail they must have shown the Greeks three thousand years before.

Some visitors found it vertiginous. Not tonight's guest. Boyce Hammond had admired the view as the sun disappeared behind the ridge of the Sierras, and then sat down to their one-on-one dinner as though he were in a diner.

They made small talk over the first courses, mostly a matter of casual questions on Atwater's part and short, though polite, answers from Hammond. Hammond was clearly baffled by the array of silverware astride his plate, and once he had gripped a fork, he stood by it, refusing to relinquish it to Joachim's finest, most discreet server, who was never so rude as to insist. The only exchange of interest, to Atwater at any rate, was when he enquired if the height and expansive view didn't make Hammond queasy. Hammond tossed his shoulders and said, ''Copter pilot', as though that were a full answer.

After dessert, Joachim's man brought port, and Atwater told him to leave it on the table. It was a good, aged bottle, with that inscrutable white crust that accumulates on the neck as ports come into their maturity. Atwater tilted the lip to Hammond's glass, and let the glorious grape-coloured vintage trickle across the crystal. 'The Portuguese call this *copa de morada* –"the cup of purple." Not to everyone's taste, of course, and I can easily send for something else . . .'

Hammond savoured it, rolling it in his mouth. 'Mmm. Like a second dessert.'

'My feelings precisely.' Atwater filled his own glass and tasted it. 'I appreciate your staying over with so little notice.'

'Drove over from Stockton. Can drive back any time.'

'Still.' Atwater chewed his lip for a moment. 'We've had some direct contact with Commander Conrad . . .'

'He didn't give me the details, but his orders were to cooperate with you – within the limits of what's best for the organization.'

'And who decides that?

'I handle the day-to-day. The Commander isn't young any more.'

Atwater kept his face neutral. Younger than me, but already only lucid half of the time, and reportedly afraid of flying. 'I understood that the Ethan Allen Brigade—'

'The Allens.'

'. . . was structured as a military hierarchy, so I assumed that if the top man was convinced, his orders would be followed on down the line.'

'His order was to use my judgement. I'm following that order.'

Atwater spread his upturned palms and put on his best smile, nodding. 'I understand. And I'm more than willing to lay my case out for you.' If he had to shepherd the man to wisdom, he would. 'But if you're convinced, what then? Do the Allens go along with your decision?'

'Yes.' Hammond shook his head in the affirmative, but his eyes seemed to lack conviction. 'Within the limits of our resources. Within the limits of our charter.'

'*To defend America against all her enemies, at home and*

abroad? I want to hire a select group of the Allens to hit hard at some of America's enemies.'

Hammond folded his arms high on his chest and leaned back from the table. '*Defend America* is the phrase, defend her when she's been attacked. We're Minutemen, like our forefathers – not mercenaries.'

'We've been attacked, haven't we? Mr Hammond, I think the terrorists are right about something. This really is a war between Islam and modern civilization.'

'Not all terrorists are Muslims.'

'Only the ones that count. Our leaders refuse to see this struggle for what it is, a war between worldviews. Until they do that, we'll keep losing. Our politicians tell us we're winning, but we're losing.' Atwater paused, and sipped his port. The man had unfolded his arms, but still leaned back away from the table, his chin tilted upwards.

Hammond tongued his teeth for a moment. 'I'm not arguing. What's it got to do with the Allens?'

'I want to hit back, fight terror with terror, carry the battle onto their own turf. But I need help – manpower, in particular. And I've already begun. Those bombings of jihadi training camps in the Mideast? Mine.'

Hammond stood, turned and walked to the window behind his chair. It was now dark enough outside that the window showed his reflection rather than the inky mountains. 'If that's true, you wouldn't talk about it.'

'It's a matter of trust.' Atwater filled Hammond's glass and topped up his own.

Hammond turned back to face him, eyebrows raised.

Atwater pointed his eyes at Hammond's empty seat.

'Wouldn't you like to sit back down and finish this port with me?'

Hammond sat, picked up the glass and drank. 'I don't buy it.' He tilted the glass higher and swallowed the priceless port as though it were Budweiser. 'Even if it were true, why would you tell me?' He set the glass back on the table with exaggerated caution, and stared Atwater in the eyes. 'In fact, at this point, I'm assuming you're working for the Feds. And it's no good. We're not assassins, we're not mercenaries. We haven't done a damn thing that the Founding Fathers didn't guarantee as fundamental rights in the Constitution.'

'Mr Hammond, Mr Hammond. Trust me, nothing could be further from the truth. Here, let me freshen your drink . . . Were I a pawn of the Feds, I assure you, I've already gathered enough information to nail your hide to the barn door. I know about the IRS-proof account in Guyana; I know about the arms caches in Yermo and outside Billings – hell, I even know about the cave in Kentucky. I'm not trying to entrap you. I'm trying to forge an alliance with you.' Atwater raised his own glass and drank, as if in a salute to his guest. 'One that, you'll find, matches perfectly your own goals.'

'Why should we trust you?'

'Three reasons. First, I haven't turned over what I already know about the Allens to our dear friends in Washington. Second, I do have a great deal of what your outfit lacks: money and connections. And, finally, because I'm about to let you in on my own little secrets – if you're game.'

Hammond sat and contemplated his own hands, open on the table before him, as though reading his palms might guide him. At long last, shaking his head, he said, 'I'm listening. But I'm not sure that the Allens want to go global.'

Though Atwater knew he wasn't much of a sportsman, he had confidence – with all due apologies to Jesus – in his ability as a fisher of men. He felt Hammond nibbling at the bait, and prepared to set the hook. 'Let's talk,' he said, leaning back in his chair, 'about how we can wipe terrorism from the face of the planet.'

3

Hammond

Sleeping with Earlene in the first place had been a big mistake, and Hammond had known it at the time, but he'd been lonely and drunk and too tired to fend her off gracefully. Now, almost a year after that party, it was practically like being married.

She'd been waiting for him the night before, when he'd driven in from his meeting at the Tahoe Institute. The meeting with Atwater had put him back in Stockton a day later than he'd expected – and, more to the point, a day later than Earlene had expected. Where had he been? Couldn't he have called? Did he realize how worried she'd been? It had turned into a fight, with tears ruining her make-up – too much make-up, where Hammond came from – and then a long, desperate bout of reconciliation sex that only bound them more tightly.

He clicked off the alarm before it could ring and eased himself out of bed. Earlene's breathing changed rhythm for a moment, some part of her sensing his departure. In the morning light she looked both trashy and innocent, make-up smeared by tears and sweat over a face that, relaxed in sleep, looked far younger than her thirty-six years. Guilt, now familiar as a soft old bathrobe, wrapped him in its folds. He knew he'd have to hurt her sooner or later, and that it would be kinder if he did it sooner; but her brother was Ray McCann. In the hierarchy of the Ethan Allen Brigade, Hammond outranked Ray, but Ray had fifteen years in the Allens, and was popular with everyone.

A hot shower washed away all the dried funk of the previous night, and most of the guilt as well. He had his head inside his pullover when she said, 'Boyce? Hon? Where you going?'

He tugged it down, adjusted the waist. 'Have to go into the city today. Trying to get a new shipment.'

'Can't you wait for breakfast? Or do it on the phone?'

'These aren't the kinds of guys who use the phone, babes. And I wouldn't even if they would. Fibbies probably have my lines tapped by now.' He leaned down and kissed her, and she kept her lips closed, not sharing her morning breath. 'I'll be back early this evening – I promise – and we'll go out to dinner. Maybe that Italian place you like.' He kissed her forehead and turned towards the door.

'Boyce . . . ?' He paused. 'I'm sorry about last night. I just—'

He shook his head. 'Don't worry about it. My fault.' She started to protest, but he laid his index finger across his lips and said, 'Shhh. When somebody says *It's my fault*, hon, don't argue.'

By the time Hammond finished his steak and eggs at Lou's Roadside Cafe his watch read 9.15. He climbed into his old

34

beater of a Ford – no foreign jobs, not in these parts, not with this crowd – and cruised down to the shop.

Eastside Guns & Ammo was a legitimate business, and Hammond had a valid licence for dealing firearms. He held title to the store, but it had been the Allens who had put up the capital for him to buy it from the previous owner, and all of the net cashflow went back to the Brigade, not into his pocket.

He worked the sequence of keys through the multiple locks on the armoured front door. Before he opened it he glanced up and down the street. A smart hold-up artist would choose first thing in the morning as the time to hit a store, and, despite the firepower sitting right behind the counter, gun stores were a favourite target. Over the years Hammond had concluded that 'smart' and 'hold-up artist' were mutually exclusive, but he still scanned the street before turning the knob.

The alarm system whined in his ear, but he locked the deadbolt behind himself before punching the disarm code into the keypad. With the roll-down metal shutters still covering the display windows, the shop stood in shadow, the only illumination provided by a bolt of sunshine through the porthole-window of the front door. He didn't bother with the lights; he knew his way round behind the counter and could find the panel below the register by feel.

The Allen Brigade carried on a big traffic in illegal arms, mostly as buyers. Some heavy traffic sat in caches in the desert, but what was in the shop was small, and 99 per cent legit. The other 1 per cent lived in the hidden panel Hammond had opened. Nothing exceptional: a short row of assorted handguns, serial numbers filed, barrels rebored. Throw-down guns, unremarkable and untraceable.

He chose a .38 snub-nosed revolver and an ankle holster: compact and traditional. Contrary to old cop shows, at anything more than a dozen feet you might as well be blowing spitwads through a straw. No handgun threw lead with any accuracy, but thirty-eights were especially bad; when the barrel was shorter than your thumb you might as well aim with your eyes shut.

No matter. Hammond didn't really expect problems, but any problems he might encounter would most likely be within arms' reach.

Next stop: the Oak Hills Branch of the San Joaquin County Public Library, over on Main. He arrived just as the doors opened at ten.

At one of the public-access Internet terminals he connected to a website selling greeting cards. He double-clicked on the icon of the All-Season Jumbo Pack and, when the new page popped into view, he held down the CTRL key and typed a code number. A pause, a flicker and then the screen cleared, displaying only a blinking cursor.

He typed in a password and a routing code, and the screen responded with 'Type Customer Comments in Field Below'.

From his hip pocket he pulled out a folded BART timetable and a route map of the San Francisco bus system. He opened both and spread them flat, easing out the creases with the flat of his palms.

He left his car in the Doubletree parking lot near the Berkeley Marina and pulled on the agreed-upon green baseball cap.

The smell of estuarine muck rose in his nostrils as he clomped down the dock towards a set of the visitor slips. Only a hint of a breeze touched his face, so the forest of naked masts sat abandoned beneath the afternoon sun.

Two long sailboats were tied up in the seaward slips. On the bow of the closest, teal-green letters spelled out *Penelope* and, below that, 'Freedom Boat Rentals'. In the slip directly across the planked walkway a high sport-fishing yacht rocked, its fibreglass hull squeaking against the rubberized fenders.

Hammond paused and rolled his shoulders. A familiar tension, an undercurrent of fear mixed with an almost sexual anticipation, that buzz that came just before touchdown when landing a chopper in a gusty cross-wind. He leaned over, rapped on the deck of the *Penelope* and called out, 'Tea time.'

Scrambling sounds came from the galley below, and three men emerged onto the deck beyond the mast. Their hesitating hops from the deck onto the dock showed that none of them were sailors.

O'Toole, a red-haired man with the stance of a veteran carthorse, he recognized from the photos. The two men flanking O'Toole were new to him, and he tried to file their faces away in his memory. Dark, wide-browed, possibly Slavic, with the barest touch of an Asian slant to the eyes; except for the Marine buzz-cut one wore, they might have been bookends.

'How'd you know which boat?' O'Toole asked, his eyes narrow.

Hammond shrugged. 'Not too many rentals out here

today.' All three of the men had on loose navy sports coats, unbuttoned, and he noticed the bulges under the left armpits. 'Either you don't have the money with you, or somebody's got really big pockets.'

'It's here.' O'Toole shifted his feet. 'We hand it over at the same time we get the goods.'

Hammond chuckled and shook his head. 'You know it doesn't work like that. Your people and my people agreed.' He let his smile fade. 'This ain't COD.'

'How do we know you'll deliver?'

'I stay here until you're happy.'

The dark man with the buzz-cut took a step forward. 'And how do we ensure it works?' His root accent – Hungarian? – was submerged under a British slur.

'How do you test if a hand grenade is still good?' Hammond asked. 'A SAM ain't a used car. You don't get to test-drive it.'

The men glanced at each other.

'Look,' Hammond said, 'you're not comfortable, we'll call it off. You people came to us, you agreed to terms. This money doesn't go into my pocket, and I'd just as soon go home.' He clasped his hands behind his back and put on a bored expression, running his tongue over his teeth.

The men huddled and conferred in whispers for a moment, and then O'Toole faced him again, colour showing under his pale skin. 'Fine. But I'm warning you—'

'Let's not engage in threats, all right?' Hammond reached into his coat pocket, and all three men tensed. 'Cellphone, okay?' He flipped it open, punched a speed-dial code, and when Alvorsen picked up he said, 'Come get a tall cool one.'

38

He paced back and forth, hands behind him, studying the sky. The buzz-cut Slav clambered back onto the *Penelope* and emerged a few moments later on the dock, a backpack dangling from his hand. 'Here it is,' O'Toole said. The Slav advanced with his arm outstretched, as though to hand Hammond the backpack.

He shook his head in refusal. 'Don't give it to me. Wait a second.'

A motorboat throttled down to marina speeds gurgled in the harbour, and Hammond saw Alvorsen's blond hair and beard as the man swung the little boat in a wide arc around the end of a neighbouring dock. He pulled up at the end of *Penelope*'s slip, and Hammond jerked his head in Alvorsen's direction. 'He's your guy.'

Alvorsen motored away with the backpack, and a few minutes passed before Hammond's phone rang. 'Smooth sailing,' the voice said. 'We'll be leaving the baby with you now.'

A longer motorboat, a Boston Whaler, puttered down the harbour and docked at the end of the slip. It tied up, and Hammond watched Skittle and French, two of the Allens, struggle with the long wooden crate up onto the dock.

As Skittle cast off, the two Slavs hurried down to the coffin-sized crate and hefted it, edging their way onto the deck of the *Penelope*. Hammond caught a motion on the deck, the duck of a head back into the galley.

More than three people, then. Hammond kept facing the *Penelope*, stretched his arms above his shoulders with a yawn and then clasped them behind his head. He pulled both hands into fists and freed up three fingers on his right hand, and his little finger crept out to join them. Four. There might be more, but that was the best he could do; he hoped the folks at his back were paying close attention.

He dropped his hands to his sides. 'That's done,' he said to O'Toole, 'so I guess I'll be moseying along . . .'

O'Toole shook his head. 'Stick around while my boys have a look.'

Hammond made a show of glancing at his watch. 'I have to read them the instruction manual, too?'

'Just wait.'

He paced. Indistinct voices drifted over from the *Penelope*, and then her diesel auxiliary started.

'I guess we'll be leaving you, then,' O'Toole said. 'The damned thing better be in working order.'

Hammond nodded and started back towards shore, trying not to hurry. A glance back at the *Penelope* showed O'Toole and one of the Slavs on the dock, puzzling over the way they'd tied the boat.

Across the dock a bullhorn crackled from the tower of the sport-fishing boat. '*Do not move. Put your hands in the air. This is the FBI*—' Hammond hoisted his hands over his head, but as he did so a rifle shot boomed and he turned to look back. A rifleman crouched on the deck of the *Penelope*, aiming at the fishing boat, and O'Toole had dropped to one knee, pistol in hand.

The fishing boat bristled with rifles, a good half-dozen, and Hammond caught a glimpse of blue baseball caps. A ragged volley of shots rang from both sides of the dock, and Hammond dropped his arms and dived for the water. As his feet left the decking he heard rifle slugs crack into the wood behind him.

By the time he'd pulled himself out of the bay alongside one of the nature trails, the shooting was long over, and ambulance sirens were converging on the marina. Water sloshed in his shoes at each step. He knew no one would be looking for him, but he saw no need to be conspicuous; he worked his way through the underbrush for as long as possible before crossing the parking lot to his car. He stripped and changed into his track suit and running shoes before driving to the Rockridge BART station.

When the time came, he boarded BART and rode under the Bay, jumping off at Market Street. He walked back up to the Hyatt, rode the elevator to an upper floor of the parking structure, rode another elevator to ground level, and walked out through the *No Pedestrians* entrance to the garage. He caught the streetcar at the Embarcadero turnaround, jumped off a short distance up California Street and took a ten-minute walk south to a bus stop. He bought the *Chronicle* while he waited through two buses, and then he caught the third, asking for a transfer before taking a seat towards the rear.

At the next stop two men boarded. The second one wore a blue fisherman's cap and sat down near the exit doors in the centre of the bus. Hammond didn't recognize him, but the man opened his own copy of the *Chronicle*, found the sports section and folded the rest of the paper onto the seat beside him. Hammond did the same. The bus turned and headed crosstown, passing four stops before the man pulled the bell-cord.

The man in the blue cap got off alone. Hammond waited two more stops, jumped off alone, walked two blocks east and then rode a bus north, climbing off on Polk Street above Van Ness.

The Polk Street Bar & Grill was such a product of the fifties that, in the shadows inside, it seemed to be in black and white. The cracked Naugahyde upholstery must have been the original stuff. At a booth towards the rear, the man removed his fisherman's cap and placed it on the centre of the table: I'm clean, no tails.

Hammond went to the men's room and slid the revolver into the pocket of his windbreaker. He'd dried it as best he could after his unexpected swim, but he hoped he didn't need it; you couldn't count on damp revolvers.

He made sure the fisherman's cap was still on the table-top before he joined the man in the booth. He slid across the seat, the cracked fabric snagging his jeans, and eased his hand into his pocket, fitting his fingers around the pistol grip. 'Very casual,' he said, 'just pull out your creds, put 'em in the newspaper, push it over.' The man's square face wore the impassive countenance favoured at the Bureau, but his eyes showed that he'd been startled by the demand. He gave a slow blink, eloquent as a shrug, before he obeyed. Hammond used his left hand to lay the folded newspaper down on the seat beside him, opened the thin wallet by feel and then darted a glance down. ID from the FBI, or a damn good facsimile. The tension in him eased a little, and he studied it more closely. Townley, James P. SF District Office.

He refolded the wallet in the newspaper and pushed it back across the table. While Townley retrieved his ID, Hammond crossed his leg and moved the .38 from his pocket back into his ankle holster.

The snap of the closure made Townley stare. 'Jesus, Hammond.' The slightest flare of nostrils. 'A little excessive, isn't it?'

'Where's Troy?'

'His wife's having a baby.'

A baby. Christ. He didn't even know Troy had got married. 'Then why didn't they send somebody else I know?'

'We would have sent Jacobsen, but he took a bullet in that little scuffle this afternoon. Plus, people get transferred. There's only about four guys in the office who know you personally any more.' When Hammond just stared, he added, 'We tried to get Troy, we really did. Even called him at the hospital. He says hi. It's a girl.'

'How's Jacobsen?'

'Jacobsen'll be okay. He's the one who shot at you, by the way – thought it would help keep your cover.'

'From who? The dead guys?'

Townley shook his head. 'Not dead. Five on board. Three are still with us.'

'What the hell happened out there today?'

'You didn't walk away as soon as we expected. They looked like they were getting under way. And something tipped one of them off that we were there.' Townley pursed his lips.

'I didn't so much as look at the fishing boat—'

'Didn't say you did.'

A waitress came to the table, a full-up goth who, against the fifties décor, could have been a skinny Elvira, Queen of the Night. They ordered two draft beers, and Hammond waited until they'd been delivered to continue. 'Why didn't you just take them out in the bay?'

'Think about the logistics. Think about them dumping the goods. And way harder to take anyone alive if they chose to fight.' Whatever he saw in Hammond's expression made him add, 'It wasn't my call – I'm not a field guy. But now we have tape, we have video. Airtight.'

'Almost blew my cover.'

'But didn't.' Townley sipped at his beer, and when Hammond stayed silent, he said, 'Your message this morning said you had developments on the Tahoe front.'

'It's what we figured when I got the invite. Atwater's trying to forge an alliance with the Allen Brigade. He wants us to do work for him.'

'What, exactly?'

Hammond made a throw-away gesture with his hand. 'Not sure yet. Serious money, though. What I am sure of is that he's up to his elbows in it overseas. These fight-terror-with-terror attacks in the Mideast? The ones the Arab press are claiming must be the Israelis? They're his.'

Townley sat up straight. 'How do you know?'

'He told me. Didn't give the how of it, but took credit for it. Guy seems convinced that Islam is going to destroy world civilization. Keeps comparing it to the Christians and the fall of Rome.'

'We figured something was up with him. A week before he invited you, there was activity all over your cover records. Professional work, too. Looked into your birth records, your school records, even bribed his way into your service records.'

Townley scratched behind his ear. 'Probably has all your W-2s and 1040s by now.'

'Jesus.'

'Had to spend serious money and pull strings on high to get it all.' Townley drank from his beer mug and licked his lip. 'Not to worry. The harder people have to dig to get misinformation, the more they trust it. Your cover is bulletproof.'

'My body's not.' Hammond hadn't really wanted a beer, and now he pushed it further from him, leaving a wet stripe on the table. 'You've got O'Toole's bunch buying a SAM, you have the Allens selling it to them, plus everything else I have on them. It seems to me this is done.'

'Actually . . .' Townley looked down at the table. 'Actually, we're going to keep the O'Toole bust under wraps for a while.'

'What the hell for?' Hammond realized he had almost shouted, and he glanced around the room and lowered his voice. 'I don't get it.'

'We're a lot more interested in finding out who O'Toole was fronting for. Somebody out there wants a surface-to-air missile, and you can bet it ain't for self-defence. We follow up on that and we might bring down a major terror network.'

'Follow it worldwide, for all I care. But take care of business at this end first.'

'What is it you want?'

'I want to come in. I want the Bureau to roll up the Allens, and Atwater with them. I want to take a vacation as the real me, and spend my back pay.'

'Troy said you'd say that.'

'And Troy knows why. They told me it might be more than a year—'

'Yes, they did.'

'But they didn't tell me it would be more than *three*. I want a life again, before what I'm doing now *is* my life.'

'It's too soon. I know it's tough – the folks upstairs know it's tough – but, frankly, you've done too good a job. It looked like things were wrapping up, but now with Atwater in play . . . well, that would be quite a bust.'

'You don't know tough unless you've done it, okay? What the hell do you folks want? I've given you the Allens, stone-cold solid, and now Atwater has confessed to me that he's been blowing people away overseas—'

'It's not enough. Not enough. Your hearsay won't cut it, not with someone his size.' Townley put on a softer expression. 'You yourself said you're not 100 per cent on why he wants an alliance with the Allens. But it's got to be domestic, right?'

'Does it matter? Let the Bureau charge in with warrants. I've given you everything you need to look up his asshole with a mirror and a magnifying glass. Do it.'

'Boyce . . . I'm sorry. You've done an amazing job. When you come in, you'll be able to write your own job descriptions for the rest of your life. But, man, don't give it up yet, don't stop digging when you're ten feet from gold.'

Hammond flagged down the waitress. 'Glass of Cabernet?' he said. She frowned at his full beer mug, but nodded and headed off towards the bar. He saw Townley watching him without expression. 'I'm sick of fucking beer.' He pushed it further across the table. 'All yours. So, is that final? I can't come in yet?'

'Not for me to say. I can tell them you're making a formal request, but I think you know what they'll say.'

'Yeah. Stay right where you are.'

'No. They'll tell you to bring them Rex Atwater's head.'

'What the hell do they want, signed confessions?'

'Tape would be good. Money trails, solid witnesses . . .'

The waitress put down the glass of wine atop a paper napkin, sloshing a bit, and the dark-red liquid spread out towards the edges of the white paper. 'I want immunity for a few folks,' Hammond said. 'Some people've been good to me the past three years.'

'You going native on us, Boyce?'

Hammond stared at the soggy red napkin and reached for the glass. 'I said I want immunity for some folks.'

'Look, we're not talking about little fish here. Atwater, he's Moby-Dick. You hook him and help us reel him in, and they'll give you about anything you want.'

'Yeah? You got your coffin ready?'

'Huh? Is that some kind of threat?'

'No. You know, *Moby-Dick*, at the end?' Hammond studied Townley as the man shook his head. 'You should check it out, you'd learn a lot about fishing. And flotation devices.' He put the wine glass back on its napkin without taking even a sip and slipped out of the booth. 'Wrong time of day for me to be drinking, I guess.'

'There's a big coffee-and-tea joint around the corner.'

'Caffeine ain't gonna fix it. Guess it's time to toddle on home and cut myself.'

'What?'

'You wouldn't understand – you're not a field guy, remember?' He watched Townley's eyes, and fancied he could read the man's thoughts: *Boyce Hammond has been out in the rain too damn long.* Screw him. Hammond leaned over, slapped a hand down on Townley's shoulder, relished the brief, suppressed flinch he'd hoped for and said, '*Out* is what I'm looking for. You run this upstairs, okay? You tell them to bring me in, before I come in on my own – because I will, pal, I will.' He grinned and leaned in, speaking in a conspiratorial voice. 'A whale isn't really a fish anyway. It's a mammal.' He patted the man again in a solid, good-doggy way, and turned and left the bar.

4

Gerald

The voice of Ottensamer's clarinet sang out above the orchestral background, the cry of the woodwind plaintive and yet somehow victorious, and at last the moment came when Fedosejev swept both arms high, even his baton hand palm upwards as though to hurl the music into the sky, and the full final force of Mozart's A-Major Concerto rolled through the hall, the ending progression of chords predictable yet satisfying, a massive airborne craft brought down to a safe landing.

Gerald joined in the applause as the lights of the Konzerthaus came up halfway. Ottensamer and Fedosejev took deep bows, disappeared stage right and then, after the appropriate interval, reappeared on the stage. Fedosejev opened one hand towards the soloist as if disclaiming any personal role in the success of the performance.

In the seat to his right, Viktor was clapping politely enough, but when Gerald stole a glance at that perfect profile, the man gave him a raised eyebrow. Gorgeous as Viki looked in evening clothes, Gerald knew that his friend would rather be clubbing it up crosstown than listening to what he called *Grossmuttermusik* – grandma's music – and Gerald felt a surge of affection.

The house lights came up to full and the audience began to rise, gathering up purses and programmes, but then the lights fell again, catching half of the patrons already on their feet. A tuxedoed official was on stage, apologizing in German – most sorry, his deepest apologies, but there was an important announcement . . . A murmur of discontent rose from the crowd – the Viennese took their music seriously, took Mozart most seriously of all – and this was irregular in the extreme; irregular, ill-bred and offensive.

Gerald was so occupied trying to translate the grumbles around him that if Viktor hadn't elbowed him he might have missed the official saying, '. . . *Herr Doktor Gerald Graves* . . .' The man on the stage repeated himself in Austrian-accented English: if Dr Gerald Graves was in the audience, he should make himself known to an usher; there was an emergency.

He doubted that anyone in the crowd apart from Viki knew him, but when the house lights rose to full again, he felt conspicuous and embarrassed. At least they'd used his title: people would probably assume Gerald Graves was a medical doctor, and that he was racing to save a patient's life, a matter that might, in the eyes of the Viennese, just barely justify an announcement intruding into the afterglow of a Symphoniker concert.

How had they known he was here? Mathilde, no doubt, the section secretary; she knew his plans and schedules better than he did himself. But why the hell hadn't they just paged him? He followed his neighbours as they worked their way towards the aisles, Viki close behind him, but as he walked he pulled the pager from his hip pocket and glanced down, keeping the gadget hidden in his palm. Cripes. Instead of setting it to vibrate before he'd arrived tonight, he'd turned it off completely.

He thumbed the power switch and the damned thing was still set on alarm, so it sang a little digital song as it came on. All around him music lovers searched the crowd with looks of deep disapprobation; and a few who were close enough to Gerald to be certain he was the culprit edged away. He clicked it over to vibrate, and cast his eyes down and read the display. *01* – from Head of Section – and then *505*, report to office.

He used his free hand to dig his keys out of his pocket and then twisted round to press them into Viki's palm. 'Take the car. I'll call the apartment when I know what's happening.' Viki gave his hand a surreptitious squeeze, and Gerald almost gave him a little kiss, but then thought better of it; Austrians weren't keen on public displays of affection even between straight couples, much less between two men.

The pager buzzed and this time the display read *666*, the official code for a radiological emergency. He pushed through the crowd, no longer worrying about being polite.

The first usher he found led him to a driver, and the driver hurried him through the Art Nouveau foyer and down the steps to a car idling at the kerb. A parked car on the Lothringerstrasse after a concert was a major impediment, and two policemen were waving traffic out away from the kerb lane. That bone-snapping Mitteleuropean cold had already worked its way through his evening clothes, and Gerald pulled open the passenger door and jumped into the front seat, praying that the heater was on full force.

When the driver got behind the wheel, Gerald asked, 'Did they say where?' The driver shook his head. Great. Could be a minor spill at the RadLab of a hospital, with a couple of hot mops and buckets, or it could be Chernobyl II.

The driver shifted gears and turned the wheel as though ready to pull away from the kerb, but waited. The rear doors flew open and two more passengers piled into the back seat, big men, their winter clothes so heavy that beneath them they might have been bears. The driver steered the car out into the traffic. The door locks thunked shut all around the car, and Gerald tried flipping the toggle on his lock and then tugging on the door handle.

Instead of rounding to the side of the Stadtpark and heading for the Danube bridge, the car turned right. Gerald tried to think through his rising tide of panic. Everyone at IAEA nowadays had been schooled in abduction response, and he tried to remember what he'd been taught. Stay calm – too late for that – identify yourself and try to ascertain who has taken you hostage. 'I'm an American citizen . . .' he said, and then, realizing this was a claim that might not help, added, '. . . and accredited to the United Nations.'

The man on the left had a German accent. 'We know who you are, Dr Graves, and it is my duty to collect your badge, your pager and your ID card.'

Gerald opened his mouth and shut it again. Impossible. Were they claiming this was legal? 'Who are you?' he asked.

'I'm going to see some ID from you before I turn over anything.'

The man twisted his mouth in a look of indifference. 'No. You are not. It is you who are being arrested, not I.'

Being arrested. If true, it was far better than being abducted. But why the elaborate ruse? Of course, his apartment building had impeccable security, and the IAEA offices were guarded round the clock.

'Is one of you with *Stapo*?' he asked, probing for any connection with the Austrian federal police. 'And if not, what right do you have to just, just *grab* me like this?' The growing sense of outrage made his voice shrill in his own ears. 'In fact, if you have some reason, some legitimate reason, to arrest me, why not just come to my office?' No answer came, and fear opened in his stomach like a parachute, jerking his anger to a sudden halt. He swallowed. 'Where are you taking me?'

The other man in the back seat spoke up and, to Gerald's surprise, his words had an Arkansas twang. 'The airport. DOE's revoked your clearances, and FBI wants you home. Now hand the man what he's asking for.'

'There's some kind of mistake here. Department of Energy seconded me to IAEA for another round of three years, I'm barely through with the first six months. You must be—'

'Listen up, boy. I don't know what you're wanted for. Don't really care. You're being picked up under the Patriot Act, and that's enough for me right there. Now give the man what he wants or I'll take great pride in blowing your brains all over the dashboard.'

Gerald fumbled through his wallet until he found his card

53

and swipe-badge, and passed them back over the seat. His mind had been working fast, but without much efficiency, and he still had no idea, not even the slightest glimmer, of what was happening or why. 'You know,' he said, trying to keep his voice conversational, 'I really do think you – or somebody – must have me confused with someone else. Because I'm certain that—'

The American leaned forward and his voice came round the headrest of Gerald's seat. 'You just shut up, yeah?' Gerald heard a metallic click, and some intuition told him it was the sound of a pistol preparing for action – a hammer being cocked or a safety catch being eased off. 'Don't give me a fucking excuse.' There was a squinch of cloth against leather seats as the man leaned back. In a quiet voice, perhaps addressed only to himself, the man added, 'People like you make me sick.'

In some obscure park along the frosty banks of the Danube they forced him out of the car, and he stood shivering as they cuffed his hands behind his back and gagged him. Another pair of cuffs bound his ankles together, and once they'd loaded him into the trunk, a third set bound his wrist cuffs to his ankle cuffs.

If they planned to kill you, he told himself in the darkness of the trunk, they would have done it already. Easier to transport a corpse than a prisoner. Now try to remember the turns the car takes, they taught you that. But as time passed, he began to believe that the cold itself might do him in; little heat leaked back from the car's interior, his shivers progressed into something near convulsions and he lost track of any turns or manoeuvres.

He remembered a tilt, as if the car lumbered up an inclined driveway, and then feelings of acceleration that made no sense, but the bite of the cold gradually lessened. After a time he sank into something akin to a trembling sleep.

They'd probably been airborne an hour or more when they popped the trunk open and dragged him out.

Gerald had a dozen friends who could have told him exactly what sort of plane they'd put him on, but he'd never been one of those who awaited the next edition of *Jane's Military Aircraft* or browsed *Aviation Weekly*. Whatever combination of letters and numbers it might have been designated by, it was huge enough that it could have carried several of the limos they'd arrived in – so huge, in fact, that there was a walled-off compartment the size of his apartment kitchen where they left him, alone, in the single airline-style seat, up against the side of the plane. Plenty of leg room compared to most transatlantic hauls, but with his legs chained to ringbolts on the floor, and his wrists shackled to the seat armrests, he wasn't able to appreciate it.

Two chairs flanked the door opposite him, hard functional chairs bolted to the floor. There were no windows; if not for the inward slope of the wall at his back, it could have been an interrogation room in some Third World country.

They didn't leave him alone for long. First to enter was a Marine, dressed in fatigues, a pistol holstered on his belt. Without a word he sat in one of the chairs and watched Gerald with what seemed like a total lack of curiosity.

A few minutes later, the man with the Arkansas twang

entered and stood between Gerald's legs, looking down into Gerald's eyes. The man's head was too big for his body, and his fists seemed to be balls of knuckles and veins. 'Now, boy. Who you work with?'

'IAEA. The International At—'

The man backhanded him across the face, and Gerald's hands jerked against his cuffs in a vain effort to shield himself. 'Don't fuck with me, you little faggot. I want names.'

'Names of *what*?'

The man slapped him again, and Gerald tasted blood in his mouth. 'This is one long flight, boy, and I got long enough to hurt you to death.'

His fist smashed into Gerald's mouth, and he gasped in pain as he felt his lower lip split open.

The man grinned. 'So you just take your time, boy.'

'Jeb!' A thin man in a rumpled black suit stood in the doorway. 'Get away from him.'

'Get back up front, Frank, and let me handle this.'

'Dammit, Jeb, that's an order. Leave off. Now.'

Jeb backed a step away from Gerald and turned. 'What do you care about, our country, or fucking protocol?'

'Out. Now.'

Gerald frowned as he noticed something dripping from Jeb's knuckles, and realized it was his own blood.

Frank stepped aside, and Jeb stomped out of the room. He turned his head to watch Jeb go, then leaned down to set an accordion-top briefcase beside the empty chair. 'Sergeant – undo Dr Graves's arms, and bring him something to clean up.'

After his wrists were unshackled and the Marine left the

room in search of towels, the man flipped open a wallet and dangled his FBI photo ID in front of Gerald's face. 'Frank Welch. And I do apologize for my colleague's behaviour – it's hard to restrain people when we're under this much pressure. Can I have the sergeant get you anything – something to drink, maybe, or a blanket?'

Gerald blinked, and then, as he remembered his training classes, he laughed, sputtering specks of blood onto the front of Welch's white shirt. 'Jesus, it's just what they told me would happen. Deliberate disorientation, maybe a little torture, and then good-cop, bad-cop.'

'What who told you?'

'Took UN classes. What would happen if we were kidnapped.' Gerald grinned, and he felt blood drip off his chin. '*By terrorists*,' he added.

The man was too professional to flinch, but his total lack of reaction told Gerald he'd hit a nerve. The Marine returned, handed Gerald a towel with impartial courtesy, and shut the door before settling into his seat.

Gerald wiped his face, and winced when the rough terrycloth dragged at his injured lip.

Welch addressed the wall just above Gerald's head. 'Now that we're in the air we're in US territory, so I can formally tell you that you're under arrest for security breaches, and for disclosing classified nuclear secrets.'

Gerald's astonished laugh came so suddenly that the man took a step back. 'My God, somebody really sent you guys chasing after the wrong rabbit this time. Nuclear secrets?' He shook his head. 'I'm the guy who constantly gets called on

57

the carpet for bitching in public the US hasn't done enough on the non-proliferation front.'

Welch studied him for a moment, chewing the inside of his cheek. 'Fine.' He sat down, unbuckled the briefcase and dragged out a thick binder that he opened on his lap. 'Suppose, then, that you start by explaining who gave the *Guardian* all the background about Brazil restarting their weapons programme.'

'Sure, that was me. Also talked to *The Economist*, the *International Trib* – pretty much anybody who'd sit still and listen. Since neither our government nor IAEA seemed inclined to do anything about it, I figured I'd see if I could get the European press stirred up.'

'That's it, then?' Welch leaned back and crossed his legs. 'You admit it?'

'Admit what?'

'Disclosing classified nuclear information.'

Gerald sighed. 'Look. I'm the one who figured out Brazil was restarting their diffusion plant. On my own time. From unclass sources.' He watched Welch's face and saw no signs that he was scoring any points. 'It's nothing that any idiot couldn't figure out from the trades and *Chem Engineering Weekly*. Hydrofluoric acid? Who needs hydrofluoric acid? An alkylation plant in a refinery, though most of those are still sulphuric, but you only need fresh charge on start-up, and Brazil only has one anyway, just a couple of thousand barrels a day. Or you can use it to etch glass. Right. You could do an Art Nouveau number on every window in Brazil and not use up these kinds of volumes. So, what do you conclude?'

'I'm not following you.'

'Uranium hexafluoride. They've restarted their gaseous diffusion plant. The one they supposedly dismantled. And IAEA doesn't want to check it out, even though I wrote a memo outlining what was going on, using data from *public*, *published* sources. So I sent the same memo back to DOE, to try to get some action from the other side of the pond. But the White House – yeah, lots of talk about eliminating weapons of mass destruction, but do they bother about what's happening in Brazil?'

Welch pursed his lips and pushed them sideways, showing that he was unimpressed. 'Brazil *is* our ally, you know.'

'So's Pakistan. Boom-boom.'

Welch blinked, and then tilted his head to the side, dismissing the topic. 'As they say, tell it to the judge. Your ex-wife has also agreed to testify about various kinds of irregularities in security during your marriage – classified documents at home, discussion of classified information over the phone . . .'

'That's bullshit.'

'She's volunteered to testify.'

Gerald was willing to believe that she was vindictive enough to lie on the stand, but he doubted that she could be convincing. 'Lynn's idea of a security breach is having a tele-marketer get her cellphone number. There's no security violations and no nuclear secrets. If that's all you've got, you better turn this plane around.'

Welch stood. 'You may be telling the truth, I don't know. But if I were in your shoes, I'd be pretty damn nervous. These charges come right from the top, straight out of the AG's office. And that means they're going to go after you with everything they've got.' He dumped the binder into his briefcase, latched it and opened the door. 'And no matter what you think, having your ex testify will make you look like Benedict Arnold.'

'She won't testify,' Gerald said, 'once she realizes that guys in prison can't send alimony cheques.'

'Yeah? Department of Justice has already seized her house and frozen her bank accounts.'

'Jesus!' Gerald tried to jump to his feet, but rebounded when he reached the end of his shackles. He sat down hard. 'Are you guys fucking crazy?'

Welch stepped through the doorway. 'You decide you want to confess and set up a plea, you send for me.'

'I'm not pleading to anything. I'm not *guilty* of anything!'

The man paused with a hand on the doorknob. 'May not mean as much as you think.' He started to say more, hesitated, and then sighed. 'Listen. I can't tell whether you're feeding me a line or giving me the gospel. But here's some free advice about Washington these days: it ain't about being on the side of right. It's about being on the right side.'

5

East of Suez

The Burj al-Arab Hotel in Dubai claimed to be the tallest hotel in the world. It sure as hell had the highest atrium; when Carla tilted her head back she could see up for the length of at least two football fields. The way the three walls of the hotel – one of them glass – curved inwards to meet at the apex made it look even taller, as though the lines of the building converged in the distance.

She tilted her head down when Lamont Richter returned from the breakfast buffet, his plate laden with grilled tomatoes, madamas, leben and triangles of pitta. 'When in Rome, huh?' she asked.

He settled into his seat, taking a quick look at her own plate of eggs and potatoes. 'Fact is, I originally hail from Rome. Rome, Georgia, that is.' He lifted knife and fork and set about cutting his pitta into bite-sized pieces. 'Beautiful Floyd County.'

'I did some stuff at Benning,' Carla said. 'Swell climate.'

'Ah, but the spring's lovely. It's the other fifty-one weeks of the year that get you down.' Richter had finished cutting his tomatoes, and he began to fork together a bite: a chunk of tomato, a bit of leben, several madamas beans and a piece of pitta, all pushed onto the tines in sequence like a miniature shish-kebab.

Carla glanced skywards again. 'Wonder how long it'll be before someone flies a plane into this one.'

His voice was amused, his Southern drawl exaggerated. 'Now, why would they do that?'

'Big target. And I'm sure somebody in the Gulf thinks Dubai is the centre of godlessness in these parts. Bars. Women in dresses, without headscarves.'

'Like yourself. You do look quite nice, by the way.'

'Look like fuckin' Barbie.' She glanced down at her pearly silk business suit. 'Well, Muscle Barbie, maybe.' Spending an entire afternoon in Versace with Richter's assistant Ellen had been one of the low points of her adult life. She wasn't quite the right shape for anything in the store, and she'd had to stand there forever while they chalked in little lines to make alterations.

'What did you wear when you were escorting ambassadors? Surely you didn't travel in combat fatigues?'

'Nothing this goofy.' Carla felt her cheeks beginning to redden; even as a little girl she'd felt less self-conscious naked than she did dressed up like a goddamned Easter basket. She leaned down and retrieved the accordion folder from where it leaned against the leg of her chair. 'Here.' She held it over the table toward him. 'You should probably have this back now. Everything's in there.'

Richter placed the folder in his lap. 'And?'

Carla had spent the previous two days studying the documents – photocopies, for the most part, seemingly from a dozen different sources. Many were fragments of official memos on 8½ x 11, with the headers and footers missing and occasional phrases redacted into oblivion by a felt-tipped marker – probably CIA, DOD, NSA. Others were in English but on A4 paper – most likely NATO goodies – and there were a fistful of government memos in Arabic. Two final pages were in Hebrew with English translations attached. Mossad, presumably. Whoever had put the package together was wired in to Spook Central. 'I'm good to go.'

'With respect to your brother, of course, there's no guarantee that this particular crowd . . .'

'They're in the same business.' Carla wriggled. She'd forgotten how damned uncomfortable it was to have a bra digging into your flesh right below the armpits; stretch fabrics were relentless. 'They're the same,' she said, 'they're all the same.'

Carla slapped her notebook closed with an air of finality. 'We're a big company,' she said. 'If we're happy with the quality and the price, we can get round the sanctions one way or another.'

The conference room held an oval wooden table large enough for twenty participants, but Carla looked across its five-foot width at only two other people. Daoud smiled and nodded – this was exactly what he'd wanted to hear – but Rashid, the man from the Syrian Ministry of Industry, didn't change his dour expression. 'Your government seems intent on hurting our people, hurting them as much as they can.'

Carla waved this away. 'That's politics. This is business.'

When Rashid looked even more dogged, she added, 'Listen. Just a year before he ended up being Vice-President, Dick Cheney was in the UAE talking to the Iranians about what his company could do in developing their offshore gas resources.' She paused. 'That's the *Iranians*. If the future VP can play ball with the Iranians without anybody calling foul . . .'

Daoud nodded so hard in agreement she thought he might injure his neck, but Rashid muttered to him in Arabic, 'I don't need to sit and debate politics with a koos.'

Koos: cunt, pussy. Hole. *Elif air ab tizak*, she thought, *a thousand dicks up your ass*, but kept a bright baffled smile on her face as though she didn't understand a word.

Daoud was flustered, and scanned her face for any sign of comprehension. 'My company would like to take you to lunch today at our club, one of the finest down on the Ghouta—'

'Thank you, but no.' She resisted the urge to grin as both men tried to hide signs of relief; clearly, like many Arab men, they considered it vaguely degrading to eat with a woman in public, and it was more so if they were seen to be doing so in front of their peers. Carla had a headscarf covering her blondeness, true enough, but she knew she would be an embarrassment to both of them. 'I have a telecon with my people in New York.'

'Perhaps some other time, then,' Daoud said.

She rose from her chair. 'If you can send those files to our European HQ, I'll have my team start running the numbers.' My team. Start running the numbers. Christ in lederhosen, a week with Richter's folks had been enough to make her sound like a total MBA jackass. Just to top it off, she added, 'Nothing's cast in concrete yet, but I'll make sure one of my *boys* gives this top priority.' Both men stood. 'Oh, and by the way – if you could make sure that the driver this time understands English? We had an *awful* time getting to my hotel yesterday.' Carla gave Rashid her best smile, silently wishing *Yela'an Mayteen Ahlak*, may God damn all your ancestors.

It was her fifth day in Damascus, and so far Carla had managed to keep her afternoons and evenings free. Her alter ego Jennifer Brown, VP for Textiles at FiberCorp International, was in great demand with the Syrian industrialists, even if FiberCorp's sending a woman might have been perceived as a slap in the face.

Which made it even sweeter to turn down their invitations with the regret that she was too busy.

Le Meridien Damascus was located perfectly for tourists, not far from the Old City, and close enough to the centres of power for business travellers. For Carla, it was something of a disaster, miles from where she needed to be, but it provided good cover.

She pushed open the door to her room. The fretted grille-work on the headboard of the bed and the tessellated bathroom tiles suggested that the room was in the Middle East, but only in the most gestural way. An envelope had been pushed under the door, along with a short fax. She plucked them up, tossed her notebook onto the bed and kicked the door shut behind her.

The envelope held a Meridien cardkey.

The scrawled fax told her that a Mr C. Heston had called, and wanted her to call back at 212–248–4725, extension 43.

She sat on the bed, lifted the phone receiver and punched the button for the hotel's voicemail. Her only message purported to be from a Bill Brady, who had been happy to let her know that the company stock had just passed thirty-two.

A simple code, but easy for a one-off affair. Start past the third two – so after 212–2 – grab the next three. Okay, 484. Extend by forty-three, that made what? Three plus four was seven, eight plus four was twelve, carry the one, five . . . 527.

She kicked off the dumb-assed heels she'd worn all morning, stepped out of the room and padded down the hotel hallway to the stairwell, feet bare except for the layer of nylon mesh that came with the pantyhose.

If there were a moment where things might have gone totally off the rails, she figured it would have been upon opening the door to Room 527. She was ready to pull her sheath skirt to the top of her thighs so that she could use her legs for something other than tottering along, but there was no need. The room was deserted but for a shopping bag on the nightstand.

She carried the bag back to her room, turned the deadbolt and spread the contents out on the bed. A Makarov automatic pistol. Figured the Syrians would still be working with artefacts from the Soviet era. She hefted it, felt the cross-hatched grip catch at the skin of her palm, a nice, satisfying friction, a gun's way of saying *I'm here for you, babe*. Just above the grip a bifurcated triangle had been incised into the metal, enclosed in a perfect circle. This wasn't just export-grade, this was the real thing, Soviet military issue, probably from the seventies. A collectible in some circles, but more important, reliable. Short of a direct nuclear hit, this puppy would still be tossing metal in a thousand years.

The silencer was less authentic, without any identifying marks. The tube was most likely a Bulgarian or Chinese knock-off, strictly bargain-basement, but it screwed on with a clean, oily smoothness that verged on erotic.

The gas mask was a floppy, foldable job, probably for civilian emergencies. The disposable screw-on canister, the size of a tin of chewing tobacco, wouldn't hold out for more than thirty minutes, and wouldn't hold out at all against nerve gases. It ought to do fine; with any luck, she wouldn't need it.

Richter's guy apparently hadn't understood the rest of her requests. The holster was olive-green nylon mesh with a Velcro closure at the top – nice enough, but cumbersome in an emergency. Too short to accommodate a silencer. The knife was a thing of beauty, a supple leather sheath, a wicked curved blade, and a handle inlaid with ivory and carnelian; more about looks than wet work. The high-test monofilament line was serviceable, though she would have preferred a slightly thinner strand.

She used the knife to cut the nose out of the holster and then dropped the pistol in a few times, silencer and all. The extended barrel snagged when she pulled it out. No big deal; she wasn't planning on any *High Noon* scenes.

Carla stripped off her business clothes and fetched her jeans from the closet, where the maid had folded them on top of her suitcase. As she bent to step into the pants she caught a glimpse of her body, still a little flabby from months of hard boozing. Three or four obvious scars on her legs; one puncture wound on the side of her belly that might have been taken for a sloppy appendectomy. As a counterpoint, high on her waist, the encircling red marks made by the unaccustomed squinch of pantyhose.

She bent her elbow, tilted her fist up and flexed, hoping to see her pectoral show some cut. The cord of tendon from her armpit stood up, quivering and rigid, but disappeared into the soft fat of her breast without coaxing forth a single striation.

Jesus. She could have used another month or so in training, maybe two.

She shrugged, pulled her jeans up and zipped them. *It is what it is*.

People claim Damascus is the oldest continuously inhabited city on the planet – though the Chinese dispute this, as some obscure point of pride. Whatever its age, old and new coexisted. Women covered their hair, but women in headscarves atop Western attire walked side-by-side with women draped in shapeless black robes. Enough tradition continued that there was a citywide lull in activity in the early afternoon, the Middle Eastern equivalent of the siesta, when those who could retreated from the heat and let their lunches settle.

Summer hadn't yet descended, but the air was hot. Carla's taxi driver had taken a route so indirect that it would have made any New York cabbie blush with shame, cutting through a corner of the Old City, and then paralleling the meanders of the Ghouta, the gardens that traced the banks of the Barada River as it lost itself in a thousand ditches and canals. Through the window Carla inhaled the scents of a spice market together with the rank humidity of the river, a mixture like the odour of leftovers after sitting out too long.

At the Hotel Qasim, a small hotel patronized by Syrians as well as Europeans one step up from the hostel crowd, she paid off the driver and pushed through the front door like any brazen tourist woman, daypack slung over one shoulder.

Ten minutes later she emerged in a full chador, a black tent surmounted by an engulfing hood, with only a mesh opening for the eyes. A rattling city bus carried her to the Saahat Khorshid, halfway up the rocky slope of Jebel Qassiun. A dozen afternoon idlers – all of them men – sat at the cafés around the square, toying with their tiny cups of coffee as they gazed out across the sprawl of Damascus in the valley below.

There were some expensive neighbourhoods on the mountainside, but most of the slopes were covered by the homes of the working poor – charmless concrete or stuccoed apartments and townhouses sharing common walls, rising only two or three storeys, and dressed in colours so drab that it was impossible to tell if a given wall had been painted or was simply dirty. Carla headed east, and though the rows of buildings continued, the streets narrowed and the pavement ended. The hardpan soil of the road was gullied from rains long past, but now the saffron dust rose with every step and gathered on the hem of her black robe – a hem she had distinctively frayed on the left side so that 'Ali', her associate, could recognize her despite the anonymous garb.

The district seemed deserted. Those not at work in the town or factories below were shuttered in their houses. The sunlight gave any surface it struck a harsh glow. The shadows in the street were like slices of the night sky by contrast, and Carla paced down an empty roadway carpeted with polygons of light and dark.

Damascus was, at least in diplomatic terms, terrorist-central; every little splinter group of every Middle Eastern political faction maintained an office there, with the full knowledge of the government. Back in 2000 there been an uproar when an Israeli newspaper had published the addresses of fifteen of the roughly forty-five terrorist groups represented in Syria; the Syrians had complained that to identify these groups publicly was an incitement to violence. But most of those outposts were political in nature, housed closer to the city centre.

Not this one. Carla was hunting practitioners.

The single-storey safe house sat on the north side of the street, right at the edge of the town. Their squat beige warehouse sat fifteen yards past the end of the road, off in the rocks and sand. Syrian rue stood in scraggly knee-high clumps – *esphand* to the Iranians, *haoma* to the Parsees, the seeds a sacred incense according to her Culture & Customs instructor, ages ago.

It all looked like sagebrush to her.

There had been only two planning meetings with Ali, her assistant, both times in hotel lobbies, though she'd seen him from a distance every afternoon of the previous four days – one of the few pedestrians she'd sighted as she shuffled up and down the streets and through the narrow alleyways that separated the blocks. Carla had never worked with someone she hadn't trained with, and the thought made her a little nervous. She'd never had to trust her back to a stranger. Yet the man sounded like a professional, and he had all the details.

The safe house was a one-storey apartment tacked on to the side of a series of two-storey townhouses. The front door opened into a living room, used as an office, with a large bedroom to the right. A hallway ran back from the living room, with two more bedrooms to the right, a kitchen to the left, a bathroom at the end of the hall.

One desultory guard on the rooftop patio of the warehouse – she'd seen him there every day; another just inside the door of the safe house, both with walkie-talkies, both sloppy in desert-tan fatigues.

Inside the safe house, her four targets. Three of them were FIG, the Libyan extremist group working for the overthrow of Qaddafi on the grounds that he was insufficiently Islamic. Carla had nothing against FIG – let 'em kill each other if they liked – but these three had temporarily abandoned the struggle against Qaddafi to funnel explosives and arms to the jihadis in Iraq.

The fourth target was a former member of the Abu Nidal Organization, the group that had carried out the *Achille Lauro* hijacking; the people who had shot a wheelchair-bound man in front of his wife just to teach the world a lesson.

Carla needed to dispatch the rooftop guard on the warehouse. Once that was done, Ali would toss a gas grenade through the kitchen window of the house. Carla would pick off her prey as they poured out the door. Ali would handle any that came out bedroom windows or tried the back door out of the kitchen – though, since that's where the gas would be, it was an unlikely escape route.

It should be closer to an execution than to a firefight. Only if the targets failed to appear would she pull on the gas mask and go in hunting.

A few blocks from the end of the street, she saw Ali squatting in an alleyway over to her left, smoking. He stood as she passed and then slipped away to the north, around the backside of the townhouses.

The guard on the warehouse rooftop slouched against the waist-high patio wall, slurping at a soft-drink can. A kid, really, careless and arrogant, with the merest scruff of beard on his face. He glanced down the road, his eyes passing over Carla without any apparent hesitation or interest.

She'd grown used to this over the last four afternoons. Her outfit proclaimed her to be female, traditional and probably old, and the result was like some form of ghosthood. Wouldn't be much of a challenge to be a male cross-dresser in Syria, would it? She not only could have been a man beneath the robes, she could have carried enough armaments to lay siege to a small fort.

The guard crushed the empty can and tossed it down onto the gravelly sand, where someone would scavenge it later for the aluminium. She recognized the demented red-and-blue yin-yang sign. Pepsi. It would have to be Pepsi, of course. Coke had been banned in most Arab countries since the day they opened a factory in Israel.

Carla shuffled off the end of the street, towards the building, heading towards barren terrain where no one but a goatherd could possibly have any business, but a glance through the mesh eye-slit of her veil showed that the guard saw her no more than he would have seen a pigeon. The hours she'd spent on courses on camo and concealment: what a waste. All she'd needed to do was dress like a woman.

She walked on past the warehouse and then edged round the back, facing the empty slopes of Jebel Qassiun off to the east. A concrete stairway led up to the rooftop. As she had four times before, Carla moved into the shadows beneath it. She drew out the monofilament line, two feet of it, either end tied to the barrels of cheap ballpoint pens. She tugged on the makeshift handles and felt a satisfying twang.

She checked her watch, and then sat down on the dusty ground and waited.

After what seemed like fifteen minutes she checked her watch again. Five minutes, of course. She rolled her shoulders to loosen them. How could she be sure all her targets would be in the safe house? What if the warehouse guard didn't come downstairs today? What if—

She could almost hear Jill beside her. *Goddammit, Smukowski, once you start a move, stop thinking. It's a bobsled run. Thinking doesn't do shit to slow down the bobsled, but it sure as fuck slows down your reactions.*

Concentrate on your breathing. Even it. Listen to your pulse. Wait.

Twenty minutes. The guy's bladder habits had been regular four days running. He'd give a heads-up over the walkie-talkie before he came down the stairs, and then she'd have her window of time, the length of an average piss, before the guard at the safe house started to wonder . . . but the sonofabitch on the roof must have put on a pair of incontinence briefs that morning. Another half-hour and people would be moving around again, all over town.

Drop it. Come again tomorrow. Game cancelled due to rain.

No. Do it.

She stood, stretched and then walked up the stairs, hunched over like an old woman.

The rooftop patio was bare but for a half-dozen wooden tubs in the centre. Someone was growing eggplant. Carla doddered over towards the plants, keeping her head down, but watching the young guard from under her eyebrows, her gaze hidden by the mesh of her veil. *Pick up the walkie-talkie and call in*, she found herself urging him, even though it was the last thing she wanted him to do, *don't you have any discipline, don't you have any respect for procedure, don't you want to stay alive . . .?*

'Eh?' He straightened. 'No one allowed,' he said in Arabic, his North African accent thick. 'Eh! Move on.'

She affected not to hear him, leaning forward over the plants as if inspecting them. She moved around the circle of tubs to his side, and leaned in again, her back to him.

'You can't hear?' His footsteps came up behind her. 'Clear off!'

She lifted a young green-purple eggplant dangling from a stem and squeezed it.

'*Eh!*' He bumped her hip with the butt of his rifle, and not gently.

Carla spun on one foot and swept the other one back, catching him just above the front of his ankles, and he pitched forward and hit the patio face-down. She had the line around his throat in a second, but the robe of the chador slowed her, and she fumbled getting her knee in the centre of his back, giving him time to claw back at her and even get a grip on the fabric of the robe.

She jerked up hard and twisted, and his instincts made him let loose of the chador and scrabble at the thing cutting into his windpipe, and she had him. She leveraged with her knee and tried not to think as he went into his final convulsions, his legs hammering, his whole body arching up from the floor.

She removed the garotte. It had cut a thin line of red into his neck, and blood began to well up in the smooth skin. Maybe eighteen years old, twenty?

A kid.

Think about it later. He could get a call on the walkie-talkie at any moment. Move.

At the bottom of the stairway she heard a sound from the main street, a car climbing the grade. She stopped and listened. Heavy motor sounds, the round growl of a diesel, but a small one. The sound came closer, and didn't turn off onto any side streets. The crunch of the tyres on the dirt road ceased. The motor died, and a car door opened and slammed. Then a second door.

Carla crept to the front corner of the warehouse and peeked out at the street. A dusty black Mercedes, an early-eighties model, was parked in front of the safe house, and the front door stood open. A man in a wrinkled suit – the driver, no doubt – leaned against the car, chatting with the guard, whose bulk filled the doorframe.

The car had government plates.

She saw Ali peek round the northern corner of the apartment, twenty yards away. He shook his head.

Too late to bail now; somebody was already dead. Oh, sure, she could slink on back to the hotel, but they'd never get a second shot at this bunch . . . She raised her forearm through the slit in the robe and flagged it forward twice, open-palmed. Go.

Ali shook his head again, and drew his fingers across his throat. Carla repeated her gesture.

He shook his head once more, waved goodbye and disappeared.

Shit. She took a deep breath. Well, come on, girl. Do it or head home. Every second you wait is a second when the door guard might call the guy you killed.

Carla pulled her arm inside her robe and eased the Makarov out of its holster.

She squinted, trying to adjust her eyes for the indoor lighting she knew would be coming. The veil already acted like a cheap pair of sunglasses.

She didn't run across the street from the warehouse, but she didn't move with the halting gait of an old lady, either. By the time she'd crossed half the distance to the car, the guard had glanced her way, and by the time she rounded the front corner of the car, both the driver and the guard were frowning at her. An interesting problem in logistics: the driver appeared to be unarmed, so it would make sense to shoot the guard first, but in terms of sequence it made more sense to shoot the driver, then the guard, so that she would already be aimed into the doorway. But the guard was armed, and some-what alert . . .

The driver parted his lips to say something to her and she shot him in his open mouth from four feet away, a muffled blat from the silencer, and she corrected for the kick of the barrel as she continued to swing the gun towards the guard as she ran the last steps and squeezed off a round into his shocked face.

The guard fell back through the doorway of the safe house and she jumped over his body into a cacophony of voices, her robes billowing out as her feet hit the floor. She fired at the silhouettes within, going for the chest, her vision indoors too uncertain to go for headshots. Strong kicks from the gun, but only that flat spitting sound at each shot, the reports so quiet that in between the cries of alarm and pain she could hear the chiming of the brass cartridges as they rained onto the floor. Three down, four; someone crouching behind a desk, coming up with something in his hand . . .

Five down.

Two in the doorway, five in the room, that made seven; the Makarov was an 8+1, which left her two rounds, one already chambered. She wheeled side-to-side, scanning.

At least two of them were still alive, one of them gurgling, another clutching at his chest.

The room seemed to be a combination office and living room. The wall opposite opened into a hallway; to her right was a closed door.

She vaulted over a body and headed down the hall, pistol still extended.

To the left, a bedroom, two beds, the door open. A door

on the right, barely ajar: she eased past it, peeked into the two open doors towards the end of the hallway. A kitchen. Another empty bedroom. A bathroom at the end of the hall.

She came back down the hallway towards the living room, paused outside the ajar door. She hid her body against the wall and eased it open with her toe, then dropped to one knee and leaned pistol and face into the room.

An office. Desks. Shelves.

Groans and choking sounds came from the office.

One more room to check, the one directly off the office. She stepped across the body in the hallway.

A stunning, shocking pain in her left calf. Carla fell to the floor and curled back around on her side, gun extended.

It was one of the Libyans, propped on one elbow. She took deliberate aim and shot him in the forehead.

The pain in her leg still jangled, and she reached back and swiped at her calf with her free hand, and then cried out as she dislodged a short blade from her flesh. She dragged the damned hood off and threw it down in disgust. No peripheral vision. How the hell did they expect women to do anything if they were half-blind all the time? She levered herself up with the heels of her palms and her good leg and limped towards the closed door.

This time she flung the door open and entered Makarov first, ready to fire.

It was a small room, and there was a figure on a cot facing her, his hands tied behind his back, a gag in his mouth. One of his eyes was swollen shut, but the other showed unmistakable surprise at seeing a blonde woman in a hoodless chador, aiming a pistol at him.

Carla left him for the moment and hobbled back out into the office, where she checked faces and then cut throats with her handsome damascene blade.

She'd bound her calf tight with bandages from the bathroom – too tight, from a first-aid perspective, but the extra pressure made it possible to walk with no more than a wince at each step. She donned the chador hood again before she stepped through the front door to drag the driver inside.

The warehouse at the end of the street was exactly that, a warehouse. At first she found only truck parts and drill bits, but the crates stacked in one corner turned out to be explosives – just dynamite, for the most part, but one box yielded the unmistakable motor-oil smell of plastique. Probably not genuine C-4, but a decent imitation: Swiss or French. Fuses, timers and detonators, even some fancy long-range radio-frequency units.

She hesitated. It was enough explosive power that it might – just might, who knows, this was a pile of crates, not shaped charges – take out this end of the street along with the warehouse.

She didn't have time to cart them off to a safe distance, and didn't intend to leave them for whoever came next.

The wound in her leg went off like an alarm. Fuck it. People like this had killed Kevin, and if innocent folks chose to live next to people who patrolled warehouses with automatic weapons, they'd have to take their chances. She uncrated the plastique and started wrapping the long, oily rolls around a crate of dynamite.

*

She flipped on the light in the small room and stood over the captive. All his fingernails on one hand had been ripped out, and it looked as though someone had recently been working at his fingertips with a blade. An Arab, from what she could see of his profile, probably Lebanese.

She sighed, and started out of the room. Not my problem, not even a situation I understand . . .

Shit. She turned back, leaned down and undid his gag. He cried out when she pulled the cloth away from his lips, and it was easy to see why: it tore scabs from lips that had been shredded. She whispered in Arabic, 'Do you hear me?'

'Yes.' The word came slurred from his broken mouth.

The enemy of my enemy is my friend.

Stupid thinking. And she didn't want it announced to the world that a woman in a chador, a blonde woman, might be an assassin.

It was either that, or shoot him in the head. She spoke in her most generically accented Arabic, closest to a Cairo gargle on the glottals. 'Listen very closely.' She knelt beside the bed and slid her blade between his wrists. 'I'm going to cut you loose. You're going to get up and walk out of here in front of me, and then keep on walking, without looking back at me. Then go far away.' She began to saw at the bindings but paused. 'Tell no one how you were released. Make up a story. Understand?'

'Yes.'

She cut through his bonds and helped him to his feet. She urged him a few feet forward. 'Go.'

'Alhamdullilah.' She could hardly understand the word;

the man's teeth had been shattered. *You will be blessed for this.*

'Go.'

After the man stumbled out into the street, Carla let herself out the back door in the kitchen. The neighbourhood was beginning to stir as she made her way down the alleyways and streets, back towards Saahat Khorshid and her bus ride down the mountain.

Just before she arrived back at the square, she turned the dial on the RF transmitter she'd stolen from the warehouse. Carla was the only person in the vicinity who didn't look eastwards towards the sound of the explosion.

6

Atoms for Peace

A freak spring thunderstorm had left Washington's streets littered with tree branches that evening, and the driver had to
slow to edge the limousine around some of the larger fallen
limbs. Gerald realized he'd had his face almost pressed to the
glass of the window, looking out at the wet city and ignoring
his benefactor. He turned and looked across the plush seat to
where Lamont Richter sat.

Richter raised one eyebrow. 'Seems we picked a nasty
night to fetch you out.'

Gerald watched as Richter undraped one long leg from
the other and recrossed them, right over left. Everything
about the man seemed so cultivated – from the refined Georgia drawl to the way the grey suit hung on his lanky frame –
that Gerald's fingertips tingled. He'd never been attracted to
older men (hell, according to his friends, he was practically
a chicken hawk), but Richter really had it, had it in that maddening way that some straight guys did. Gerald wet his lips
and said, 'Most beautiful night I've ever seen. Of course, I've
been looking at cinder-block walls for almost a month.' He

paused, and then added, 'Mr Richter, I really – well, I just want to say that I can't possibly even begin to thank you enough for what you've done . . .' *Just want to say that I can't possibly even begin to thank you enough?* Gee, what eloquence. Are you going to drop your hankie next?

Richter waved the issue away with a tranquil toss of his hand. 'Don't thank me, thank Atwater. And all of the other folks you'll be meeting tonight. I'm just a consultant . . . and it's *Lamont*, please, not Mr Richter.'

'What happens now . . . Lamont?'

'To what?'

'To the charges against me?'

'I expect they'll vanish like the dew. That was an illegal snatch in Vienna, and the Austrians are doing themselves a Chinese Lion Dance about it.' He looked over at Gerald and chuckled. 'And there's no FBI fellow named Frank Welch, either, so the whole thing smells. By the time our legal bunch is done, the Adminstration'll be ducking back into their burrows and pulling the dirt in after them.'

Gerald glanced down at his tux – the same clothes in which he'd been arrested and flown across the Atlantic, clothes that had then been wadded up and stuffed into a box by whatever jailers had been holding him. Under the shield of the Patriot Act, of course, the folks in the Justice Department didn't need to use much haste in making clear where you were being held, or by whom, or why . . . but whoever his captors had been, they apparently didn't include pressing and dry cleaning in their budgets. 'I look like an idiot. Plus everybody there will be in suits, not formals, right?'

Lamont laughed, a laugh of surprise and genuine amusement. 'You look fine. And, *son* – this is your fan club, here. You could come dressed as Che Guevara or Minnie Mouse and they wouldn't fluster the least bit.' He tilted one finger at Gerald, as though he couldn't be bothered to move his whole hand. 'We both know you're pale from living too long in Vienna . . . but add the rumpled tux, and the bruises on the face, and you look just like the prince who's been rescued from a year in the dungeon.'

Richter studied him a moment more, and added, 'The ineptly removed bloodstains are a particularly nice touch. Remind me to make sure we get good photos tonight – the lawyers will want them when we sue everyone who can even spell *Vienna*.'

The limo eased over to the kerb, and Gerald realized they had pulled up next to The Mall, not far from his former Department of Energy office in the Forrestal Building. 'The reception is here? Where?'

'Right there.' Richter tilted his head towards one of the red-brick buildings.

'In the Smithsonian?' He watched Richter half-shrug. '*In the Air and Space Museum?*'

The driver had scurried out and opened Richter's door, and the clean sharp smell of the earlier thunderstorm rolled into the car. 'You prefer Natural History?'

'How the hell do you get to hold a party at the Smithsonian?'

'I assure you, *I* don't.' Richter pronounced *I* with a lazy emphasis that turned it into *Ahhhh* . . . He hoisted himself out of the deep seat cushion, stepped out of the car and then

84

ducked his head to peer back inside. 'It's done all the time, by certain kinds of people. Why not? Smithsonian's public property, isn't it? Problem is . . . some folks seem to be more public than the rest of us.'

Gerald had friends who'd met Reagan, and friends – mostly another set – who'd met Clinton, and all of them described the same thing: a genial, feel-good presence that got bigger and bigger, and an ability to pay attention to you in a way that made it seem you were the only other person in the room. Whatever the origins of that narcotic aura, Rex Atwater had a limitless reservoir. Gerald felt himself grinning from the moment that Atwater shook his hand, and that same delighted grin stayed on his face as Atwater took him by the elbow and steered him towards the lecture alcove of the museum.

The room had been outfitted with a long dining table along one wall, and a buffet and bar along the other. The silver globes of the buffet dishes still sat closed, but to judge from the reaction of the crowd in the centre of the room when Gerald entered, the bar had been in use for some time before his arrival. Perhaps two dozen men and women, in suits – casual attire by DC party standards – turned and applauded. The applause was muted because most of the clapping was done with fingertips against the heel of the opposite palm, so as not to spill the drinks, but the volume of welcoming voices rose to compensate.

After a month alone in a cell, with nothing but infrequent interrogations to break the tedium, everything was a blur. Atwater escorted him through the crowd, making introductions. Gerald had heard of few of the attendees, but the emphasis with which Atwater pronounced the names made it clear that Gerald should at least act as if he knew of them; made it clear that anyone with real connections would know these were real players. There were lawyers, environmentalists and the expected assortment of politicians; but there was also a handful of folks who must simply have been born rich, people who were introduced by name only.

An hour of hand-shaking, back-slapping and grinning had put him through four flutes of champagne by the time Atwater announced dinner. He found himself seated at the centre of the long table, alongside Atwater. After weeks of what must have been Kraft macaroni-and-cheese, Gerald applied himself to his food, nodding as Jake Powers, from the Brookings Institute, and Linley Jarrow, an attorney, boiled over with Washington gossip. Only when Powers gave Gerald a pointed look and said, 'This Administration might as well be *sponsoring* nuclear proliferation', did he abandon his plate.

Confident, tipsy and well fed, Gerald was in the mood for a pleasant disagreement. 'Don't blame them in particular.' He pushed his plate away and hooked one thumb back over his shoulder to the past. 'It's an old, old story.'

Linley Jarrow said, 'Seems like you'd be ready to blame them for quite a bit, considering.'

'I am. And if you can help me crucify them for their lock-me-up-to-shut-me-up policy, I'm all for it.' Gerald smoothed his hair back. 'But I was talking about the bigger picture.' He realized that people up and down the table had suddenly tuned in to the conversation, and he raised his voice a little. 'Look. This goes way beyond party politics.' He started into his standard litany, Nuclear Proliferation 101. The huge escalations in the Soviet and Chinese arsenals because of confrontations with JFK and Reagan; the failure to help the Russians dismantle and control their inventories under Bush, Clinton and Bush. 'Truth is, the last people who really did anything right were Nixon and Carter.'

The Senator down the table laughed. 'Isn't everyday you find them on the same side.'

There were chuckles, but Powers persisted. 'How long is it, do you suppose, before a terrorist group gets their hands on one of those Soviet-era bombs?'

The table became quieter. Gerald had answered this one a hundred times before, and his reply had always infuriated his superiors at DOE. 'Somebody has one already. Probably three to five groups have acquired one.'

The hubbub that followed his words surprised him; only Atwater, Richter and the Brookings man seemed nonplussed. 'Is it that easy?' Atwater asked. 'When should we expect them to nuke DC?'

'Ownership and delivery are very different matters. They're big, and heavy, and the detonators are complex, and to really flatten a city they have to go off high above the target. You need missiles, or a bomber, and some good technicians—' Gerald realized he was getting both grim and pedantic, well outside the bounds of dinner-table talk.

'I don't need to sell my Rock Creek place, then?' someone down the table called.

There was laughter, and at the far ends of the table some whispered conversations started up again. Gerald stared at the tiny fan of a shrimp tail on his plate.

'So there's no imminent danger?' Atwater asked.

Gerald raised his head. To hell with it. He'd give them the full horror show. He talked about the Eisenhower Atoms for Peace programme, the missing kilos of plutonium, the medical radiologicals, the piles of waste from power plants . . . and dirty bombs. Suddenly it was all too much. No exercise in a month, drinks, a heavy meal – and now here he was again, singing the same song he'd been singing for the last fifteen years. He threw up his hands and leaned back in his seat. 'Nobody even knows where it all is. Nothing's going to happen until we lose a city.'

'And why don't we do something to change that?' Powers asked.

'Great idea. A couple scientists and a PC aren't enough.'

'We agree. We're assuming we'd need to start with at least ten full-time scientists and engineers, maybe ultimately staffing up to double that level – if that many qualified people could be found . . .'

Gerald opened his mouth and then shut it. That would involve a budget of – hell, at least two or three million a year, just in salaries. Plus rent, overheads, equipment, travel. He glanced round, ready to object on cost grounds, and then smiled at his own naivety. They might not understand nuclear science, but the group gathered here knew everything there was to know about money. 'The scientists and engineers are out there. I personally know a dozen who'd leap at the chance.'

Atwater patted the table with an open palm, as though he were calming a large dog. 'We're hoping you can give us some guidance in that regard, and at least sit on the Board of Directors.' Atwater smiled, and it once again felt to Gerald as if they were alone together. 'We're also hoping – and we don't need an answer now, you can mull it over – we're hoping that you might be willing to run the place.'

Gerald hadn't been to church in decades, but suddenly he believed in God again.

The guests had been picked up by their chauffeurs, and Richter was bundling Gerald off to a hotel in the care of his driver. Atwater stood alone in the half-lit museum gallery, nursing a cocktail and studying a special exhibit on the *Enola Gay* and the bombing of Hiroshima. It had been a good night, maybe a perfect night. Most of the work had been done for him by the earnest, do-gooder crowd he'd assembled. All it had taken from him was the slightest nudge here and there.

Richter sauntered up with a tumbler of Jack Daniel's in his hand. 'I like a man who isn't afraid to drink like a woman. Is that a pink Martini, Rex?'

Atwater raised the glass. 'A Cosmo. Cranberry juice's good for your bladder.'

'Didn't know you had bladder problems.'

'This is why I don't.'

The only sounds were the distant clink of dishes being gathered up by the caterers. The two of them wandered without speaking through the gentle dimness, and out to the centrepiece of the museum: Lindbergh's plane, suspended from the ceiling. They stared up at it and sipped their drinks. 'I always forget—' Richter began.

'. . . how small it is.' He'd been thinking the same thing. Small, flimsy, fragile. Memory always transformed *The Spirit of St Louis* into something monumental. 'You could tear it apart with your bare hands.'

'Take a little work, but I grant your point. Course, breaking things is always easy.' Richter sniffed. 'How do you feel about our boy Dr Graves?'

'Still might have been easier to hire someone, and tell them the truth.'

'The people you want aren't for sale. You can buy techies from Russia. But Gerald's got the whole picture.'

'Except the picture of what I want to do.'

'Even better. He's a True Believer, just like the crew you had in here tonight. You can trust him – not like people who are in it for the money.'

'I thought *you* were in it for the money.'

Richter chuckled. 'I don't recall,' he said, 'that I ever insisted on being trusted. Just paid. But people motivated by morals, or revenge, they're effective. Look at our little female Terminator in the Mideast. Damascus, Amman, Karachi. Effective.'

'We need to bring her home for this. What she's doing is just swatting flies.'

Richter laid his hand on Atwater's shoulder, and the touch was so unexpected Atwater felt himself flinch. 'Rex. We're really making a dent. Field a few more agents like Carla, and let the effects pile up. Put these other ideas on hold, see how it plays out.' The hand lifted from his shoulder.

'Ah, Lamont.' Atwater shook his head. 'Thing is, I'm a True Believer, too. History sometimes gives a man the means proportional to a task, a task that someone has to do. This one's mine, my legacy.'

Richter tilted his head back to gaze at Lindbergh's plane. 'Don't expect them to name public schools after you.'

'Don't need it. And let 'em try to sort out why Almighty Allah allowed it. But I *will* be remembered.' He took a breath and found he was trembling with an emotion he couldn't identify. 'I'm going to be the man who nuked Mecca.'

Richter sucked his teeth for a moment, still considering the plane, and then looked at him with a shrug. 'It's your nickel,' he said.

7

Rabbits

Hammond watched Ray McCann squint down the barrel of the 30.06 and take aim at the line of cans and bottles on the distant fence. With deliberation, McCann squeezed the trigger – a squeeze, not a tug – and let his shoulder roll back with the recoil. His shoulder rolled forward on the bounce as though it were glued to the riflestock, and McCann squeezed off another.

Even with ear-guards on, the boom of a large-calibre rifle was too damn loud. Hammond edged further away. The third in the line-up was a bottle, and the shards of glass glinted in the sun as they flew, a miniature fireworks display.

Out of a dozen, McCann might miss one. The man was good, there was no doubt about it – one of those big fat guys who could do a few things with the delicacy of a jeweller. A matter of practice; McCann could shoot all day long without even a hint of boredom, while Hammond grew weary even thinking about shooting targets.

They stood on a brushy slope in the Panoche Hills, five miles from any public road. Panoche: Hammond had looked it up once and found that it was Spanish for slabs of the rawest grade of sugar, hard and grey-brown. A good name, at least for this particular valley – not a spot of green anywhere.

McCann finished his row, and Hammond felt Earlene tug at his sleeve. He slid off the ear-guards. 'Hon?'

'You guys ready to eat? I sure am.'

Hammond started to answer, but McCann overrode him. 'Later on. But right now, why don't you fetch us a couple of cold ones? We're gonna need more targets.'

Earlene didn't bother to answer him. 'I'm going to have something to eat,' she told Hammond, and turned and headed upslope toward the shelter.

'Who put the frog in her panties?' McCann asked. 'What's so tough about bringing a couple of beers?'

McCann had a habit of ordering women around as though the simple fact of their gender meant they were all in the service industry. His wife took it without even a whisper of complaint, but Hammond suspected that she harboured fantasies of pushing the man's head into her deep-fryer. 'Jeez, Ray, what do you expect? She's your sister, not your wife.'

'Ain't *your* wife, either.'

Hammond let that stand. What the hell was McCann trying to suggest, that it was time for the two of them to get married? If McCann was trying to defend his sister's maidenly virtues, he was jumping in too late, too late by probably twenty years and by more guys than Hammond cared to think about. He scratched the top of his head with his ear-guard. '*I'll* go get the beers.' He turned and trudged up the hill, sweat breaking on his forehead the moment he began walking.

The shelter was called the Porch, because that's what it looked like – a crude porch sawed off from the front of a house and then abandoned out here. Two steps up, four posts supporting a slanted roof, and a boarded-in back. Earlene sat on one of the benches and leaned on the back wall, a paperback in one hand and a sandwich in the other. As he reached the steps, Hammond heard McCann pop off a few shots, probably at some small rodent unlucky enough to poke its head out of its burrow.

The Porch seemed dark after the harsh sunlight, and he stood still, blinking as his eyes adjusted. 'I think I'm going to take the car and head home,' Earlene said. She dog-eared a page and put the book down. 'I'm bored.'

He sat down beside her. 'I told you we'd just be shooting.' He draped an arm around her shoulders and she snuggled in. Her hand still held the sandwich, and she held it up for him to take a bite. Turkey, cheese and lettuce, slathered in a mustard so hot it made his eyes water. 'Why'd you want to come, anyway?'

'Because it feels like I hardly see you any more. But I didn't think you were going to spend *all day* playing soldier.'

'It's business, Earlene. I need to talk to Ray.'

'Doesn't look like business. Looks like a couple of clowns shooting at cans.'

He sighed. 'It takes a while to work up to talking to your brother.'

''Cause he's an asshole. I don't understand why you hang out with him.'

And how are you going to feel when I put him away for fifteen-to-twenty? 'Because I need to. I work for the Allen Brigade, it's my job. I—' She cut off his sentence by pushing a corner of the sandwich into his mouth and he obediently took another bite.

With her other hand she took his free wrist and guided his hand to her breast and cupped it there. 'C'mon,' she breathed in his ear, 'let's just *go home.*'

Her nipple was hard against his palm even through the T-shirt and bra. He knew better than to pay much attention to that – Earlene had been born with stiff nips – but it still had the usual effect. She was thirty-six, but sexually she'd got stuck at somewhere around age seventeen, and always came on as though they were both involved in some private, exciting, dirty little secret. And he'd laugh, as he did now around his half-chewed mouthful of sandwich, but he always responded in kind, sliding back down the maturity banister to become a sweaty-palmed boy again. 'C'mon,' she whispered, 'we can go back to our place and *do stuff . . .*'

He disentangled himself from her and swallowed his food. 'Seriously, Earlene.' He realized he sounded a little breathless, and that she was watching him with a small look of triumph. 'Later. This really is important business.'

She puffed air from her lips, aiming it upwards as though she were trying to blow non-existent bangs from her eyes. 'I don't understand why you do all this stuff. I mean, you're a smart guy, Boyce, and I could be smart, too. I could. Who cares about the Allens? Why don't we just go somewhere together, and live like normal people?'

'Maybe some day.' *That's nice, Boyce. Lead her on even*

95

further, dickhead. 'There's – there's a thing coming up, and, well, things will be different after that.' *There, that clarifies it*. 'Look – I just can't explain right now. But I tell you what – you take the Taurus on home, I'll ride back with Ray, and tonight we'll go out to dinner: Italian, champagne, whatever you want.'

She smiled, but then bit her lip. 'Aren't we supposed to be watching our money this month?'

He put his arm back round her and hugged her tight. Access to money wasn't a problem for him, but the difficulty of explaining where it came from had made him live like a pauper for the last three years. 'I'm expecting . . . sort of a windfall. Money's probably going to be easier from now on.'

She cuddled up against him. 'Money don't matter. All that matters is that I'm with you.'

Earlene had a gift for making him feel lower than dirt.

McCann patted at his jacket where it lay between them on the bench until he found his cigarettes.

'What is it with you and the damned jacket?' Hammond asked. 'You expecting a cold snap this summer?'

McCann lit up and sighed out a wide cloud of blue-grey smoke. 'Cigarettes, matches, ammo – what'm I supposed to do, carry a purse?'

Hammond twisted the cap off another Michelob – McCann's idea of an exotic brew – and handed it to Ray. The big man accepted it with a grunt and settled back on the bench, his rifle leaning beside him. The two of them stared out of the Porch at the reddening sky beyond the Coast Range. 'What I need,' Hammond said, 'is the names of twenty of our most reliable men. Preferably former military, preferably not too old. Above all, men who can keep their mouths shut.'

'I can give you fifty, easy.'

'There's more. They need to be willing to do something big for America. Something dangerous. And they have to be able to leave work for at least a month, maybe more.'

McCann spluttered in the middle of a gulp. 'That cuts it down.' He wiped his mouth with the back of a massive hand. 'Cuts it down to fuckin' zero, is what it does.'

'I see. The Allen Brigade – the first line of defence against tyranny. Ready to die for America. But don't ask 'em to miss work.'

'Fuck you, Boyce.'

Far off, an owl called. Hammond wondered where it could be; there wasn't a tree in sight. Did Panoche have those owls that lived in burrows, like he'd seen down in Texas? 'Anybody who signed up would be well paid.'

McCann held up a silencing hand and whispered, 'Hold it.' Slow and smooth, he reached for the rifle and eased it up to his shoulder.

Hammond squinted downslope to where McCann's attention was directed. At first he saw nothing but low, cow-trampled dead grass, but then he noticed a flicker of movement. 'The rabbit?' he asked.

'Yep.'

'Forget it. Way too far.' Too far and, even if it weren't, Hammond was in no mood for another deafening boom. He held his hands over his ears as McCann took aim.

The expected thunder of the gun came, and at first Hammond was sure McCann had missed, but then the rabbit was punched into the air and flung a dozen yards down the hill, the compact body unravelling into ribbons of flesh as it took the impact of a round designed to stop a grizzly.

'Jesus.' It seemed like a safe reaction. Hammond swallowed, and then reached down for his own beer. If guns didn't exist, would folks like McCann wander the countryside with sledgehammers, pounding unwary wildlife into bloody pulp? 'Hell of a shot,' he said, and realized he meant it.

McCann put the rifle down on the bench and patted it with an air of satisfaction. 'Practice.' He picked up the beer, and then asked, 'What the fuck is this you're getting us into?'

'Counter-terrorism. Taking the war to the terrorists.'

'Who are we working for, the Feds? I thought that was their job.'

'Not doing too good at it, are they?'

McCann searched around the inside of his lips with his tongue, as though a good reply might be hidden somewhere between his teeth. 'Who are these people? Get more specific.'

'I can't be, because I don't know the details yet. But it involves making a lot of the bad guys dead.'

'How the hell can we sign on for something without knowing what it is?'

'You'll get to meet one of the people behind it at Town Hall tomorrow, but the Commander's satisfied with the arrangements.'

McCann stared at him, and Hammond kept his face impassive. Both of them knew the Commander grew less lucid with each passing day, and had one foot in rest-home heaven, but no one in the Allens would ever admit the fact. 'When'd you talk to him?' McCann asked.

'Last week. And he agrees that we ought to keep this strictly West Coast. There's good folks in Carolina and Montana, but he's trusting you and me to make decisions on this. Says we ought to know the men involved like the backs of our hands.' Hammond paused. 'Which is why we have to have you on this. I'm Johnny-Come-Lately here.'

McCann's shoulders slumped and Hammond watched the man's mouth work with words unsaid. 'He don't—' McCann shook his bulky head. 'He don't talk to me much any more.'

Uh-huh. 'Cause Dad likes me best, I suppose. 'Doesn't talk to anyone much. Talks to me more than most, but that's because I'm his gofer.' Hammond pulled out his trump card and slid it onto the table. 'I'll tell you one thing, though.' He reached over and put his hand on McCann's beefy forearm. 'The Old Man's made it clear to me that when he's . . . when he's gone, he'd like to see you take his place.'

McCann went rigid, and Hammond retrieved his hand. The man sat and stared into the deepening dusk, and Hammond felt sick about what he was doing. He tried to concentrate on the image of the rabbit's shattered body, cartwheeling through the air, shredded flesh throwing out droplets of blood . . .

When McCann turned towards him, the man's eyes were wet. 'And you're . . .' McCann gulped. 'You're okay with that?'

Hammond tried to play it right down the middle, acting the part of a disappointed man trying to be brave. He looked away from McCann and shrugged. 'Sure. I – well, I think it's the right choice.'

He heard McCann's heavy exhale and felt him shift his

body restlessly on the bench. And this year's Oscar for Best Actor in a Deceptive, Backstabbing Role . . . Hammond was seized with a wild urge to leap up and just run, run far away, drop it all and move to Canada where no one knew him – no, grab Earlene, why the hell not, slutty but more decent than any other woman he'd ever known, without question more decent than his ex and God knows more decent than he deserved – just grab Earlene by the hand and book a flight to Australia and start over, start a life growing things or making things, something where at the end of the day you could see what you'd done, count carrots or widgets or whatever, and feel satisfied as you went to bed, putting your head on the pillow without wondering when it would all be over.

'You're a good guy, Boyce,' McCann said.

For a moment Hammond was unable to speak, and when he did it was with a thick tongue. 'Just doing my job.'

They sat in the silence for a time, waiting for the moment to pass, until finally McCann asked, 'You said whoever we picked would be well paid?'

'Ten grand up front. Forty more at the end.' More money than any of this crowd had ever seen in one place. 'Possible bonuses.'

McCann whistled. 'That's a different situation.'

'Yeah. And it means we need to pick solid guys, not cowboys who are going to ride through town, whooping it up and shooting off their guns because they've struck it rich.'

'Guys who can keep their mouths shut? That cuts it down to maybe fifteen or twenty – and some of them might need a good talking-to first.' McCann chewed his lip. 'I want to be one of them.'

Hammond shook his head. That was a complication he didn't need. 'You'll get full pay just for helping set it up . . .'

'It ain't the money. I mean, you're going to be part of it, aren't you?' He waited for Hammond's answer. 'Aren't you?'

'Yeah. But, Ray – there's not much room for big dogs in this one.'

'I can take orders. Shit, four years in the service, twenty in the Allens – you think I can't take orders?' He drained his beer and threw the bottle off into the brush. 'You think I won't take orders from *you*?'

'I'm not going to be in charge.'

'Who is?'

'Somebody else. Somebody from the outside.'

'Who?'

'I don't know yet.'

'You don't know much, do you?'

Hammond laughed. 'Ray – I don't know shit.' He thought about it. McCann always meant extra headaches, but whatever Atwater had in mind, once there was enough evidence for a watertight case, the Bureau would come in and roll everyone up. Ray McCann was going down either way. 'Hell, if you can behave, join the party. But keep in mind we're *both* going to be taking orders.'

'I'm a big boy, I can handle it. When do you need the list?'

'Next few days?'

'You got it.' McCann tugged open the lid of the ice chest, and there was a wet, sucking sound as the vacuum broke. 'Want another beer?'

'Nah. I need to get back. I'm supposed to take your sister out to dinner.'

'That so? Guess I'll drink this one while I drive, then.'

'I'd just as soon not get arrested. Earlene'd be real pissed.'

'Hey, I'll finish it long before we hit pavement. And Earlene'd forgive you for anything.' McCann stood, twisting the cap off his Michelob. 'Truth is, you're the best thing ever happened to her.'

Yeah, that's me, Hammond thought. The best thing ever happened to anybody.

In the little office at the rear of the Grange Hall, Lamont Richter considered all five of the straight-backed chairs before choosing one, and Hammond half-expected the man to spread a handkerchief on the seat before sitting down. 'I do apologize for being late,' Richter said. 'My driver isn't used to navigating through the wilderness.'

Hammond hitched his hip up onto the corner of the formica-topped desk. 'I'd hoped to have time for a bit more of a chat. Maybe we can come back here after the meeting?'

'Perhaps.'

'I'd hoped that Rex Atwater might come, too.'

Richter gave a thin smile. 'Rex doesn't tend to show up in . . . insecure situations.'

'We've got an entire militia out in the auditorium. Seems safe to me.'

He crossed his legs and interlocked his fingers over his bent knee. 'I meant from an intelligence point of view.'

'We're solid there, too.'

'Oh, really?' Richter raised his eyebrows. 'It's come to our attention that just recently the FBI arrested some – customers? clients? – of yours down at the Berkeley Marina, and almost arrested one of your people.'

How could he know that? Inevitably there had been a brief spot in the papers – you can't have gunfire in an urban centre without some coverage – but it gave no details, and certainly no mention of the Allens . . . Hammond realized he was holding his breath. He played for time by saying, 'You seem to know a lot.' *One of your people* . . . that meant one of O'Toole's bunch, one of the inner circle of the Allens, or, as a remote possibility, someone from the Bureau. No, not the Bureau, and not the Allens, because they'd have been able to give his name. 'Why don't you tell me more?'

'Mr Hammond, it's my business to stay informed, but it's not my job to pass it all on to you. Let me turn that around: Why don't *you* tell *me* more?'

Hammond considered. 'All right. O'Toole's bunch contacted the Allens through one of our arms buyers, but they never had any names on our side, and the only direct contact was at the Marina. Somebody on their side slipped up, and the Feebs were laying in the weeds.'

'And who was there from your side? Convenient that despite all the gunfire, your man got away unscathed.'

'Unscathed?' Hammond pulled up his shirt and displayed the horizontal gash along his left side. After he'd returned from his meeting with Townley, he'd sliced himself with a box-cutter and then done some exquisitely painful work with a rat-tail file, and the result was gorgeous: a scabbed groove, with reddened, angry flesh to both sides. 'If they'd aimed a bit to the right,' he said, dragging his shirt down again, 'we wouldn't be having this little talk.'

'My condolences,' Richter said, without any hint of sympathy. 'If we're going to do business, though, this kind of thing has to stop for the duration, do you understand? We're not going to get tied up with any of the Allens' illegal activities.'

'All our activities are rights guaranteed in the Constitution.'

'The authorities beg to differ. In any case, if you expect us to work with you—'

'And if you expect us to work with you, you'll need to get more specific. And I'd like the men to hear it from Rex Atwater himself – what he plans, and why they should sign on for it. All this talk of overseas assassinations, and—'

'Mr Hammond. Please. If you expect Atwater to come put on a public pep rally—'

Someone rapped at the door, and Dodge stuck his head in. 'Speaker's here.'

Hammond rose. 'Maybe we can continue this afterwards. Dodge, would you get Mr Richter situated? I have to find this guy's damned bio-notes.'

He waited for a full minute after Dodge and Richter left before locking the door. Then he crossed to the rear of the room and shouldered the filing cabinet a few inches to the right. The loose panel in the wall came away, and he checked the voice-activated recorder. The readout had advanced by a good five minutes. He'd have to wait to find out about the quality of the recording.

As Hammond remembered, Richter hadn't committed himself to much, and had done little to incriminate Atwater – and the remark that they didn't want to be involved in any of the Allens' illegal activities was the sort of thing that would make a defence lawyer weep with gratitude. Still, it was a decent start, and he'd get Richter back in there after the meeting for another try.

And then, somehow, he'd have to get Atwater himself.

Sitting on a folding chair amongst the three dozen Allens gathered in the Grange, Lamont Richter looked like a city politician come to hustle votes. Telling the men that Richter was a delegate from the Commander himself gained him immediate respect, but Hammond noted that the Allens left a small island of empty chairs around Richter's seat.

They'd been through the singing of the national anthem, and Hammond stepped onto the low stage and walked over to the podium and tapped the mike. 'Normally we'd move to general business, but since we have visitors this evening, we'll be postponing that.' He consulted the index card in his hand. 'Tonight we have a very special speaker. He holds a master's degree in business administration and has lectured to audiences all over the western states. I'm sure every one of you will want to take home a copy of his book *Freedom's Death Knell: America and the New World Order*. Without further ado, a round of applause for James Brattleson . . .'

Hammond shook hands with the man as he climbed onto the stage, and then Hammond took his own seat in the front row. Richter would be getting entirely the wrong impression of the Allens, he reflected, as Brattleson started speaking. A speaker was a once-a-year affair at best – most meetings featured inflammatory video documentaries.

'. . . but this book –' Brattleson held up a copy of his self-published tome, '– only scratches the surface. The connections between the Bushes and international banking, the Bushes and international oil, the Bushes and international terror, are all well established, but what isn't so widely known . . .'

Like most of the militias, the Allens had started in the fifties as a bulwark against the coming communist invasion, and the collapse of communism had left them without an enemy. The New World Order had somehow seeped into the Commander's mind as a looming threat, and now the Allens were a kind of dropped stitch in the fabric of American politics: conservatives who hated Bush.

Kowinski hustled down the front row and knelt beside Hammond's seat. 'Police,' he said in a harsh whisper. 'Three cars.'

'Who?' For a moment, Hammond had the wild hope that the Bureau had at last decided to act.

'Sheriffs. Jack's heading out to stall 'em.'

Hammond stood and cleared his throat. 'Excuse me.' He waved his hands for attention. 'Folks. I've been informed that the County Sheriffs have just pulled into the parking lot.' Several people rose to their feet, and a hubbub of questions broke out. 'Hey!' he shouted. 'There's nothing illegal going on here, so I want everybody to stay in their seats and stay calm – *100 per cent calm*, and I know you know what I mean.' Translation: those of you carrying guns should leave them in their holsters.

He met McCann's eyes across the audience and nodded towards the entrance as he headed there himself. Passing the stage, he saw that Brattleson had a dazed look.

Three deputies came through the door, though McCann's

bulk blocked them from full view. McCann stepped back and intercepted Hammond a few steps away from the cops. 'They have a warrant for Bill Sutton,' he said. 'Some money thing.'

'Then we'd better hand him over, right?' He waited for McCann's nod. 'Okay. You fetch Sutton and keep him mellow, and I'll talk to the audience.' He snagged the arm of McCann's shirt as the man turned to go. 'You know any of the cops?'

'Firestone, a little.'

'Then escort Sutton out, try to get details.'

Hammond strolled back up towards the front and raised his voice to fill the hall. 'Folks. It's a personal matter. Nothing to do with tonight.'

Brattleson spoke through the mike. 'Thought they'd finally come for me.' There was polite laughter, though most of the audience had turned in their seats to watch McCann and the deputies escort Bill Sutton from the room.

As soon as he managed to get the lecture rolling again, Hammond slipped out into the parking lot where McCann waited. He was surprised to find Richter already standing there as well. 'What did you find out?'

'Embezzling, for Chrissake, down at that body shop,' McCann said. 'But they raided his place for evidence, and they also found . . . stuff.' He raised his eyebrows and glanced at Richter.

'It's okay,' Hammond said.

'Assault guns. Grenades. Some other toys.'

'Christ.'

'I don't mean to pry,' Richter said, 'but how much damage can the man do?'

'He's not inner circle,' Hammond said.

McCann lit a cigarette, and his words came out in smoke. 'He knows a lot.'

'And how much . . .' Richter searched for the right word, as though he were seeking a euphemism for a delicate matter of hygiene. 'How much *pressure* can they apply?'

'Plenty,' McCann said. 'He's got a record, forgery or some damned thing. And I'd bet his Vegas jones has something to do with the money he's been lifting.'

'Then I'd suggest Mr Hammond ought to come with me and bail him out.'

Hammond chewed his lip and nodded, as if just grasping the possible consequences of Sutton's arrest.

'It's going to cost major bail money,' McCann said. 'Janine split with the kids more than a year ago, he's got priors, the place he's in is rented. What they call a serious flight risk.'

'I'm not so concerned about the money as the . . . security implications.' Richter rubbed his long hands as though giving them a quick wash.

'We'll find out what he said, and who to,' Hammond said.

'Well, then.' Richter held out his hand to McCann, who considered it for a long moment before realizing he was being asked to shake it. Richter then took Hammond by the elbow and steered him through the parking lot full of pickups towards the chauffeured black Mercedes.

8

Real money

The blinding-white beaches of Abu Dhabi aren't covered with sand grains, but instead with *oolites* – tiny carbonate ovoids and spheres, smooth and perfect, closer in weight to dust than to sand, individual bits of geology so light that they cling to skin and hair and clothes by static electricity and coat beach-goers like a gritty powdered sugar.

Carla had showered off before returning to her room at the Sheraton, but even so, as her skin dried she shed a continuous rain of pinpoint-sized eggs. She peeled off her modest one-piece swimsuit, tossed it onto the bathroom floor and padded naked over to the minibar, leaving behind footprint traces outlined in the faintest white.

A vodka-tonic, her first drink in months. She slumped down into the desk chair and let the warmth of the first sip linger in her mouth before she swallowed. A good feeling. Earlier today in the locker room of the health club she'd checked out the other women – Western women, of course – as they'd changed, and realized that she was the only one in the room who hadn't been cultivating her pubic hair in some fashion. Trimmed back or bikini-waxed, carved into a downward-pointing arrowhead or, in one case, shaved entirely: it seemed that all the women in the room but Carla had tended the hair on their crotches as though they were French formal gardens, intended to impress any visitor who might happen through. By comparison Carla felt lumpish, scarred and overgrown.

She took another drink. Karachi had been bad. She'd learned her lesson in Damascus: don't count on people you haven't trained alongside. And she had taken out the training camp at the edge of the city exactly as she'd planned. She took care of the two sleepy sentries around three in the morning, and then went about her business.

The first, small explosion she triggered drew the jihadis outside; the second set off the shaped charges of plastique she'd clustered in a semicircle, packed with ball bearings. Seventeen men were shredded as thoroughly as if they'd dashed through a minefield.

She'd set off the radio-frequency charge from near the end of the roadway, cloaked and veiled, lurking just outside the last apartment building.

And then, from out of nowhere – no, it wasn't from out of nowhere, it was from that shed, equidistant from her and the barracks building of the camp – a single raghead, cloth tucked on top of his head untidy as a bird's nest, with an RPG on his shoulder.

Carla whipped the pistol from beneath her robes and took aim, but he fired off the rocket. An idiot, an amateur: he aimed at her as though it were a bullet, as though he might hit her directly with the grenade.

If he'd fired it at the ground anywhere around her, she would have been dead. She squeezed off the first round and went into automatic mode, firing without much hope at this distance, and she heard the irregular whine as the grenade cut through the air a yard to her right.

The explosion threw her forward. She hit the ground hard, her fist still clenched on the pistol, pumping out the last rounds. Behind her there came a rumbling and then a long sliding crash.

Concrete dust rolled across her as the apartment building collapsed.

There was a long silence. Carla pushed herself to her feet. She'd brought the man down. Sheer luck, that.

She started beating the chalky dust from her dark robes, and stumbled back down the road towards the massive labyrinth of Karachi. Down the street, doors flew open and people began to pour into the streets, trying to understand the explosions.

From the ruins of the apartment building as she passed, she heard sobbing.

She'd wandered the alleyways of Karachi for three hours before she'd dropped the robes and made it back to her hotel. Now, two days later, safe in Abu Dhabi – that clean, false, Disneyland of a country – she tried to sort it out. *She* hadn't fired an RPG at an apartment building; *they* had. But they were firing at her. Should she have foreseen it? Was it her fault? Or just one of those things . . . ?

Was she even doing any good? Sure, bad guys were dying. But there were thousands of them, maybe tens of thousands. What had she killed, in total: probably thirty?

More than ever, she missed Kevin. Her brother could have told her how to think about this, could have made sense of it all, could have told her she was okay, could have told her what to do next. If not for Kevin she'd still be stuck out in Burns, Oregon, under the thumbs of their religious-nut parents. What would she be now – a cashier at the Rite-Aid living in a double-wide trailer, married to whatever slob had been willing to settle for her, who'd been decent enough to settle for her, even though she wasn't Kelsey Jo Williams or Laurie Maycox or Lynne Perry or any of the other vapid bitches who'd ruled her high school?

Was this better? She'd never wanted to be the one who set up the big plans, never wanted to be the one who decided what was right and wrong. All she'd asked for was to belong. And when she was with Killer Jill and the rest, she'd had it; when she was part of Special K, she'd had all she'd needed. And Kevin had always given her that, too, the sense that she was okay; but they'd murdered him, the fucking ragheads had murdered him, when all he was trying to do was keep them from killing each other.

You want to be martyrs? Fine. I'll help you.

She took a deep drink and relished the heat rolling down her throat and into her belly, and she looked down, half-expecting to see her stomach glowing, and saw instead her nastiest scar and the bush of her pubic hair, with a thin trail of finer hairs running up from her groin towards her navel. Ugly. And not getting prettier as time went by, not by a long shot.

Knuckles rapped at the door. She put down her drink and

strode over, a little wobbly on her feet – who would have thought half a drink could make you woozy?

Through the peephole she saw that it was Richter. Shit! She'd said she'd meet him in the lobby an hour ago. 'Just a minute,' she shouted, and then dashed to the closet for a robe. 'Sorry,' she said as she opened the door. 'Come on in.'

Richter, impeccable as always in a charcoal suit, said, 'I can wait downstairs . . .'

'No. Come on.'

He did, shutting the door behind him. Carla turned her chair to face away from the desk and sprawled back in it. For a moment she thought about trying to hide her drink, but she decided to hell with it, and hoisted it off the desk blotter and into plain view. 'Sit down,' she said, nodding her head at the bed, 'sit down.'

Richter sat on the corner of the bed. He raised an eye-brow at the drink in her hand, but said nothing.

'Want one?' she asked.

He chewed on the inside of his cheek for a moment. 'Sure.'

Carla squatted down in front of the minibar. 'Name your poison.'

'Scotch, if they have it. Rocks.'

'Lessee, we got Johnny Walker Red, *annnnd* . . . more Johnny Walker Red.'

'Fine.'

Once she'd got him a Scotch on the rocks she sat down in her chair and lifted her vodka-tonic, a little defiant, one leg crossed over the other, ankle to knee, as unladylike as possible. Richter's face showed no real expression. The thick terrycloth robe felt heavy and hot on her body despite the air conditioning and she felt the urge to throw it off; she doubted that she'd feel any more naked without it.

'How are you, Carla?' he asked, his accent at its most courtly.

She knocked back the rest of her vodka-tonic and busied herself making another without answering. Back in the chair, she said, 'I don't know. I'm better with a team. And . . . well, after a while it starts to seem hopeless, you know? I mean, there's only one of me.'

'We're pleased with what you've accomplished. Pleased and, frankly, astonished. We did use a few people before you, you know – paid people.'

'I'm paid. Paid better than I ever have been.'

'Yes. But, the money – that's not really why you're doing this, is it?'

She shook her head.

'Unless you have an objection,' Richter said, 'we'd like to pull you back to the US to work on something a little bigger.'

There was something about Richter's manner that was so smooth, so insinuating, that Carla wanted to resist him on principle. 'What is it? But I've got to warn you – I'm a soldier, even if the US Army doesn't think so any more.'

'Meaning?'

'I don't kill Americans.'

'We don't anticipate that killing Americans will be necessary.'

'Who the hell is *we*, anyway? This is getting too weird. Way beyond killing a bunch of thugs.'

'Come back to the US. Take a few days off, and then I'll

introduce you to the Man Behind the Curtain. He wants to meet you.'

Carla let her head loll back and stared at the white ceiling. For a moment the uneven plaster seemed to portray a ghostly army in procession, but when she sought individual faces, the figures blurred back into the paint. 'So this isn't your money? Is it CIA? Or who?'

Richter chuckled. 'I don't have real money.'

'Seems like you do all right to me. What are you worth, a million bucks?'

'There's money, and then there's serious money. Serious money starts in the tens of millions. That kind of money I don't have.'

'Then who does?'

'You'll meet him. And, you were complaining that there's only one of you. We have the nucleus of a small commando unit.' He finished his drink and stood. The ice in his tumbler clinked as he put it on the desktop beside Carla's. He looked down at her, and she felt a sudden, inappropriate quiver of sexuality – him standing over her in his suit, her sprawled back in the desk chair, naked under her bathrobe, the two of them together in her hotel room. 'What we don't have yet,' he said, 'is someone in charge. I think it's time, Carla, that you started giving some orders, making some plans.'

Questions swirled in her mind, but all she said was, 'I'm not saying yes until I know more.'

'That's fine, I can wait. Oh, and Carla: if you ever decide you want to go back in the Army, our lawyers tell us that you might have a decent shot at reinstatement. *Disproportionate penalties relative to existing case law*, or some such mumbo-jumbo. Be an uphill slog, but . . .'

Carla felt as if a vast arm had squeezed the breath from her chest and then released her. 'I don't believe that,' she managed to say.

'Don't matter to me. I'd just as soon you stayed on our team and let the military fend for itself. Any case, we can talk about it on the plane.' Richter's expression was impassive and yet managed to suggest, in Carla's eyes, a mixture of disapproval and irony. He turned and walked to the door, pausing when his hand reached the knob. 'If you're planning to get drunk,' he said, 'do it soon. We fly out at seven in the morning.'

The Naval Postgraduate School in Monterey looked like a classic Californian university, red-tiled roofs supported by tall stuccoed walls that shone white in the sun. Carla'd expected some of the features of a military base, but collegiate civvies outnumbered uniforms, and she was waved in the direction of Jill's classroom with a casualness she might have met at any Cal State campus.

A superficial glance at Killer Jill McMillan's glossy black skin and long, lean build suggested that she might be magazine-beautiful, but a second look revealed that her shoulders were too wide, her thighs too muscled, for a Paris catwalk. Add a nose that had been broken and poorly reset, and a dusky-pink keloid scar that ran off-kilter from her lower lip onto her chin, then top them off with a pair of eyes sharp and shiny as obsidian: Carla had seen men's eyes ladder their way up the rungs of Jill's body and then shy away when they arrived at that hard face.

The door opened, and students wandered out, split about evenly between male and female. A dozen, from their postures and haircuts, had to be Navy or Marines, but only a few were in uniform. Many of the others looked to be foreign, mostly East Asian, or were dressed as Washington bureaucrats, which in Carla's view qualified them as a special breed of foreigner.

Carla felt herself backing away from the open door, sidling back towards the wall, as though the door were a sluice-gate directing a powerful current against her body.

Killer Jill came through the door last, alongside a Chinese man. She had on a tailored teal-green suit, and heels that jacked her up above six feet, and Jill's head was tilted to the left, nodding as she listened to what the shorter man said. A limp-leather valise, deep burgundy, dangled from her right hand, and Carla saw those long, strong fingers twitch and then tighten on the handle as Jill noticed and then recognized her.

For a moment it was as if God had turned down the volume knob on the universe. Jill was patting the man beside her on the shoulder and saying something, but her impassive eyes were fixed on Carla, and then Carla's heart swelled as Jill's lips parted and gleaming white teeth showed through, and Jill opened her arms and Carla stumbled into them, pressing her cheek against Jill's chest, feeling the woman's chin come to rest atop her head, feeling the valise knock against her back.

On the way to the restaurant, in Jill's SUV, Carla leaned back and listened as Jill recounted the history of the last two years. K-Force was gone, demobbed, wiped off the Army's map during what Jill called *Bush Two*: 'Girls don't get to hang out in the clubhouse any more.' Most of Carla's cohort, though, had gone on to better things; the bulk of them were still military, in the clandestine bodyguard business, shepherding semi-secret US envoys around the world, but some of them had climbed into command positions in the Army. 'Me,' Jill said, 'me, they don't know what to do with. So when these sailors asked if I could come teach for a year, they were happy to toss me across the country. Army'd be even happier if I got hit by a truck.' Jill glanced at Carla and winked. 'When I first saw a figure standing in the hall, I figured you were a paid assassin.' For a moment Carla thought that Jill must have seen into her soul, and something must have shown on her face because Jill hastened to lighten the moment by adding, 'Knew the brass wouldn't hire you for that, though. You always was a pussy.'

The restaurant was a chi-chi place down on Cannery Row, done up in varnished blond wood, and Carla winced as she read the menu. The problem wasn't the prices, though they were steep enough to cause shock. It was the blackened this and the caramelized that, the aioli and arugala and framboise, and the fact that everything had been drizzled upon with something else. There were only two pages in the menu, but the cushioned leather folder that held them must have been upholstered by Rolls-Royce.

'If that expression on your face is because of the prices,' Jill said, 'relax. I'm buying.'

Carla shook her head. 'No, no. I'm picking up the tab, money's not a problem. It's just –' she closed the weighty menu, '– I have no idea what any of this stuff is.'

'For real? You want me to order for both of us?'

Carla nodded.

''Kay, girl. But with our haircuts, people are gonna get the wrong idea. This is California – I order for the both of us, it might make us legally married.'

Carla smiled as much as the remark seemed to call for, and then watched Jill study the menu. Her dark eyes scanned the pages with no apparent rhythm – abrupt, pattern-breaking moves, as unpredictable as the running manoeuvres they'd been taught for charging armed emplacements. Jack-rabbit runs, they'd called them: head your torso one direction and then break hard to the other side with your legs. Lead the enemy's aim to the right at the same moment as you snap to the left.

Jill's eyes stopped jack-rabbiting and she slapped the menu shut. 'You drink wine? White okay?' The sharp report of the menu must have attracted a waiter because Jared soon appeared, his attempt to recite the evening's specials cut short by Jill's waving hand. Salads, sea-bass, orange roughy, side vegetables, Sauvignon blanc, dessert to be decided later. Jill's voice of command hadn't diminished: when she finished her list, the boy knew he'd been dismissed, and he gathered up the menus and retreated without another word.

Most of the small talk had been exhausted on the drive, and Carla couldn't find the words to begin. The questions were simple. *Am I crazy to even think about reinstatement? Am I fit to command?* And, above all, *Am I still 'one of us'?*

Jill saved her by saying, 'My, my. So "money's not a problem", huh? I'm figuring you didn't marry Bachelor Number Two, so there ain't many choices. There's private security . . .'

Carla thought she was keeping her face expressionless, but Jill must have seen denial there, because she moved on. 'There's The Company.' Carla swallowed and shook her head.

Jared arrived with the wine and an ice-bucket, but Jill's withering glance made him dispense with the formalities: he popped the cork, set it down beside Jill's plate, poured two full glasses without going through the ritual of tasting, and then drilled the bottle down into the chipped ice as he backed away.

Jill sipped her wine. 'So I guess you're a merk, then. National hire? Or are you private?'

Outside the military, *mercenary* was a term of abuse, but Jill said *merk* as though it were just another job designation, like *librarian* or *fireman*, and Carla felt grateful. 'Private,' she said, and picked up her own glass of wine. It was dry and astringent on the tongue, and she ached for the oily feel of vodka or gin.

'On our side, I hope? You killing bad guys? Or don't you care?'

'Bad guys.' Except for folks who get killed by accident. And, oh, yeah, maybe a kid here and there. To hell with sipping; she took a long, hard drink. 'I care.'

'Good. And you can definitely buy dinner.' Jill spun her wine glass by its stem, and Carla found herself hypnotized by the revolving patterns of light it cast on the wooden tabletop. 'You know, girl,' Jill said, 'you broke my fucking heart.'

Carla closed her eyes. 'I know. I deserved to get booted. Everything you taught us about putting your temper on hold . . . I screwed the pooch.' After the court martial she'd cried every day for weeks, until she'd convinced herself that her lifetime supply of tears had been depleted, but now, as she opened her eyes, she realized they were wet, and she swallowed hard and prayed, prayed that the tears wouldn't come again, not here, not now, not in front of Jill.

'I'm not talking about what you went on trial for. You understand that?' Jill gulped her own wine and then hoisted the bottle from the ice-bucket, handling it like a fat-necked 32-ouncer of malt liquor. 'Your brother's dead and some dickweeds are celebrating it? I might have fucked 'em up, too. Anybody can lose it.' She filled her own glass and then waited for Carla to offer hers, filling it so high that a little sloshed onto Carla's thumb. 'What broke my heart was your big prima-donna vanishing act.'

'I know you sent me a note . . .'

'Fuck.' Jill ground the bottle back into the ice. 'Fuck that. Not just me. Your whole cohort. Everybody you trained with. Any time any of us talk, it's *where's Carla, anybody hear from Carla, anybody find Carla yet . . . ?*' She picked up her glass, started to drink and set it down again. 'Shit. It was *family.* My blood relatives can go fuck. But you were real family. Not the Army – screw the Army. You girls. And then you just took off.'

Carla felt her face go cold, and then hot, a blush spreading down her cheeks onto her neck. 'I was . . .' Why is my mouth moving without making words? 'It was the same for me.' She realized she'd been holding her breath. 'I was just so ashamed. I figured – well, I thought I'd screwed it up for all of you.'

Jill's face, never soft, could have been an asteroid, stony, cold and distant. 'That an apology?'

'Guess so. 'Cause I'm sorrier than you can imagine.'

'Don't be telling me what I can and can't imagine.' Despite the edge of the words, the vigilance on Killer Jill's face evaporated, and she lifted her wine glass again. 'Don't overrate yourself, Smukowski. Think *you* could fuck it up for all of us? Think again. K-Force was on the way out from the day it arrived. The boys want all the girls out of their sand-box, and it's gonna go on like that until the day Wal-Mart sells dicks as screw-on attachments.'

After Carla came back from the restroom, Jared arrived with the salads. 'Now, who wanted the pear, goat-cheese, and caramelized pecan, and who—'

'Set 'em down and we'll sort 'em out,' Jill said, and Jared clonked down both salads in the centre of the table. 'We're going to need a couple more bottles of this juice.'

'Fine.' He lifted the wine bottle from the bucket and eyed the remaining ounces. 'Just signal me when you're ready, and—'

'No.' Jill took the bottle and poured the remaining wine into her glass. She thrust the bottle into his hands and said, 'Two more bottles now, and another ice-bucket, pronto. Got it?'

'Yes, ma'am,' he said, and scurried away.

Jill interlocked her fingers and put her elbows on the table. 'Now, honey, what's up with you?'

Carla explained that she'd become involved with an off-the-map, secret mercenary group, and that Richter had raised the possibility of reinstatement in the Army.

Jill was shaking her head before Carla had finished. She washed down her mouthful of salad and asked, 'Right off-hand, you remember the Army ever admitting they made a mistake?'

'The guy I'm working for said they have lawyers who say I might have a case . . .'

'Lawyers.'

'. . . because the punishment was way out of line compared to the crime. It was assault, off-duty. Happens all the time.' She could see that none of this was convincing Jill. 'And he said a couple of Senators might be willing to put in a good word for me. That might change things.'

'US Senators? No shit?' Jill put down her salad fork. 'Yeah, that changes things, all right. Congress got no authority over military courts, but you can bet the generals don't mind a little horsetrading.' She grinned, showing teeth like a dog ready to snap. 'You seem to be doing pretty good for yourself. What makes you so damn sure you want back in? And, Senators? Who the hell you mobbed up with, anyhow?'

She didn't know who her real bosses were, not yet, though Richter had promised she'd be meeting them soon. 'Some rich guys who don't like terrorists. And, yeah, I want back in. You said it. It's family.'

'K-Force is history. Why not stick with what you're doing?' Jared wandered by to see if they were done with their salads, and Jill waved him away.

'I've . . . I don't know. Collateral damage. There's been civilians killed.' She stabbed some greens with her fork, began to raise it to her mouth and instead laid it down on the plate with a loud clink. 'They kill ours, too. But . . .'

Jill made a tired sound, as though steeling herself for something tedious, but when she spoke there was conviction in her tone. 'Best situation: strictly military versus military. Never happens except in the movies – and maybe a couple of tank battles out in the Sahara before we were born – but that's the ideal, yeah? Now, take real life . . .' She snorted. 'It ain't a boxing match any more once the other guy pulls a knife. Once he pulls that knife, it's your *job* to pull a gun, if you got one. Once they break the rules, there ain't no rules – except to win.'

'But where do you draw the line?'

'The other guy draws it. I know the politically correct types half a century later expect me to get all teary-eyed when I hear about Hiroshima or Dresden. Well, you say *Hiroshima*, I say *Nanjing*. You say *Dresden*, I say the *London Blitz*.' As Jill's voice grew more contentious it had also swelled to at least classroom volume, though still short of her full parade-ground bellow. A man at a nearby table stared as though he might say something, but she turned her gaze on him and he hastily looked down at his food. When Jill's face swung back to Carla, her expression was unapologetic, but she spoke in a tone more appropriate to a restaurant. 'Look, I ain't saying you have to turn into some kind of monster. But if you stay all Marquis-of-fuckin'-Queensberry, you're gonna lose. *I* say, if you don't care if you lose, don't bother to fight in the first place.' Jill seemed to realize she'd been pontificating, and grinned. 'Maybe I just don't like losing, huh?'

Carla took a gulp of wine, wishing it were something

stronger. 'It isn't just that. They want me to train a whole little squad of merks. Run 'em. Give orders.'

'So?'

Jill's bland reaction was maddening. 'So, I'm not good at that kind of thing. I'm not, I don't know, qualified.'

'You're not qualified? I've seen you run squads, seen you lay out strat and tacks. You're as good as any of 'em.'

'You don't know me. I screw up.'

'The fuck I don't know you. I taught you which direction to wipe, girl.'

'But—'

'Everybody screws up. Class is about how you recover from your screw-ups.' Carla began to interrupt, but Jill jabbed her index finger across the table, right at Carla's face. 'You *do* this, girl. It's about time you grew up and took some real responsibility. When you're in charge, at least you can't go running off.'

Carla realized her mouth was gaping and shut it, and felt her lips, like oil spreading on water, sliding into a silly smile.

'What's with the grin, Smukowski?'

'It's just like old times. You telling me what to do. Me figuring I'd better do it.'

'If it were old times, I'd put my size-ten boot up your size-eight ass. I spent years making you one of the best, and you come in here whining with this *I'm not qualified* crap.' She poured more wine into both glasses. 'Now tell me about this squad you're pulling together. Men, women, or both?'

'Don't know. Haven't met anyone yet.'

'If you don't get to pick from people you know, pray for men. They're easier.'

Coming from the former leader of K-Force, this was baffling. 'How? And, then, why'd you volunteer to run all of us?'

'I thought women were better soldiers. Still do. But easy they ain't – you gotta to deal with each one individually. Guys are like a bunch of dogs: they got a pack order and a top dog. You come in and kick the crap out of the top dog, the whole pack is yours.'

'And how do I do that?'

'However you can. In the service, you just bust their balls until they give. Wear 'em down. In your case, well . . . you private-sector types got a lot more latitude. Hurt somebody. Where the hell is dinner, anyway?' She waved two fingers in the air as though she were pledging the Boy Scout oath.

Despite the years, despite the civvies, despite the trendy restaurant, it felt as though they were on the same team again. 'Jill. I really do appreciate this. Not just the advice, the way you're . . .' She frowned, unable to find the right words.

'Oh, you think all is forgiven? Uh-uh. Not by a long shot. For starters, this fairy-assed limp-leather briefcase –' she gestured at the floor, '– has my address book in it, fifteen, twenty addresses of people who been wondering where the hell you been. So the first thing you need to do is write some letters – and no word-processor form letters, either, you sit down and write 'em out by hand, and kiss some ass. Then,' she said, 'then maybe we'll see about forgiveness.'

Carla cringed as she imagined the process: her clumsy scrawl, the repeated explanations. But Jill was right, as always. It needed to be done. 'Yes, Mom' was all she could think of to say.

'Hey, Jared?' Jill kept her voice quiet, but her tone stopped the waiter three tables away. 'You gonna bring us some fish? Or do we need to walk down the street to the Aquarium and catch our own?' She turned her face back to Carla. 'Now. Tell me some war stories.'

9

An army of genies

After a dozen years working for government and international agencies, Gerald had forgotten what private funding could achieve – and how fast it could move. Atwater and the other donors hired Start-up Facilitation Expeditors, a San Jose firm that, despite their clunky name, moved with hallucinatory speed. Within a week of Gerald being prised out of Federal custody, the new Critical Path Institute had a fully furnished office in McLean, and a few days later he returned from a series of job interviews at his office to find Viki waiting in his bed. Within a month he found himself reviewing a draft of Critical Path's *Interim Report on Immediate Threats from Radiological Terrorism*.

A slapped-together job, to be sure. Only one of the eight co-authors of the study had actually arrived to take on her job at Critical Path. Most of them needed to give notice to their employers, arrange to put their houses on the market or wait until their kids' school terms had ended. But all of them had rallied to the challenge of getting a document on the table, even if the work had to be done long-distance.

It hadn't required much new research. Every one of the scientists he'd recruited had been crying in vain about these dangers for a decade or more. Their gas pedals had been mashed to the floor for years. All Gerald had to do was release the brake.

The long chapter on the former Soviet Union was disturbing, but none of it was news to Gerald. The world inventory of missing commercial radioactive packages, mostly medical and food-industry, was familiar in principle, but seeing the list of more than three thousand missing packages laid out in one place made him feel nauseated.

What jarred him the most, though, was the report out of Indonesia. On the entire drive from the office back to Georgetown he ticked off a mental list of the TRIGA research reactors around the world, and wondered how many of them had been diverted to abortive nuclear-weapons programmes. By the time he stood in his kitchen, pouring a brandy, he had settled on a total of two dozen.

Something was ready to go wrong.

He wandered upstairs in a trance. Viktor was already in bed reading, propped against the headboard with all four of the pillows. 'Why so gloomy?' Viki asked, his Austrian accent changing *why* to *vie*. 'I give you pillow, also. Better?' He leaned forward and pulled a pillow from behind his shoulders and tossed it on Gerald's side of the bed. He patted the mattress. 'Come.'

Gerald sat down and kicked off his shoes. 'Let me tell you a bedtime story.'

'Ah, Märchen?' Viki asked, *Oh, a fairytale?*

'Indonesia.' He leaned over and ran his fingers through

Viki's thick, dark hair, and tousled it as though patting a child. 'They went for the bomb under Sukarno, way back in the sixties. Officially renounced their plans after the Suharto coup.'

'A good thing?'

'A good thing. Except they didn't give up. Continued using their TRIGA research reactors, to bombard heavy targets, for . . . well, years. We knew they had the six kilos of enriched uranium that LBJ gave them – but they used it to produce a couple of hundred kilos of other radioactive garbage. We've only found out because they've decided to get rid of it, give it back to the US.'

'Americans want radioactive garbage?'

'If it was ours to start with. Ship it into Concord, California, drag it up to Idaho Falls by rail.'

'Where then is the problem?' Viki asked. 'The bad stuff is found, and now she has a home.'

Gerald leaned forward, elbows on thighs, and rested his forehead in his hands. 'India diverted material from its research reactors to help make their bombs. Iraq did it too, and right under the noses of the IAEA inspectors. But this . . .' He groaned and sat up. 'I thought we knew what was going on, at least how much material in the world had gone missing. But now I realize that probably a dozen, two dozen nations were doing what Indonesia did at one time or another. And most of them had bigger reactors. There's thousands of kilos of highly radioactive stuff out there that no one ever counted, *thousands of kilos*.'

Viki reached across the bed and put his hand on Gerald's shoulder, and only then did Gerald realize how rigid his body was. He forced out a long exhale before he continued. 'I've spent my whole career trying to stuff the genies back in their bottles, and now I learn there's a whole extra army of them hidden out there. How do you say *Armageddon* in German?'

'For Armageddon we say Armageddon, how else? But also we say *weltweite Katastrophe*.' Viki's hand slipped from his shoulder, and Gerald heard Viki's hardback novel drop onto the floor beside the bed. 'Truly? That bad?'

'No. I'm exaggerating. It's not the end of the world.' He paused, trying to understand what he was feeling. 'But for the first time I'm sure that something terrible's going to happen, people are going to die. I've said that for years. But now I *know* it.'

He heard Viki sit up and scoot across the mattress and he felt those strong arms encircle his shoulders, smelled a hint of goaty male odour beneath that soap-scrubbed scent. 'If it is not Armageddon, if it's not Armageddon on this night,' Viki whispered, 'then I think that you should take off the clothes and come into the bed.'

Gerald couldn't think of a single reason why that wasn't the best thing to do.

10

Enola Gay

Whenever he returned to the lodge at the Tahoe Institute, Atwater wondered why he bothered with the outside world. From his den, the floor-to-ceiling windows showed the whole sweep of the valley where it plunged eastwards towards Reno. How long did he have left on this planet anyway, ten years? Twenty? If he cashed out all his non-essential holdings, he'd have at least three hundred million, and still leave behind a solid corporate empire for his heirs to squabble over. He spun his desk chair round from the window to face the room. 'Maybe I'll just retire.'

Over on the sofa Lamont Richter laughed. 'And maybe my Shetland pony'll win the Derby.' Although Atwater was dressed in Levis and a polo shirt, Richter had arrived at the breakfast table in a white linen suit, nice enough down in the dining room, but it now looked absurd against the rustic pine and dark upholstery of the den.

Atwater tilted the corner of his mouth, acknowledging the truth of Richter's remark. He tapped the cover of Gerald's

Interim Report where it lay on his desk. 'So. What do you think?'

'I think,' Richter said, in his laziest drawl, 'that I ought to say *I told you so*. No way we'd have gotten this much, this fast, without a True Believer.'

'So say it.' Atwater leaned back in the chair and interlaced his fingers, releasing the index fingers to tap against each other as he spoke. 'Where do we go from here?'

'We've hired good people,' Richter said. 'Let Carla and Hammond sort it out.'

The yellow mid-morning sunlight had shifted enough that the room had become bright and monochromatic, like an underdeveloped sepia-tone photograph. Atwater pressed a button on his desktop console and held it down as blinds rolled along their tracks from either side of the window. He kept his finger down until the light pouring into the room was cut by half. 'You're sure they'll buy in?'

'Hammond and the Allens are certified, true-blue loonies. You just wave the Stars and Stripes a little and they'll come running, especially when the money's so good. Carla . . . well, you'll have to convince Carla. Shouldn't take too much.'

Atwater unlaced his fingers and stood. 'And what else do we need: a missile?' He turned and looked out of the window to the forested valley.

He heard Richter hoist himself up from the couch and wander towards the window. 'Leave it to the folks you've hired.' From beside him, the man said, 'Hammond's a Marine pilot. And our Miss Smukowski is a death-and-destruction machine, one of the best America ever made. You're the one who claims true genius is all delegation.'

'If you've got the right person for the job.'

On his right, he heard Richter sigh beneath his breath. 'Rex. People like Carla, they teach them how to make anti-personnel mines out of apples and shoe polish. What did al-Qaeda hit us with? Hijacked airplanes. If the lady says she wants a missile, then I'll buy her one – I've got sources lined up – but let her figure out how to tackle it.'

Atwater chuckled. 'Apples and shoe polish?'

'You know what I mean. What did McVeigh hit Oklahoma with? Diesel fuel and fertilizer. There's more where that came from.'

'You're right.' He gazed out of the window, not really seeing. The gargantuan *Interim Report* had been just what he'd hoped for, but now, having read it, he was appalled at the sheer volume of deadly material scattered around the world. Scattered around his own country. 'That report made uncomfortable reading, didn't it? I mean, there's tons of this stuff out there.'

'Lucky for us.'

'Right now, sure. But when you think about the long term . . .'

'Don't. Truth is, Rex: I had your kind of money, I'd buy myself a whole county of New Zealand and a modest but well-chosen harem, and just get away from it all. Because even with the World War One trenches, even with the concentration camps, even with Hiroshima and Rwanda and Bosnia and all the rest . . . well, my guess is the twenty-first century is going to make the twentieth look like Woodstock.'

The restaurant – a private dining room atop the San Francisco Hyatt – had been chosen to impress her, to sell her, to close the deal. Atwater considered himself a pro at reading people, but for the first half of dinner Carla had him stumped.

She carried herself with a calm physical confidence he'd seldom seen – no swagger, just self-assurance, and her body language never changed. She'd glanced at the view when she'd first come in with Richter, frowned at the menu for all of ten seconds before telling him she'd have whatever he had, and then leaned back in her chair, watching him. Her face – a pretty-enough face, if she'd cared – never gave anything away, and it took Atwater a good half-hour of chit-chat to realize that only her eyes would give him any kind of tell-tale.

Once he'd learned to read them, though, those blue-grey eyes were eloquent. Shadows chased across them, fear lurked behind them, and inchoate pain drifted through them like rainclouds; but the darkness was often illuminated by flashes of anger, pride and what he interpreted as a sense of justice. At odd moments her gaze would dart across the dining table to Richter, as though seeking his approval or permission.

By the end of dinner the three of them had put away two bottles of wine, and by the time they rode the elevator to the helipad atop a bank building he thought he had the basics straight. Patriotic, in a simple, clean way; deeply distrustful of religion; lonely and wounded, though he couldn't say how or why.

The Sikorsky S-76 was the executive limousine of choppers, and this one was palatial. The craft could have seated a dozen, plus two up front, but this one had a mere six seats in the rear. Atwater had it done up like a small cocktail lounge rather than an aircraft – three plush armchairs, their backs to the wall, faced three more on the opposite side. Low mahogany tables sat between the burgundy-velvet seats, matching the mahogany wet bar at the rear. Seat belts on the chairs and gimballed drink-holders on the tables were the only real clues that you were looking into an aircraft cabin; even the tinted windows had been squared, replacing the usual porthole look.

Once they were airborne he fetched glasses and a crystal decanter of real cherry brandy, served out drinks and sat down in a chair opposite Carla and Richter. He picked up his discussion from where he'd left it dangling in the restaurant. 'My point is that Western civilization is cutting its own throat. Our enemies hit us as hard as they can, but we're supposed to strike back in a limited, perfectly accurate, fair way . . . and always apologize. Do you remember during the invasion of Iraq, when all of the Arab press was crying out *they're deliberately targeting civilians*? And the White House responds with patient denials, instead of saying, *Christ, if we were deliberately targeting civilians, do you think there'd be anybody left alive to bitch?*'

Carla's eyes showed a glimmer of amusement. 'Politicians,' she said, 'don't say things like that.'

'Ours sure don't. Do you believe in evolution?' He waited for her to nod and then went on. 'Survival of the fittest. Not the most just, not the most moral. Take our policy, take the enemy's policy – in the long run, guess who ends up dead.' He sat down his glass and opened his palms towards her. '*This is not a war against Islam*, President Bush kept saying. Well, why the hell not? Islam has a war against us, no matter what their apologists claim.'

'I'm with you there.'

They all sipped their drinks in silence for a moment. 'Carla, have you ever thought about the *Enola Gay*?'

'Huh?' It was clear that this question was wide of anything she'd anticipated.

'The plane that dropped the bomb on Hiroshima.'

'I know what the *Enola Gay* was. I'm just not sure what you're asking me.'

'Would you have done it? Piloted the plane, dropped the bomb . . . ?'

'Orders are orders. Bombardiers don't get to pick their targets.'

He smiled. 'Suppose you *had* gotten to pick.'

She dragged her free hand back through her hair in irritation. 'Jesus, Atwater. Spare me the hypothetical bullshit.'

Jesus, Atwater. She seemed uncowed by who he was, and unimpressed by the surroundings. Of course, he thought, in her old job, escorting clandestine envoys, she'd stayed in the best hotels, and been present at meetings of the powerful. It bothered him. It bothered him that, from what he could see, she might as well have been in a McDonald's, and it bothered him more that he could neither charm nor overwhelm her.

He sat back and crossed one leg over the other. 'Let me try putting this another way. In World War Two, what kept the Japanese going was their faith in their god, the Emperor. Say it's 1942, a month or two after Pearl Harbor, and you have a chance to kill the Emperor and destroy the Imperial Palaces, just wipe Japanese Emperor-worship right off the map. Would you do it?'

He watched her eyes move as she searched through the question. 'This sounds like a trick, but when you put it like that . . . sure.'

'That's what we'd like to do to Islam.'

Carla sat up straight, her mouth open, but no words came. She slumped back down in the chair and frowned. 'No. I had to spend some serious time learning about this stuff. There's no equivalent of the Emperor in Islam, and there's two big sects and a dozen minor ones, who quarrel endlessly over who and what is holy, with only a few exceptions . . .' She sat up. 'Jesus. You're talking about goddamn *Mecca*, aren't you?'

Atwater saluted her with his glass.

Carla scrunched her hand down over her eyes, massaging hard. When she pulled her hand away, she put her drink down on the table and locked her gaze with his. 'Look: are you fucking crazy? I can blow away a few dozen ragheads here and there, but I can't march into Mecca and—'

'We're not anticipating you going there in person.'

The helicopter lurched. The pilot's voice came back from the cockpit. 'Sorry. We're getting into the Sierras. There's liable to be a few more.'

Atwater brushed away the interruption with a wave of his hand. 'We're anticipating delivering a small nuclear device.'

'Jesus.' She shook her head. 'This is a joke. I mean, you can't just pick up a nuclear bomb and—'

'Not a classic atom bomb – a dirty bomb, a radiological device.'

She shook her head. 'Too rich for me. Mecca, there's

what? There's way more than a million people there nowadays.'

'We're not talking about a thermonuclear blast, Carla. Think 5 per cent explosion and 95 per cent radioactivity. Something small, local, that will make their holy-of-holies too hot to visit for a thousand years.'

Carla drained her glass and put it down on the table again. 'This is . . . a whole different scale of thing, guys. This isn't a one-girl show. You can't run this with a handful of people and some small arms. And it's nuts.'

Richter spoke up for the first time since they'd entered the 'copter. 'We're not asking you to do this with a Cub Scout troop. Hire whomsoever you need. In any case, you don't have to decide tonight. You can take some time and think it over. But . . .' He reached down to the side of his seat and lifted up a copy of the *Interim Report*. 'Let's take a few minutes and go over some of our ideas, and then you can take this as a little bedtime reading when we get to the Institute.'

'Uh-huh,' she said. 'And what's our next target after this job, the Vatican?'

Atwater leaned forward and refilled her tumbler. 'Nobody worships the Vatican – and not all Christians are Catholic.'

Carla chewed her lip. 'Muslims think the Kaaba's holy, but it's just a rock. Strategic significance, zero.'

A good salesman knows when to employ artifice, and when to get out of the way and allow sincerity to flow though. Atwater abandoned gamesmanship and let his voice speak without restraint. 'The Kaaba is the beating heart of Islam. Cut it out, and the whole religion will die. Not in a moment, not even in a generation, but in time. In a hundred years Islam will be like Zoroastrianism. And it will hit the fanatics hardest, and soonest.'

He paused, letting it sink in, and waiting for his own passion to subside a few degrees. 'And,' he said, in a calmer voice, 'if it's the hand of a woman that brings about the destruction of Mecca – well, that would be even sweeter, don't you think?'

Once they arrived at the Tahoe Institute, it was clear to Carla that Atwater would be perfectly happy to continue haranguing her until the sun rose. She excused herself, saying that if he wanted an answer from her, he'd have to wait until she'd had time to read the *Interim Report*. They saw her off to a bedroom, where she found her bags had already been delivered from the helicopter.

She sprawled on the bed and paged through the *Interim Report*. It looked authoritative enough, but she was too preoccupied to digest even small bites of the information. Atwater's scheme was probably feasible, given time and resources. The question is whether his plan was genius or insanity, and she didn't want to decide by herself.

Her hand dug into the outside pocket of the suitcase and found her cellphone. She flipped it open and heard it chirp its annoying digital song as it powered up.

To her surprise, the reception icon showed good connectivity. But then it only made sense there would be a cell tower on the grounds; from what Richter'd told her about people who attended seminars at the Tahoe Institute, they were the kind of folks who'd go into cardiac arrest if deprived of their mobile phones. She fumbled through her papers until she found the scribbled note with Jill's home phone number.

Given what she knew about Richter, she thought there was a better-than-even chance that someone might be listening in to her calls, but after considering it, she decided she didn't care.

It took four rings before Jill answered. After Carla announced herself, she said, 'I want to ask you about something.'

'Make it quick. I'm one minute out of the shower and about ten seconds from bed.'

'Have you ever thought of leaving the service? The people I'm working for would hire you in a second, put you in charge, and they pay top dollar—'

Jill laughed. 'Hey, woman. Your mind and your mouth ever think about having a little get-together? Just a few days ago you were talking about trying to get reinstated, now you're asking me if I wanna quit?'

Carla nodded to herself. 'Yeah. Dumb question, I suppose.'

'You suppose right.' Jill let out a long yawn. 'Sanchez is private-sector now. You need a playmate, try calling her. But, Carla . . . ?'

'Yeah?'

'I trained you to be a leader. That means making the hard decisions yourself.'

After they ended the call, Carla stood. Her body wanted to move, but it seemed too late to go for a walk without arousing the staff, or, worse, Richter and Atwater. She didn't want to talk, she wanted to think. For a time she found herself pacing the length of the room, flexing her muscles, clenching and unclenching her hands, unable to impose order on the thoughts that tumbled through her mind.

It ain't a boxing match any more once the other guy pulls a knife.

She stopped. With deliberation she sat on the edge of the bed and took off her boots, letting each one clump down onto the floor. The perspiration of a long day clung to her body, but a shower could wait until tomorrow; right now there was work to do.

Stripped to her panties and undershirt, she climbed into bed and opened the *Interim Report*.

I I

Overnight delivery

By their third meeting, Boyce Hammond decided he'd had more than enough of Rex Atwater. It wasn't that the man was annoying; far from it. But Hammond's mother had gone through a religious period in his youth, and had dragged him along a half-dozen times to see evangelists when they toured his part of Ohio. Atwater was cut from a finer cloth than any of those tent preachers, but the tailor's pattern was the same: he was riveting and charming and plausible even while spouting the most arrant nonsense.

Hammond had been expecting a big revelation this time, and Atwater had exceeded expectations. He'd imagined that the old man would pitch him a scheme for hunting down terrorists inside the US, a whole unit of the Ethan Allen Brigade Dirty-Harrying their way across America.

Instead, over dinner and drinks on the Top Floor, Atwater had made a long, convoluted speech about culture wars and the rise and fall of empires, culminating in the conclusion that Islam could be wiped out by destroying Mecca.

Delenda est Carthago, Carthage must be destroyed – even

Hammond could have quoted that. History hadn't been his major in college, but Atwater's lecture had him biting his tongue. He doubted that nuking Mecca would make Islam evaporate. When did the Romans pull down the Temple in Jerusalem, sometime in the first century? Despite the fact their holy-of-holies had been obliterated, there still seemed to be a few Jews knocking around the planet two thousand years later.

But arguing would only arouse suspicion. Instead, he nodded and looked impressed, and fought down that small part of him that wanted to respond to Atwater's crackpot enthusiasm by jumping up and crying *Hallelujah*!

The end of this job was near. Atwater described to him the possible sources of radioactive material, and the 'female Ranger' they were bringing in to manage the commando squad Hammond had been assembling. Female Ranger? No such thing. But the overall scheme was so loony that once even the basics got into place, the Bureau would finally be able to storm in and lock up everybody in sight, and Hammond would be free to . . .

To what? It had been so long since he'd had a real life, he didn't remember what his goals had been. Moonlight shimmered on the ceiling of the glass hexagon above their heads, and Hammond reflected on what great targets the two of them would make against the black backdrop of the mountains. People in glass houses.

He must have looked pensive, because Atwater said, 'I know it's a lot to take in, all at once, and I know that it's a heavy burden to pick up. But our government isn't protecting our civilization – none of the Western governments are willing to defend our heritage – and someone has to. So it falls to us.'

'Who's this "female Ranger", and when do I get to meet her?'

'We thought Carla would be here when you arrived, but she had to attend to some personal business. She'll most likely be back tomorrow night. Is there a problem in you staying over?'

'How long?'

'We figure through the end of the week.'

That should set Earlene's motor running for sure. And if she somehow discovered he'd stayed over to meet up with another woman, that'd be rocket fuel in her carburettor. This was getting too strange. He needed to get to someone in the Bureau soon, sooner than he could arrange a trip into San Francisco. 'I'll need an Internet connection.'

Atwater shrugged. 'Easily done.' His tone was agreeable, but his eyebrows lifted, and Hammond realized that Internet maven didn't fit the profile that Hammond had cultivated with such care.

Two birds with one stone. 'My girlfriend will chew my butt off if she thinks I'm staying one minute longer than necessary. I thought I might send her some stuff to ward off the storm – a card, some chocolates, maybe some roses.' Hammond smiled his best self-deprecating smile. 'I think I can manage that much without having to call Bill Gates.'

Atwater relaxed and smiled in return. 'I'm not sure I could. One of the problems with getting too much money – technology keeps leaping ahead, but it's always easy to pay someone else to do it all for you.'

'I could live with problems like that.'

'Um-hmm. I know you aren't in this for the money, Mr Hammond. But, at the risk of being a little crass, if we pull this off, I can guarantee you won't have to worry about money any more.' Atwater stood and handed him a thick spiral-bound document. 'This is the *Interim Report* I talked about. You'll want to at least skim it before Carla gets back here. Come along and I'll show you where you can get on a computer.'

Atwater led him downstairs to a communications room right off the main auditorium and then bade him goodnight.

Once he was alone, Hammond logged into the greeting-card site. He had to assume that any computer in Atwater's lodge was monitored, probably with a keystroke-capture program. Even if the strokes weren't captured on the local computer, there could be a 'bridge troll' lurking on a server somewhere down the line, a program that grabbed any packets emanating from this address; NSA was reputed to have thousands of these, and he had to assume that what NSA could provide, Atwater's security people could buy in at least some watered-down form. That not only ruled out clear communications through typing, it also eliminated the usefulness of code. A half-page of gibberish would look mighty suspicious if anyone stared at it.

The usual way of avoiding keystroke capture was to call up a virtual keypad – a picture of a keyboard on the screen – and click out his sentences, letter-by-letter. A local keypad-capture program would see only clicks . . . but a bridge troll in the right place, running a *TraceRoute* program, might still see encrypted bytes. Hammond stretched and yawned, buying time. Even if he gambled that no trolls were waiting downstream, there was always the risk that secret cameras were installed in the room. There was no point in searching the room for minicams: if the cameras weren't there, then it was a waste of time; and if they were there, they'd record his search in all its suspicious detail.

There was no safe way to send a full message. The best he could manage was to arrange a clandestine meeting. He hopped to the *Friendship Packages* page and sent an *Economy Pack* to his home address. He specified Friday afternoon as *Latest Delivery*, and typed 'A little something before I come home from Tahoe' in the message box.

The door swung in, and Lamont Richter stood there. 'A little computer work?' he asked.

'A gift for my girlfriend. She gets lonely.'

'Now that's mighty sweet.' Richter leaned against the doorframe, and Hammond noticed him eyeing the screen. 'I wanted to have a few words with you about the gentleman they arrested at your meeting the other night, that Mr Sutton?'

'I told you, we talked to him. The cops never asked a word about the Allens.'

'Yes.' Richter brushed something invisible from his lapel. 'Yes, you said that. But further enquiries – and the fact that Mr Sutton agreed to visit the District Attorney's office this coming Friday – suggested to me that Mr Sutton might not have been entirely honest with you.'

The news was startling, though not entirely unwelcome, and Hammond let the surprise show on his face. 'I don't know what your sources are, but – but, I'll get through to McCann. We'll handle it.'

'Fortunately, that won't be necessary. It seems that our friend was driving while intoxicated last evening and met with a fatal accident.'

Hammond stared.

'The carnage of the roadways. Fifty thousand people a year.' Richter lifted his hand, palm up: what could one do? 'It could happen to anyone.'

If there was a threat there, and Hammond thought there was, the man was smooth enough not to dwell on it. 'No, it couldn't,' Hammond said. 'But it could happen to anyone who drives drunk.'

With Richter watching, he jumped to the *Sweet Greetings* page and sent Earlene a box of Godiva chocolates, overnight delivery. Hammond hated his job, but taking Richter down was going to be all pleasure.

He decided to save the roses for two days hence, when he'd have to let Earlene know he wouldn't be home as soon as he'd promised.

Hammond had even more time to read the *Interim Report* than expected. Carla Smukowski didn't show up the next night, but rather at midday on the day after. She tromped into the dining room as he finished lunch with Atwater and Richter. A slim, dark woman trailed behind her, listing sideways to counterbalance a huge duffelbag.

'Lamont,' Carla said, with a nod. 'Mr Atwater.' She focused on Hammond and came round the table to shake his hand. 'You must be Boyce Hammond. That over there is

Lorraine Sanchez.' She repeated everyone's names for Sanchez's benefit, and then said, 'Lorrie's gonna be helping us on this whole thing.'

Atwater smiled and rose like a good host, but Hammond could see Richter searching for words. 'Uh, Carla . . . ?' he began.

'Lamont?' She stood with her hands on her hips. Hammond had been sceptical about the capabilities of Richter's pet Ranger, but now, watching her easy stance and detecting a vigilance beneath it, he was prepared to re-evaluate his beliefs.

'Is she . . . ?' Richter began again, 'Is your, uh, friend, one of your old . . . *squad*?'

Carla shifted her stance just a bit, and that was enough for Hammond to make up his mind. The way she balanced on her feet spoke of sudden violence, the same barely concealed edge that a certain kind of smiling bar-fighter carried. 'Yeah, Sanchez here was Special K. Though she quit quick enough – never was much for the crawling-through-the-dirt bit.'

All three men considered Lorrie Sanchez, who looked more *Indio* than Spanish, a sharp Aztec nose dominating her slender face. She was slight, seemingly too slight for Special Forces work. When she smiled she didn't show her teeth, and one side of her mouth twisted upwards. 'The dirt always fucked up my nails,' she said, her voice flat, and then dropped her duffel with a thud.

Hammond's eyes darted to her nails, which were chewed to the quick.

He fought back a smile as he watched Richter flail his

mental arms to regain his balance. 'Have you apprised Ms Sanchez,' Richter asked, 'of exactly what we're planning?'

'Yeah. She's okay with it.'

'Carla . . . it might have been better if you'd let us know first.'

Carla smiled, an artificial smile that dared anyone to step across some invisible line. 'Now, hold on here. You guys said I was in charge, and I could hire anyone I needed. And I need Lorrie.'

Atwater held up placating palms. 'We're not questioning you. We're just taken a little offguard. Ms Sanchez, it's a delight to have you on the team. Do you two need lunch?'

'We had food in the car coming up from Reno,' Lorrie said. Hammond detected no hint of a Latina accent, but there seemed to be a trace of Midwest nasality. 'What I need's a shower.'

Carla shook her shoulders to loosen them. 'No kidding. Took about fifteen different flights to get from DC to Nevada.'

Atwater gestured back at the broad hallway with an open hand. 'The rooms to either side of yours should be ready. If anything's missing – well, Carla, you know how to ring for anything you need.'

Carla nodded and headed back round the table towards the hallway. Lorrie hoisted her duffel from the floor with a grunt.

Richter cleared his throat. 'Carla?'

She turned back towards them. 'Yeah?'

'I assume this means that you've signed on, as it were? That is, that you're committed to our . . . project?'

To Hammond, her eyes seemed to focus on him, and that reptilian gaze almost made him shiver. 'Sure,' she said. 'Let's make some history.'

They spent the rest of the afternoon rooting through the *Interim Report*, trying to sort through targets. Atwater and Richter began as eager participants, but when Carla and Lorrie insisted on working through dinner, sending down to the kitchen for sandwiches, the two men excused themselves, leaving Hammond to work with the women.

He kept his comments to a minimum. Fundamentally, he didn't care – the whole operation would be rolled up before it ever got under way. His only goal, via occasional quibbles, was to steer as much as possible back to the US; the more that happened on US soil, the more watertight the charges.

'Delivery,' Lorrie said, 'is a completely different issue. Right, Boyce?'

Startled, he realized she was addressing him. 'Um, right.' He rubbed his palms on his face to gain time. 'Two separate things,' he added. That seemed safe enough.

'Oh, yeah?' Carla asked. 'It seems to me the hot goods and the delivery system are two sides of the same coin. I mean, if—'

Carla's question was cut short by the arrival of sandwiches, chips and beer. They munched in silence for a while, and then Carla asked, 'You have a problem, Boyce?'

He shook his head and gulped his beer. Had she detected a hinky undertone to his comments this afternoon?

'You have some kind of bitch with taking orders from girls?'

The best kind of question, one he could answer with honesty. 'No. None. Done it before.'

'A service issue, then? Marines don't want to listen to the Army? You *are* a Marine, right?'

'Was.'

'Right. Like jarhead is something you get over.' She crunched a mouthful of chips and washed them down with a swig of beer. 'You got any redeeming features to sort of cancel out the whole Marine thing? They teach you something in there? To dance, maybe, or fold napkins?'

He shrugged. 'I fly. 'Copters and light aircraft.' He lifted his sandwich and took a bite. Earlene would like this food, he thought, avocado and provolone and whole-grain bread and . . .

'Do you, now?' Carla glanced sideways at Lorrie, and the exchange of expressions made it clear that the two of them knew this already. 'Then I'd like to hear your opinions on how we get two or three bombs to Mecca from, say, fifty miles out in the Red Sea. No missiles. Something under the radar, or undetectable by radar. Something where we come back alive.'

He eased the sandwich onto his plate so its thick layers remained intact. 'It'd be a lot easier if Congress hadn't given them AWACS. The Saudis can see way over the horizon.'

'We know that,' Lorrie said. 'We've only brought it up about ten times now.'

He closed his eyes and tried to look lost in thought. Play it as though it were real.

Right, Earlene's voice whispered in the back of his mind,

this doesn't have anything to do with trying to impress these ladies, now does it?

He breathed out and opened his eyes. 'Okay. Lorrie said that delivery and procurement were two separate issues. I agree, and I'll go even further. There's two separate issues in delivering a bomb successfully – getting it there, and not getting killed in the process of getting in and out . . .'

For the first time that day, Carla and Lorrie were listening to him with some degree of respect, and he started to think about the problem in earnest.

Richter and Atwater sat at one end of the oval table, toying with their after-breakfast coffee, and they greeted him with nods of their heads. Across the room, Carla and Lorrie showed as huddled silhouettes against the morning light. Hammond took a seat at the table, facing the broad bay window.

He squinted at the bright sunshine. The women sat together on the cushioned window-seat, poring over their notes, and he realized that both of them wore T-shirts, shorts and running shoes. The previous evening he'd begun to drown in his inner sea of guilt – he'd liked Carla and Lorrie from the first, and had come to respect them as they worked together – but now he decided to hell with them. If they got up and went running at 6 a.m. after a working and drinking binge, then as far as he was concerned they deserved to be locked up.

Atwater and Richter chatted with one another while Hammond ate breakfast, and by the time he wiped up the last of his egg yolk with the corner of his toast, he had relaxed into a more charitable frame of mind. Richter made conversation by asking a few questions about how Hammond had become involved with the Allens, and Hammond answered them as though he were unaware that Richter and Atwater had done an exhaustive background check on him.

The women wandered over to the table, and Hammond was interested to note that both of them shaved their legs, and that those legs displayed an assortment of white scars – but not the kind you accumulate from shaving accidents. Carla had one on her calf that still stood up, proud and pink, and he guessed it couldn't be more than a few months old.

They sat down at the other end of the oval table, four seats separating them from Atwater, and piled their papers in a stack between them. 'I think we've worked most of it out,' Carla said. 'There's maybe three, four good ways to go about this. All of them cost serious money.'

Atwater made a throwaway gesture. 'Money's the least of the problems.'

'You may be sorry you said that,' Lorrie said. 'I assume you boys can dummy up some sort of business account we can use? You don't want your fingerprints on this.'

Atwater and Richter exchanged glances and then nodded.

Carla looked at Hammond. 'I've seen your list of candidates. A little old, some of them, but they look good. We need to pick a dozen, no more.'

'I can give you twenty, twenty-five . . .' he said.

She shook her head. 'Just be extra work. Most of those we keep need to be strong swimmers. Scuba training is a big plus. You dive?'

'A little. I'm no SEAL.'

Richter cleared his throat. 'All of which brings us to the issue of general secrecy. How much do these men need to know about the plan?'

Carla seemed taken aback by the question. 'Why, all of it.'

'But, Carla . . .' Richter massaged his neck. 'We can't afford to have people talking about this. The target here is just too big.'

She opened her mouth to respond, but Lorrie spoke first. 'How in hell's name are we going to train people through all the procedures for handling radioactive material without letting them know that's what they're dealing with?'

Richter nodded in vigorous agreement while saying, 'That doesn't mean they need to know what it's for.'

'With all due respect, Mr Richter,' Lorrie said, 'you must not know much about people working in teams. We don't tell them what it's for, they're going to wonder, then speculate, and then you'll have wild rumours. Pretty soon, they'll decide that we're planning to blow up Detroit, or the Moon, or something, and your whole damned project will be floating downriver, tits-up.'

'I want people to know what they're doing and why, period,' Carla said. 'Or count me out.' Her body language said she was ready to get up from her chair and walk away, and Hammond believed it.

Atwater had been watching the interchange, drumming his fingers on the tabletop. Now he spread that busy hand flat and spoke, his voice conciliatory. 'I'm afraid I'm going to have to side with Carla on this one, Lamont. If you recall, this was one of the reasons we came to the Allens in the first place – a pre-existing organization of people who knew how to watch their mouths. Folks who can keep a secret.'

'Not perfectly,' Richter said. 'The way we managed to get all that information on their so-called "secret" weapons caches suggests to me that someone in their organization talks too much.'

Atwater inclined his head towards Hammond. 'That's one of Mr Hammond's jobs, though, isn't it? To select men who can keep quiet. At least until the job's done.'

'And after?' Richter asked. 'If it gets traced back to us? The nature of my business means I've built places to run to. What about you, Rex? Can a billionaire disappear?'

Atwater smiled and shook his head. 'That's a risk I'm willing to take. I'm not carrying a gun in this operation, but it's only fair that the risk runs right up to the top.'

The table fell silent for a moment. Carla seemed to be studying Atwater with a new respect.

Hammond saw his chance. 'Rex is onto something. Money's nice, but it isn't about money for the Allens, never has been. Somebody at the top who's committed, somebody they can admire – that could make all the difference.' He saw Richter open his mouth, and he hurried on. 'Once we have our team together, it'd be great if you could meet them, maybe give a little speech, the same kind of talk you gave me, give 'em the big picture. It's the kind of inspiration they might need.'

Richter groaned as though he felt a sudden pain in his belly. 'Rex . . . that's just plain, outright crazy. You've got to stay arm's length—'

'Who says?'

'Your security advisor says.'

Atwater reached his arms towards the ceiling, stretching his shoulders, and then exhaled a satisfied breath as he lowered them to the tabletop. 'Your advice is noted, but I think I'm going to ignore it.'

Richter gave a casual shrug, but Hammond saw the man's annoyed eyes dart in his direction before he said, 'A fool and his head are soon parted, but it's your neck that's being stuck out.'

Atwater smiled and nodded as if he'd just been given a mild compliment. 'Indeed it is. But if we can make this happen, I'm willing to face the consequences.' He picked up his empty coffee cup, glanced into it and clinked it back onto its saucer. He turned his face to Carla. 'Let's hear your plan.'

Carla scrutinized Richter and Hammond as if examining them for defects. 'We're pretty clear on the best option. We want to take the goods coming up from Indonesia. That gives us no more than three months. The exact sailing date is secret – but I bet you can handle that aspect of it, can't you, Lamont?'

He nodded his assent. Lorrie added, 'And we'll need blueprints of the ship – it's got to be an INF-2 class, at least, or military, or the Coast Guard won't let it into US waters with that kind of cargo – but we need detailed plans. Plus specs on the shipping casks.'

Of the possibilities mentioned in the *Interim Report*, this was one Hammond least favoured. 'Why the Indo shipment? Once it gets anywhere near a port, Coast Guard, DOE and Homeland Security will be all over it.'

'We're going to take it long before it reaches any port,'

Carla said. 'The last thing I want is a firefight with Americans who are just doing their jobs.'

'I see.' Hammond let his voice get mean, as though sarcasm might make them reconsider their target. 'And Indonesians, we can kill them, right? They're just Muslims.'

Lorrie said, 'I like Indonesians. There's a few kooks down there, but if all the Muslims in the world were like the Indonesians, we wouldn't be in this mess.'

'Why not keep it inside the US?' he asked. 'We know the turf, we speak the language, we can call up any extra resources we need. Hell, from the look of things, we could just about walk into some of these waste-disposal sites and stroll out with plutonium in our pockets.'

Lorrie sat back in her chair and considered him. 'I don't get it. "Keep it inside the US?" What's the incentive? I'd go for just about any target outside the US first.' She drummed her fingertips together, staring without a single blink. 'There's a big possibility of getting conned in the US, being set up by Homeland Security, the Bureau, someone. And if we get caught in the US, they'll assume that our intention is to attack America. Give me one reason – just one – why this would work better on our home turf.'

Hammond swallowed. 'We can keep it civilian. Why go up against the Indonesian Navy?' From the flat gaze Lorrie kept on him, he could tell he was losing ground and raising suspicions. He tossed up his hands in surrender. 'I'm just thinking of our men. Why put them in a potential combat situation if we don't need to?'

Lorrie opened her mouth, but Carla interrupted. 'If we do this right, no one will get killed. And if we do this right, the nasty stuff will never enter the US. And, *if we do this right*, it may be that no one will ever know that the hot goods are even missing.'

She glanced at Richter, and then at Atwater, as if waiting for either of them to contradict her. Both of the men smiled, Atwater avuncular, Richter lazy and amused.

'Okay.' Carla stood and leaned the heels of her palms on the table. 'Here's what we're going to do.'

Hammond realized she was telling them, not asking, and he understood that nothing he could say would derail her plans now. He eased back in his chair and relaxed.

In the late afternoon, Hammond headed west on I-80 in his old Ford Taurus. He station-hopped the radio, trying to maintain reception as he drove down to the Central Valley.

He took the freeway off-ramp in the tiny town of Colfax, and without pause crossed the road to the on-ramp. A hitch-hiker stood there, his cardboard sign reading 'SF.'

Hammond pulled over and leaned across the seat to open the passenger-side door. The man hoisted his backpack and clambered in, slamming the door. Troy looked at him and grinned. 'You going to the City?'

Hammond eased the car back onto the ramp and accelerated as well as the gutless old bucket would allow. 'Not all the way, but I'll get you a few miles further on.'

Troy pointed at his own mouth and raised his eyebrows. Hammond shook his head in response, and laid his index finger across his lips.

They listened to the radio until they reached the outskirts of Sacramento, where he turned off the freeway and cruised down one of the parallel surface streets. 'I'll need to stop here for gas,' Hammond said. 'Plus I need to hit the restroom. Remind me to check the oil and water before we split, this junkheap sucks 'em down by the gallon.'

'No prob,' Troy said. 'I'll even check 'em for you while you're in the bathroom.' He unzipped his backpack and unloaded his e-sweeper and his wand, an elongated metal horseshoe like the handheld detectors used at airports. 'Take your time.'

By the time Hammond came back and climbed behind the wheel, the man had put his toys away and stood by one of the gas pumps, several yards from the car. 'No recording devices,' Troy said, 'as far as I can tell.'

'I'd still rather not take any chances until we've had a full sweep done.' He nodded at Sue's Diner in the adjacent lot. 'Let's talk over lunch.' Hammond pulled the car out of the station and parked it.

Troy met him inside the restaurant door. 'Jen and the baby are fine, thanks for asking.'

'Uh-huh. Where do I need to drop you?'

'Can you think of a good reason to drive to San Fran?'

'Nope. I need to get back to Stockton and then go rent ourselves sort of a training camp, for Chrissake. *Near the water*, mind you.'

The waitress waved her hand at the line of empty booths, and they slid into one in the middle. Hammond noticed a scar on the wall where a fifties at-table jukebox had been torn away. 'Can't say I don't take you anywhere nice.'

Troy shrugged. 'I'm grateful. I'll even let you buy – you're the one with three year's back pay accumulating interest.'

'That's right. And I want out, ASAP.'

'What have you got?'

'No. Question is, what have you done with what I gave you?'

The waitress hurried over to their table, her order pad ready. Troy asked for a chicken-salad sandwich and a Coke, and Hammond said, 'The same.'

Troy waited until she had bustled back to the kitchen. 'The Richter tape from the Grange was crisp and clear. But Legal doesn't think there's much on it.'

Hammond had suspected this, but he still felt let down. 'And the money?'

'We've traced the seed money back from your Eastside Guns account. Easy to do – comes straight out of one of the Tahoe Institute accounts for speaker honoraria.'

'I didn't speak.'

'True. But he's paid for people to attend before, even if they didn't speak. He's on perfectly defensible grounds. You're going to need something bigger than that.'

'What about Sutton?'

'He was bailed with cash.'

'He's also dead. Convenient car accident. Get the CHP or somebody to take a close look.'

Troy blinked a few times. 'I can have Forensics—'

'No. Don't take the Bureau anyplace near it.' Hammond leaned forward and put his palm down on the tabletop. 'Richter knew about the Allens and the whole Berkeley Marina cock-up.'

Troy blew out a breath. 'Does he know you were there?'

'I told him.' Troy opened his mouth with protest written

on his face, but Hammond added, 'He might have known already.'

'Do you think he knows you're with us?'

'No. I don't think so. He seems to know a lot about the Bureau, but I don't think he's that well wired-in.' The waitress returned, juggling plates and glasses onto the tabletop, asked if there would be anything else, and then slapped down the check before retreating. Hammond chewed his lip. 'I want a few things. I want Richter to go down hard. No plea-bargains. And I want immunity for a few of the people in and around the Allens.'

'Townley told me. Shouldn't be a problem. Richter, though . . . if they need him to get Atwater, I can't make any guarantees. Give me a solid case on Atwater, something big.'

'It's big, all right – we're talking nuclear – and I want the plug pulled soon.' He shook his head. 'The guy's as daffy as Saturday-morning cartoons.'

'Tell me your tale, and I'll run it upstairs. This is too big for me to call the shots.'

'Soon, Troy. You got that? Real soon.'

12

Predators

'Gianetti,' Carla said, 'you're up.'

The twelve-minute course: net-climbing, a quarter-mile sprint; a rope climb leading to horizontal bars, then tyres to run through, alternate feet in each tyre; a big clamber-and-jump-off platform leading to an underwire belly crawl; then an eighth-mile sprint, a trench crawl and another, final eighth-mile sprint. A close duplicate of the first course she'd trained on, all those years ago, and Richter'd had it all in place by the time she arrived at Rancho Del Mar three days ago.

A man stepped out from the dozen Allens crowding around the start post, and Carla tried to memorize his face and tie it to his name. Gianetti – an easy one, looked and moved like a New York street hood, even though he hailed from Seattle.

He cinched the chest band on his pack and nodded. A forty-pound backpack. Not full regulation size, no need to overdo it, but a little extra riding you the whole time.

Carla raised the stopwatch. 'Mark . . . set . . . *go!*'

Gianetti ran towards the net. Carla looked out past the men, across the half-mile of fields to the sea-cliffs above the Pacific.

She had to admit that Richter had delivered everything she'd asked for. Space, seclusion and even accommodation; a hundred yards behind her, on the road to Highway 101, were the buildings that had once constituted Rancho Motor Court – two strips of white stucco bungalows, ten to a side, that faced off across a gravel drive wide enough for a children's soccer game. A dining hall at the rear, a relic of years the motel had been converted to a dude ranch, united the two rows into a deep horseshoe.

All this, thirty minutes north of the docks at Santa Barbara. Yeah, the site was perfect. She had her doubts about the people.

Whoops and catcalls from the men pulled her eyes back to the course. Gianetti had fallen in the tyres and was struggling to regain his feet.

She'd met each of them individually when she'd arrived, assessing their skills and temperaments. All of them had previous military experience, but at the end of four hours of interviews she felt something was out of balance. It wasn't just a matter of age, though the youngest of her team was over thirty . . .

Thinking back to her early days in Georgia, it all came into focus. Today's Army was nothing if not diverse. But what she had here was a squad of middle-aged white guys.

It made sense, once she thought about it: what kind of clowns signed up for an underground militia?

She'd gathered, during the interviews, that their excitement over the money, and their enthusiasm at a chance to get back at *them damn Moslems*, didn't extend to her presence. It seemed logical now; she might be the most elite soldier any of them had ever met, but she was still a girl, *gee-yoo-arr-ell*, girl. A lose-lose situation – if she weren't as tough as they were, then she didn't deserve respect, but if she were tougher, they wouldn't want to hear about it.

Her biggest stumbling block right now, though, was a problem of command she'd never anticipated: How the hell were you supposed to remember everybody's name?

McCann, the big, older guy; Skittle, short for Steve Kittle, fast and nervous. Big Jones and Little Jones. Alvorsen, pudgy and blond-bearded; French, the dark guy who studied everything around him as though there might be a pop quiz. Madden, Slater, Simonsen, Dodge, Kowinski – she had the names on her tongue like a mantra, but she couldn't swear she could match them with faces.

The reason for the worldwide custom of stitching soldiers' names onto their fatigues had become obvious, and she vowed she'd spend an hour with their files later, concentrating on nothing but marrying mugshots to monikers.

Gianetti came stumbling in at twelve minutes twenty-three seconds, and let his pack thud to the ground behind him. He leaned over and put his hands on his thighs, gasping, and then looked up at her. 'Under twelve and a quarter,' Carla said, and stuffed the stopwatch back in her pocket. 'One of the best today, but not good enough.' A half-circle of a dozen sullen, sweaty men stared at her; off to her left, leaning on an old fence pole, Hammond watched her, his hand above his brow to shield his eyes from the August sun.

She raised her voice. 'Listen up, folks. We got times here that range from almost adequate to total crap.'

She heard a murmur of discontent move through the group. She clasped her hands behind her back and stood as tall as she could – five-seven and three-quarters, even in boots, nothing compared to Jill's approach to six feet, and shorter than any man on the grounds – and strolled in their direction. 'Twelve minutes is *adequate* – not good, *ad*equate. You guys think you're the last line of defence for American freedom?' She snorted. 'Shit. A decent beach-volleyball team'd be tougher.'

One of them, she thought it was Little Jones, said, 'Yeah? Show us how it's done then.'

She could shout him down or ignore him, but this was still a direct challenge. It had to be dealt with. Either she'd need to chop the man down to size . . . or ace the training course herself and put them all to shame. She bought time by staring at him without speaking. What would Jill have done? Who knows? Jill trained people who'd fought for the privilege of lining up in front of her. But the men standing here weren't the best and the brightest; they looked more like the cheap seats at Pro Wrestling Nite.

Jill wouldn't be here, she reminded herself, because Jill wouldn't fuck up the way you did. And if Jill could talk to you this instant, she'd tell you to *get on top of it, now*.

She heard a few other voices chiming in to agree with Little Jones, asking to see if she really had chops, but they sounded as though they were coming from underwater, garbled and distant. *Get control of yourself, that's the first thing*.

If she ran the course, she might fuck up in front of everybody. Low risk, but it could happen. And it might be a mistake to give in to their challenge – after all, who the hell was in charge here, anyway: her or this gang of wimpy white boys?

What would she want, if she'd been given a new, unproven leader, if she'd been asked to obey someone with no rank? She found herself nodding before her conscious mind had even reached a conclusion, and found herself pitching her voice high and loud and saying, 'Okay. We don't know each other. So let's start now.' She glanced over her shoulder and snapped out an order. 'Hammond. Get over here.'

She lifted Gianetti's backpack and swung it onto her shoulders. She cinched in the shoulder straps, only a little – she wasn't that much smaller than he was – and clicked the quick-release on the cross-chest band into place. She snapped the waistbelt, shook her torso, and the pack slithered on her back like a child hanging onto her neck. Not what you wanted – you needed it to be on your back like the hump on Quasimodo, part of you. She jerked on the take-in strap, and it tightened, squinching her breasts. Too damn tight, tight enough to constrict her breathing, so she loosened it . . .

Screw it! Getting someone else's gear just right on your own back could take twenty minutes. If she kept them standing there while she fussed, she'd lose them.

She sensed Hammond standing by her side. Her fingers dug through her pockets for the stopwatch and slapped it into his hand. 'Reset it.' She hunched over, exhaling as deep as she could on each breath.

'You ready?' he asked. She nodded, staring at the ground. 'Then . . . *go!*'

She launched herself with everything she had, but it felt as though the air had become a gelatinous mass, holding back her arms and legs. It felt all wrong, running a course alone, no one alongside her to compete against. *That's a problem we can fix, just tell Richter we need another set of everything, running in parallel.*

She leaped at the net and clutched her hands high in the webbing, kicked one foot down into the mesh and heaved herself up onto the cross-pole, landing hard on her belly and then arching and rolling her hips up and over and letting herself fall, giving a last tug at the net as she dropped, just to cushion the force on her ankles, and she hit on the balls of her feet, let her knees flex way down to absorb the force – textbook-perfect, but for the fact that Gianetti's pack rode too loose, and when it swung to the side she felt a slicing pain as her left ankle twisted in her boot.

Treat it like a wound. She lunged into the quarter-mile straightaway.

A quarter of a mile is an eternity, nearly a minute for the fastest runners on the planet, unencumbered; closer to two for the best of the crop wearing boots and packs and in the middle of a course. At every other footfall she winced at the pain, knowing that running on a sprain would only make it worse. Despite the fearsome twinge in her ankle, despite her laboured breath, the straightaway gave her long enough to think, long enough to decide it was stupid to run this because they'd provoked her, long enough to ask if it really mattered anyway.

Long enough to get angry. She'd proved herself getting into Special K, had proved herself in finishing training, had proved herself over and over again, too damn many times, and now what did she have to show for it? A bunch of losers, a bunch of losers who demanded she prove herself again, to them, as if they knew anything – a bunch of dick-swinging morons whose only claim on life was the fact that Y-chromosome sperm swim faster.

She hit the rope high – the higher you catch it the less footage you have to climb – and she said, '*fuck! – fuck! – fuck!*' as she yanked herself up, hand-over-hand, and leaped out to the horizontal bars.

Playground rules: swing hard and skip every other rung, and at least her feet weren't pounding the ground, but it was only seconds before she was jouncing through the tires – *knees high, knees high!* – wincing every time her left foot touched down, until she leaped for the patchwork cross-braces of the climb-up platform.

A long drop, and she tried to take all of the force on her right foot and convert it into a fall-forward as soon as the sole of her boot touched the ground. She rolled in a shoulder-somersault, angling her head to the opposite side to protect her neck, and came up with her left knee and right foot on the ground. She threw herself forward and started into her belly-crawl five feet early, as though she were taking real fire. When she dragged herself under the last strand of barbed wire she pushed to her feet and started running again, and even though she knew it slowed her down, even though she knew it was tougher on her ankle, she started jackrabbiting as though

169

there were bullets flying, until at the end she dived into the trench.

Rocks crushed into her knees and elbows and she churned dirt like a gopher fleeing a coyote until she pulled herself from the trench and started running.

Pain was everywhere. The fire in her ankle had become familiar, but other parts of her body now clamoured for attention. Her shoulders ached, but no, that's referred pain, it's only your diaphragm cramping, and that pain around your heart, no, it's your cervical vertebrae pinching; roll your neck, let it loose and run, you stupid cow, run harder, you've already blown it, you're too fucking slow, but you've got to beat the fat guys . . .

She tripped, recovered and stumbled onwards to slap her hand on the waist-high finish post, and then she leaned there sucking air.

'Nine forty-eight,' Boyce announced.

Jesus. 9.48. When she was in shape she could do 8.30 on a course like this, even a personal best at 8.05. Now she was at 9.48, and she wasn't sure she'd live. She wanted to drop to her knees and gag, but she'd be damned if she'd do either in front of this bunch. She felt the pressure building in her gut, and vomit erupted into her mouth, bubbly as a baby's spit-up, but vastly more acrid. With deliberation she swallowed it, and then swallowed again, trying to wash away the taste.

She forced herself to stand up straight and take in a deep breath. 'Where I come from—' she began, and then stopped to pant. 'Where I come from, anything over eleven is . . . is *humiliating*.'

There was no obvious response from the semicircle of faces, but it was hard to see: her vision pulsed in rhythm with her heartbeat.

'What does crawling under fences have to do with our operation?' This time she knew it was Little Jones, his square face set in a petulant expression.

Nothing, really. Running courses on land wasn't relevant, but having a unified, capable team was. Having them dance to her tune was even more so. 'Who the fuck asked you?' She paused to swallow grateful lungfuls of air. 'The next time I say "piss", I expect golden liquid on the ground, whether you have time to unzip or not.'

'And suppose we don't want to take orders from you?' McCann asked.

Carla sighed, and then shut her mouth and moved her breath into her nose. When she was sure her voice wouldn't tremble for want of air she said, 'Did somebody give you boys the idea this is a democracy? Here's the picture. I asked for twelve of you. I only need eight.' She paused and let that sink in. 'I'm not going to drill you for the next two weeks, I've got other things to do. But anyone who isn't under twelve minutes two weeks from now is out. And if we don't have at least eight left, then I quit.' She scanned the faces, seeing nothing, wishing her blue eyes were as opaque as Jill's black glare. 'And don't get any ideas. Without me in charge, the money guys will call this off, and you losers can all go home and milk your goats.'

She headed off towards her bungalow, not limping, but biting the inside of her lip each time her weight hit her left foot.

*

Three hours later her mind was in a manual on rebreathers and her foot was deep in a bucket of ice when a knock came on the door of her bungalow. It was a little surprising. She'd put out a *Do Not Disturb* sign, not caring to have anyone know she'd needed to ice her ankle. 'Yeah?' she shouted. 'Who?'

'Lorrie,' a voice replied, muffled by the door.

Carla pulled her foot from the bucket and hobbled over to open the door. When they released their greeting embrace, Carla asked, 'When did you get here?'

'Couple hours ago. We been screwing nuts on bolts. What's with the foot?'

'Nothing.' She limped back to her chair, her lower leg so numb she couldn't feel the floor beneath her heel.

'We've got the goodies, and we're all set up on the field out back. I figured you'd want to be there for the demo.'

Most of the swelling had gone down. When Carla had wrapped her ankle in a tight support bandage and laced up her boot, it felt good enough to walk on without favouring it.

Out past the obstacle course a large rental truck sat parked in the sparse brown sage. The men stood in a half-circle beyond the truck, and between their shoulders she caught glimpses of dark grey metal. 'We've got four of them,' Lorrie said, 'four of the flyers, that is. Cost some extra money, of course, but I figure there's a decent chance we'll screw up one or two between now and D-Day.'

They pushed their way into the circle and Carla studied the ultralight. At first glance, it looked like an overgrown hang-glider, too light, too fragile for the job they had planned. Yet it wasn't a hang-glider; the broad, overarching wing was solid, not fabric, and there was a skimpy fuselage of the same material stretching back to the tail. A single seat was bolted on just behind the engine, so the pilot's legs would almost embrace the motor, a weirdly sexual image, a motor-cycle of the air.

'Whisper-power motor,' Lorrie said, 'and fibreglass every-where except the engine and the wheels. Minimal radar profile.' She gestured back over her shoulder with her head. 'Three more in the truck, just need to bolt on the wings and tail.'

Hammond stepped forwards and stood between the two of them. 'Still big enough to catch on radar. Probably give about the same bounce-back as a small helicopter.'

'Sure, if that was all,' Lorrie said. 'But we've done the motor in electro-conductives.'

'Stealth paint? Where the hell'd you get that?'

'Brazil,' she said, in a nonchalant voice. 'It isn't B-2 qual-ity, but we aren't trying to hide a B-2. Sure, there's still a signature.'

'How big a signature?' Carla asked.

'About like having a Mylar balloon blow past,' Lorrie said. 'The problem comes when we add the payload . . . though we can paint that, too.' She glanced on past Carla and searched the crowd. 'Yo! Alvorsen. Where's my goodies?'

Alvorsen – blond beard, a little pudgy, an easy one to remember, Carla reminded herself – trudged over and handed Lorrie a pair of gloves and a set of flight goggles.

Lorrie pulled on the gloves and shouted for someone to cast off the plane. Two men hurried over to unclip the cables that staked the ultralight to the ground. Carla gritted her teeth. It annoyed her how readily, even eagerly, everyone seemed to be obeying Lorrie's orders.

With the goggles atop her head, Lorrie looked like an aviatrix from the early days of flight. She shooed everyone back and climbed into the pilot's seat, her slim legs straddling the engine. Once she was buckled in, she pulled down her goggles and cranked the engine. After the grating sound of the ignition, the low hum of the engine and the smooth swoosh of the propeller seemed delicate by contrast, and as the aircraft eased down the field Carla realized she could hear the sounds of weeds crushing beneath the wheels.

When Lorrie lifted off into the bright afternoon sky, there was no sudden change in motion or thrust. It was as though the ultralight were a leaf, wafted up on a passing breeze, passive, light, weightless. She steered the plane through a wide upward spiral, and the low speed and near-silence reinforced the illusion that the craft was being carried by air currents.

While they watched, Lorrie took the ultralight out past the edge of the seaward cliffs, turned south to fly along the hidden beach and then glided downwards, disappearing from sight. With no visual sign and no engine sound, this created the uncanny feeling of a magic trick, and this was reinforced a minute or two later when Alvorsen exclaimed and pointed to the north, where the ultralight had reappeared, heading back.

'More like a glider than a plane,' Hammond said. 'Smart woman. How'd she end up in the Army?' Seeing something in Carla's face, he hurried to add, 'I mean, I was a Marine, I'm not dissing the service. But she seems . . .'

'Probably needed the college money. Her mom's a cleaning woman.'

'That explains joining up. Doesn't explain going all the way to Special K.'

She pondered this for a moment. It was so obvious to her: if you could qualify, then it was almost a duty, like being invited to compete in the Olympics. 'I suppose people told her she couldn't do it. She didn't stay long after we got our patches. She's one of the few who ever quit.'

'She's something.'

'She is,' Carla said, and she felt a tugging sensation as she did so. Lorrie *was* something, but so was everyone in Special K. Christ on a carousel, am I jealous?

Lorrie slowed the plane to what seemed like a fast walk before she landed. To Carla's amusement, there was scattered applause as Lorrie rolled out of her seat and pulled off her goggles. 'Alvorsen, Jones, stake this baby down.'

Lorrie sauntered up between Hammond and Carla and said, 'So, buy me a beer?'

Carla realized, with some surprise, that Lorrie was asking for her approval. She turned and draped her arm over the woman's shoulders. 'Anything for you, Amelia.'

'I still have a few questions,' Hammond said.

'Come on along,' Carla said. 'You're legal age, ain'tcha?'

The dining hall was filled with dark varnished tables and benches, just a little too smooth and shiny to be classified as picnic benches. To Carla, it was reminiscent of a pizza parlour from the seventies, one of those whose decorators had been torn between a medieval and a Roaring Twenties motif. It was a good half-hour before dinner, and they had the place to themselves, though the sounds of the cook and his assistants banging away in the kitchen echoed into the hall.

Lorrie and Carla took seats on opposite sides of a table. Hammond had pulled a six-pack of bottles from the cooler, the cardboard holder still dripping, and he slung it onto the tabletop and sat down beside Carla. *Pacifico*. He twisted off a top, clomped it down in front of Carla, twisted another and slid it to Lorrie. Once his own was in hand, he said, 'Ultralights I've seen before always sounded like power lawnmowers. But if the radar profile's as small as you say, no one will know this one's coming. Like I asked Carla before, what's a brain like yours doing in an outfit like this?'

Lorrie neither smiled nor bristled, only stared. 'I've thought about asking you the same question.' Carla glanced at her in surprise; though Lorrie's tone was causal enough, Carla knew that the question was dead serious.

'What do you mean?' Hammond asked.

'You're a smart guy. What are you doing with the Allens? I can do math, and it don't add up.'

'Okay.' He set his beer down on the table and rolled the bottle between his palms. 'I did my time in the Gulf. Some other places, too. And I've seen what happens to people in places where the rulers are the only ones who have real weapons.'

'Huh,' Lorrie said.

Whatever was happening between the two of them, Carla wished they would cut it out. 'Will these planes carry enough weight?' Carla asked.

Lorrie nodded. 'These are technically two-seat trainers, not legal to fly solo. They'll handle it.'

'Still doesn't solve the problem that matters to me,' Hammond said. 'How's a pilot going to get in and still get home?'

'Simple,' Lorrie said. 'No pilots.'

'GPS guidance?' Hammond swigged his beer. 'I don't buy it. What about contingencies, what about sneaking between hills, what about staying low?'

'Remote-piloting,' she said. 'Remember when they hit that carload of al-Qaeda guys in Yemen a few years back? The missile was fired from a Predator unmanned jet. The guy flying it – if you can call it flying – was sitting at some console a thousand miles away.'

'Yeah, yeah, I know what a Predator is. Question is: who the hell are you, the Defence Department? You think you can buy those controls from some catalogue?'

'Predators move at jet speed. That's tricky technology. But if you don't mind staying under fifty, sixty miles an hour, you can get remote-piloting controls custom designed a dozen different places.' Lorrie folded her arms and gave Hammond a smug look. Score one for the girls, Carla thought.

'And I suppose that no one's going to put it all together?' Hammond gestured at the room with his beer. 'Nobody's going to figure out what we're doing?'

'They already have. The folks designing the controls think we're flying spectrometers over oil and gas pipelines up north, looking for leaks.' She raised her bottle and then swallowed, in no hurry at all. 'The folks who modified the ultralights – well, nobody said anything, but they charged us double because they knew exactly what we were doing. It's clear we're drug smugglers.'

Carla laughed. 'Can't think of a better trial. Before we fly these puppies in some hostile country, let's give 'em the acid test: let's fly 'em into the US from Mexico. If NORAD doesn't catch them, I'm betting Mustafa won't have a clue.'

She and Lorrie grinned at each other. 'Hell, we're going to be setting up a base in Baja anyway,' Lorrie said.

'One more question,' Hammond said. 'How the hell are we going to launch these? Have you contracted for a mini-aircraft carrier, too?'

'They're amphibious. I've already bought floats. They add seventy-five pounds a pair, but we can handle that. That, plus extra gas tanks, plus a four-hundred-pound payload.'

Carla raised her bottle and she and Lorrie clinked them across the table. Hammond joined in belatedly, so he had to chase the two bottles with his own.

As the sun headed down, the dining hall turned dark, darker than logic dictated. Even though golden light still flowed through the windows, the stained beams and slats of the walls and vaulted ceiling sucked up every photon, as though the diners were on a picnic in the void of space.

The three of them had the table to themselves over dinner. With six long tables seating eight each, and a total of fifteen diners, the hall wasn't even half-full.

Carla held up her end of the conversation, but her eye was on the table where Ray McCann sat. Six of the men had joined him there, including Little Jones and Madden, the pair she had singled out as the biggest troublemakers.

Skittle and Gianetti sat at a table of their own: furtive, skinny, dark, they hunched forward over their food and talked in low voices, as though they were planning some second-rate robbery. Outsiders, she guessed, not on anyone's side. Slater, Big Jones, and Alvorsen formed a trio at a table in the corner; they seemed at ease with the world and with one another, and she figured them for possible allies.

Odd how, once she'd started to classify the men into friend and foe, the names she'd had such a hard time remembering became clear in her mind. McCann, Madden and Little Jones were the problem, and Simonsen, Dodge, Kowinski and French were signed on to McCann's team.

When she'd first arrived and been confronted with a basic lack of respect from the men, Carla had wondered if Hammond had been sandbagging her, if he'd been unwilling to share authority. She'd changed her mind since; he treated her with unfailing regard and, in front of the men, took her requests as though they were orders.

All of the Allens deferred to both Hammond and McCann, but Carla had enough time in the military to recognize respect based on hierarchy, and Carla could see that the men respected Hammond because of his position. McCann, on the other hand, enjoyed the respect given a ringleader or rebel, the recognition due an oversized personality.

Mess-hall lawyers, Jill had called them – folks who always knew better, who always had an opinion, and who gathered the malcontents around them the way a stick on a pond accumulates a ring of lesser debris.

Seven out of twelve over at McCann's table. The numbers weren't reassuring. She needed to take him down a peg or two. But should she do it alone, or in front of his cheerleaders? She'd know better if she waited and watched a few more days, but she didn't know if she had a few more days, not if she wanted to turn these bozos into a team.

'You aren't eating,' Lorrie said to her.

'Late lunch.'

She listened with one ear while Lorrie and Hammond argued about the benefits of small planes versus ultralights. Odd, really. Hammond had been the one, back in Tahoe, who'd first suggested ultralights for delivery, and now he seemed to be making every effort to discredit his own idea.

Over at the other table, McCann made some comment, and his listeners erupted into loud laughter. He sat in their midst with the patient, glowing face of a stand-up comedian waiting for his audience to quiet down.

Not in front of the men, she decided. It didn't matter to her if she humiliated McCann in front of his fan club, but the circle around him needed something to draw them together. She didn't want to knock their emotional compasses off course.

Losers. A roomful of losers. Herself included, she realized – maybe everybody in the hall except Lorrie and Hammond.

She knew why Lorrie was there. When they'd met at Lorrie's office, the woman's black eyes had glittered at the first mention of fighting terror with terror. Carla had been in the hotel room with her when she'd called back to her office at TLI, Technology and Logistics International, and told them she was going on indefinite leave from her Junior VP position. Told them; Lorrie's voice hadn't allowed for any negotiation, and Carla was certain when this was over that Lorrie would be welcomed back without hesitation.

Hammond, on the other hand, was a puzzle. Good-looking:

it had been a couple of years since she'd had sex that didn't require batteries, but she'd decided she wouldn't mind taking him for a spin around the block. Intelligent enough, too, and Lorrie was right, he just didn't fit in with the Allens. Most men were made up of less than met the eye, but Boyce Hammond . . .

Right. A man with a dark past, a man with a secret sorrow. Get a grip on yourself, Smukowski.

Carla nodded to her companions and mumbled the appropriate words before she stood and carried her tray to the back of the hall. She dumped them into the tub with no attempt to muffle their clatter.

She stretched as tall as she could and stomped her way towards the front doors, disregarding her protesting ankle. When she passed McCann's table she nodded, a short bob of the head, and, neglecting her urge to grab the man by the throat and take him apart right then, continued on. Slater, Big Jones and Alvorsen smiled from their table, and Skittle and Gianetti favoured her with nods of their heads.

Five on my side, plus Hammond, Lorrie and me. Eight for us, seven for them.

But I need them all, and I'm going to have them.

As the door closed behind her, she heard a burst of laughter. She couldn't be sure, but she felt that it was aimed at her, and she thought she knew who was responsible.

13

Lorrie

It is a puzzle to geographers that Switzerland, a land-locked nation, should be one of the world's most important manufacturers of diesel engines for ships. But then there was really no logic that predicted the country would be a leading *chocolatier*, either, or that such a famously neutral nation should be a key source of mercenary soldiers, so Lorrie Sanchez added Taneli Filip Karvonen to Switzerland's list of enigmas. A Finn with a refined British accent, heading a firm of naval architects in Geneva – why not?

He cleared his throat and again gave her that patronizing smile from behind his desk. 'My first thought was that your people must be having us on, Miss Villalobos. We've been through your specifications, though, and . . . well, no one would devote these kinds of resources to a prank.'

You've also cashed our retainer cheque, Lorrie thought. She shifted in her chair and smoothed her skirt.

When she didn't respond, he continued. 'I'm sure you'd be willing to allow as it's an odd request, though. Ramming hasn't been a factor of consequence in naval warfare since the

Battle of Lepanto.' He smiled again. 'That was the sea battle between Venice and Turkey, where—'

'Fifteen seventy-one AD,' she said. 'And I'd have to disagree. Right offhand, the Battle of Hampton Roads in the Civil War was won by an ironclad running down two wooden ships. The invasion of Guadalcanal was shortened when the *Kiwi* rammed and sank a Japanese submarine.'

Karvonen steepled his fingers into the prayer position and then tapped the tips against one another while keeping the heels of his palms pressed together. Was he applauding her, or just nervous? 'Hmm. Apologies. I see I'm dealing with something of a scholar here. Oughtn't make assumptions . . . Might I ask for more detail on what you have in mind, the exact purpose of these . . . unusual calculations?'

'You can ask.' Lorrie turned her head and looked out the window to Lake Geneva, glassy under the summer sun.

'Hmm.' He smacked his lips with an air of decision. 'Between you and the candlestick, then. But you are aware that what you're asking has no precise answer? Certainly with these reinforcements you can puncture any hull at those speeds, much less a cargo ship . . . but the rate of water gain will depend on the degree of penetration, how high the seas are running, the distance and frequency of the wave-to-wave maxima . . .'

'Give us ranges and conditions, then.' Lorrie dug through the inside pocket of her suit jacket and pulled out a pack of Capitano cigarettes together with a sheet of paper folded in quarters. She tossed the cigarettes onto the desktop and opened the sheet of paper. 'Assume at least an hour afloat, maybe even two. Give us pumping rates needed to keep it zeroed out.'

'"Can do," as you Yanks say.' Lorrie saw him study her for a reaction, the unstated question being *You sound American, but are you?* His eyes focused on the pack of Capitanos, and he nodded to himself as though that settled it. 'Obvious, though, that your goal here isn't sinking an enemy . . . You wouldn't perchance be related to Admiral Villalobos, of Chile, would you?'

Lorrie did her best to give a tiny flinch before she shrugged.

'Ah. Best not said, eh? Still and all – might I guess this would have something to do with the Argentinian border dispute?' He tossed it off with a casual air, but she saw his eyes scanning her face for any tell-tales. 'Create an accident in Chile's claimed territorial waters, bit of an international incident, enough time to get TV crews on site . . . ?'

She kept her face impassive. The details of the story the man was inventing for himself were better than any cover she could have devised, since every element of the story was in precise accord with his own suspicions.

He leaned back in his chair with an air of satisfaction, and then shot his cuffs as though he'd finished a task. 'Well, then. Shan't pry any further. Nod's as good as a wink, and all that. Under the circumstances, though, the matter of payment is a little delicate. Might I suggest that—'

'If you'll take the commission, we'll wire the full fee to your bank this afternoon. If you can make the timeline, that is.'

'Readily. Indeed, I think we can have it in your hands inside of a week. Unless there's anything else . . . ?'

'Nothing. Just what's in the papers and blueprints.' Lorrie stood and he rose from behind his desk and came round to shake her hand.

'Glorious weather this week,' he said, as he escorted her to the door. 'Will you be staying in Geneva long?'

'Not long,' she said. 'A little tourism, and then I'm off.'

'We'd be happy to sponsor a lake cruise, if sightseeing is on your schedule. We've got, as you might imagine, any number of watercraft . . .'

'Wish I had the time, but no.' Lorrie hit him with her best smile. 'Just an hour or so to catch a bit of Gothic architecture, and then it's off to the airport. Mr Karvonen – a pleasure doing business with you.'

From the lake, the sharp verdigris-covered tower of St Peter's Cathedral dominates the centre of old-town Geneva. The church has been added to over the centuries; a Roman core supports Gothic and neoclassical additions, and the whole hunkers down amidst more pedestrian buildings like some massive chimera.

This was the epicentre of the Reformation, where John Calvin preached his fiery sermons damning the corruption of the Church of Rome, and it remains a destination for the few Protestant pilgrims who care about the history of their break-away faith; but, Lorrie reflected, sitting in the dimness of the chapel, it was still a Catholic cathedral – Catholic workmanship, Catholic architecture, Catholic-hewn stones beneath her feet.

No sermons were being preached from Calvin's pulpit that day, and the tourists who wandered through were hushed and reverent. She'd been worried that she wouldn't be allowed to sit there, that some profession of Calvinism might be demanded from her, but her presence in the empty pews was respected by visitors and churchmen alike.

Jill, Carla and the rest thought she'd retired from K-Force to pursue her career, and she'd been content to let them go on believing that. But it hadn't been the lure of money that had drawn her away from the Army.

Her lover of those days had used condoms, she'd made sure of that, but somehow a squadron of his sperm had breached those defences and crept silently into her womb. When her period was late, she didn't worry: heavy training can do that, especially when you get low on body fat. But when she missed two in a row, she checked . . .

She'd been baptized, catechized and confirmed in her youth, but it had all been for the sake of her mother; Lorrie'd been a closet atheist by the time she was thirteen. A quick and quiet abortion seemed in order, and she undertook it like a trip to the dentist.

A few months later, on assignment in Colombia, the dreams started.

The terrain was never the same. Jungle, tundra, forest, desert, even what appeared to be other planets. What was constant was the crying baby, off in the distance, the baby crying for her, and every night she'd search, frantic with fear and guilt, and awaken in the morning drained.

She knew it was all over for her. Exhaustion and stress had made her lose her edge, and she wasn't sure that she hadn't lost her mind as well. Going to a shrink would spell the end of her clandestine escort work, so at the first opportunity she headed back to the States and left K-Force. The girls who were in town, including Jill, had given her a big send-off party, and she'd been bright and chipper and smart-assed and had gone back to her hotel room and cried herself to sleep.

And in the dream that night she'd found Michael, the most beautiful baby in the world, floating in a basket at the edge of a river. She'd never even considered baby names, but she knew the moment she lifted him from the water that he was Michael.

She found a good job with an engineering and logistics firm, and returned to the Church. From the viewpoint of the external world, she prospered, but her real life started every night when she went to sleep and held Michael in her arms, nursed him, and finally watched him take his first steps. And his life expanded: often she was aware of his presence during the waking day.

When he began to speak, she became frightened. The first psychiatrist started her on antipsychotic meds, but they made her depressed without eliminating the dreams.

The second shrink, Dr Louise Wegner, had a very different approach. 'It's only one voice, always the same voice?'

Lorrie slumped in the overstuffed chair, weary. 'Yes.'

'Does the voice threaten you, berate you, tell you you're unworthy or evil?'

'No!' She sat upright, offended. 'Never. I'm telling you, it's like a son, a friend, a companion. Sometimes he helps me solve problems, problems in my work, and—'

'This may not be a mental illness, you know.' Wegner rapped her fingers on the arm of her chair. 'In psychosis, the voices typically hound the patient, tormenting them. But many sane, creative people have a kind of voice that helps them along – a narrator, a muse, an angel of sorts.' The psychiatrist smiled. 'You need not believe in the supernatural for this to be real. Think of it as a part of yourself you've personified – your intuition, perhaps, or your conscience. If it helps you rather than harming you . . . then I'm not sure why you're here.'

At long last Lorrie spoke to a priest, and his was the final word: 'If it led you back to the Church, then why doubt it is a gift from God?'

From the day Carla had arrived in her office to recruit her, Lorrie had known this was the task appointed for her.

Gifted, they'd called her back in school, and a gift it was. These last few weeks her brain seemed to sizzle with ideas, and as soon as a problem was proposed, she'd see a dozen possible solutions. If there were some doubt which road to follow, Michael helped her to choose. Intuition, or God's blessing: it didn't matter what you called it.

There was no longer any fear in her: does the hammer fear striking the nail? She was a tool, doing what she had been forged to do, and there is no deeper satisfaction, not in this life.

'I thought this was a Hollywood thing,' McCann said. His bulk loomed between Lorrie's chair and the stage. 'Calabasas ain't Hollywood.'

'Sit down and cool your jets,' Alvorsen said from behind her. 'Anyway, Hollywood means the industry, not the town.'

McCann patted down his coat to retrieve his cigarettes and lighter before draping it over the back of the chair to her right. He lowered himself into the seat with a grunt. 'Looks more like a first-grader Christmas pageant.'

Lorrie had to admit the set-up wasn't impressive: an outdoor stage perhaps thirty feet wide sat against the evening sky, with two metal cubes squatting near the centre, each of them higher than a tall man's reach. Their surfaces were scored by a series of horizontal vents, and if she'd seen them atop the roof of an office building she'd have taken them for the central air conditioning units.

Neil Lansky, her consultant, emerged from between the two cubes and came forward onto the stage, his skinny frame dwarfed by the equipment. He crouched at the forward edge of the stage and fiddled at the knobs of a small control panel, for all the world like a roadie at a low-rent rock concert.

He stood up, stretched and then waved his arms. 'Excuse me.' Lorrie saw that Hammond, Carla and Kowinski were still standing off to the side chatting. Lanksy raised his voice. 'Excuse me.' He paused, making sure he had everyone's attention. 'It's time to take your seats. Now, this is all perfectly safe, but *you must stay in your seats*. Don't under any circumstances come any closer to the stage. Sit down, relax, and in about five minutes we'll start 'er up.'

French sat down to her left, leaving an empty folding chair between them. He shot a glance in her direction, and then scanned the stage, tugging his earlobe. Lorrie had picked Alvorsen and Kowinski to come along because they were the most technically inclined of the Allens; she'd added French because she wanted a third man trained on the equipment, and there was something in the way French studied everything without ever speaking up that suggested some intellectual depth.

McCann had been invited because Carla had insisted. As the others chose seats, McCann lit a cigarette, and a whiff of acrid Capitanos touched Lorrie's nose. 'I gave you those as sort of a joke,' she said. 'I didn't think you were going to smoke them.'

'They ain't half-bad for Mexican stuff,' he said.

'Chilean.'

'Same difference. So this guy's some kind of military expert? Looks like a geek to me.'

'He isn't a military expert, and he *is* a geek – an alpha-geek, a lord among geeks. Just keep your butt in the chair and, I promise, you'll learn something.'

McCann started to say something, but speakers beneath the stage boomed out the opening chords of 'Also Sprach Zarathustra', the three full-octave jumps stacked atop one another, and then, on the *ta-da!*, twin fountains of flame roared from the roofs of the cubes, reaching three storeys into the evening sky.

The pillars of fire dropped away, but then walls of flame burst from the sides of the cubes and rolled out far past the right and left edges of the stage. The flames pulsed; they surged back and forth like high orange surf. Lorrie felt sweat bead on her face. 'Jesus Christ!' McCann yelled. He'd leaned his face close to her ear, but even so she could hardly hear him over the earth-shaking roar.

The flames sucked back into the cubes and then they exploded from the front panels, grasping out from the stage with fiery fingers, and though Lorrie knew it was coming, she recoiled. She looked from side to side, and was amused to see in the yellow-orange light that half her companions had tilted their seats back onto two legs to retreat from the flames, though they'd been too slow: the flames were gone before anyone had reacted.

Now the cubes were surrounded by fire on all sides, but these flames were docile by comparison with the great gouts of fire that had gone before. They guttered and danced and spurted, and beneath them might have been anything – a house, a bus, a pair of haystacks.

A human scream rang out across the sound of the flames, and it was a moment before Lorrie realized it must be amplified, possibly even recorded. Between the cubes a figure burst through the flames, human in shape but engulfed in fire, and staggered forward, flailing its arms, and between the tongues of flames the flesh was a glistening blackness.

McCann and French both jumped to their feet. The flaming figure stumbled forward a few yards and then tumbled down into some invisible gap in the stage floor.

French and then McCann sank down into their seats. Lorrie grinned at French, and he shook his head as if to clear it.

The head and shoulders of a shadow peeked up from the floor of the stage, and Neil Lansky peeled the clinging mask from his head. He braced both palms downward and hoisted himself up onto his knees, and water poured from his black-clad body as though he'd clambered onto the deck of a swimming pool.

He strode forward, and his gait was now cocky enough that Lorrie half-expected him to high-five the air. Lansky dropped to one knee near the control panel and picked up a cordless microphone. His voice was a little breathless, but confident. 'Now, the point I want to make here, before I shut things down, is that pyro is about half-audio.' He turned a knob and, although the flames behind him continued their gyrations, the omnipresent roar dropped to a mere whoosh. It felt cooler, even though Lorrie's intellect told her the heat hadn't changed.

Lansky stood up. 'I'm going to shut this down and pull off this suit. Wine, beer, refreshments on the table behind the stage.'

Neil Lansky sat with his legs dangling over the edge of the stage and gestured at their semicircle with his goblet of Chardonnay. 'You know, I'm cutting my own throat here, but, frankly, I'm surprised you aren't going CG. I mean, 90 per cent of everything nowadays is digital. ILM could do this as cheap as I can. Cheaper.'

Lorrie shook her head. 'Digital fire just doesn't work on screen.'

'*You* know that. *I* know that.' He lifted his wine glass and gulped, and Lorrie wondered if he drank wine at home as well, or Orange Crush. 'People who know film can tell. But your average audience?'

'They can tell.' She gave him a smile. 'They don't know it consciously, but subliminally, they know.'

'I hope you're right. And I hope the rest of the industry works it out soon. Seems sometimes like I'm in a dying racket, here.' He ran his hands over his eyes as though dispelling an evil vision. 'You don't need to *buy* the gear, you know. I can lease it to you for, well, however long. Where are you going to run this, Escondido tank? Baja?'

Lorrie caught Carla's eye and winked. 'We'll be doing *something* in Baja, but probably not this. We may go far foreign. I'm not sure it'll pay to ship the equipment both ways.'

'What did you say the name of your bunch was?'

'Mecca Films. We're an indie.'

'Mighty well-heeled indie.' He shrugged. 'It's your money. I've got most of the stuff on hand here to meet your specs.' He picked up his wine glass and put it down again without drinking. 'What the hell, it's not like I need three suites any more. Pyro work's getting scarce.'

'When can you deliver?'

'Couple of weeks.' He sat silent, staring at the ground, and then shifted his gaze enough to stare at her feet. She'd worn open-toed pumps, and her toes felt naked. 'You guys need anything else?'

Kowinski leaned forward. 'That suit you were wearing, that whole stunt thing? How hard is that to learn?'

Lansky's eyes lit up like propane torches. 'Firesuits? They aren't dangerous, as long as you follow certain protocols, and, man, do they make an impression on an audience. If you want to be trained . . .'

The man's voice receded in Lorrie's mind as he continued his lecture, and she looked at Carla and they both nodded. This was going to work.

14

Gog and Magog

On the phone, Prescott Wainwright had been blunt: it was important, it was urgent and it needed to be discussed face-to-face, preferably at the Cosmos Club. Atwater hadn't the slightest idea what the topic might be, but Wainwright was one of the few people in the world who could command Atwater's attention at his whim.

Atwater had reached the bottom of his Cosmopolitan and was contemplating another when Wainwright hustled into the bar, harried as usual. The man was rotund, with a face that gleamed with perpetual moisture, and the way he peered round the barroom reminded Atwater of a myopic groundhog, searching for his shadow.

Shaking his head, Atwater rose to his feet and waved. The man brightened with recognition and hurried across the room with his hand outstretched. Atwater clasped it and shook. 'Press,' he said, using the man's nickname, 'it's been months.'

Wainwright answered by dropping his weight into a chair

and gasping for breath. 'Scotch, rocks, double,' he said, once he could manage it. 'Christ, I hate DC summers.'

Atwater signalled for a waiter and then slid into his own seat across the little cocktail table. 'Is there somebody who doesn't?'

'I want to move the seat of government to some place civilized.' He wiped his forehead and his hand came away wet. 'Maybe Europe. We're contracting out everything else, why not government, too?' His gray summer-weight suit was rumpled and hunched up round his shoulders, and Atwater was amused that anyone could make a thousand-dollar tailored suit look like it came off the rack at Kmart. But he knew better than to assume he was dealing with a clown: Wainwright was the quintessential Washington player – from very old money, with no axe of his own to grind, he knew everyone in the town and was a vital force in easing each new administration into the Washington milieu. Wainwright stood, bowing slightly. 'Sorry, Rex. Call of nature I put off all through crosstown traffic.'

Atwater ordered drinks and then leaned back and breathed in the atmosphere of the Cherrywood Bar, the heart of the Cosmos Club. Though the Club had moved headquarters a half-dozen times since its founding in the 1870s, it seemed to Atwater that the Townsend Mansion had grown up around the Cosmos Club on Embassy Row the way a shell encloses a lobster, an organic housing integral to the organism itself. Inside, nothing fundamental ever changed. Oh, a photo of a new Nobel or Pulitzer laureate might have been added to the Hall of Honours, but the Club felt frozen in a time both more adventurous and more genteel, as if at any moment Teddy Roosevelt or Rudyard Kipling might stroll through the doorway and settle into one of the overstuffed chairs in the library.

When Wainwright trundled back from the restroom and dropped into his seat, Atwater asked, 'How's Min? And the kids?'

Wainwright sagged a little lower in his chair, hoisting the shoulder of his jacket even higher. 'Charlotte's finished college and now seems unsure whether she's a lesbian or wants to date fellows from the wrong side of town. Prescott Junior has an MBA and is doing his best to maladminister the family fortune into oblivion.' The drinks arrived, and he lifted his tumbler and saluted Atwater before taking a long sip. 'Ahh. Better. Min's the same as always, except that she's decided she was put on this planet to prolong my life. She's after me to lose weight, and it's easier to try than to argue. But look at me. Six weeks on that damned Atkins thing, and I'm *up* fifteen pounds. Back when I was on high-carb, high-fat, high-booze, I was thinner.' The ice in his glass clinked as he raised it again, and condensed moisture ran across his knuckles and dripped onto the table. 'You, Rex? I suppose you haven't lost any money, despite this lousy economy . . .'

Atwater said the right things, and they spent a quarter of an hour catching up on mutual acquaintances before a slight change in Wainwright's manner, an increased focus of his eyes, told Atwater that they had reached the moment when the man was prepared to get to the point.

'I had dinner with Jake Landau two nights ago,' Wainwright said.

'Jake Landau?'

'Don't suppose you'd know him. He's got one of those silly-assed Special Legal Counsel slots they slip you into if they want to pay you six figures, but don't want to specify what your job might be.' Atwater saw that beneath his jovial demeanour, Wainwright was ready to drop his bomb, and it came as expected. 'Mr Landau's *real* job is as chief advisor and confidant to ol' Cotton Mather himself, our nation's charming Attorney-General.'

This could mean a thousand things, Atwater told himself. Perhaps they hadn't liked some of his stock trades over the last couple of years; the no-brows in the SEC and the Justice Department were often hard-pressed to tell the difference between legitimate insight and insider trading. Or maybe they were ready to hit him with some sort of anti-trust suit and break up his holdings. Or . . . 'And?' he asked.

'And he told me the wildest story. Now this is under tight wraps, but it seems that there's some plot to blow Mecca right off the map. Can you believe it?' Wainwright's big grin had his eyes peering out past folds of flesh, but Atwater felt those eyes studying him with no humour at all. 'Of course, I assumed it was all a big joke. But your name was mentioned.'

'In . . . what sort of context?'

'Only by inference. The name mentioned directly was Mr Lamont Richter. And Mr Richter, of course, heads his own firm. Now, it's well known that you've often used his services – why, some folks even assume you're his main source of income – but any link between you and this supposed plot is nothing more than conjecture. Right?'

Atwater's heart pounded as though he were hiking up the

path to the Tahoe Institute, and he breathed deep to calm himself. 'Of course.'

'Just what I told Landau. But he was insistent. I said, "Look, Jake, I *know* Rex Atwater, and I have to tell you that if he were involved in even the *wild*est scheme, he'd set it up so you never ever heard about it." Right?'

Wainwright's smile was big and false and Atwater gave an equally false chuckle. 'So, what does the Justice Department plan on doing about this?'

'Well. It's a wild rumour, and only a few people know about it, so . . . nothing. But if the rumours continue to grow – that is, if the wild suppositions are constantly thrust into the AG's face – then I suppose they'd have to do *something*.'

'But there's no plans?'

'No plans. In fact . . .'

Atwater raised his eyebrows and waited.

Wainwright leaned forward so that his belly pressed against the tabletop. 'You know our AG these days.' He whistled a few bars of 'Onward, Christian Soldiers'. 'If such a wild plot were true, I'm not all that sure that the AG wouldn't think – in a purely private capacity, of course – that it wasn't a pretty damn good idea. But, then, if the plotters were so sloppy that they rubbed his nose in the facts more than once, I suppose he'd have to take some official action.' He picked up his tumbler of Scotch and relaxed back into his seat, and the shoulders of his suit stuck to the chair back and rose up level with his ears. 'If you understand what I mean, Rex.'

'You've made yourself abundantly clear. But, after all, it's just one of those silly Washington rumours, right?'

'Yeah, but you know this town.' Wainwright's grin had

retreated to a knowing smile. 'Even the crazy talk turns out to be true once in a while.'

Richter leaned on the starboard rail of the *Million Dollar Baby* and looked across the water to the California coast. 'So, how does it feel? Ready to buy a cap with gold braid?'

'Amongst the afflictions that rich men impose on themselves,' Atwater said, 'boats are right up there with golf.'

'Best get accustomed to it, Mr Onassis. You now own a freighter, a big tender, and this forty-three-footer.'

'I'd damned well better not be the owner of record,' Atwater said. *Million Dollar Baby*, indeed. Next he'd find himself wearing gold chains on his neck. 'How long do we have to stay on this kiddy ride?'

'Just up to Santa Barbara. But I thought this would be a good venue for discussing . . . current developments.'

Meaning you're still sweeping other venues for bugs, I suppose. 'I think Wainwright's misreading the situation. If the Justice Department has wind of what we're up to, they're going to come after us with everything they've got.' An erratic bounce of the waves brought the scent of brine.

Without turning his gaze from the coast, Richter said, 'I disagree. Don't surprise me one little bit that our blessed Attorney-General is willing to wink at it. Probably sees the Hand of the Lord behind it all.'

'Spare me. Nobody that credulous gets to his position.'

Richter turned and cocked his head. 'No? Well, you sure don't hail from Georgia –' he exaggerated it into *JO-jah*, '– 'cause if you did, you'd have met a hundred just like him. Tend to be our town fathers and our representatives down at the State Assembly. Any kinda noise out of the Middle East . . .' He flicked a dismissive hand in an easterly direction. 'The slightest rumble over there, and every one of those boys is dead certain it's the armies of Gog and Magog, a-massin' on the plains.'

'That's comforting. But even if the AG thinks we're carrying out God's Will, he'll come after us full force if he decides anything will go public.'

'Goes without saying. Politics trumps Jehovah any day of the week.' Richter arched his long arms over his head and stretched, balancing against the roll of the ship. 'But maybe nothing will go public.'

'We have a leak of some sort already. And if we succeed . . .' Atwater sighed. 'Oh, well. If we succeed, I'll be happy to face the consequences.'

'I won't. But if we succeed, I think the problem just might solve itself.' Richter gave only the slightest smile, that smile that Atwater had learned meant *I've got an idea*. 'The assassinations we carried out? Who got blamed? Mossad, the Israelis. Some pollsters did a survey a while back, and about a third of the Arabs still believe that Israel set up 9/11, to make the Arabs look bad. So if we plant a few clues pointing in that direction . . .'

'No.' Atwater shook his head. 'The truth will come out sooner or later.'

'Not necessarily the whole truth. Listen, Rex: even if you aren't worried about what happens to you after, our side is going to have to hand the AG a little old fig leaf to cover himself.'

'Like what?'

'The Israeli angle is an obvious one. But if you want to confuse a coonhound, just hand him too many things to track all at once. So we need to feed Justice a whole slop-bucket of false intelligence. Let me think on it a few days.'

'Meanwhile, how do we plug this leak?'

'I can pull the chains of my contacts in Justice and the Bureau, but chances are slim on that side. Endangering sources or agents is the first deadly sin with that crowd.' Richter hoisted himself out of his slouch in the chair, and leaned one elbow on the overstuffed arm. 'Our best bet is from the inside out. Who do you trust?'

'You, me. Hammond, Carla.' He considered. 'Lorraine Sanchez, I suppose.'

'I don't trust anyone completely, not even you or me. Sanchez checks out so far. But on Carla and Hammond my people did everything short of a colonoscopy before we even contacted them. So we should come clean with them about this, first thing. They're running bigger risks than we are.' Richter paused, and wet his lips. 'There is another possibility, of course.'

'Oh?'

'We could drop this whole expedition. Or put it on hold until we know what's what.'

Atwater was taken aback. Richter had been pushing ahead on all the logistics for a month now, and had been reporting that everything was running smoothly and ahead of schedule. Was the man getting nervous? 'Is that your recommendation?'

'No. Not at all. But it's my job to put everything on the table for you, and remind you there's options. It's not too late to back down or slow down. Another six weeks or so, and we'll have reached the point of no return.'

'Would our chances of success be higher if we delay things to sort this out?'

'No. I don't think we'll ever have a better plan, and I don't think we drop off the AG's radar screen by waiting. Moving ahead knowing there's a leak is risky, sure. But when you're on thin ice, you don't stand still.'

Atwater chuckled. 'What does a Georgia boy know about ice? But you're right. Full speed ahead, and we'll look for our leak while we go.'

'You realize that when we find the man responsible, he'll have to meet with a fatal accident. Are you okay with that, Rex?'

Atwater leaned back on the couch and folded his hands on his stomach. A shame to kill someone who probably thought he was just doing his duty. And Carla wouldn't like it; despite the dozens of corpses she'd left in her wake, she'd made it clear that her fellow citizens were off-limits. Any killing would have to look like an accident even to her.

'Rex?' Richter asked again.

Atwater clucked his tongue and sighed. 'Cost of doing business, I suppose.'

Once he'd said it, the idea didn't bother him so much.

15

Digging for coolth

The mechanic came out of the garage, wiping his hands on a rag. He looked over at Hammond and Kowinski. 'The brown Taurus?'

Hammond raised his index finger.

'You want to come in the office, I'll explain the charges.'

'Sounds bad,' Kowinski said. 'I'm gonna sit down and have a smoke.'

Hammond followed the man through the shop and into a cramped office. They dropped into a pair of broken-down desk chairs. 'Why didn't you come alone?' the man asked.

'Couldn't be arranged.' Hammond gave him a tight smile. 'Try this business yourself some time.'

'Hmph.' He glanced round the office. 'Had a hell of a time getting cooperation, here.' A long sigh. 'Okay. Your car isn't bugged, I can guarantee it. *But* . . . there's a GPS unit and battery pack up under the muffler, sealed in tight.' The man watched Hammond's face, and Hammond had the feeling that he enjoyed the look of whatever he saw there. 'Neat a job as I've seen, by the way – straight out of James Bond.'

'Shit.' Hammond searched his memory, trying to recall every place he'd driven since the meeting at the Tahoe Institute.

'You want me to pull it?'

'Huh? No. No, leave it alone. And thanks.'

Out in the parking lot, while they waited for the garage to bring the car down off the rack, Kowinski asked, 'How bad was it? Does it need more work?'

'There's more they could have done, but . . .'

'Yeah, there's always more they can do.' He flicked his cigarette butt and it bounced across the asphalt, showering orange cinders. 'Mechanics. Bleed you dry if you let 'em.'

'So you flew?' Chazz asked.

Hammond had left Carla, Lorrie and Richter in the rear of the Sikorsky with the excuse that he wanted to ride shotgun. In truth, he wanted to get away from them – the metal golf ball in his pocket had him on edge, and the seat up front gave him a chance to try to memorize their flight path.

'I flew,' Hammond said, 'but nothing like this.' Chazz looked at him with a sceptical expression, and Hammond glanced round, trying to see the bones beneath the skin, the chassis beneath the opulent decoration. 'Except . . . frankly, it looks like an old S-70.'

'Bingo! The S-76 is just a Blackhawk, all dressed up to go to town. You look close, you can still see the little girl underneath the hooker get-up.'

'Nah.' Hammond shook his head at the control panel and the stick. 'All different.'

'Oh, sure – nice digitals now, and a great nav system. But

I tell you, if you had your fingers on these sticks, it'd feel like you'd just been called up to active duty.'

Hammond glanced to the rear where Carla, Lorrie and Richter were studying reports and fold-out plans. 'Don't remember anything on duty that was quite this swank.'

'Yeah, this is a sweet job. I know I'm just a glorified taxi driver now, but, hell, back in the service we were mostly glorified bus drivers, right?'

Below, desiccated and eroded hills stretched to all sides, without a single tree to give a sense of scale. 'I hear you,' Hammond said. 'Where the hell are we, anyway?'

'Nowhere. Hundred miles south of Ensenada, inland. Pretty soon now I'll move a little west, and we can follow the coastline on down. More scenic over there, but usually bumpier.' He winked. 'Don't want the ladies to spill their drinkies.'

They approached the Baja coast from the seaward side. A small bay, less than a mile across, eased its way into the shore, its mouth wide open to the Pacific. Inland, the curve of the coastline was echoed and then amplified by a horseshoe of barren hills, their tops eroded into sharp peaks.

Between the hills and the sea a handful of adobe walls sat crumbling, their colour the dun-grey of the surrounding slopes. Yet there were signs of modern life. A new Quonset hut, perhaps seventy feet long, gleamed silver amongst the ruins like a giant pipe buried to half its diameter. In the bay a rust-bucket of a cargo ship rocked at the end of a T-shaped pier, and a pair of electric utility carts carried construction supplies from the pier onto the shore.

Chazz set the S-76 down fifty feet in from the pier, a stone's throw from the Quonset hut, and Hammond saw a few men in front of the building sheltering their eyes from the inevitable dust storm of a chopper landing on bare soil.

Richter was the first down the stairs, and he conferred with one of the dusty men over on the shady side of the building as the others unloaded themselves and stood in a sun-dazed half-circle, wincing in the heat and the glare. Hammond fumbled for his sunglasses.

Impossible to tell how long the buildings had been abandoned, but three dead palms stood among the walls, their fronds long gone.

Richter came back, showing no signs that the heat affected him apart from the sheen on his forehead. 'Good crew, I must admit. Running well ahead of schedule. Be ready to move in any time after a week from now.'

'What is this place?' Lorrie asked.

'Bahia San Andres. We've got ourselves a ninety-nine-year lease on it, so if any of you want to bring your grandkids here on vacation when this is all over . . .'

'No thanks,' Carla said.

'Seems like a good omen, though,' Lorrie said. 'St Andrew is the patron saint of sailors and ventures on the water.'

'How did people survive here?' Hammond asked.

Richter grinned. 'I confess the weather's a little inclement today, but it's not usually so bad. Was a time this was a prosperous little fishing village. Then, back in the forties, the wells dried up.' He made a large gesture at the bay. 'Water, water everywhere, and not a drop to drink. Beefing up the pier and getting a major water tank ended up being our biggest expenses.'

They wandered together for a while and gradually drifted apart, like a group of tourists fanning out to pursue their individual interests. Hammond headed further inland. Behind the ruins lay a hard, flat plain that he realized must have been a large plaza or square. Beyond that the spiky hills sloped upward, and by scrambling up their crumbling feet, he had a view of the bay.

It was more protected than he had realized at first. A few hundred yards out, foam surged, and he saw that the remains of the ring of hills on the south ran out under the sea, forming a natural breakwater. In fact, the hills kissed the water at both ends of the bay; Bahia San Andres would be hard to leave except by sea.

He studied the gravelly slope around him. There were no big rocks or crevices within easy reach, no good place to plant the device.

He looked seaward again. A long, narrow outcropping of rock, maybe ten feet high at its peak, ran like a wall parallel to the hills on the northern side of the town, and Hammond saw Carla troop over it, the friable ground sliding under her boots. On the north the rocks were bigger, the hillsides littered with boulders. He decided to head in her direction.

By the time he arrived where she'd breasted the outcropping, she was gone, but he saw what had drawn her. Four small adobe houses, better preserved than in the main town, stood between the outcropping and the slope of the encircling hills.

He scrambled down the northern face of the outcropping

and looked in the half-ruined buildings for signs of Carla. It seemed she'd moved on.

If this site ever became an active camp, these adobes would probably be a popular place – popular enough that the gadget might be discovered. He walked north through the ruins and looked up the steep slope. The boulders there were shoulder-high.

He worked his way through the stones, perhaps twenty yards up from the valley floor, before he came to a pile of boulders that offered a dozen dark crevices. He turned and scanned the surroundings. A thousand yards to the south, though mirage-like heat waves, he saw the chopper, and two figures beside it, one of them Richter in his white linen suit.

Hammond fished the ball from his pocket and squatted behind the boulders, hidden from the valley. Two hemispheres of shiny metal joined by a groove at the equator of the ball, the device seemed impossibly perfect and symmetric amidst the chaotic geology of the hillside.

His mouth felt gritty inside, and he spat and then watched as his saliva vanished from the rock where it fell, evaporation so rapid in this heat that it looked like a time-lapse sequence from some science film.

You're getting overheated, dehydrated, he told himself. C'mon, you know the signs.

He grabbed the hemispheres with the thumb and index finger of either hand wrapped round the edges of the equator, and he twisted. A single, loud snap, as though he'd broken a stick. That opened the seal and activated the chemical battery. The little GPS unit inside would remain silent unless queried by code from a passing aeroplane, but when that query came it would shout its coordinates across the radio waves, answering back to calls from anyone within two hundred miles. In theory it could do this for the next fifty years, long after Boyce Hammond had been laid in the ground.

He used his thumbnail to hook the nub at the north pole of the ball, and drew out three feet of thin wire. The antenna. He stood, and wedged the wire in the space between two of the boulders, sawing it into place. Then he let the ball tumble down into a dark crevice.

'Hey, Boyce!' Carla's voice. He stood up so erect he almost toppled backwards.

He squinted down at the adobe house, out across the big outcropping.

'No. Up here!'

He looked up the slope of the hill to perhaps twenty yards above his own elevation, and saw Carla, hands on hips, standing in front of a cave. She waved. 'Come on up.' Dizzy with the heat, he turned and started to fight his way up the slope to where she stood, but she shouted, 'No. Go back down by the houses. There's a path.'

He half-clambered, half-skidded his way back down the slope. Seaward of the adobes he found a well-worn path that made its way among waist-high boulders. Above the mouth of the cave, the hill's slope ran nearly vertical, and he eyed it with distrust, but there was a flat landing where Carla stood, probably built with rocks excavated from within.

'What were you doing down there?' she asked. 'It was weird.'

'Animal. Saw something . . .'

'You better come inside, ace.' She took his arm. 'You sound cooked.'

'Is this a cave,' he asked, panting, as he let himself be led, 'or a mine, or what?'

'Little of both, I guess. I think it's natural, but somebody enlarged it. Watch your head.'

They had to keep their chins against their chests to avoid the ceiling. He probed carefully with his foot at each step, fearing stumbling, but the floor of the cave was level and smooth with dust. The shade felt like a swimming pool after the pounding heat outside.

Thirty or forty paces in, enclosed in the darkness, Carla stopped and let go of his arm. 'This is as deep as it goes.'

'I can't see a damned thing.'

'Did you take off your sunglasses?'

He laughed and took them off. 'Jesus, this heat has fried my brain. Cooler in here, though.'

'Yep. I'll bet that's what this place was for. Couldn't have been looking for gold in all these crumbly piles of dirt. Guess they were mining coolth.'

He felt sweat on his forehead – sweat that had been vanishing instantly back in the sunlight. 'Can see why.'

'Home, Sweet Home.'

There was something oddly erotic about the two of them alone in the cave, he found, like the classic fantasy of the two last people on Earth. He pushed the thought far, far away. 'Not our home too soon, I hope. And not for too long.'

'By the time we get here, there'll be diesel generators and air con. Anyway, c'mon,' she said. 'After the Gulf, Baja's like Club Med, right?'

*

Once the Sikorsky had levelled off over Bahia San Andres and sailed forward on its course back to California, Richter called for Hammond to join them for a chat. He unbuckled, nodded to Chazz and walked, head bent under the low ceiling, back to what he now thought of as the lounge – though cocktails had been abandoned in favour of bottled water.

Carla and Richter sat to the starboard side, facing Lorrie, and he dropped into the armchair nearest her. Carla tossed him a litre of Evian, and he caught it and smiled his thanks.

Lorrie said, 'You must be pretty dried out, Boyce. You were scouting the place like you were exploring for oil.'

Was Lorrie suspicious about him, or was he reading too much into her normal, sceptical manner? He avoided answering for a moment by taking a long drink and then sighing with satisfaction. 'Old habit. I was taught when you set up a camp you get to know the terrain.'

'Good habit to be in,' Carla said.

Richter took a long drink from his bottle and then screwed the cap on before setting it between his legs. 'I'm sure you folks noticed I resisted bringing any of the rest of the squad. That's because I needed a little time in private with you all, with the management team, as it were.' He clasped his hands round the bottle. 'I'll come straight to the point. There's a leak, and the kind of information that's leaking has to come from inside the team. At the risk of sounding a note of melodrama, there's a traitor in our midst.'

'How do you know?' Carla asked. Her head glanced from side to side, and Hammond saw a pugnacious look settle on her face. 'Where does this come from?'

'Sources in the Justice Department.'

'What exactly do they know?' Lorrie's voice was calm; she could have been asking for a zip code.

'Too much,' Richter said. 'Even our target.' Carla sucked in a sudden breath, and Richter glanced at her with a fond smile. 'We're not blown yet. Not sky-high, in any case. To them it's still sort of a wild rumour. But we need to find the man responsible and figure out some way to keep him quiet from here on out.'

'You're the pro,' Lorrie said. 'What do you suggest?'

'To start tracing back from the outside, you need to feed your team some misinformation. Feed half of them one bad fact, and half of them another, and swear them to secrecy. When the bad info gets fed out, we'll be able to narrow it down to six. Split the six into two groups of three, and feed more bad facts . . .'

'Binary search,' Lorrie said.

'I'll have to assume that's a term of art, and that we're talking about the same thing.' Richter uncapped his bottle and took a long sip, and then methodically seated it between his legs and capped it again. 'This approach takes three or four passes, and that can amount to a long time. So while we're waiting, if you can decide amongst yourselves who the culprit might be . . .'

All three of them stared at Hammond, and it seemed as though they all knew. He tried to keep his face impassive, but he felt as though his skin began to flush with guilt.

'Well?' Carla asked. 'They're your guys. Do you have any guesses?'

Hammond tried to swallow, but his throat felt solid. He shook his head, trying to look thoughtful, and at last his larynx came alive again. He looked down at his knees. 'I'm . . . I'm stunned. I've known these guys for years now. And if they wanted to turn us over to the authorities, they've had plenty of chances before . . .' He forced himself to raise his head and look round into the eyes of the other three. 'I just don't know.'

'Well, then,' Richter said, with the light tone of someone trying to move a discussion along, 'something to think about. In the meantime, we need some *good* bad information: items juicy enough that our mole can't resist feeding them on, but not so outlandish that he becomes suspicious.'

'What are we going to do when we find him?' Carla asked. There were a dozen unasked questions in her voice, and Hammond thought he heard something like fear in her tone.

Was Carla suspicious of what he'd been doing amongst the boulders? Did all three of them suspect him? He cleared his throat and tried to sound ruthless. 'Geneva Convention doesn't apply to spies,' he said. 'If you're in the wrong uniform, they just shoot you.'

'You're right about that,' Lorrie said.

The helicopter set them down at the airstrip in El Centro, and then whisked Richter away again. They piled into a rented Jeep that Lorrie had left there and drove south to Calexico, where they ate at a Mexican restaurant just on the Californian side of the border. Lorrie and Carla drank Dos Equis, but Hammond stuck to Coke; he'd be needing his vision sharp that evening.

The women kicked around limp conjectures about the

possible mole, and Hammond tried not to notice Lorrie's dark gaze resting on him. Both seemed unwilling to commit themselves to saying anything bad about any individual Allen, but Hammond could detect a note of hostility in Carla's voice whenever she mentioned McCann or his closest pals. Not surprising; the man had been handing her a rough time ever since she arrived.

Every so often they'd look to him for confirmation or reaction, and he'd fork up another mouthful of enchilada and shrug: I'm as baffled as you are.

With Lorrie at the wheel they drove north through the endless agricultural fields of the Imperial Valley as the summer sun lingered in the west. She steered the car over a small bridge that spanned a canal, and Hammond saw their truck and trailer parked in the field beyond. Whatever crop had grown there – wheat? alfalfa? – had already been harvested, leaving a flat, inscrutable stubble like a morning beard.

Alvorsen and Big Jones had the ultralight assembled and staked down against the mild evening breeze. Nearby, the controls sat on a table, along with the battery and the virtual-reality goggles. Hammond had tried the gear three times back at the Rancho, on brief flights, and he hadn't cared for the sensation.

The controls mimicked the sticks and wheel of the plane itself, but they protruded from an anodized box. A dish antenna was bolted to the right side of the box like a miniature satellite-TV receiver.

The pilot controls of the ultralight had been dismantled and replaced with a black servo-mechanism that sported another antenna, plus a pair of tubular video cameras that looked much like department-store security cams.

He nodded to Alvorsen and Big Jones and sat down in the chair before the controls. The goggles were heavy, a good five pounds, supported by webbing that sat atop the head like a hairnet. He plugged the feed cable of the goggles into the control box and fitted them onto his head.

The paired screens inside the goggles showed him the view through the plane's cameras, grainier than real life, but with 3-D depth perception. Reasonably convincing, except that when he turned his head, the picture before his eyes didn't change. 'If they were smart,' he said, 'they'd have the cameras swivel when I moved my head, so I could look around.'

'Too much bandwidth involved already,' Lorrie's voice said from behind him. 'Even the Predators and other military UAVs are strictly look-ahead.'

'Bet it makes the pilots unhappy.'

'Probably so. But it beats getting shot at in person.'

'We unstaked?' From the murmurs and movement, he guessed the answer was no. Someone's denim-clad thighs, probably Alvorsen's, crossed through the camera's field of view.

He waited, and after a moment Lorrie said, 'You're good to go.'

He groped for the controls and fired up the engine. A smooth hum from a dozen feet away, nothing at all like the lawnmower sounds of most ultralights. He grasped the wheel and guided the plane down the field.

Disconcerting. The plane bounced from side to side over the uneven ground, and he saw the bounces, but didn't feel them. When it lifted into the air he saw the change in angle, but didn't sense the distinctive thrust of take-off in his gut.

The sun was gone, but there was moonlight aplenty, and he increased speed and then saw a judder in the camera as the plane hit its first crosswind.

He kept low, above power-line height, but well below sensible air-lanes. Around him he heard the others walking, their feet crackling in the stubble, but he was in the night sky, flying across a patchwork of farms.

After about twenty minutes he reached the border fence west of Calexico, and crossed it at around thirty feet above the ground. All the while his compatriots were talking amongst themselves at some distance to his rear, probably leaning against the truck or perched on the rear of the trailer, and he felt as though he were in two places at once, or perhaps nowhere at all.

He flew ten minutes down into Mexico, then turned and made for the border further west. He crossed into the US, still staying low, made a long curve into US air-space and then weaved westwards along the border in a long, easy sinusoid.

Ahead a few miles he saw the stacked-rock cities of the Jacumba Mountains, the corridors of piled granite bright under the moon, and he looped south of them into Mexico and skirted their edge, hugging up to the rocks as close as he dared. At any moment he expected to see the lights of a small aircraft coming at him, or even a jet, but he seemed to be all alone on the border.

The ultralights had been his idea, suggested simply because of the logic, and now he regretted his contribution. He'd never expected the Bureau to let things play out this far.

This stretch of border was monitored by some of the most sophisticated radar anywhere, up to and including the Air Force radar itself, and he was cruising its length at about fifty miles per hour without so much as a who-goes-there. If they *had* been drug-runners, as the aircraft customizers had assumed, they'd be in the money: four hundred pounds of goods per trip. He had no doubt that this trick could get past Saudi AWACS, and he was frightened to realize that the same trick could be played back against the US.

He toyed with the idea of a deliberate crash, but he couldn't afford it, not in this new atmosphere of distrust. If anyone had to seem gung-ho from here out, it was him.

Worse at the moment, his neck hurt. The weight of the goggles was poorly balanced, straining the back side of his neck and shoulders, and after an hour the stress had blossomed into a headache. 'Anybody got an aspirin?' he asked, his voice too loud in his own ears. What his eyes saw was rock and desert, and he had the odd feeling he had shouted into empty space.

Crunching footfalls, and Carla's voice. 'Open.' He obeyed, and her fingers pushed a tablet onto his tongue. 'Coke, or beer?'

'Coke.' Beer and flying never mixed, and neither did beer and headaches. He felt the rim of a can touch his lips and tilt, and he swallowed, dribbling some onto his chin. He took a hand off the controls and wiped his mouth.

'Where are you?' she asked.

'Just passed miles of warehouse-sized rocks, so the dozen lights below must be the town of Jacumba. Just re-entered the US.'

She patted him on the shoulder and he heard her trudge off.

He headed back through the Jacumba Mountains, riding sixty feet above Interstate 8, following the tail lights through the long curves.

When he approached the lights of El Centro he left the freeway and headed off to the north-east. 'You guys should hoist up that beacon,' he said, 'because I don't really know where the fuck I am.'

He heard a flurry of activity back by the truck. His vision entered the endless quilt of fields, and he flew for five minutes before he asked, 'You winking at me yet?'

'A few minutes already,' Lorrie's voice said.

He took the plane in a few easy leans right and left before he located the harsh flashing light. 'Gotcha.'

The plane swooped in past the truck and trailer. He looped back round and touched down, rolling up to stop twenty feet away, with the nose of the plane pointed at the table, and he realized with a shock that he was looking at himself sitting behind the tableload of controls.

He pulled off the goggles and rolled his head to loosen his muscles. The other four ran past his table to stake down the pilotless plane he'd been flying moments before.

The idea worked – *his* idea worked. It worked too damn well. In his mind's rating scale, the schemes of Atwater and Carla and Lorrie moved from merely nutty to dangerously insane.

If the Bureau and DOJ were going to continue to twiddle their thumbs, then he'd have to find a way to force them to act.

16

Pacific waters

The *Harcourt Global* – now rechristened the *Princess Mishail* after the Saudi Princess executed for adultery – was a classic tramp steamer from the fifties, four hundred and twenty feet from stem to stern, riding with her deck twenty-five feet above the waterline in ballast. The bridge and mess sat far aft, like a two-storey office building dropped down on the ship's tail. An ungainly beast: when she made only two knots, as she was doing now, she wallowed like a sea-cow, but with the new engines and screws, Carla had seen her do twenty knots.

Carla watched the *Princess* from the stern of the former *Million Dollar Baby*, which now bore the name *San Andres*. There couldn't have been two ships more different. *San Andres* might be carrying a training crew, but her lines and her teak trim showed clearly that she was a luxury boat slumming it.

It was one of those rare days when the Pacific lived up to its name, flat and slick; the only ripples beneath the hull came from the *Princess Mishail*'s wake, damped by a half-mile of sea distance. Lorrie had a half-dozen of the Allens practising with the deck derrick, and Carla saw the big crane snag a crate from aft, reel it up and then swing in a slow circle over the water before it stabilized and lowered its package into the main cargo hold amidships.

The sun blasted down from the afternoon sky, and Carla felt her face burning even through the slathered sunscreen. If they didn't hit the water again soon, she'd have to shed the wetsuit and get a hat.

She turned as McCann came back on deck, zipping up his wetsuit. No one's looks were flattered by a wetsuit, but McCann looked like a hippo reared onto its hind legs. ''Bout time,' Skittle said, and stood up from the bench.

'Hey, they should put flaps in the back of these damn things,' McCann said.

Carla surveyed her crew. McCann huge next to wiry Skittle; Little Jones slumped on the rail beside the ever-inscrutable French; Alvorsen, his face already burned beneath his blond hair and beard; Kowinski wearing his perpetual squint. 'Okay, listen up. We ain't Navy SEALs here, so don't push the envelope. Go to two atmospheres and straight oxygen is poisonous. Thirty feet down, and most of you are going to get damn sick. Some of you might get convulsions below twenty. So pay attention to your BCDs.'

'BVDs?' Kowinski asked. 'Ain't that what my grandma called my underwear?'

'Your grandma probably called *your* underwear "panties", Kowinski,' Alvorsen said.

Carla resisted sighing, and said, 'B-C-D. Buoyancy Control Device. Not a *life jacket*. Not a flotation vest. You want to be neutrally buoyant, and how much air the BCD takes to do that varies with the depth.'

'Convulsions? I hate these rebreathers,' Little Jones said. 'I'm not even going on this part of the operation. How come I gotta do this?'

McCann snickered. Carla stared at McCann while she said, 'We never know who'll need to do what.'

'Right,' McCann said. 'We might even need to run obstacle courses out in the ocean.'

Little Jones and Kowinski laughed, Alvorsen and Skittle pretended to find something interesting about the deck, and French just frowned.

She exhaled a controlled breath. She'd thought the situation had been getting better, but the new regulations after Richter's news about the mole had soured attitudes even further. No phones, confinement to the Rancho Del Mar base except on approval, visits cut down to Saturdays only, no solo travel at all . . . No matter that she and Lorrie and Hammond had all agreed on them, Carla still took the heat. She needed to do something.

Sort it out later. Do this now. 'We're fifty miles out from Santa Barbara. Anybody goes into convulsions they'll probably be dead before we can get help. So don't go there. Stay at fifteen feet, no deeper.'

She locked eyes with each of them in turn, waiting for someone to say something. When no one did, she continued. 'Masks, weapons bags and your rebreathers are all on a line running stem to stern under the ship. Your gear is in order. First one in the water swims to the front of the line, second one to second position, and so on. Swim to your position, get the breather on your chest, get the mask on and clear it. Leave your weapons bags hanging until we're ready to swim, and don't pump anything into your BCDs until we head out. Don't overinflate 'em, or you'll have to make bubbles when you back off. We hold here for ten minutes and then swim three hundred yards west-south-west, where Hammond will be waiting in the Zodiac. Got it?'

A mixture of nods and stares. 'Okay, then,' she said. 'And one more thing. Next time we practise this, it will be nighttime, and we'll probably have rougher water. And when we do it for real, Christ knows what we'll have. So this is as good as it gets. Enjoy.'

She watched them struggle into their fins and then hit the water, twenty seconds apart. Skittle, McCann, Little Jones, Kowinski, French, Alvorsen. She leaned against the stern rail and tugged on her own fins, and then slap-slapped her way over to the open port-side gate. She pulled in a deep breath and jumped.

Away from the coast the Pacific waters were chill, even in August, but today they felt refreshing. A slight negative buoyancy with the weightbelt: she could feel herself continuing to sink. She opened her eyes in the burning salt water and kicked up towards the hull, steering herself back towards the stern. She saw the fuzzy silhouette of her gear hanging on the line next to what must have been Alvorsen.

She fit the mouthpiece between her lips, twisted the flow knob open and exhaled. On the inhale the air came sweet and smooth. Waving the tips of her fins to maintain position, she slid her arms through the shoulder straps, and the rebreather, two stubby cylinders in a hard plastic shell, came and hugged her chest like an infant.

She undid the clasp holding the mask to the line, hitched

the rubbery band back over the rear of her skull and fitted the mask to her face. The increased pressure drove water up her nose, and she exhaled by instinct, remembering at the last minute to clamp the mask against her face. A few bubbles rushed out of the mask's purge valve, and her eyes and nose were in air again.

Those were the last bubbles. She looked towards the bow: a long row of humanoid figures at various angles, swinging in slow motion from the line. No horizon, and no floor, just sun-filled water fading to dark blue in any direction but up.

To anyone used to scuba, it was freakishly silent without the roar of the exhale. True, your breath was still loud in your own ears, but after a few moments your mind discounted that and began to hear the arcane sounds of the sea – odd little snaps and pops, whistles and creaks, which seemed to come from everywhere and nowhere. Beneath it all she heard the low drone of the *Princess Mishail*'s engines, the rumble of cavitation from her props.

Then she heard something more patterned, more guttural, possibly closer at hand.

Alvorsen had turned in her direction and she saw his throat and cheeks moving in rhythm with the sound, *Boom-boom Boom-boom* . . . the theme from *Jaws*.

She smiled around her mouthpiece and flipped him off with her free hand.

Carla's tray was still loaded with uneaten food, but she nodded to Hammond and Lorrie. 'Catch you two at break-fast, okay?' She stood, lifted the tray, stepped her legs over the bench and headed back towards the wash-up tubs.

As she'd expected, there were loud murmurs and a burst of laughter from McCann's little clique. She dumped her tray and sauntered over to their table. 'Something funny?' she asked.

McCann looked up at her with his smug, pudgy face, and she wanted to bust his nose right then.

'It's a guy thing,' he said, 'you wouldn't get it.'

'Maybe you should explain, 'cause I'm fascinated with guy things,' she said. 'For example, are you always the pillow-biter, McCann, or do your buttfuck buddies here let you take a turn on top sometimes?'

Madden let out a surprisingly high-pitched giggle, and Little Jones whistled. McCann's face was framed in thick sideburns, and she watched colour crawl across his skin. 'Go ahead, run your mouth. You're just lucky I'm not the kind of guy who hits women.'

'Really? Because you seem like exactly the kind of guy who hits women.' Carla leaned in closer and lowered her voice. 'As long as the women don't hit back.'

McCann's nostrils flared as he tried to control himself. His eyes darted to the side, and Carla realized Lorrie was standing at her shoulder. McCann's mouth worked for a moment. 'Fuck you,' he said.

'Wake me up if you ever do.' Carla made a fist, raised it in front of his face and let her little finger pop up and waggle to and fro. 'I want to be sure I notice.'

The men around McCann were silent now: this puerile little exchange seemed to mean something to them. Her peripheral vision caught McCann's fists clenching and rolling, but she kept her gaze locked with his. 'I could rip you apart,' he whispered.

She straightened up and smiled a smile so tight it felt as if it might fracture her face. 'You know where to find me.' She backed away and headed for the door. Halfway she stopped and called back to Lorrie, 'I'm out messing with the training course if you need me.'

It was the end of Magic Hour, the honeyed glow preceding sunset that moviemakers swore added life to even the most insipid scene. Carla leaned on the creosoted starting post and sighed. McCann wasn't coming. She'd spent an hour playing out strategies in her mind. If he got a grip on her, she'd be in trouble. Six foot three, she figured, and maybe two-eighty, two-ninety, even three hundred pounds. Up at those sizes, who could judge? As far as she was concerned, once you were looking at weights over two-fifty you were in the land of wildlife documentaries. But it wasn't going to happen.

Her feet led her back towards her cabin, half-relieved and half-disappointed. She didn't want to fight with the man – there was too much risk he'd try to damage her, and too much risk she'd have to hurt him bad to stop that from happening. But another week of having half her men undermining her seemed like too much to bear. Maybe she should just head for his cabin – hell, call him out, even if his friends were there . . .

He grabbed her hair as she passed the corner of the dining hall and jammed the cold barrel of a revolver right beneath her ear. 'Let's take a walk,' he whispered. He jerked her round and began marching her back towards the field. 'Some hot-shot commando.' He screwed the barrel tighter into her flesh. 'I could do anything I want with you.'

Anything I want? Was this drifting in that direction? If he tries to turn this into rape, all bets are off: I'll blind the sonofabitch. 'So you got a gun. All that proves is that you're afraid of me.'

His hand in her hair shoved her and then pulled back, hard. 'Why are you trying to piss me off?' He kept marching her towards the training field.

'How come you keep busting my chops? Where's the percentage? To pull this off, we need to be a team.'

'*We* already are a team.' He started to say something, and then settled for, 'You're not one of us.'

'An Allen? Or a man?'

'Either.'

'You're right about that,' she said, 'and I'm better than both.' She tried to keep her voice level. 'I'm a soldier, not some weekend warrior playing dress-up.'

'So says the Army. So you can run some obstacle course faster than me. So what?' His voice grew louder as he warmed to his topic. 'The Army's full of shit nowadays. Girls and niggers get promoted right over the heads of deserving white guys, no matter how good the white guys are. Keep the faggots in Congress happy.' His breath was uneven, verging on ragged, and Carla realized that he must at least half-believe the horseshit he preached.

Before them the western sky had turned bloody, and the long shadows the rope-climb threw on the ground were growing wraithlike. She thought about provoking him further, but decided to let him do it himself. 'That so?' she asked.

'I've served with coons. They talk big, but they ain't worth squat when the chips are down. And everyone knows you can't count on women. What's gonna happen if there's a crisis and you happen to be on the rag, huh?' He asked this of the world, not her. 'There ain't one of us who'd trust a woman to watch our back. Specially some dyke.'

She could scream for help. Somebody would come, and she didn't think he'd shoot her, not for screaming, but that would wipe out what little authority she'd established. Yet the man was big, and underneath the fat he probably carried twice as much muscle as she did. This was a stupid, dangerous game, but one she needed to play. 'Yeah? Who would you trust? Some fat boy who ain't even got the guts to look me in the eye – even when he's got a gun?'

He jerked up so hard he nearly lifted her by her hair and then threw her face-first to the ground.

She rolled onto her knees and faced him, darting glances from side to side. The climb-rope dangled a few yards to her left, and beyond that the horizontal bars; no real cover. The gun was a snub-nose .38. She could run: with a snub, in the deepening gloom, his chances of hitting her would be low.

It was wrong to let him get close a second time, and if Jill had been there she'd have shot Carla herself, just for sheer stupidity. But she stood her ground.

'Wish now I'd invited the men out to watch,' she said. He was about five feet away, and if he were smart he'd stay right there. 'Gonna shoot me? Is that what you're gonna do?'

He stepped up in front of her and held the gun two inches from her face. 'Shut your mouth,' he said, 'before I stick this fucking gun in it.'

Despite the confident words, she heard a tremor in his voice. He's afraid. Good. Let that build. She waited, staring up into his face rather than at the pistol. Even in the dimness she could see fear and anger battling in his eyes.

Christ, he might just shoot me.

She knew she was faster. Chances were she could knock the pistol to the side and step in, put out his eyes or crush his trachea . . .

No. Only as a last resort. Let him play it out for a while.

McCann reached towards her chest and straight-armed her in the sternum. She staggered back two steps and he followed. 'Not talking so much now, are you?' he asked. 'Hunh?'

He shoved her again. 'C'mon, you titless wonder. Speak up.'

Suddenly Carla saw him as the playground bully – the same overgrown, petulant, fat-faced brat, the same push, push, push.

But with a gun, she reminded herself.

Never wrestle with a man, Jill's voice said.

He pushed her again, his voice demanding something. *Sorry, Jill.* Carla let her left shoulder spin back with the force of his shove, but planted her feet. Her left forearm swung up, sweeping both his arms to the side. His momentum carried him forward and she reached her right hand up and grabbed his left ear, digging in her fingernails and jerking down with her full body weight so that he stumbled to the side like a locomotive derailing and fell on his knees.

McCann screamed and reached for his bleeding ear, but Carla's hands were long gone. She gave him a hard chop at the base of his skull – lower and she might have broken his neck – and slipped back behind him and booted him in the right kidney, a solid kick that would have him pissing blood for a day or two.

McCann's left hand clutched his wounded ear, and his gun hand instinctively reached back to grope at the throbbing pain where she'd kicked him. She stepped in and jerked his right wrist up behind his own back, prising the pistol from his grip as she did so. She used her left hand to yank his arm up into a painful version of a half-nelson.

His left hand abandoned his ear and reached back, clawing at her, and she jammed the barrel of the gun against the base of his skull and thumbed back the hammer with an unmistakable click. 'Keep your hands to yourself.' He went back to clutching his ear, and she pushed harder with the gun. 'Do you know how many men I've killed this year?'

McCann whimpered, and in the twilight the blood flowing down through his fingers formed black streams.

'That was a question. Do you know how many men I've killed this year?' The smell of crushed sage rose in her nostrils; McCann must have fallen in a bush.

'No.'

'Neither do I. Maybe twenty. Maybe thirty.' She leaned her lips close to his right ear and whispered, 'Don't make me add to the list.' She waited before going on. 'I want to get along with you, McCann. I really do. What I'd like best of all is if you'd be my right-hand man, and keep the rest of the guys in line. And we can do that. We can forget all about this – no one will ever know – and start off tomorrow as partners.'

He started to say something, but she cut him off. 'No, no, don't make hasty decisions. Sleep on it. And while you do, keep in mind that I could have done this in front of everyone.' She paused. 'If we're going to get along, we start tomorrow. Got it?'

'Got it,' he said in a shaky voice.

She released his arm and backed away. 'If we're not going to get along, then you'd better not be here in the morning. Because I *will* kill you if I have to. Got it?'

'Got it,' he said, still on his knees, still not looking at her.

She opened the revolver and dropped the speed-load clip into her open palm. After pocketing the ammo she snapped the pistol shut and tossed it like a Frisbee. It skidded through the dust and came to rest in front of the man.

'Tomorrow, then.' She started back towards the bungalows and paused. 'McCann? Styptic on the ear. Then ice everything.'

Back in her bungalow she waited for an hour, her own sidearm on her lap. When McCann didn't come seeking vengeance, she stripped and took a hot shower.

17

Dead in real time

Lorrie bobbed in the water in the shadow of the *Princess Mishail*, surrounded by a half-dozen of the Allens plus Carla. They wore thin wetsuits and light flotation vests, which let them ride low in the cool water, and Lorrie could have stayed there the rest of the afternoon. 'Okay, gang,' she said. 'We have to be letter-perfect on this in the next two days.'

'What happens then?' Alvorsen asked.

'This tub heads south to our base and stays there until we head for the Red Sea. So practice time is limited.' She paused. 'Of course, you can always practise when she's docked in Bahia San Andres, but the water down there's a little sharkier.'

Big Jones and Kowinski raised their eyebrows in alarm at this, and Carla laughed. 'She's jerking your chain, guys.'

'Am not. There *are* more sharks down there. I never said they were more dangerous . . .' She grinned. 'Okay. She just used that lever to pump air into the chamber. Carla, you want to show 'em how it's done while I jabber?'

Carla nodded and swished her arms to face the looming

side of the ship. Lorrie watched as Carla raised the zinc-grey firing tube, about the size of a tennis-ball can. The big three-pronged grappling hook protruded from the mouth of the tube like a nasty bouquet.

Carla pressed the release and there was a dull *thoomp* as the pressurized air blew the sabot out the end of the tube. Lorrie saw the hook and sabot rise high and arch over the railing, carrying the cable behind it. There was a clank as it hit the deck.

'Now, she's going to set the ratchet,' Lorrie said. Carla rolled to the side and sloshed her hip up out of the water, showing the climbing belt round her waist. She turned the ratchet, and the cable started to reel back in to the pack strapped to her belly. 'The force of blowing it out has tight-ened the spring inside, so it reels in on its own . . .' The hook latched onto the upper rail with a clang. '. . . but it only takes up the slack. Don't think it's going to drag you upstairs.'

The spring had been strong enough to move Carla up against the ship. Carla looked over at her. Lorrie nodded. Carla braced her feet against the steel in a horizontal squat, grasped the cable with both hands, straightened her legs and began walking up the side of the ship, almost perpendicular to the hull. 'It won't climb the thing for you,' Lorrie said, 'but it'll hold on to whatever you feed it, and it won't let go.' Carla leaned back and spread her arms, feet braced, her whole weight supported by the cable and climbing belt.

'That is,' Lorrie said, 'unless you decide you want to come down fast.'

Carla bent her legs and pushed off, swinging out a little as she did, and released the ratchet with a twist. She fell, and as she plummeted she lifted her arms above her head and brought her legs beneath her so that she hit the water like a spear, feet first, and vanished.

Lorrie waited until Carla broke the surface and shook the water from her face, and then she said, 'You'll notice that the cable is still attached – and the drop should have rewound the spring. Carla? You want to show 'em how it's done in the major leagues?'

Carla rolled to her side again to show that she was twisting the ratchet, and let herself drift to the ship as the mechanism reeled in the slack. She paused there a moment with her hands on the cable and her soles planted on the hull.

Then she ran up the side, hand over hand on the cable, until she lunged at the railing and threw herself over the rail and onto the deck.

It had only been a matter of seconds, but Carla was gone. The unbuckled climbing belt swayed below the grappling hook on two feet of cable.

'That,' Lorrie said, 'is how you do it.'

Carla reappeared by the railing and began buckling on the belt. 'And that,' she shouted down, 'is why we have quick-release buckles.'

Lorrie put her fingers in her teeth and gave a loud wolf-whistle, and she was surprised and pleased when, floating beside her, Alvorsen and Kowinski applauded.

Carla bowed, climbed to the top rail and dived back into the ocean.

Lorrie finished setting up her movie screen, computer and LCD projector in the empty dining hall, just in front of the kitchens. She popped up a graphic on the screen and walked back among the dining tables to check the focus and visibility. Decent enough, if everyone moved in close.

The entry doors swung open and Carla came in, trailed by Hammond. 'Talked to Richter,' Carla said.

'Yeah?' Lorrie could tell Carla had something on her mind, so she sat down on the bench at a table and nodded her head at the seats opposite.

Carla and Hammond sat. 'The news is complicated,' Carla said.

'Not necessarily bad, though,' Hammond said.

Lorrie put on her best listening face and waited.

'I told you Richter's sources in Jakarta were seeing perishables loaded aboard ship?'

'Yeah. You had your panties in a bunch thinking they might be leaving early.'

'With good cause,' Carla said. 'They already weighed anchor. Two weeks early. And they're making fifteen knots so far, when we'd figured on thirteen-five.'

'Shit,' Lorrie said. That threw everything off. 'That gives us, what, maybe two weeks?' The men were coming along fine – today had been their best training day ever – but two weeks . . .

'It's not that bad. Because there's other things going on.'

'C'mon, Carla, don't good-news bad-news me.'

'Told you it was complicated. Not only did the ship sail early, it headed off in the wrong direction. Richter's people got their speed estimate from ships that talked to it while it headed just north of New Guinea.'

Lorrie blew out a puff of breath. That made no sense. No

one could run a perfect Great Circle out of the island-studded, reef-bound South China Sea, but any route from Jakarta to San Francisco that made sense went far north, curving well above the Hawaiian islands. New Guinea was due east.

'It's headed for Guayaquil,' Carla said.

'Ecuador? Why on earth?'

'Double duty,' Hammond said. 'According to Richter's folks in DC, picking up some medical isotopes the Ecuadoreans don't want to own any more.'

'I don't get it.'

Hammond twitched his shoulders in the slightest of shrugs. 'Indonesia's poor. Washington's tight-fisted. Somebody's cut a deal to defray some of the freight.'

Lorrie rubbed her face and sighed. 'I thought we had it all worked out – where the goods were. Now we've got another cargo . . . Do we know how it's stowed?'

Carla shook her head. 'Not yet. Shouldn't matter much, med isotopes aren't going to need a giant cask, but Richter's going to try to get more info. The point is, even though they're running faster than expected, they're taking the long way round. And the route will be—'

'Up the coast.'

'Exactly.' Carla grinned. 'The Coast Guard will meet them once they enter American waters, down around San Diego. So they'll be hugging the coast . . .'

'And waltzing right up to us.'

'Yeah. So instead of a four-day sail each way for us, we can snag them in maybe one day in, one day out . . .'

'And no cold-assed water.'

'No cold-assed water.'

Lorrie shut her eyes and offered up a silent prayer of thanks. Even when things seemed to go wrong, in truth the Lord was smoothing the way before them.

Lorrie took a seat amongst the men in the front row, and watched Carla step in front of the screen. She seemed more at ease with herself these last few days, Lorrie thought, more in command. Something had changed.

'Just a few words before I hand over to Sanchez,' Carla said. 'I know you folks don't know every detail of the plan – though I promise that you will before we go into action together – but I do have some news. The *Pontianak Laut* has sailed, and is under way. And that means that we are definitely going for it.'

'Nuke Mecca!' Alvorsen shouted, and several of the men laughed.

'Now there's a bumper-sticker for you,' she said. 'It's a long ride from here to the Red Sea – almost ten thousand nautical miles. But I think I can promise you that we'll all be suffering through the shitty climate offshore of Yanbu and Jeddah before mid-October.'

'Yeah?' Little Jones asked, a nasty edge in his voice. 'And who's going to sail us through the canals, and do the long-distance nav? Or maybe you're a sailing master too?'

'Shut up,' McCann snapped. 'Give the lady a break. I want to hear what she has to say.'

Little Jones looked as though he'd been slapped. Things really *have* changed, Lorrie thought.

'We're hiring a jobbing captain to get us there. He doesn't

236

know why, and he doesn't want to. And we have enough navy types in the bunch here to stand watches and steer when we're in blue water. Point is, we're really going.'

Lorrie heard a murmur of approval run through the group.

'Any other questions?'

Madden, usually silent, said, 'One. Ponti-whatever it is. What does it mean?'

'*Pontianak Laut*. I asked the same thing when I first heard it, and our friends found out for us. *Laut* is ocean. A *Pontianak* is some kind of an evil female thing. Steals children. Casts spells.'

'*Sea Witch*, then?' Hammond asked.

'Close enough.'

And thou shalt not suffer a witch to live, Lorrie thought.

'Lorrie?'

She stood and strode up to where Carla had been, then turned to face the squad. She had expected to see Carla sitting in the seat she'd just abandoned, but instead she was one row back, next to McCann.

Lorrie blinked a few times at the unexpected sight, and then gathered her wits.

'This is a real-time radiation dosimeter.' She dangled it from a necklace chain, and let the room get a look at the slab of plastic, the size of a playing card, but for its quarter-inch thickness. 'This big blue square changes colour when it absorbs radiation. Goes from yellow to orange to red. It's cumulative. You wear it for a year, it tells you how many rads you've taken that year.' She raised an eyebrow. 'Not whole rads. Microrads, hopefully.'

She spun the chain around her index finger and the dosimeter badge whirled like a tiny propeller. 'This isn't like Washington's terror alerts. This goes yellow on you, you've had more than enough. Orange, and you probably want to give Mom one last call. Red, and nobody's gonna pick up your body to bury it.' Lorrie popped the badge up into her fist as though she were snatching a recoiling yo-yo. She raised it between thumb and index finger and held it out to the audience like a tiny sign they needed to read. 'Used to be they used special photofilm for this. Had to wait to hear from Fotomat whether you were dead or not. Nowadays, you can figure out if you're dead in real time.'

Uncomfortable chuckles echoed in the room.

'I'm not fooling about this. Anybody here not had a dental X-ray?' She surveyed the men. 'Remember what it felt like? Kowinski?'

'It – it didn't feel like nothing.'

'That's what a lethal dose of radiation feels like, too. You don't know you're getting it. Get a big enough dose, though, and you won't feel too good right afterwards. Get a medium dose – cancer, blood diseases, all kinds of lovely things.' The faces were all sombre but stoic. 'I hope I'm scaring you. I want to scare you into learning every aspect of this procedure, especially the safety procedures.'

She picked up the remote control. 'Will somebody dim the lights?' She clicked the power button and stepped out of the path of the beam from the projector. She advanced to the first diagram. 'This is a Class B transport cask, same basic design as the ones we'll be dealing with. The drill up in Concord would be to unbolt it from the floor of the ship and hoist the whole damned thing onto a train, but we'll be popping the lid to get at that little capsule inside. Capsule looks small, twenty-four inches long, but it weighs a couple of hundred pounds. But that's chicken feed. The lid of this cask weighs sixteen hundred pounds, that's one thousand, six hundred . . .'

She watched the faces of her audience as she talked, and every one of them stared at the screen in rapt attention.

This might work, she thought, we really might be able to build a team out of this bunch.

The Lord moves in mysterious ways, His miracles to perform . . .

18

A troop of Japanese

Atwater crossed the living room of his Watergate apartment and pulled open the closet. 'Where the hell is that hat of mine?' he asked over his shoulder.

'Where'd you last see it?' Richter asked from the front doorway.

'On my head.'

Richter slouched against the doorframe. 'I keep track of a grand number of things for you,' he said, 'but your hat wasn't mentioned in my job description.'

Since he wasn't in truth looking for his hat, Atwater realized there was no need to look in the closet, but it gave him something to do. 'Well, I want it. Can you help me look?'

'Sure.'

Atwater heard Richter shut the apartment door, and he closed the closet door and turned. Richter ambled round the living room in a slow circle.

'You sure you brought it back here?' Richter asked.

'Pretty sure.'

'Hmmm. Well, speaking of things that *are* in my job

description, I met with one of my acquaintances the other day, and he'd heard the craziest rumour about you.'

'Let me guess. I'm marrying my ex-wife again.'

Richter chuckled. 'Not that crazy. No, this guy said that some people in the government, probably DOJ, think you're trying to hijack nuclear materials, some sort of terrorist scheme.'

Atwater laughed, and found himself surprised by how easy it was to be amused by it. It *was* absurd, after all . . . 'What are they smoking on the Mall these days? Where in hell did they come up with that?'

'Probably got it confused with one of those medical isotope things your company was doing with Canada. Or maybe somebody garbled something from one of those seminars Tahoe Institute is always holding.'

'Pretty funny.' They chatted a while more about the absurdity of the idea, until Atwater said, 'Looks like I was wrong. Maybe I left it in the restaurant.'

'You can afford another, Rex.'

'Sentimental value. I got divorced in that hat.'

In the rear of the limo, Atwater said, 'How long before you jerk out that bug?'

Richter had sprawled back in the other corner. 'Let it sit. Pulling it looks just a mite suspicious.'

'Nonsense. Industrial espionage. We could even call the FBI in and ask them to pull it for us, see who was spying on us.'

'Could do. But I think it's a lot more fun feeding them bullshit. And if they ever decide they want to start proceedings against us, it'll be pretty hard to convince a jury of our guilt. Our innocence will be right there on tape. In fact, this is perfect. We need to start scripting some material, build us some fine alibis for every little thing we've done, or ever might do.'

Atwater gazed out the side window at the passing Potomac, its waters caramel-brown under the summer sun. He knew Richter was right, but he still wanted to grouse: it was damned annoying having people listening in on his private life. 'So I can expect bugs everywhere, I suppose? From now on, we'll only be able to talk freely in the car?'

'I imagine our friends, whoever they are, will probably try for the car, eventually. But having drivers waiting 24/7 makes it a little sticky for the other side. So far, the only places they've hit are the Watergate and your Palm Springs place.'

'Who are they?'

Richter lifted a lazy hand and wiggled the fingers in dismissal. 'Most likely the Bureau, but Justice has a whole passel of other possibilities. Whoever it is, we should have pissed 'em off pretty good. What say we drive out to Maryland, maybe Annapolis, hook us up some seafood at one of the little restaurants?'

'Why not? Don't seem to be able to talk in my own apartment.'

'Now, now, Rex. That's the Tahoe Institute's apartment. You don't want the IRS starting to think you have beneficial control, do you?'

On the drive, Richter filled him in on the latest information from his contacts around town. He still hadn't been able to determine if the AG was receiving his reports from the FBI, or if they originated elsewhere, and the Bureau itself was impenetrable as always when it came to undercover operations.

'I don't get it,' Atwater said. 'We've pulled plenty of info out of Justice before, even out of the FBI.'

'Not about undercover ops, not from the Fibbies. And you can bet they aren't letting any operational details filter uphill. Nobody trusts the politicians. But here's the most interesting part.' Richter explained that Carla, Hammond and Lorrie had planted two false rumours among their own men – one that the Israelis were involved, the other that a Hindu group was providing support. 'Here's the result: *both* of the rumours have made it into DOJ reports.'

'What does that mean?'

'Could mean a lot of things. Could mean we have two moles. But it's a tad bit simpler to assume we have one mole, and somebody else can't keep his mouth shut.'

'But Carla and Lorrie and Hammond knew both stories. Could mean that one of them is the mole.'

'Rex, you're tired. Your thinking is just a touch fuzzy.' Richter looked over at him, peering like a doctor looking for signs of disease. 'Yeah, all three of them knew both stories. But they knew the stories were false. These were obviously reported back by someone who thought they were true, because they're being reported upstairs as fact.'

Richter was right. He *was* tired, tired and dull-witted, and starting to think like a frightened old man. He rubbed his face. 'Maybe we should have gone the other route. Take some serious money, and just buy a warhead and missile.'

Richter's head started shaking even before Atwater had finished his sentence. 'We've been over this turf so many times we're wearing a path. This is our best shot by far. Just stay with it.' He smiled. 'I have some good news, too. DOJ and Homeland Security are all wound up because they suddenly have wagonloads of information about nuclear threats around the country – Idaho Falls, the Carolina dump site, five or six reactor sites, even some planned assaults on weapons dumps. They're going batshit.'

'But they've got a full investigation running on us.'

'Yessir, they do indeed. And now they have seven others. And by the end of this week, they'll have maybe fifteen.' Richter gave him a wry grin. 'The Japanese have a saying, though it can't hardly be ancient. They say, *It's illegal to cross the street against the light – unless everybody does*. That pretty much sums it up. We're crossing against the light, but now we got us a whole troop of Japanese folks milling around us. By the time they get this sorted out, our little job here will be history.'

'I hope you're right.'

'I hope I am too,' Richter said. 'Obviously.'

19

Dying on the vine

Mid-afternoon, and Hammond had finally found the dining hall empty. Carla and Lorrie had been gone for a few days, taking Alvorsen and Dodge, the two most experienced sailors, to run the *Princess Mishail* down to Bahia San Andres.

He stepped off the top of the giant freezer near the end of the serving line and hoisted himself onto one of the massive beams that supported the roof of the rustic hall. The wood must have come from old-growth timber – the beam was so wide that Hammond could kneel atop it with both knees.

Carla and Lorrie were due back that evening, and Hammond wanted to praise the Lord for that small mercy – another day with no one but the Allens to talk to and he might rig up a sock puppet to chat with. Even better, it was Friday. That meant that Earlene would be there tomorrow, there and in his bed. Not that sex was the only attraction, not at all. Being apart from her six days a week had made him realize how much he missed her companionship, the little noises she made as she padded round the house, even just the smell of her in the room with him . . . though at this moment he was overjoyed to be alone.

He planted the roll of transparent wrapping tape on the beam, and then slid the solid-state recorder, slim and hard as a cigarette case, out of his back pocket. He'd wheedled and insinuated, pleading the needs of the men for high-level leadership, until Carla had prevailed on Atwater to come give a pep talk to the men four days hence. Then he'd have him – him and Richter both, with any luck, convicted out of their own mouths.

He ripped off a swathe of tape and pasted the recorder to the top of the beam. He pulled the little remote from his pocket, flipped up the Plexiglas shield and clicked the button. A red LED glowed on the recorder, and then died when he clicked it again. Good. Now all he had to do was find a convenient location for the mike, and . . .

There was a noise off in the kitchen. Too early for the cooking staff. Hammond waited, making himself small, making himself immobile. He tried to keep his breathing inaudible, tried not to breathe at all, and for a giddy moment he was eight years old again, lying flat along a branch of the old walnut tree, watching Cousin Billy, the *It* of the moment, stalk across the yard, looking for hide-and-seekers . . .

Footsteps. He turned his head slowly, slowly as a flower follows the course of the sun, and saw Skittle emerge from the kitchen and open the big refrigerator to steal an off-hours beer.

A gunshot cracked from outside, too close at hand to be out on the training ground. Hammond jerked, and knocked the roll of tape off the beam. Skittle dropped his beer can to the floor and looked up at Hammond as though Jacob's Ladder were rolling down from the sky.

Hammond yanked the recorder off the beam and stuffed it into his hip pocket, tape and all. Skittle stared while Hammond jumped down onto the roof of the big refrigerator and then dropped to the floor. His sidearm was on his belt, just in case anything happened while he was planting the bug, and he pulled it now. Skittle's eyes grew wide. 'Come on,' Hammond ordered, 'and keep your mouth shut.' He ran for the front door, unlocked it and threw it open.

He half-expected fifty agents in SWAT gear, but what he saw instead were the Allens clustered at the door of Number 12, down at the corner of the gravelled motel parking court. Whose cabin was that? French? Kowinski?

As he elbowed his way through the packed bodies, he heard someone – McCann – shouting.

At first all Hammond could see was McCann's wide, beefy back, standing as close to the centre of the room as the bed would allow. Hammond edged to the side, and he saw that McCann towered over French, who lay slumped to the floor, his shoulders propped against the back wall. The man's hands clutched at his belly, and blood welled crimson over his fingers.

'What the hell's going on, Ray?' Hammond asked.

McCann still held a snub-nose .38 pointed at French. 'Sonofabitch is ATF.'

Hammond turned to the crowd at the door. 'Gianetti, get me one of the big first-aid kits.'

Gianetti nodded and ran.

'He don't need no first aid,' McCann said. 'What he needs

is for someone to decide if I blow his brains out here, or somewhere else.'

Hammond edged up beside the big man and whispered. 'I need to talk to him, Ray. I need to know what he's told them, what's happening. And then, I'll take care of it, okay? But not until we have what we need.'

McCann's jaw was set hard, his teeth clenched in anger, but he nodded his head.

When Gianetti returned with the kit, Hammond had him help pull French away from the wall and lay him out on the floor. French groaned and gasped, and then yelped as Hammond pulled his hands away from the wound.

Nasty. Gut-shot on the left side. But Hammond had 'coptered back worse cases from the battlefield and seen them live. 'Hold his hands down,' he said to Gianetti. He loaded up the syringe with an ampule of lidocaine and slid the needle in near the wound. 'Tell me about it,' he said to McCann. French shrieked as Hammond's thumb jammed down the plunger.

'He went into town to snag the smoker bunch a few cartons of whatever. Even though he doesn't smoke, Simonsen went along as his double, wanted to pick up some Jim Beam. Stopped in a restaurant to grab some food.' Hammond listened, but as he did so he also swabbed blood from French's belly. A bad hole, and no bleeding from his back. The round was probably still lodged inside, along with fabric from the man's shirt. Infection city.

'So, this fuck says he wants to go outside for a smoke. Simonsen doesn't think anything of it, but then French doesn't come back for maybe fifteen minutes, and you can't see him outside the window, so Simonsen decides to take a gander out the front of the restaurant and he sees dickweed here down the street talking to Nagel.'

Through McCann's explanation, French had whimpered as Hammond tried to staunch the bleeding with pad after pad, and, if not for Gianetti's grip on his arms, the man would have pushed Hammond's hands away. For Hammond it was almost as though he were ministering to a wound of his own. It would be easy for him to end this way, bleeding out on the floor in a room full of trigger-happy yahoos.

'Jack Nagel?' Hammond asked.

'How fucking many Nagels you know?'

The ATF man had been after the Allens for years, and had been following Hammond for what seemed like ages. If French had been meeting Nagel, there was no doubt that French was a traitor. Or a good guy, all depending which side you were on. 'And then?' Hammond asked.

'And then Simonsen didn't say anything, but they drove back here, and he came and told me, and I came down here to demand an explanation and the sonofabitch *drew* on me.' There was incredulity in McCann's voice, and Hammond's own thoughts echoed it – what kind of a moron would go up against Ray McCann when it came to firearms?

'This is no good,' Hammond said to Gianetti. 'We're going to need to get his shirt off, wrap him round and round to get enough pressure on him that he doesn't bleed out.' He glanced over his shoulder. 'Madden, Slater. Give us a hand.'

By the time they finished it, French was weeping with pain and Hammond's hands were gloved with blood up to the elbows. 'Get him in the back of my car,' Hammond said.

'You want him cuffed?' Madden asked.

'Does he look like he's going anywhere on his own?' Hammond asked. He looked at McCann, nodded at the pistol. 'Is that a throw-down?'

'Of course.'

He held out a wet, red hand. 'Gimme. Skittle, you're driving.' He stepped into the bathroom and turned on the cold water in the sink to rinse the blood away.

French continued to whimper as the tyres of Hammond's Taurus crunched down the gravel drive, but Hammond knew that after the shot of lidocaine it had to be fear rather than pain. He could have used a few days to think out his strategy – a gut-shot Federal informer or agent in the back seat, Richter's GPS tracker under his car . . .

What the hell! It was probably ready to blow sky-high anyway.

At the wheel, Skittle seemed on the verge of tears. As they hit the asphalt, he said, 'Boyce – I'm not good with this. I mean, I've got a record . . .'

'Uh-huh,' Hammond said. 'Are you packing?'

'Yes.'

'Give me your piece.' Skittle hesitated. 'Give it to me.'

Skittle reached down, keeping his eyes on the road, and undid his ankle holster and passed Hammond his revolver. 'Look, Hamm,' he said, 'I'm a two-time loser already, and this is California—'

'I know. That's why I want you along.' Skittle shot him a look of utter confusion and then looked back to the road. 'Get us to Santa Barbara. The business stretch off 101.'

He turned and looked over the seat to French's wan face. 'What are you going to do to me?' the man whispered.

'Get you to a hospital, if you just cooperate. Let's start here. Are you really ATF?'

'I don't believe you.'

'Okay.' Hammond sighed. 'Okay, listen, both of you. I'm with the Bureau. I've been undercover in this pissant operation for three fucking years.' The car swerved, and then steadied as Skittle took in this information. 'You, Steve – I can ensure you walk out of this mess, no charges, but you have to help me. Otherwise you'll go Federal on the first raps, and then, when you're so old you're wearing diapers again, Sacramento will swoop in and put you away under three strikes. You with me on this?'

Skittle stared out the windshield at the oncoming lines on the asphalt. His lips moved with no sound, and Hammond was surprised to realize that the man was praying. At last he nodded. 'Okay.'

'Now, again,' Hammond said to French, 'are you really ATF, or what?'

French snorted, and then winced. 'I guess so. I mean, they been paying me. And also not busting me for . . . some stuff. I mean, this is right up their alley, all the guns and shit.'

'And Nagel's your contact?'

'Yeah. Don't like me, though.'

'How much have you told him?'

'Till today I couldn't get ahold of him for about two months. Told him there was this big deal. All kinds of money and weapons.'

'Did he know what we were doing?'

'No. I didn't really have time to explain it all. Told him it was big, that I needed to have a long meet, but all he wanted to know was how many guns? How much explosives?' French stopped talking and closed his eyes in pain. 'I was supposed to have an accident next week, fuck up my leg, need to go to the hospital to tell him everything . . . and here I am. One week early.' He laughed, and then coughed, and then started crying. 'Jesus, I'm gonna die . . .'

'You're going to be okay.' Hammond scrounged through the glove box and found a pencil and a scrap of paper. He pulled out his wallet and jerked a folded fifty-dollar bill from beneath his driver's licence. After scribbling a number on the paper he tossed it and the fifty onto Skittle's lap.

'What's that?' Skittle asked.

'Dinner money. You pull off where I say, drop us near a phone booth and keep on going, all the way down to Ventura. Find a nice steakhouse and then call this number and tell the recording the name of the place. Nothing else, just the name of the place.'

Skittle nodded, watching the road. 'What then?'

'Drive all over town, I mean *all over*, and then go back there. Have dinner, maybe a couple drinks, and wait.'

'That's it?'

'Yeah. And nothing else. Don't call anybody else, don't do squat. You help me with this and you'll walk out of here with at least some of the money you were promised, but you fuck me up on this, and you'll hang – and I swear, Skittle, I'll be pulling on the rope.'

French gasped in pain when they dragged him out of the back seat and onto the kerb, but Hammond ignored him and pushed his way into the phone booth. He dialled 911, gave their location and then punched in Troy's direct number.

After the third ring, Troy's voice said, 'Bishop.'

'Me. The operation's blown. Santa Barbara General, right now, jet or 'copter down.'

'Jesus. Are you—'

'Do it.' Hammond dropped the handset back into the cradle.

The police and the ER people were all over him, but he finally convinced them it was an FBI matter and that Troy was on his way. Eventually they left him in a doctor's examining room with a Santa Barbara cop posted outside the door.

Hammond was near-certain the last fig leaf had been stripped from his cover, and he welcomed the prospect, but basic tradecraft told him he had to ensure there were no loose ends either way. He hitched his butt up onto the crinkly paper that covered the examination bed. Skittle could probably be controlled – for a while. The GPS in his car – all it would show was a drive from Rancho Del Mar to Ventura, and then round and round in Ventura for a while. No hospital on the route for Richter to check on . . . He yawned. Too much to work out.

He was asleep, his hands thrust into the pockets of his sweater, when Troy arrived. Troy's credentials disposed of the need for a guard, and the two of them retreated to the hospital cafeteria for coffee in styrofoam cups.

Hammond sipped his coffee and made a face. 'Blech. Let me get a Coke or something.'

Troy looked impatient, but said, 'Sure, whatever you want.'

Hammond left Troy at the table. While standing at the self-serve soft drink machine, he slid his hand into his sweater pocket and turned on the recorder. He had a gut-shot ATF informant on his hands, on top of a militia training camp and a nuclear plot; it occurred to him that it might be nice to have a record of his orders from the Bureau.

'The best way to pick everybody up,' Hammond said as he sat down, 'would be if we could organize something big in town, where everybody'd come unarmed, and then—'

'Hold it.' Troy had his hands upraised, palms out, as though he thought Hammond might charge across the Formica tabletop. 'Washington doesn't think the time is ripe.'

'Huh?' For a moment Hammond couldn't make sense of the sentence. 'What the hell are you telling me, Troy?'

'They want Atwater with both hands in the cookie jar.'

'Christ, he's already in it up to his elbows! How much more do they need?'

Troy shook his head in sympathy. 'I know, I know. And it would be perfect if you could get the recording you had planned. I'm sorry, Boyce – I'm not sure what they're all thinking back there, but—'

'I don't give a flying fuck what they're thinking back there. Somebody damn near got killed today.'

'Listen, Boyce—'

'No, *you* listen. That could have been me with a bullet through my gut. I'm the guy on the ground here, I've still got a recorder someone saw me plant, and I'm pulling the plug.'

Troy sighed and looked down at the table. 'Told 'em that's

what you'd say.' When he looked up again he seemed to have trouble meeting Hammond's gaze. 'Okay. This isn't me talking, this is Washington. We've got the goods on all of the Allens, from your reports plus other sources. If you pull out now, we're going to take them all down, take them down hard. Families and girlfriends included. We have enough on most of the wives to indict them as accessories, and fifteen kinds of obstruction of justice—'

'Now, wait, you promised that—'

'Things were different then.'

Hammond found that his hands had clenched into trembling fists, and he clasped them in his lap to make sure he didn't bust Troy in the mouth. He exhaled and then, keeping his voice as even as possible, said, 'You said I could have full immunity for a few people if I stayed the course.'

'You can. But they've decided the course is a little longer. Jesus.' Troy massaged the bridge of his nose. 'Listen. If you ride this out, you can have all of them, get-out-of-jail-free. Earlene, the Allens, even Smukowski and Sanchez.' He sipped his coffee and grimaced. 'Sure, a couple might have to testify, and we'd roll up the weapons, but no formal charges. All they need upstairs is Atwater and Richter.'

'They've already got 'em, for Chrissake! What more do they want?'

Troy gave a weary shake of his head. 'I don't know. But I can tell you one thing: all this is happening at the very top. Get somebody Atwater's size involved, and it gets political.'

Hammond leaned back from the table. 'Maybe you haven't explained it very well.' He held up his hand, measuring out a quarter-inch between his thumb and cocked index finger. 'We're this far from operational. This far. Smukowski's actually whipping these weekend warriors into a dangerous force. Their whole plan looked crazy to me, but I'm telling you, it just might work, and if you don't roll it up now, in a few weeks we might actually be hijacking a ship with enough nuclear material aboard to—'

'And would that be such a bad thing?'

Hammond stared. 'What do you mean?'

'So we grab everybody *after* they have the goods. I'm not saying that's the plan, I'm just playing what-if. Makes a better story, doesn't it, than just foiling a conspiracy?'

'I don't believe what I'm hearing, Troy. Are you saying you're going to risk letting the Allens get their hands on a nuke?'

'Let's not exaggerate. It's not a bomb. If needed, we can grab everybody in the act, on the way to play pirates.'

'Once it's out of the US, it's out of control.'

'Don't be melodramatic. And I'm not saying we're going to wait that long, but even if we do, once it's out of the US, we can use the whole US Navy if we need to. Even your girl Smukowski isn't going to argue with a destroyer.'

'Fine. As long as we're playing what-if, what if things don't go as planned, and the Allens end up with radiological weapons, sailing off towards Mecca?'

Troy laughed. 'C'mon, Hamm. It's ten thousand sea miles to Mecca. Takes a month or two to get there, and has to go through Panama and Suez both. So, even in the worst case, we snag 'em along the way.'

'I don't like it.'

'I don't like it either.' Troy looked down at the tabletop again. 'But I'm not running this show any more.'

Hammond picked up his Coke and drank. It tasted good for a moment, but it was flat, and the aftertaste was ugly. He'd never thought the Bureau would use Earlene against him, certainly not in such a blunt, horse-trading way. But now at least he wouldn't be scheming to put away the people who trusted him. And he'd grown to like and respect Carla and Lorrie . . . 'How do I know these folks will keep your word? About not indicting?'

'You're their star witness. You don't testify against At-water, or testify only as a hostile witness, it makes their case look shaky, doesn't it? They'll give you the little fish. They don't matter.'

'You still trust these weaseldicks, Troy? Remember, it could be you sitting over here instead of me.'

'I trust the Bureau. But this all comes down from higher than that.'

Hammond chewed over what he'd heard, wishing he had the weekend to spend pondering. But if he was going to main-tain cover, he didn't have more than a few hours. 'Okay,' he said at last. 'This thing with French knocked a big hole in our boat, and I've spent all day bailing like crazy. How do we make it watertight again?'

The simpler the story, the better. They'd questioned French, and the guy had bled out. They'd driven the body to Ventura. Skittle had scored a vial of crack, and they'd dumped the body, sans bandages, along with the vial and McCann's throw-down gun. Drug-related shooting. Nagel would be suspicious, but he wouldn't be able to prove anything.

He rehearsed Skittle on the story over and over as they fought their way through a late-night traffic snarl on 101. He couldn't count on Skittle for long, but he wouldn't have to: they'd agreed that Skittle would take a bad fall in the next few days, a leg injury, and Troy would make sure that the ER sent him to a hospital bed with some bogus tale. Troy would also plant a short news item about a body in Ventura, and make things right with the ATF – and ensure they got the hell out of the Bureau's operation.

Not perfect, not watertight, but the best they could manage.

It was pushing eleven by the time they arrived back at Rancho Del Mar, but the lights were on in the dining hall. Hammond found that most of the Allens were gathered there, and they told him that Carla and Lorrie had been back for a few hours.

Hammond told them their cover story, and Skittle threw in a few comments such as, 'Man, it was nasty.' The guy wasn't a bad actor, and his everyday nervous demeanour played well in the situation.

'But what about the ATF?' McCann asked. 'Is Nagel going to swoop in here with warrants?'

Hammond shook his head. 'French wasn't an agent, just an informer, and a pretty half-assed one. Nagel's going to be suspicious when French shows up dead, but that's different from having evidence. If Nagel had anything solid, he would have come after us before this.'

He sat through an hour of discussion and speculation,

unwilling to leave Skittle to answer questions on his own. Most of the men thought French couldn't have died enough times to make them happy, but a few – Dodge, Slater and Big Jones, in particular – sat quiet and scared. A boundary had been crossed; it wasn't just playing soldier any more.

When the crowd headed back to their cabins, Hammond did the same. He realized he'd left the bedside lamp on, because a trickle of light escaped round the edge of the curtains.

He stepped into the dim room and saw Carla sitting on his bed, her back against the headboard. A fifth of Smirnoff, two-thirds empty, sat on the end-table, keeping company with a bottle of Schweppes' tonic water and a glass.

He closed the door. Carla was dressed in an athletic undershirt, olive fatigue trousers and combat boots, and she glowered at him through red-rimmed eyes. 'You killed him, hunh?' Her voice was slurred with drink. She turned and planted her boots on the floor. 'We killing our own now? 'Zat it?'

'Carla, look—'

She climbed to her feet. 'Fuckin' South America, now, hunh? Soldiers killing their own people?' She pointed a wobbly finger at his face. 'Who the fuck you think you are, huh? Don't even talk to me first? Who the fuck you think you are?'

He stepped towards her with his hands open in front of him. 'Carla, let's sit down. We need to talk.'

Her eyes seemed to go out of focus for a moment, but when they tightened back in on him, she said, 'You *son-of-a-bitch*—' and swung her fist at his face.

He blocked the punch and grabbed her wrists. She was drunk, but he knew she was still dangerous, and his stomach clenched in fear as she twisted her arms in his grip. He must have an edge on her in strength, but it felt slight. 'Carla, *listen*—'

She grunted and swore as she struggled, but then she seemed to give up. He puzzled over whether it was safe to let go of her wrists, and she kicked his feet out from under him. He crashed onto his back on the bed and, without understanding how she'd managed it, he found himself with Carla straddling his waist, her knees pinning his wrists down on either side of his body.

'Don't you fucking move,' she said. Her hands clenched and unclenched over his chest.

'Goddammit, Carla,' he said, keeping his voice low, but giving it all the urgency he could muster, 'you need to listen to me.'

'. . . the fuck were you thinking?'

'Dammit!' He bucked his hips up, not to try to escape, but to get her attention. 'Listen. We didn't kill him. We didn't kill him. Do you hear me? We didn't kill him.'

Her eyes narrowed, and then her gaze searched his. 'You didn't.' It was somewhere between a question and a statement.

'We didn't.'

She sat back onto her hips atop him, and when he wiggled his wrists from beneath her knees she made no effort to stop him.

'Listen,' he said. 'I have to let the men think I killed him. I have to. But I didn't.' She continued to study him. 'I got him

260

to a medico the Allens use sometimes, got him patched up. This time tomorrow he'll be in Canada, away from us, and beyond the reach of the ATF.' He repeated this, with variations, a few more times, and he felt the tension leaving her body. More important, after his years of daily lying and deception, he thought he knew how to recognize trust, typically misplaced trust, and he saw it growing in her eyes.

'We didn't kill our own,' she said.

He reached down and patted her knee. 'We didn't kill our own.'

There was a long empty moment as he waited to see which direction she might tip, and her eyes went inward, blank, and then, to his astonishment, she hunched forward onto him and started crying.

He gathered her in his arms and let her sob, her face pressed into his shoulder. Relief? Sorrow? Her own arms hugged around him, and her tears came harder, and he realized how strange she felt in his arms – female, but hard, strong, chiselled. His hands felt the cords of muscles contracting in her back with each powerful sob.

Without intending to, he found himself rocking her, patting her, even murmuring the nonsense syllables used to calm children, and after a time she quieted, sniffling, and let herself be gentled.

It almost seemed as though she'd gone to sleep, but she roused herself and wiped a hand across her eyes and nose. She looked into his face, her own face a wet, flushed mess, and then she led her mouth to his and kissed him.

Not a quick peck, and not a friendly smooch, either, but

an open-mouthed, tongue-thrusting, clinging kiss, her mouth still hot from her tears. He kissed back.

They broke apart to breathe and he said, 'Carla, I don't think we should—'

She looked up into his eyes and swallowed. 'Please—' she said, and he could see that this was costing her something immense. 'Please?'

God knew he wanted to. He kissed her, and used his hands to peel her shirt up under her arms. Her breasts barely existed, but her nipples were unmistakably female beneath his palms.

The combat boots were enough of a struggle that it would have been funny if their mutual urgency hadn't been so great, but at length they were undressed and she lay back on the bed. Her body was scarred, and too wide in the shoulders, and too muscled round the waist, and yet superb, and she spread those powerful legs and pulled him into her without any preliminaries.

At first it seemed freakish to him, almost homoerotic, having someone so brawny moving beneath him, but inside she was soft and yielding, as much a woman as any he'd known; and she was drunk, and desperate, and fearless, and the force of her desire soon abolished any qualms he had.

He came too soon – to be expected under the circumstances – but Carla soon convinced him, without saying a word, that a second round was needed. She wasn't a skilled lover; she hadn't an iota of finesse; but her raw enthusiasm made up for everything.

Afterwards she gave him a vague, sloppy kiss, dropped her head back onto the flattened pillow and fell asleep within a few breaths. Stretching his arms, Hammond found that his muscles trembled as though he'd been through a long session in the gym.

He rolled onto his side and studied Carla. Her expression showed none of the softness or innocence he treasured in a drowsing lover; even asleep, her face was troubled and unyielding, though her lips bore just the hint of a smile. A self-possessed face, an ungenerous face, yet somehow compelling, even beautiful, and it was hard to resist reaching for her again.

Great. As though his life weren't already complicated enough.

20

Carla's Navy

So good, so good, so good. Even with the slight hangover, Carla hadn't felt so good in years. She propped herself up on one elbow and admired the rise and fall of Hammond's chest in the early morning light.

She was smart enough to know that most of the intensity of the previous night had been the strength of her own yearning, the months – no, the years – she'd gone without sex. But some of it had been him, too, and she felt a little jealous of that woman Earlene, who had him on an ongoing basis. Not that she had any desire to get in the middle of anyone's relationships; she knew she wasn't made for living with other people.

But she wouldn't mind taking him out for a few more test-drives.

Hammond stirred, rubbed his eyes and saw her watching him. 'Hey,' he said, 'how ya doing?'

She reached over and touched his cheek. 'I'm great. Even if last night was a little weird. Haven't done that in ages.'

'Made love?'

'No, cried.' She sighed. 'Hadn't gotten fucked in ages, either, though. That was awesome.'

'*You* were awesome.'

She felt an idiotic blush spreading up her neck and onto her face, and she turned her head away.

'Carla . . . you know, I'm sort of—'

'Involved. I know. I wasn't picking out china patterns or anything.' She looked back at him and smiled. 'But if you're ever inclined, I'm game for a rematch.'

He started to say something when there were footsteps outside and a hard rap came on the door. His eyes widened in alarm. 'Shit,' he whispered, 'it's Saturday.'

She raised her eyebrows in enquiry.

'Earlene.'

The knock came again and they both waited in silence until they heard footsteps trudging away across the gravel. 'She'll go down to the dining hall to look for me,' he said.

Carla kissed him on the cheek and rolled out of bed. She wiggled into her panties and socks. Hammond sat up. 'Well, don't sit there,' Carla said, 'get up and shower. Change your sheets.' She pulled on her trousers and shirt, and sat down to yank on her boots. 'I'll stall her.'

She headed towards the rear of the cabin, by the bathroom. 'Where are you going?' he asked.

'Out the back window. I thought guys did that all the time.'

'Only in cartoons.'

'I'll get her some breakfast, give you some time.'

'Carla. Thanks.'

'The pleasure, as they say, was all mine. Now get your butt off the bed.'

Earlene was on her way back from the dining hall by the time Carla reached the end of the parking area. 'Hi,' Carla said. 'Earlene, right?'

The woman seemed pleased to be recognized. 'Right. And you're Carla. Do you know where Boyce is?'

'I imagine he's still sacked out.'

'I knocked . . .'

'He had kind of a tough night last night. He's probably out cold. We had sort of an emergency . . .' Carla put her hand on Earlene's shoulder and steered her back round towards the dining hall. 'Let's get us some breakfast, and then we'll see if we can't rouse your man.' She stood a little distant as she guided the woman, worried that she might smell Hammond's odour; God knew Carla's nostrils were filled with it.

Over breakfast, she decided she saw what attracted Hammond to Earlene. The woman was friendly and smart, but had a kind of wide-eyed wonderment at life that Carla found adorable – and if Carla found it adorable, a man must have found it irresistible. On top of that, if you'd jostled her, Earlene would have dripped hormones the way a bush shed dew in the early morning. The make-up was a bit much, though.

It would have been easy to be envious, but Carla realized that she and Earlene were from different species. It was like envying a dolphin, or a bird – sure, flying along or porpoising through the brine might be fun, but they were different sorts of animal from her.

There just wasn't any point in dwelling on it.

*

All of the Allens had visitors on Saturday, which left Carla and Lorrie as the two singlets, so they grabbed a six-pack and headed down to the sea-cliffs. On the way, Carla explained what Hammond had told her was the truth about French's fate.

'Where you want to sit?' Lorrie asked.

'Some place on the edge, but with real rocks. I don't trust this crumbly stuff.'

Lorrie pointed, and Carla nodded assent. 'You believe him?' Lorrie asked.

'Yeah,' Carla said, 'I think so. What is it with you when it comes to Hammond, anyway?' She lowered her hips onto a wide boulder.

'I'm not sure.' Lorrie climbed onto a neighbouring rock and sat cross-legged. 'I still don't understand why he's with this outfit.'

'And he thinks the same about you. But it doesn't seem to bother him.'

'I understand *my* reasons.' She sighed. 'Fine, so you believe his story on what happened yesterday. Doesn't really solve our problem here, does it?'

'Nope. In fact, no matter what happened yesterday, if the ATF had someone on the inside, we've got big troubles.'

Lorrie twisted the top off a bottle and leaned over to hand the beer to Carla. 'At least we know who the mole was.'

'There's that.'

'Only thing is, I understand from talking to the guys that Hammond was claiming French never really told his runners much about our little project.'

Carla gazed out across the Pacific, straining to see Santa

267

Rosa island to the south. 'Hammond was trying to keep everybody from losing it, flying into a panic. I guess we need to talk to him some more. But his girlfriend is here today . . .'

'Does it matter much?'

'I don't get you.'

'Seems to me,' Lorrie said, 'that if the ATF was onto any aspect of this operation, even if they were only after the Allens and their weapons caches, we've got a cloud hanging over us every day. As long as we stay here.'

'Gospel truth. As long as we stay here.'

'Are you thinking what I'm thinking?'

Carla laughed. Lorrie couldn't possibly be thinking some of the things Carla was thinking right then, since part of her own mind was still riffling through images from the previous night. 'I guess we're both deciding there's only one obvious way to maintain the integrity of the operation.'

'So. You're in charge. What are you waiting for?'

'For tomorrow,' Carla said. 'Sunday, at lunch.'

Carla surveyed her domain from the landing of the cave. Bahia San Andres was a living port again. *Princess Mishail* was moored at the top of the T-shaped pier, her stern thrust back further than the distance of the planking, and *San Andres* rocked at right angles to her, tied up to the tip of the T's right arm.

Out in the channel *Sturmkönig,* their old oil-rig tender, lay anchored fore and aft. Two hundred and seventy feet long, she was as thin and sharp as a needle, born to cut through the North Sea's furious winter waves. A practised eye would have noted that her prow had been sharpened and reinforced, as though she had been retro-fitted for ice-breaker duty, and her sleek lines were as out of place as a polar bear against the calm turquoise of the bay. The other ships had been rechristened after purchase, but *Storm King* seemed like a fine name for their predator.

Beyond *Sturmkönig*, *Easy Angles* rode at anchor outside the reef. It was a bareboat sport-fishing charter out of Cabo San Lucas, and though Carla disliked the name, *Easy* wasn't theirs to rename. Within a couple of weeks *Easy Angles* would be back in her home port, with every sign of having been used to land fish, and at the moment she could see that Dodge and Simonsen were using her for just that purpose, both of them kicked back in their chairs with a pole in one hand and a beer in the other.

Carla's Navy, Lorrie had taken to calling it, and though Carla was Army to the bone, she found that playing Admiral suited her fine. The problem was a shortage of captains and sailors – the full team totalled fourteen, including Lorrie, Hammond and herself.

Over the past two weeks the squad had shaped itself into a real team. They weren't K-Force or a team of Rangers, but they knew their moves, and they acted like soldiers rather than a gang of middle-aged street punks.

She wasn't sure when the turning point had come. Perhaps it had been her little talk with McCann; perhaps the day French was shot. Or it might even have been the Sunday lunch when she announced they were abandoning Rancho Del Mar and moving to Bahia San Andres – with four hours to pack.

She'd been prepared for consternation or even open argument. What she saw instead were nodding heads, some faces grim, others smiling, and she heard a murmur of satisfaction run through the dining hall. Surprising, but on reflection it made sense: the kind of men who joined up with the Allens must have harboured some fantasy that one day they'd be called upon to be heroes, and now it was happening, the Real Thing.

There were a few hold-outs, of course. Skittle looked nervous rather than satisfied, but Skittle always looked nervous. Kowinski wore his usual squint. And Hammond, sitting in the rear, seemed disconcerted. Maybe his nose was out of joint because she hadn't consulted him before making this announcement; maybe he thought that having fucked her brains out two nights before gave him some special say in the decision-making process. If so, he'd have to grow up: fun was fun, but business was business.

Now, on her tenth morning in Bahia San Andres, the morning sun felt good on her face, though in a few hours it would be unbearable. Since they'd come to Baja Camp, they'd adopted the lifestyle of desert animals, moving about morning and night and sleeping through the hot part of the day, bedding down in their air-conditioned Quonset hut from 11 a.m. to six in the evening. This suited Carla's needs perfectly; all their open-water training was now done at night.

The boom of a large-calibre rifle echoed up from the base of the mountain. She smiled to herself; McCann was still at it. She took a few steps down the path and mounted one of the waist-high boulders.

They'd turned the long strip of land between the northern wall of mountains and the outcropping dyke into the arms-training range, and it had become McCann's domain.

He kept his beloved 30.06 and its ammo in a room of one of the adobes behind the outcropping, and he might amble over and take a few shots at any time of the day, popping holes dead-centre in the hay-bale targets.

The Allens as a group were gun-nuts, but at the outset she'd pondered long and hard over the standard armaments for this operation. She'd settled on the discontinued – but still available – Heckler & Koch MP5, the notorious Room Broom. It threw only nine-millimetre rounds, but once you depressed the trigger it threw them at dazzling rates of fire – a weapon with little in the way of finesse, but with an unrivalled ability to shred everything in an enclosed space. The unit was small and light, the 40-round clips popped in and out with German-machined solidity and, even though Carla intended to work with waterproof bags, it was a comfort to have a gun that remained reliable after a good salt-water dunking.

They hadn't been able to practise with the MP5s back at Rancho Del Mar – rifle shots were one thing, but machine-gun fire would have brought in reports that Santa Barbara County had been invaded. McCann made up for lost time, running the men through blind courses where they had to step out or jump up from behind boulders or walls, locate the targets and shred them before McCann judged that these imaginary opponents would have squeezed off their own shots.

Carla hadn't bothered to standardize the sidearms; the various Allens were comfortable with different pistols, and she let them use their favourites on a BYOB basis, Bring Your Own Bullets. McCann also insisted on ongoing rifle training

– this also BYOB. She couldn't envision a situation in this operation that would call for long-distance shooting, but being prepared never hurt.

Indeed, if everything went according to plan, the only shots fired during this operation would be fired in practice. Jill's First Rule was *Nothing ever goes according to plan*, but if events hewed even to the general outline of the plan, no one would be killed in getting the goods – and no one but Carla's team and her employers would even know the goods had been taken.

The main Quonset hut had been honeycombed with floor-to-ceiling partitions, giving everyone their own room and a sense of privacy from prying eyes, but there was no corresponding protection from prying ears: the partition walls were thin, and there were substantial gaps where the walls met floor and ceiling. If she ever had a chance to go skin-to-skin with Boyce Hammond again, Carla thought with some regret, it would have to be somewhere else. He'd taken to night-prowling the rocks on the hillslopes surrounding Bahia San Andres. Maybe some night she'd drag along a blanket and ambush him amongst the boulders.

She knocked on Lorrie's door, but received no answer, so she headed down to the pier.

The big dormitory Quonset was the only large onshore building, but there were two buildings on the water. The equipment shop, about the size of a one-car garage, floated atop two long steel pontoons. It was anchored twenty yards south of the pier, and moored to the pier itself by a floating walkway; when the day came that they'd sail for Mecca, the plan was to hoist the entire shop onto the deck of the *Princess* and lash it in place.

The other floating building was the explosives dump. This had been erected on a small barge, and sat anchored fore and aft far out in the bay, closer to the reef than to the shore. They'd brought ten times the explosive power they envisioned needing – there weren't many wholesalers between them and their final destination – and keeping the whole deadly operation far offshore gave Carla a measure of comfort.

It was a long tromp down the pier to the shadow of the *Princess*'s hull. She waved hello to Slater and Kowinski, sitting out their watch on the deck high above her, and then turned and climbed down the rope ladder to the floating walkway.

The bay was calm, but the planking of the walkway still undulated. Ropes were strung at waist height along the full length, supported by posts every ten feet, but Carla trained her sea-legs by keeping her hands in her pockets.

High tide was approaching, and she saw the shadows of sharks gliding a few feet below the surface. They were a mixed bag – hammerheads, a few tigers and a number of thin, tan reef sharks she couldn't identify. She'd never thought of sharks as creatures with daily routines, but the sharks of Bahia San Andres were as regular as suburban commuters: when the tide was on the make they crowded into the bay, cruising the pier, but as soon as the ebb came and the hard currents began to run out of the bay, most of them retreated to the deep water beyond the reef.

Despite her protestations that only the tiger sharks were

dangerous, some of the Allens could barely bring themselves to cross the walkway to the equipment shop. The real dangers were outside the bay, where there were rocky islands covered with basking sea lions. That was Great White country . . . but, since they were still doing underwater training out there, she saw little advantage in bringing up the fact that they'd all be safer in the bay.

She found Lorrie and Alvorsen in the shop, fiddling with what looked like a giant wok. Behind them the four ultralights sat partly disassembled in their long crates, and two extra Zodiac inflatables were folded against the wall. 'You guys going to put the planes together sometime soon?' Carla asked.

Lorrie shook her head. 'I've decided to leave them crated until we're through Suez. Less chance of damaging anything. Gianetti and Simonsen are both pros in flying remote now, along with Hammond; Kowinski and Slater check out okay, too.'

Carla was suddenly conscious of how much she owed Lorrie, and how many of the technical details she'd left in the woman's hands. Where would they be now if Lorrie hadn't dropped into the picture? 'So where do we stand? What isn't ready to go?'

Lorrie knocked on the giant wok and it rang. 'The containers. I'd like to give 'em a test run.'

'How do you do that?'

Lorrie gestured at the back wall of the hut. 'Grab one of the scored jobs, will you, Alvorsen?'

The man returned with what looked like a stainless-steel antibiotic capsule, scaled up to two feet long. A U-shaped handle was welded to either end. He swung it up with a grunt and rolled it onto the table. 'Eighty pounds, packed with sulphur. Decent duplicates of what's in the casks – but those will weigh more like a few hundred.' The surface had been crisscrossed with deep grooves, and Lorrie ran her fingers along the cuts. 'There's the touchy part, of course. Scoring the real thing. I've put guards on the saw blades so we can't accidentally slice too deep, but it needs to be done from behind shields, lead gloves, everybody takes turns.' She laughed. '*That's* something for the last minute. The babies need to stay in their cask as long as possible, and we need to weaken the structure as late as possible.'

'What's this about test runs?'

'Oh. Well, the general theory is that this bowl gets packed with a thick layer of plastique, then a layer of dispersant powder and then more plastique packed right around the hot goods. Slap on a couple of impact fuses –' Lorrie jerked her head at a small crate by the wall, '– and cover with your favourite tarp, and you got something that goes *fooom*!' Lorrie's hands flew from chest level to above her head, spreading apart all the while. 'Most of the energy goes up and out, and the dispersant starts degassing . . . not so much boom, but a big, big footprint.'

'You're keeping the impact fuses here?'

'Didn't want to keep 'em under my pillow. Sure as hell didn't want to store them in the explosives dump.'

'Like keeping matches with your dynamite,' Alvorsen said, and then shut his mouth and looked down as though suddenly shy. Carla smiled. Over the past month Alvorsen had turned into Lorrie's acolyte.

'So,' Carla asked again, 'test runs?'

'Oh,' Lorrie said. 'Well, I believe the math, and I believe the physics, and I also believe I'd like to blow a couple of these up and see what the real spread is, see if everything works as predicted. See how far the pretty yellow sulphur scatters.'

That didn't sound like Lorrie. 'And what if it doesn't work?'

'Oh, it'll work, it'll work. I'm mostly afraid it'll work too well. We want to take out the sacred grounds and make them too hot for comfort, not spread it too thin.'

'Or kill too many people.'

Lorrie shrugged. 'Of course not.'

Carla pondered for a moment. 'Sounds like a good idea. We can use a distraction.'

'Natives getting restless?'

'No. Overtrained.' Seeing Lorrie's frown, Carla said, 'Never thought it would be a problem with this bunch – no offence, Alvorsen – but they're so ready they're about to pop. We need to *do* something.'

'And making things go boom is a good distraction.'

'Always. We have enough plastique?'

'Plenty. Not sure how to set off the impact fuse, though . . .'

Alvorsen chuckled. 'Have McCann shoot it.'

In response to Lorrie's raised eyebrows, Carla said, 'He could probably manage it. Just about any distance you like.'

'Man.' Lorrie shook her head. 'This is the lowest-tech high-tech operation in history. It's like Hints from Héloïse around here.' Carla blinked at her in confusion – who the heck was Héloïse? – and she saw that Alvorsen shared her bafflement. 'Forget it,' Lorrie said. 'I need to remember you guys have limited educations.'

21

Rising seas

Lorrie hadn't intended to fall asleep. She'd planned to lie on her cot for thirty minutes and let lunch settle – the 1 a.m. lunch required by their upside-down daily schedule – while she reviewed the overall plan in her mind for the ten-thousandth time. Instead, her eyelids had closed, just for a moment, and she was in the dream.

If dream it was. Her visions of Michael now lacked the shapeless miasma of the dream state: they were somehow both distant and yet clear, like the video conferences they'd held back in her office.

You're ripe for betrayal, he said.

Our traitor has already been found out, she said.

Don't believe you're safe. Don't believe your mission is safe.

What should I do?

You have the tools. Why hesitate? Begin the work.

But we've begun—

No. You're waiting. Strike now.

Then he was gone, and her eyes opened.

She climbed off her cot and made her way down the hallway and through the small dining area, nodding at Slater and Big Jones where they played poker at a table in the corner. The doorknob turned in her hand, cool from the perpetual air conditioning, and she stepped into the warm, dark night.

Since she had been outside, back around midnight, the world had changed. A growing breeze came from offshore, and an unfamiliar sound sang in parallel with the unending hum of the diesel generator.

Waves. She climbed behind the wheel of one of the electric utility carts, switched on the headlamps and drove down towards the beach, near the point where the pier collided with solid land. The seas had risen enough that small breakers rushed up the shingle and sand, hissing as they withdrew. At the end of the pier, the bulk of the *Princess Mishail* rose and fell, black against black, her silhouette visible only as it alternately hid and revealed low-lying stars in the west.

She looked up. The stars glittered in the blackness, without a hint of clouds, but there was no doubt that, off to the south-west, a major storm had the seas running high.

They were ready. They were ready and hadn't known it themselves. But now the seas were high, high enough to put fear into the hearts of sailors if anything went wrong with their ship . . .

She parked the cart back at the dorm and set off in search of Carla.

Smukowski wasn't in her room, and the workshop was empty except for Alvorsen and Giannetti, who were retrofitting hoses to extend through *Sturmkönig*'s forward hatch.

Lorrie had just climbed to the top of the long outcrop on

the north of the valley – the long dyke the men had nick-named the Great Wall – when two shadows ambled out of the adobe ruins by the shooting range. In the same way one can recognize an acquaintance when too far off to make out features, the most primitive part of her mind recognized Carla and Hammond by the way they moved – though that movement seemed easier and more relaxed than usual, verging on intimate.

She raised her hand. 'Carla.' The two shadows were perhaps fifty yards away, but in the silence of Bahia San Andres, with no sounds other than the drone of the generator and the low roar of the surf, there was no need to shout. The figures paused, whispering, and then Carla detached herself and began hiking in Lorrie's direction, while Hammond waved and made off towards the main camp.

Lorrie sat on a short boulder and waited, perched atop the long upthrust dyke. Far off, the surf made a white line that highlighted the reef protecting the bay.

Carla squatted down onto a rock beside her. The woman's face never gave much away, never had in all the years Lorrie'd known her, but of late – ever since the men had begun to shape into a team – it had worn satisfied expressions, and tonight Carla looked satiated, filled with life, comfortable. 'What's up?' she asked.

'Just thinking.' Lorrie wasn't sure how to raise the topic. She couldn't tell Carla of her dreams, and intuition was something she herself had been noted for scoffing at. 'It probably doesn't make sense . . .'

'Your thinking's the best thinking I know. Just let me have it.'

'I'm concerned. The whole thing with French felt wrong – how much Hammond said the man had passed on compared to how much Richter thinks Justice knows. I don't feel secure, even down here. What if we go after the *Pontianak* and somebody's just waiting?'

Carla stretched like a seated cat, arching her back, a move that looked out of place on her. 'Why wait? Why not grab us here?'

'I don't know. And I don't feel safe here, either, just sitting. Waiting.' She sensed Carla's body coming to attention. 'You said yourself that everyone was getting overtrained. I think we should consider moving the schedule forward. And doing it just the way you moved them here. No notice, just deployment. That way if someone outside knows our schedule, they'll have it wrong. And if there's still someone inside, they won't have time to tell anyone.'

'Nobody can get anything out of here. Even if somebody smuggled in a cell, there's no reception.'

'There's the radios on the ships.'

'Sort of,' Carla said.

'How do you mean?'

'I pulled their fuses the day we arrived. I'll put 'em back when we need 'em.'

Lorrie stared at her, and she saw a hint of a smile form on Carla's lips. 'You devious little weasel,' she said. 'When were you planning on telling me? What if you got hit by a bus?' It had been a smart move, but she was surprised Carla had done it without consulting her first.

'Hey, I knew you'd never set sail without spares, and you know where everything's kept.'

'True. But I still think we should move up the schedule, just in case.'

'Hmph.' Carla sat silent for a long moment. 'We can't control *Pontianak*'s speed, though, and that's the main variable . . .'

'No. We can't control her speed, but we can control where we take her. We're planning to take her close. But back when we thought she was coming on the great-circle route across the North Pacific, we were willing to run three or four days . . .'

'You've worked this out, haven't you? Just give it to me.'

Lorrie sighed. 'The further we get from base, the wider we'll have to sweep . . . but I'd say leave early and push south. Instead of waiting for her to waltz by, take her when she's as far from the US as we can still manage. And doing that means leaving days earlier, so if there has been a leak . . .'

Carla stood. 'Which means leaving when?'

'Tomorrow? Next day?'

Carla's strong hand clapped down on her shoulder and squeezed. 'You got it. C'mon and give me a hand.'

Lorrie climbed to her feet. 'With what?'

'Sorting out the last-minute logistics without telling anyone.' Carla swung an arm around Lorrie's shoulder and hugged her up against her side. 'Tomorrow night soon enough for you?'

'So we're going? Just like that?'

'Hey, you're the only one I trust, girl. They're shaping up good. But you're the only one.'

22

Fearsome verses

Prescott Wainwright was late, but Atwater was unconcerned. Even when Press showed up on time, he always arrived in such a breathless hurry that he appeared to be late anyway.

Across the table Richter clinked the ice in his tumbler, hinting that Atwater might do well to order them another round. Atwater caught the eye of the waiter and swivelled his downward-pointing index finger over their glasses as though stirring the air.

Richter looked round the Cherrywood Bar. 'Nice place. Refined. What do you have to do to join up? Other than shoot you an elephant or win a Nobel Prize?'

'I'm not sure. At some point they just invited me.'

'Hmm. They seem to have missed me. Maybe I should check my mailbox more often.'

Wainwright arrived seconds behind the drinks, rushing his portly frame across the room like a goose preparing to take wing. As always, he was perspiring, and Atwater wondered how someone who seemingly jogged and sweated his way from place to place could remain so rotund.

He and Richter rose from their seats and went through the formalities before the three of them sat down together. 'Scotch?' Atwater asked.

'Don't really have time . . .'

'For a *drink*?'

'Oh, hell. You're right. Double Scotch, rocks.' Atwater signalled for the waiter again, and Wainwright seized one of the cocktail napkins from the table and mopped at his forehead. 'Okay. Fine. Listen. According to Jake Landau, it looks like the rumours about you were just the first of the silly season. Apparently there's more nuclear plots afoot in this country than there are political parties in Berkeley.'

'And . . .'

'And, so there's no logical reason for the Justice Department to ride your case.' Wainright took his drink from the waiter's hand before it touched the tabletop and took a long sip. 'Mmm. There was some business about information from the ATF, but . . .' He waved a chubby, dismissive hand. 'Ever since Waco, intelligence from them comes in at a pretty hefty discount rate.'

'What are you telling me, Press?'

'There was a crazy rumour. Now there's lots of crazy rumours. Why should the Justice Department pursue one about you?'

'So it's dropped?'

'Hmm. I wouldn't go that far. The AG isn't quite that hands-on, you know. Someone way downstairs, some little groundling, will probably keep it alive. Bad form to shut things down. But let's say that there's no official concern at the higher levels.'

Atwater glanced at Richter. Richter looked content. Wainwright slugged back the remainder of his drink as though it were iced tea. 'Thanks, Press,' Atwater said. 'I know this was all nonsense from the start, but it's still decent of you to keep us posted.'

'One good turn. Oh.' Wainwright patted at his suit jacket. 'Almost forgot. I actually saw the AG the other day – party at his house, unavoidable sort of thing . . .' He dug into the inside pocket of his suit and withdrew a folded square of paper, memo-pad-sized. 'The AG told me to tell you best wishes if I saw you. And also said I should pass you this.' He handed the paper to Atwater and then stood, bumping the chair back from the table by straightening his knees. 'It's a quote from the Koran, I gather. Notice the chapter and verse.'

'The *Koran*?' Atwater asked.

Wainwright shrugged and raised his palms. 'Gotta run. Rex, Lamont. Let's have dinner sometime.'

They rose to watch the man trundle out of the bar. 'ATF?' Atwater asked. 'So maybe our man Hammond plugged the leak, then.'

Richter slouched down into his chair. 'One can only hope.'

Atwater sat. 'Quotations from the Koran? I thought our AG didn't read anything but the Bible.'

'I didn't think he could read at all. What's the damned note say, Rex?'

Atwater unfolded the page. On it, in a large font, was printed:

For it is written that a son of Arabia would awaken a fearsome Eagle. The wrath of the Eagle would be felt throughout the lands of Allah and lo, while some of the people trembled in despair still more rejoiced; for the wrath of the Eagle cleansed the lands of Allah; and there was peace.

– Koran 9:11

'Jesus.' Atwater scanned the page, and then read it again, noting the chapter and verse. The tone of the passage made a chill rise along his spine. 'Jesus. I'm not religious, but that's sort of spooky.'

He passed it to Richter, who read it and tossed it down on the table. 'Spooky that a cousin-lover like the AG is running anything bigger than a filling station. That isn't from the Koran.'

Richter said this with such assurance than Atwater believed him on the instant. 'Since when are you a Koranic scholar?'

'Can't claim as I am. But what you're looking at there is a well-known Internet hoax. Been around a fair while. Now, I may not know the Koran, but I make it a point to know horseshit, and the AG just dropped you one big steaming pile there.' Richter snorted. 'Figures he'd fall for it. He probably thinks TV wrestling is real.'

'Oh.' There had been something scary about the verse before, yet thrilling, as though he had clicked into his pre-destined place in history, and Atwater felt a touch deflated by Richter's words. 'Seemed too good to be true.'

'It's still the best news we've had.' Atwater studied

Richter, awaiting clarification. 'It's a send-off message. The Witchfinder-General himself has signed off on this. That's his way of saying *good luck*.'

Atwater chewed his lip. As always, Richter was right. And even if the verse was bogus, it did have a fine ring to it. He sat up straighter in his chair and cocked his head a bit to the side, assuming the look of a Fearsome Eagle.

23

Red sails

He'd spent thirty minutes chatting with Carla and Lorrie about the changing weather offshore, putting on a great show of being concerned that a major tropical storm might be coming. Hammond figured that would provide enough cover for what he needed to do.

He was worried, true enough, but not about the weather. He hadn't been able to contact Troy, or anyone on the outside, since that night at Santa Barbara General Hospital. The relocation to Baja had taken him offguard, and he could only presume that Troy had worked out by now that Rancho Del Mar stood deserted.

The Bureau's foot-dragging had been incomprehensible, but every day he half-expected a raid on Bahia San Andres, perhaps with the FBI riding in on the ships of the Mexican Navy. So far, the Mexican Coast Guard had treated them like VIPs, in effect dipping their flags in salute whenever they passed; Richter had the Baja politicians believing that Bahia San Andres was being redeveloped into a living town and port.

The Bureau needed an additional goad, he thought, a reminder that Carla's Navy would be launching their assault in about a week. He'd given all that to Troy – a window of dates, and the probable coordinates, due east of Ensenada – but he no longer had confidence that his colleagues would be there, either. 'Worst comes to worst we can grab them in Panama, even Suez, if need be,' Troy had said, as though a ship loaded with armed militants and radiological weapons were a bus you might catch at any number of different stops.

Hammond needed to give it one more shot. And he had a few other things he wanted to do.

He stepped out of the dormitory hut and headed down towards the pier. The sky was awash with morning light, but the sun itself still hid behind the wall of encircling mountains.

Something else worried him beyond the state of his mission, something elusive, almost a fear for his own soul. His fake concern over the weather earlier had come so easily to his lips, and sounded so true in his own ears. Misrepresenting yourself – hell, lying – to everyone around you, every day, eroded your sense of reality, eroded your sense of self.

He'd had no intention of making love to Carla again – of fucking her again, to put it in her terms – but when she cornered him up by the cave, he'd been willing and even eager. Everything from the waist down had been honest for him, no doubt about that; sex with her was different from anything he'd experienced. But in the hours afterwards his mind had been lost in a fog of rationalizations: he had to do it to stay on her good side; he had to do it for the good of his mission; he had to do it because she wanted it and needed it; and when you came right down to it, he did it because he wanted her and cared about her.

All of those reasons were true, or he could argue they were true.

Hey, they might be true.

The sand of the beach squeaked under his boots. Several times since he'd arrived he'd considered dragging Skittle onto the *San Andres* or the *Easy Angles* and making a run north for San Diego, dropping his cover and forcing the Bureau's hand. But he believed Troy when the man said that they'd prosecute everyone – everyone: Earlene and Carla and Lorrie and the whole team. So he needed to ride it out for their sakes. Lie to everyone every day, even make love to some of them . . .

Another rationalization? Just another lie, but this one to himself? He clomped onto the planking of the pier and headed towards the ladder leading up the side of the *Princess Mishail*.

But it was the truth, he realized. Criminals – terrorists, really – ready to sail to another country and commit mass murder in the name of an idea, waging a private war. Yet he'd come to care about them. He'd felt this way before, long ago, felt this way about his buddies in the Marines, felt this way in the early days as an agent in the Bureau. Camaraderie in its original sense. The Allens had shaped into a solid team, with tight bonds between them and an overarching sense of purpose; and Carla and Lorrie were as brave and fierce and loyal as anyone he'd ever met. There was no doubt they'd lay down their lives for this mission in a minute, might even lay down their lives for him. How long had it been since he'd felt that way about anything, been ready to die for something?

Had he ever?

He clambered up the ladder and onto the deck. Dodge was on guard, leaning one elbow on the seaward rail and gazing down into the water. He glanced over at Hammond, and then looked down into the water again.

Hammond wandered over. 'Something interesting?'

The man flicked his cigarette into the water, straightened and stretched. 'Just watching the fucking sharks.' He shuddered. 'Them hammerheads give me the willies, but I can't stop staring at 'em.'

Hammond laughed. 'From what I hear, they're pretty harmless. Just ugly. Carla says the only real bad guys in the bay are the tiger sharks – and even they won't bug you if you don't bleed on 'em.'

'Uh-huh. 'Scuse me if I don't test that theory. Those bug-eyed guys could ugly you to death.' The man patted his pockets for his smokes. 'So, what's up?'

'Thought I'd give things the once-over, and then see if I can get a weather forecast on the shortwave.'

Dodge nodded as if this made perfect sense, and indeed it did. Even in the sheltered harbour, the deck of the *Princess* rose and fell beneath their feet. Dodge went back to his watch and Hammond hiked down to the stern of the ship. At the two-storey tower of the bridge, a door led into the mess and quarters, right on the deck level. Beside that door, a wide stairway led down to the engine room and the aft cargo hold. He headed down, turned on the landing and then hustled down the second flight of metal steps into the hold.

The first order of business was the engine room. He cranked the handle on the heavy door and stepped inside.

It would have to be fast; he could think of no excuse for being in the engine room.

He grabbed a pipe-wrench and some duct tape from the tool cabinet, strode round to the rear of the big twin diesels and lay on his back. Using his heels to brace himself, he scooted beneath the housing of the starboard engine and found the drainbolt beneath the particle trap. The wrench needed to be opened wider – the bolt was larger than he'd remembered.

It felt as though the nut had been welded in place. His teeth gritted as he torqued the wrench. An awkward position. He banged the wrench handle with the heel of his palm several times, and then, in frustration, slammed it hard.

His wrist hurt, but the damned thing turned.

He unscrewed it to the very last thread, until he saw oil glimmer around the throat of the drain.

He duct-taped it in place, 99 per cent unscrewed, and then he wriggled out and stowed the wrench.

If the worst came to pass, and the *Princess* set sail for Mecca, the oil pressure would increase, blow out the bolt and the starboard engine would lose its lubrication and seize up. Hard to say how soon; probably not until sometime after the ship reached cruising speed. It wouldn't disable her – he didn't want her completely helpless, drifting at the mercy of the currents – but she'd have to put in for repairs somewhere nearby: Cabo, Mazatlan, somewhere.

The cargo hold was an eerie place, made more so by the dim overheads. Its football-field length was partitioned by three bulkheads that ran the width of the ship. The aft hold, back there by the bridge, was still empty except for a few crates of supplies. He strolled towards the wide doorway into the main hold, his footsteps ringing with a hollow sound.

The main hold was huge – a house could have been lowered into it with room left over for a decent yard. But the space had been filled with a labyrinth of plywood crates, some as much as ten feet high. As he walked, the hollow sound of his steps persisted; he knew that most of the crates were dummies, empty inside, knocked together to give the illusion of a tramp-steamer cargo. Walking through the corridors and alleyways formed by the plywood blocks made him feel like a titan pacing the streets of some middling Midwestern metropolis.

At the centre of the main hold, at the intersection of two main corridors of crates, sat the cask: fifteen feet across, six feet tall, a gleaming, stainless-steel cylinder weighing almost ten tons. If Carla's plan worked out, within two weeks that cask would hold two long capsules filled with enough radioactive materials to make a city uninhabitable for a millennium.

He skirted the cask, which sat like a monument at the centre of a roundabout, and headed towards the forehold. The third hold reminded him that he was inside a ship: the walls veered in towards the prow, making the room into a large, pudgy triangle. Little had been stowed here, but a workshop, with its own walls, had been constructed near the port side of the prow.

The doorways in the bulkheads were big enough to drive a truck through. He paused there, looked back towards the stern and, as though he'd heard something, called out, 'Hello? Somebody there?'

Nothing but echoes. He twisted the GPS ball and heard that satisfying crack as the battery membrane ruptured. Inside the workshop he cut himself another strip of duct tape. It wasn't hard to find a place to tape the unit down – beneath a workbench, behind one of the steel beams that reinforced the ship's prow. He fed out the antenna wire and taped it to the beam as well. In principle, the ship's hull was now one massive antenna . . . just in case.

With a long, quick stride, he headed back into the aft hold, found the interior stairs and climbed up to the bridge.

The radio seemed dead. He plopped down in the chair, flipped switches and fiddled the gain. Nothing. He clapped on the earphones to see if there was even faint static. He clicked the button on the mike, up-and-down, a dozen times. He cranked the gain to full, and revolved the tuning knob across every frequency on the band.

He heard, or sensed someone behind him, and spun in the chair. Carla and Lorrie stood in the doorway. Carla said something he couldn't hear through the muffling headset.

Hammond pulled off the headset. 'Sorry, what?'

'I asked, what's up?' Carla said.

'Trying to get the weather.'

'That's what Dodge told us,' Lorrie said. Her face wore a small, satisfied smile that seemed intended for him. 'I told you, Boyce. The storm headed off towards Hawaii. Kauai's got reason to worry. We don't.'

'What's worrying me right now,' he said, 'is that the radio seems to be dead.'

'All four of 'em are dead, every ship,' Carla said. 'We pulled a few fuses.'

Lorrie punched her fists into her lower back and stretched, yawning. 'We'll put 'em back when they're needed.'

'What the hell did you disable the radios for?' he asked, already knowing the answer. He stood. 'They're our only link with the outside.'

'Uh-huh,' Carla said. 'That's why.'

'We'll have 'em back soon enough,' Lorrie said. 'We go operational this evening.'

Hammond shook his head as if clearing his ears. 'What? Tonight?' Both of the women nodded. 'But the *Pontianak* has to be hundreds of miles away – no, make that a thousand, thousand-five—'

'There's three points on a triangle, ace,' Lorrie said, 'two other than the one we're standing on. We're heading for the south apex.'

'That'll mean *days* at sea . . .'

'Everybody's got their sea-legs,' Carla said. 'And this way, if we screw it up and she slips by, we get a few more bites at the apple.'

Lorrie nodded. 'Plus, look at it this way. If we sail towards them when they're sailing towards us . . . well, do the math. We come together twice as fast.'

'Don't look that way,' Carla said. Hammond wasn't sure what expression was on his face, but he hoped it read as disconcerted rather than guilty. 'We agreed when we left Rancho Del Mar that it would all be on a need-to-know-basis from then on.' She lifted one shoulder in a mini-shrug. 'Now you need to know.'

He still saw something unsettling in Lorrie's eyes, but guilt had a way of putting filters on your vision. She said, 'C'mon, Boyce. We got to round up the hands for the big cattle-drive.'

He spun the chair with his hip. 'How much time do we have?'

'Enough,' Carla said. 'But I want to be on the water before sundown.'

He nodded and moved towards them. The *Princess Mishail* wouldn't be part of the flotilla, so his engine sabotage would go unnoticed for the time being. But if the day came where the *Princess* sailed and the ship's engine failed, he'd now be at the top of their suspicious-behaviour list.

And if they worked it out, decided it had been him? Carla wouldn't kill him, he was sure of that. But Lorrie might. And the Allens – who knew what they might do?

As he followed them towards the stairs, Lorrie began whistling 'Red Sails in the Sunset', and it echoed off the steel walls of the bridge, down the stairwell and whispered back from the cavern of the ship's cargo hold.

24

The prize

On the three-day run south-south-west Carla had learned to love the ship. The first nights the sea was still disturbed by the distant storm, but *Sturmkönig* lived up to her name, breasting the swells with never a shudder.

Modern navies do reconnaissance from the air, but, like a convoy from the age of sail, *Sturmkönig*, *San Andres* and *Easy Angles* had been sweeping the sea for their quarry, sloping southwards in long zigzag arcs, the three ships spaced wide apart, but never so wide that a vessel could slip between them unseen.

Sturmkönig carried the largest crew: Carla, McCann, Alvorsen, Skittle, Kowinski, Dodge and Gianetti; Hammond, Lorrie and Big Jones had the *San Andres*; Little Jones and Madden trolled from the back of *Easy Angles*; and Simonsen and Slater had been left behind on the *Princess Mishail*. Carla had demanded radio chatter be kept to a minimum – and had left her scanner on to make certain – but Madden had been on the wire around sunset reporting that they'd hit a huge school of yellowtail and had landed a dozen big fish, fifty pounds and up.

She had to smile. Gutted and iced, the yellowtails would support *Easy Angles'* cover story.

The skies had been cloud-covered since they left Bahia San Andres, the sea lead-coloured by day and black by night, with never a ship or an island to interrupt the monotony. Were it not for the GPS and navigation gear, she could have believed that they'd been frozen in one spot for days, the ship anchored in place while the seas poured along past them.

At eight that evening Carla and Alvorsen had the helm when a sliver of moon glanced through a gap in the clouds. From the height of the bridge they saw that flash of light shattered and echoed for miles across the troubled sea before the clouds closed again, and then Madden's voice came across the radio. 'Found her,' he said, whispering, 'about a mile south of us.' He rattled off coordinates.

'You sure?' she asked.

'Killing our lights and going in for a closer look, but, yeah. I think so.'

'Good.' She nodded at Alvorsen, who rose from his seat to head down and roust the others. 'And Madden. You don't need to whisper. *San Andres*, you copy all this?'

Lorrie's voice. 'Check.'

'We're going to loop up north to gain angle. If *Easy* is right, we'll be getting busy in about ninety minutes.'

An hour later all the men were gathered on the darkened bridge, their wetsuits donned only waist-high, with the chest and arms dangling like half-shed skins. The running lights had been shut down for thirty minutes, and Carla's eyes had adjusted to seeing by the lights of the console and LEDs, a bank of green, red and yellow.

The men huddled forward to stare out the window at the faint, broken outline of lights that hinted at the shape of the *Pontianak Laut*. 'Looks a lot like the *Princess*,' Kowinski said.

'Close cousin,' Alvorsen said. 'That was the idea, right?'

'*Bahia, Easy* – we're on the rails,' Carla said, 'so bye for now. Gianetti, time to send some spam.'

'Gotcha.' The man strode over to the port console and flipped the switches that activated the multiband transmitter. A roar came from the radio, and Carla turned down the volume until it calmed to a steady hiss.

'Okay,' Carla said. She swallowed and tried to keep her voice even over the soup of fear and excitement that was coming to a boil within her. 'We all know how to do this now. So suit up, hand your tickets to the kid at the turnstile and buckle in.'

There were a few claps, and an undertone of nervous chuckles. She struggled her way into the top half of her wetsuit and sweat burst onto her forehead before she zipped up. In the darkness at the rear of the bridge the men were doing the same, cursing as they fought with the clingy neoprene.

The eight tall chairs had been reinforced and bolted around the perimeter of the cabin, and powerful shoulder harnesses had been installed on the seat backs. Carla snapped herself in and tightened the straps until her back was driven into the cushions.

'Do I get to drive tonight, Mom?' Alvorsen asked.

'It's your boat, navy boy.'

He grinned, his teeth red in the console lights. 'Ship.'

'Not any more. Tonight she's a missile.'

'Whatever she is, be nice to her.' He patted the wheel as though consoling the ship, and then shifted the throttle forward. 'This might be her last dance.'

When he had the engines churning at full speed, Carla felt the power vibrating up through the deck. Yet there was no perceptible increase in speed; up at the prow, sixty feet ahead of where she sat, the grey-black seas parted and rolled by as they had done for three days now. It had been warm enough before, but now, smothered in the second skin of her wetsuit and cocooned into her chair, she hungered for the coolness of those dark waters.

She lifted her binoculars and studied the *Pontianak*, now perhaps a mile distant. Through the glasses, she had a better sense of their combined speed. The *Pontianak Laut* must have been doing fourteen knots, and *Sturmkönig* must be running at close to twenty. It wouldn't be head-on – they needed the angle – but it wouldn't be perpendicular, either. Lorrie had shown her the vector maths, and if they came in at the oblique angle she'd wanted, then it worked out to, what, a little over three-quarters of their combined speed. Combined speed of, say, thirty-four knots – three-quarters of that was, what? A tough one, something like twenty-five or twenty-six knots, and a knot is 1.15 miles, so that's, what, about thirty miles an hour? That's not so fast.

An awful lot of mass involved, though . . .

Only a few hundred yards to go now, and it was clear that once they closed the distance the deck rails of the *Pontianak* would be at the height of *Sturmkönig*'s bridge, or even higher. She'd known that. Why was she surprised?

'Braces and mouth-guards,' she ordered. She wrapped the neck-brace around her sweaty throat and Velcroed it into place. 'You happy with the angle, Alvorsen?' She wasn't – the angle seemed too oblique to her – but it was his helm and she wasn't going to tell him how to steer.

He tightened the Velcro on his own collar. 'Couldn't be happier.'

She fit the rubber of the mouth-guard between her teeth and bit down with unnecessary force.

They were a gridiron-distance away when the *Pontianak*'s horn sounded, loud and nerve-jangling as an approaching train, and the cargo ship steered hard to starboard, away from *Sturmkönig*. But the *Pontianak* was no racehorse, and the turn plus her forward momentum served only to open up her naked side to *Sturmkönig*'s hard beak.

Carla had just enough time to jam the binoculars into the pocket on the armrest before the impact came.

The crash hurled her against the harness with such force she half-expected the chair to rip free of its deckbolts. But *Sturmkönig*'s forward motion hadn't stopped, and, as she watched, the ship's reinforced prow pushed its way into the *Pontianak*'s side. As the steel of the cargo ship ripped inwards there was a scream of metal wrenching apart, and *Sturmkönig* buried fifteen feet of her stem in the other ship's forward cargo hold.

The engines still churned, but they'd stopped travelling. She spit out her mouth-guard, ripped off her neck-brace and unbuckled her harness. When she stood, the motion of the deck nearly threw her off-balance; coupled, the ships wallowed up and down on the waves in a broken, spastic rhythm, and when their coupling reached a high or low point, the metal cried out. 'Everybody good?' She studied the men, received upraised thumbs all round the room. 'Get ready to move it, then.'

She heard the sounds of mouth-guards being spat out, and the ripping of Velcro, but she'd turned back to the *Pontianak*. Through her binoculars she could see men on the deck of the cargo ship, most of them uniformed. A handful of them gathered at the deckrail above the point where *Sturmkönig* had stove in their side, and they gesticulated at *Sturmkönig*'s deck in anger, as though the ship itself could somehow perceive them.

'Alvorsen, you happy?' she asked.

'Let us slide back a couple of feet, and I will be.'

'Shoot the bolts on the anchors, then. Skittle, start the forward pumps running and then get into our forward hold and see how it's doing. Everybody else, pull on some shirts over those monkey suits. Kowinski – it's showtime.'

She sat down and studied the pandemonium on the deck of the other ship. Someone on their bridge lit up a spotlight and swept it across *Sturmkönig*'s deck, searching for God-knows-what – an answer, she supposed, as to where this dark, deserted ship had come from.

The men at the deck rail were in a panic, pointing down and arguing. An odd, intimate moment: she doubted they could see into the dark bridge, but through the binoculars she could see the expressions on their smooth Asian faces, fear and anger in equal mixture. Good. Panic faster. Get those damned lifeboats into the water.

Skittle's feet rang hollowly on the interior stairs and he panted back onto the bridge. All the men in the room, light-coloured shirts buttoned over their wetsuits, turned to look at him. 'Pumps are going.' He stopped to catch his breath. 'Peeked through the foremost hatch. Water's pouring into her fast, where we're stuck in her, I mean. Even without what we're pumping in.'

'Are *we* hulled?'

'Not so's I can tell.'

'I'd be heading over the side if I were them,' Alvorsen said, 'but I don't think they're getting the message.'

'*Their* pumps are running like crazy,' Gianetti said.

'Let 'em,' Alvorsen said. 'They're still sinking.'

'What the hell's wrong with their captain?' Skittle asked. 'Is he one of those go-down-with-the-ship guys?'

'Better not be,' McCann said. 'Another ten seconds outta the water in this stinkin' wetsuit and I'm gonna climb over there and kill everybody on the damned boat.'

'Time to encourage 'em,' Carla said, still watching the *Pontianak*'s deck through the binoculars. 'Dodge, Gianetti, you like playing with fire. Man the starboard console and show these boys vents one and two.'

She heard the men work their way to the console and turn the switches, provoking the sweet whine of solenoids backing off on the hydraulic valves. 'Uno, dos, tres,' Dodge said.

The electric ignitions crackled, and down on *Sturmkönig*'s deck, to either side of the bridge, propane thundered out of the venting in flames that roared up twenty feet high. The hot orange flicker lit the lashing sea for a mile around, and in the bridge they squinted and instinctively backed away from the walls. 'Just what we needed,' McCann said, 'more fuckin' heat.'

'Lose a few pounds, Ray,' Carla said, 'and it won't bother you so much. Dodge, since they seem to think it's some kind of show, maybe you should splash their boat.'

'Done.' Carla studied the side of the *Pontianak* just above where she'd been hulled. Gasoline glistened there where *Sturmkönig*'s deck hoses had sprayed it. 'Swim time, boys. Skittle—'

'Me first?' he asked, his voice whiny.

'Okay. McCann—'

'Gladly.'

'And don't forget to—'

'Undo the clothesline.'

'Right. McCann, then Skittle, then it's Kowinski's turn . . .' She glanced back at him. His suit covered him up to the chin, like a turtlenecked leotard, and it was glossy with gel where he'd smeared it on. Atop his head his face-guard was rolled up like a giant wool cap. The man's face poured sweat. 'You sure you want to do this?'

'Yeah, yeah, yeah. But sooner's better than later.'

'All right, you three. See you in the water.'

Skittle and McCann disappeared down the interior stairs. 'Dodge,' Carla said, 'things are burning a little too evenly out there . . .'

'Sorry. I'll sputter.'

As he adjusted the controls the flames became more uneven, fluttering like wounded birds.

'There goes McCann,' Alvorsen said. Down on deck she saw McCann's bulky figure, clad in a white shirt atop his wetsuit, flee past the flames and hurl himself over the rail. A few moments later he was followed by Skittle, who dodged in close to the flames and then staggered across the deck, his shirt aflame.

'Jesus,' Carla said, 'who the hell told him to set himself on fire?'

'Who said it was deliberate?' Alvorsen asked.

'Kowinski? Break a leg.'

Kowinski exited onto the outside staircase, ran onto the deck. Carla craned her neck forward and could see him pause to pull down his hood. Now he was blind.

The man stumbled back into the fiery propane vent and immediately burst into flames himself. He ran halfway up the deck, fell, then dragged himself to the rail and then, pausing for a moment with his flailing limbs ablaze, he hurled himself into the sea.

'Christ. Christ.' Carla took a deep breath. 'Jesus, do you think he's okay?'

'I think he's a ham,' Alvorsen said.

She watched the group of men at the rail of the *Pontianak* through her glasses. They still stood there, clustered, staring at the orange surface of the sea where Kowinski had disappeared. Sweat poured from her face, and she stood and peeled the wetsuit off her arms and shoulders and let it flop down around her waist. 'Are these guys on Prozac?' she asked. 'Dodge: gimme five and six, real low.'

Flames poured out of the forward vents, ten feet high, and then the gasoline on the hull of the *Pontianak* took fire and

the men at the rail danced backwards and disappeared. Para-
doxically, as the night throbbed with even more fire, she felt
cooler, the perspiration fleeing her arms and the athletic
undershirt she wore.

'Dodge, Gianetti – you boys can go swimming any time
you want.' She looked back to see if they were good to go,
and they both stared at her. 'Remember: anybody's missing,
don't go looking. Just—'

'Hang on the clothesline and wait,' Dodge finished for
her.

'So *swim*.'

They both nodded, still staring, not at her face, but at her
chest, and then both of them turned their heads away.

She glanced down and saw that the evaporation had stiff-
ened her nipples as though she'd been rubbing them with
ice-cubes. 'Christ on a boogie board,' she said, and dropped
into the chair, 'guys never fucking cut it out, do they?'

'Huh?' Alvorsen asked.

'Just shut up, okay? I'm going to fire up the other vents,
and we'll see if the Indonesians'll bail.' She wiped sweat from
her forehead. 'When are they gonna get their goddamned
boats in the water? Is this some kinda religious thing with
these guys?'

Alvorsen said, 'It's a naval thing.'

'Glad I joined the Army, then. You sailors have soggy
brains.'

The two launches the Indonesians lowered were state-of-the-
art: motorized, decked out with rescue flashers, and no doubt

loaded with navigation and comm equipment. Carla counted thirty-two men, sixteen in each launch.

'About time,' Alvorsen said. 'They're sinking, and taking us with them. Like, soon. Jesus, I should stop the pumps. There's no reason to be feeding water into their hold any more.'

'Shit,' Carla said, 'they're heading this way.'

'We *are* between them and shore . . .'

'Well, discourage them. Let's blow a couple of the charges on deck.'

'I'm not so sure that's a great idea.'

The launches had come about and were headed towards *Sturmkönig*, perhaps not to investigate, but certainly to round the stern. 'Is it going to sink us? No? Then let's do it. I'm not in the mood for visitors.'

'Three and six? They're on that side.'

'Sounds good.' Carla looked out the starboard windows and watched the launches. 'Blow us up when ready, Gridley.'

'You got it.'

The first explosion reverberated through the ship, making the hard metal beneath her feet feel liquid for a brief, quivering moment. Carla winced and massaged her temple. The second one did the trick; the launches hesitated, like birds suspicious of a new feeder, and then veered off towards the north.

'I'm guessing we have maybe twenty minutes of propane left,' Alvorsen said. 'And their time to the horizon is more than that.'

'So they'll think we've sunk,' Carla said. 'I should get into the water. I'm worried about the guys. I'm going to shut down the jamming and call in *San Andres*, tell them to come up.' She marched over to the console. 'And tell *Easy* they're about to have guests.'

'Minute you stop the spam, the lifeboats'll be SOSing the whole world.'

'Can't have it both ways, ace.' The omnipresent roar diminished by half, and she realized Alvorsen must have switched off the forward pumps. 'We need to get the goods and clear out.'

She switched off the jamming antenna and went forward to the radio. '*Easy*, you got company, with flashers and transponders and bells on their fucking hats. Copy?'

'Gotcha,' Madden said. 'And congrats.'

'*San Andres*, come help us get the baby out of daycare, and don't take your time. We're about to get wet here.'

'Read you,' Lorrie's voice said. 'Everybody in K-Force always wondered what made you wet.'

'Sanchez, on the way up, put it on autopilot and go fuck yourself. Check?'

'Check, boss.'

Carla glanced down at Alvorsen. 'You okay here?'

'I'm fine. I'm the one who's staying dry, remember?'

'Okay. Don't forget about us. And keep this sucker afloat for a while.' She tugged her arms back into the wetsuit as she crossed the bridge, but when she opened the door and looked down she saw the bottom ten feet of the stairway had been blown away.

She reported this fact to Alvorsen, who said, 'Told you.'

She sighed and headed down the switchback of the interior gangway.

*

Dropping into the cool, salty water after what seemed like years on the bridge was a visceral release – beyond sex, beyond any real pleasure, the deep dizzy relief of a restroom after a thousand miles of busy freeway.

She swam wide of the propeller, even though it was quiescent, and guided her body to the port side of the ship before diving down.

Above her the propane flames still roared, and splinters of orange light shot down into the dark. She felt for the cable – the clothesline, they'd dubbed it – and inched herself forward until she found her rebreather and eased its mouthpiece between her lips, and fumbled at the valves until that smooth flow of air came across her tongue, oxygen massaging her lungs and salt kissing her mouth.

She squeezed into her mask and cleared it, then eased the rebreather onto her chest, and finally undid the fins and pulled their straps around her ankles.

Then she swam to the front of the line and counted down, everyone visible but wraithlike in the hot light from above. She squeezed their shoulders as she worked her way down the line: McCann, Skittle, Kowinski – big thumbs up there, the crazy sonofabitch – Dodge, Gianetti . . .

Carla retrieved her baggie from its clip on the line and looped it over her shoulder. Once she'd belted her climbing gear to her waist, she settled down to wait.

After so much time, so much tension, it felt good to hang on the line, drifting with the small currents. Somewhere out there *Easy Angles* was discovering thirty-two shipwrecked Indonesians and trying to squeeze them on board; two bewildered sport-fishermen would head back to Cabo San Lucas and, with a little bit of luck, along the way they'd foist their passengers off onto the first large boat they met.

The light from above faltered, dimmed and at last flickered out, and Carla and her men all drifted together in the dark, attached to the same thin line.

Waiting underwater, Carla thought she understood what they meant by Zen. She might be summoned out of the water to give battle, or to claim victory, or merely to die; but in that eternal moment, in the darkness beneath *Sturmkönig*'s hull, there was only the breath and the being. When the hum of the pumps started up, she was almost grieved; for a time – she was not sure how long – she had been outside herself, and it had been glorious.

She felt along the clothesline until she found the come-along, and she undid it and then swam forward, pressing a knot into each man's hand before she led them off. She glided along the hull of *Sturmkönig*, her fingertips reaching out to touch the steel every few yards; then a sharp left towards the prow of the *Pontianak*, the two ships unseen and yet looming, their sheer mass oppressing the senses.

When Carla surfaced on the *Pontianak*'s starboard side, she heard thundering fountains of water from the hidden *Sturmkönig*; from the sound of it, Alvorsen had all five sets of pumps running. Head after head broke the surface in a line alongside her. She pointed her finger at Dodge, yanked her thumb back at herself and then gestured upwards.

After handing mask and flippers to McCann, she aimed her firing tube and shot the grappling hook over the top rail. The pop of Dodge's line came seconds later. She set the hook, tugged twice and then turned the ratchet. She grinned at the men – her men, wondering if they could even see her face in the darkness – and then ran up the side of the ship.

At the top of the hull she paused, and then let herself roll under the bottom rail. As in all the drills, Dodge waited for her gesture before doing the same. Flat on the decking, she undid her baggie and pulled out her MP5 before going further.

She did a quick run-through, Dodge following a good twenty yards behind, ducking behind deck equipment to give her cover. The ship was deserted and already listed slightly to port, where *Sturmkönig* had pierced her. The jets of water arced up from *Sturmkönig*'s deck pumps, oddly gay, like the July 4th shows put on by the boats of the New York Harbor Fire Department.

She waved all-clear to Alvorsen, and then crossed back to the side where the divers bobbed in the water. 'Ahoy, mateys,' she called down. 'The prize, she be ours.'

She backed away from the rail and waited beside Dodge as they boarded. Once they stood dripping on deck, she said, 'Gianetti, McCann, get the engines going. Skittle, Kowinski, once we have power, you get the bilge pumps going, and dump ballast like crazy. Dodge, get the main cargo hatch open and then get on the derrick controls.'

Nods all round, and the men dashed towards the *Pontianak*'s stern, struggling out of the arms of their wetsuits as they ran.

Carla peeled off her own wetsuit and let it lie where it fell. She walked towards the centre of the deck, where the massive derrick stood anchored, and looked up. Fifty feet above, the arm of its crane tilted in a wide salute with each ponder-ous roll of the sinking ship.

She climbed twenty feet up the rungs and leaned back, looking to the south for the *San Andres*. Nothing showed but black sea and charcoal clouds. To the east a few stars glimmered low on the horizon, and to the north the ocean beyond *Sturmkönig*'s fountains lay deserted. The whole globe might have been nothing but this – restless water and the two ships locked in wounded embrace, with Carla and her men sitting atop it all.

25

Suiting up

Lorrie stood up in the Zodiac inflatable and snagged the rope ladder with both hands. When the slight roll was on her side, she ran up the hull, and hopped down from the top rail onto the *Pontianak*'s sloping deck. The cask lid from *San Andres*'s barge had already been hoisted up, and it lay gleaming a few yards astern like a gargantuan coin.

Carla came striding over and enclosed her in a fast, hard hug. Even in the darkness, Carla's face seemed radiant, years younger, the face of the girl Lorrie had known when they'd qualified for K-Force.

Hammond climbed onto the deck behind them, and Carla turned and wrapped her arms around him, too. His response was to freeze for a moment before returning the hug, and Lorrie wondered again what was happening inside the man's head. There were times he seemed eager to get on with business, and others when he seemed to be sandbagging the operation; times when she suspected something was going on between him and Carla, and others, like now, when she seemed to make him uncomfortable.

Maybe he was just miffed at not having been in at the kill.

'We've been monitoring the radio,' Lorrie said. '*Easy Angles* picked the crew up about ten minutes ago, and their captain tried radioing everybody in sight.'

'And?'

'And luckily the first folks he got in touch with were the Mexicans. Two parties both talking broken English. But I'm sure it's getting relayed, and once it gets back to the US, they'll scramble something to come have a look. So we'd better be miles away within, what? Ninety minutes?'

Carla nodded. 'Get the rad-suits the hell up here, then. We've already got the lids unbolted.'

Lorrie pointed down the rail, where Big Jones was using one of the little cargo hoists to reel up a package from the Zodiac. 'We're on it. Let's see what you've got.'

The hatch cover to the main cargo hold stood open in the centre of the deck, a hole fifteen feet across by thirty feet long. Lorrie edged up to the hatch-coaming, the knee-high wall around the opening, and peered in. Ceiling lamps blazed, but the sloshing water in the hold made the lights dance and wobble. When she leaned down and placed her palms on the top of the coaming, she could see the edge of *Sturmkönig*'s prow where it had rammed through the hull, well astern of the hatch.

Just below her, there they were. The two casks, their lids gleaming silver moons ten feet across, stood up three feet from the water. They'd been mounted on platforms with a ten-foot gap between the two. For a moment they seemed so bright and so close that Lorrie felt she could reach down and touch them; but of course, the lids were a fifteen-foot drop from where she crouched. In the centre of each silvery platter, a massive handle; around the perimeter, sixty bolts.

'Almost four feet of water down there already,' Carla said.

'That's not so much. I mean, the bilge must—'

'In the hold,' Carla said. 'It's four feet deep on the cargo deck.'

'Oh.' The ship was sinking faster than she'd thought. Of course, if the water got into the casks, it wouldn't matter much from a safety point of view, but it would make it complicated to see what the hell they were doing . . . Lorrie turned aside and crossed herself, the merest of gestures, and whispered a prayer under her breath. They were so close now.

A voice called up from the hold. 'Where you want these wired down?' Kowinski stood waist-deep in the sloshing water below, the two explosive bundles hoisted over his shoulder like rucksacks.

They'd been over this a hundred times on the chalkboard – either side of the hull at the ship midline, where the beams joined the floor. 'Same places as always!' Lorrie shouted down.

'Those places are under water!'

Did he think they had to light them with matches? 'You can hold your breath, can't you?'

Kowinski gave a sheepish smile and sloshed his way aft.

'Whole rad-team's suited up except Kowinski and you girls,' McCann said. He stood between them, already wearing his olive-drab radiation cloak and gloves. He had another set – fifty poundsworth each – draped over either ursine forearm.

'Okay, listen up.' Lorrie raised her voice as loud as she could without screeching. 'We've drilled this a zillion times, but I'm gonna say it again. Everybody wears their badges, and the badges don't come off until we're on the way home from the Red Sea. Anybody wearing lead, the badges go *under the suit*. Anybody not wearing lead, *clear out now*. You know your stations. Got it?' In the darkness she couldn't even tell where everyone was. 'Okay. Let's play with fire.'

She lifted the heavy robe from McCann's arm and slid her head through the neck. It hung on her with dead, flexible weight, the spiritless clasp of the lead blanket that dental assistants spread on you before an X-ray. She pushed her arms through the sleeves, and then worked her hands into the gloves that hung, suspended like children's mittens, on lines tied to the cuffs.

Beside her, Carla struggled with the gloves. 'Worse than fucking chem-warfare suits,' she said.

The light streaming up through the hatch lit their faces in death's heads, like the child's trick of holding a flashlight under the chin. 'Grumble, grumble,' Lorrie said. 'You're the one who insisted on suiting up and staying here. You're welcome to head up to the bridge.'

Carla answered by hauling the hood of her rad-cloak down over her face, so Lorrie did the same. The thick quartz eyeholes made the world look watery, which Lorrie supposed it was. With a clumsy, gloved finger she reached up under the hood, pushed the earpiece down onto her ear and pulled the mike in front of her lips. 'This is Sanchez. Check in.'

They rattled off. Gianetti, down in the little barge behind the *San Andres*; McCann and Big Jones and Carla, there on the deck beside her; and, finally, two voices of men not wearing lead – Dodge running the crane, and Alvorsen, patched in through *Sturmkönig*'s intercom. 'Kowinski?' she asked.

'Lorrie: Gianetti. He's just coming down the side into the barge to suit up.'

'Okay, let's move. Dodge: Lorrie,' Lorrie said. 'Send it down. Carla? Still want to go first?'

'Lorrie: Carla. May's well,' Carla's voice came through the speaker. 'I'm still soaked.'

The derrick whined and the big hook came down at the end of the wrist-thick cable. Lorrie watched Carla, unrecognizable beneath the hood and cloak, as the woman bent, picked up her aluminium shepherd's crook and then stepped one foot onto the big hook of the crane. She gripped the cable with one hand and let herself swing over the hatchway.

Dodge lowered her down until Carla said, 'Dodge: Carla. Enough', and stepped onto the lid of the cask. Lorrie watched her ease herself to the edge of the lid and grope her legs down into the water until she found a foothold, and then let herself down further until she was pressed to the side of the cask, shoulder-deep in water.

'Carla: Lorrie. You good?'

'Lorrie: Carla. Do it.'

'Dodge: Lorrie. Gimme a ride.' Lorrie knelt and gathered up the coil of wrap-around cable from the deck, twenty-five feet of thin steel line with hooks at either end. With fifty pounds of lead on her body, the additional twenty pounds of cable felt like a whole bag of cement mix, but she hoisted it onto her shoulder and clutched it there with one gloved hand.

When the derrick hook arrived at deck level, she stepped onto it and clasped her free hand on the cable.

The interior of the hold was bewildering after the darkness on deck. The lights bounced back from the stainless steel of the cask lids, and the swashing water broke the light into a thousand fragments and hurled them about the space in distorted patterns, like a glitter ball in some demented disco.

The hook touched down on top of the cask and she said, 'Dodge: Lorrie. Hold.' She smiled at Carla standing shoulder-deep in the water alongside the cask before she realized Carla couldn't see her face.

Lorrie knelt on the lid and slid the hook into the large handle. Then she let the wrap-around down off her arm and onto the steel lid. The rusty-purple strands of the coiled cable were startling against the mirror-silver of the cask lid. Hard to believe they were both steel.

'Lorrie: Carla. You good?'

'Carla: Lorrie. Yeah.' Lorrie scanned the rim. All around the edges giant bolts, a good three inches in diameter, had been ratcheted up until their heads stood a handspan above the surface, and their threads glistened in the crazy light. 'This thing completely unbolted?'

'Lorrie: Carla. Fuck, yes. You told us it weighs sixteen hundred pounds. It's got a six-inch lip. It's not like it's going anywhere.'

Lorrie inched over to Carla's side of the cask and handed her one hook of the wrap-around cable. When she'd paid out about half the line, she laid the centre atop the derrick hook, then uncoiled the other end and tossed its hook into the water opposite Carla. 'Carla: Lorrie. You set?'

'Lorrie: Carla. I'm not quite done moisturizing my skin. Move your butt, girl.'

Lorrie stood and braced her feet on either side of the handle, holding onto the derrick-cable with both hands. 'Dodge: Lorrie. Reel me up about two feet. Carla, no more peeking over the edge than you need to set the hooks.'

The lid stirred, trembled and then came free of the cask and she felt it wobble under her feet, searching for its centre of gravity like the world's heaviest surfboard. To the side she saw Carla fishing between the lid and the cask with the shepherd's crook, trying to guide the wrap-around hook to its target. A long moment, and then Carla edged along the outside of the cask, fished again . . .

'Lorrie: Carla. Take it to town.'

Lorrie shut her eyes. That was it? That easy? 'Dodge: Lorrie. On my word, take me up to the deck. Carla, duck and cover for as long as you can hold your breath. Deck crew, clear out. Dodge – let's ride.'

The lid rose, and there was a little tug under the soles of her deck shoes, and soon her head lifted clear of the deck, and then her waist, her legs, her feet . . .

It paused there, then Dodge reeled it back a little further and two feet of the lid's lip touched down on the deck and steadied there. She released the cable and stepped off onto the deck. 'Dodge: Lorrie. Nice landing. Gimme twenty.'

'Lorrie: Dodge. We aim to please.'

Lorrie hurried round behind the derrick's massive cable winch and crouched there, tons of steel between her and the hot stuff. In seconds, the winch jerked alive and began to wind, the squealing loud beside her, and then she heard the crane begin to rotate and extend.

She slipped out from behind the winch and looked across the deck. The capsule swung there beneath the lid, twenty yards away, suspended at the end of the triangle made by the wrap-around cable.

'*San Andres*: Lorrie. Coming at you. Heads down, boys.' Such an insignificant thing. Not even two feet long, a shiny fat capsule with a handle at either end. But filled with the heaviest stuff in existence, filled with things even God hadn't cared to create. What did it weigh, that little capsule, its body smaller than that of a young child? Two hundred pounds? Three hundred?

Lorrie knew better, but she half-expected it to radiate with malevolence, glowing Hollywood-style. Instead it dangled there, stupid and mute, above the railing, and then descended towards the little skid-barge towing behind the *San Andres*.

She heard Gianetti coaching Dodge on the approach, and imagined Gianetti and Kowinski down there with their guide cables, urging the capsule into one of the twin orifices of their own radiation cask.

'Shit!' Gianetti said in her earpiece.

'Gianetti: Lorrie. What gives?'

'Lorrie: Gianetti. Relax. Slipped undoing the hook. We're home safe. Dodge: Gianetti. Take 'er up.'

'Kowinski: Lorrie. Can you slip the probe over and get a read?'

'Lorrie: Kowinski. You're reading my mind. It's – Jesus Christ!'

Lorrie winced at the blasphemy, but among soldiers it happened a thousand times a day. 'Kowinski? Lorrie.'

'It pegged out.' She heard his breathing through the mike. 'It fucking pegged out. I'll drop the gain and poke it over again . . .'

'Kowinski: Lorrie. Negative. Keep down below the level of the cask and back the hell away. Stay shielded. You're okay, but don't go asking for it. Dodge: Lorrie. Bring it on home.' The stuff was hotter than she'd ever imagined. She pondered. 'Kowinski: Lorrie. Hammond: Lorrie. Switch places. Boyce, give him the helm, suit up in his gear, and keep your head the hell down. We got what we came for and then some, kids.'

When the lid came back over the hatch she gestured to McCann and Big Jones, and they lifted the decoy capsule – lighter than the real thing, but still a good hundred pounds – and hooked it onto the wrap-around cables. Dodge led the cable out over the hatch, and Lorrie stepped on and rode it down, where Carla guided the decoy into place.

The ship had taken on a deeper roll, and the water came up within inches of the top of the cask. Easing the lip of the lid back into the cask was a tricky business, with Carla pushing when the roll assisted her, and Lorrie keeping her legs braced wide, tilting it, with Dodge lowering the cable inch-by inch. There were four male guide-bolts, and once one of them found its mate, the lid settled into place with a hungry smack.

She and Carla rode up to the deck in turn, and then let McCann and Big Jones take over for the further cask. It went smoothly enough – McCann rode the lid up with the grace of a ballroom dancer – but Big Jones was tall enough that Lorrie had to keep telling him to crouch where he clung to the side of the cask.

Hunkered down behind the winch, she checked her watch. They'd been at it more than an hour. More than an hour, but still more work to do . . .

'Lorrie: Hammond. It's in the hole. You want me to check the heat?'

'Hammond: Lorrie. No. Get the hell away until we get the lid on. Dodge: Lorrie. Let's put it to bed.'

The crane lifted the lid of the barge cask and swayed it out over the rail. She listened to Hammond coaching it down with a sense of disbelief. No one killed, no one hurt, and Satan's own brew floating behind the *San Andres*, Satan's brew doing the work of God . . .

Hammond gave the all-clear, and the barge team began their work as the crane swung its cable back onto the deck. McCann caught the hook and bent down to hitch it to the handle of the second cask lid. He stepped on and waved at Dodge on the bridge.

Lorrie and Carla edged up to the coaming of the hatch and watched McCann ride down, the big man cloaked and hooded in lead, balanced on the cask lid like a dancer in some modernist production.

There was a scream of tearing metal and the ship lurched towards *Sturmkönig*. Lorrie fell, clutching the battens to keep from plunging into the hold. 'Alvorsen! We're going!'

In the hold, the lid swung hard to port and rang the hull like God's own bell, and McCann's feet slipped and the lid tilted like a gyroscope seeking balance. McCann's body flew up, but his hand kept a grip on the cable.

On the roll, the lid rolled towards the centre, and then swung back again, and, to her horror, Lorrie saw McCann fall towards the hull, the cask lid rushing after him. It slammed into his calf and his transmitted agony rang in her earpiece as the edge of the huge disc pinned him there. He toppled backwards, but was held upright by the crushing force on his leg until the next roll of the ship released him and he fell into the flooded hold.

'*San Andres*, stand off! Alvorsen, give it some throttle!' Lorrie struggled to her feet and saw that Carla had already thrown off her rad-cloak and balanced on the wall of the coaming. 'Carla, you can't—'

Carla dived, her body aimed at the ten-foot gap between the two casks.

26

Leverage

Carla's reason told her the dangling cask lid had paused at the apex of its swing, that it would soon fly back to port, that it would be gone before her body could smash into it, but it took an effort of will to dive straight at the shining steel.

How deep would the water be now? Five feet? Six? Maybe more – the damned lid was still right beneath her – even if it was seven feet, it was too shallow, too shallow for a real dive, not even a cannonball, that might shatter her knees if she hit bottom . . .

It was all she could do not to try to twist her body away from its trajectory towards that silver disc.

The lid moved ponderously and then gathered speed and she shot past it with a yard to spare, and she spreadeagled herself as if skydiving and sucked in a breath.

Her body smacked down on the water. Despite her clenched teeth, the force drove most of the air from her lungs, bubbles rushing past her face. She surfaced, took a gasping inhale and then jackknifed into a dive.

She opened her eyes in the burning seawater. The slosh of

the water and the swing of the lamps made the shadows leap out like grasping arms. Carla felt a sudden despair. Only moments left, and the black-and-white underwater world around her stuttered madly, a film jammed in a projector.

She swam along the floor of the hold towards the port-side hull, frog-kicking her way forward, and only seconds before she would have headed for the surface for another breath, McCann stumbled against her.

He danced on one leg, fighting his rad-suit. Carla grasped his calf, shoved her head between his legs from behind, squatted and stood up with the man riding her shoulders.

McCann's bulk was light enough in the water, but her throat gave those tight peristaltic contractions that meant her body was about to panic for lack of oxygen. She did as she'd been taught: grimace hard and screw up the face muscles to draw motor-neuron activity away from throat and diaphragm.

He needed time, time to fight free of his hood, time to suck air. But she felt the burning begin in her chest. Another few seconds, just another few seconds . . .

She eased back down to her knees, fighting the urge to fling him from her shoulders. Her head ducked down and back, and then she vaulted upwards, air spilling from her mouth before she reached the surface.

She drew in two long, whimpering breaths, and then she felt a hand under her armpit, buoying her up. Big Jones was there, leaning out, his other hand clamped onto the rim of the lidless cask. She nodded thanks and dived down again, this time grasping the nape of McCann's rad-cloak and hauling upwards with all her might. Her right hand groped towards the surface, and Big Jones clutched her wrist.

Hammond was kneeling atop the barge's cask-lid in his rad-suit when it happened. He heard Gianetti say, 'What the hell?' and then heard the wail of tearing steel as the *Pontianak* listed to port.

'Hold tight!' he shouted. The hull of the big ship tilted away from the barge, but the wave bucked them hard. Gianetti stumbled over Hammond's back and fell into the sea.

He heard Lorrie's voice over the headset, crying, 'Alvorsen! We're going!' and then, '*San Andres*, stand off! Alvorsen, give it some throttle!' Hammond's gloved fists clutched at the bolts of the lid and he leaned out to where Gianetti had fallen.

Nothing. He dragged off his hood and stared. With his rad-suit on, Gianetti must be a thousand feet down already.

There was a jerk as the tether to the *San Andres* went taut, and Hammond realized that Skittle was towing them away from the *Pontianak*.

The cask was sealed, and the lead suit he wore now seemed more dangerous than any amount of radiation. He struggled his way out of the suit with exaggerated care, keeping a tight grip on a bolt with first one hand, then the other. Then he lay down on the cask lid and looked back at the water where Gianetti had vanished, hoping to see a figure break the surface.

He made his way across the cable-walk above the tether and onto the stern deck of the *San Andres*. Skittle had the wheel, and Kowinski stood beside him. Hammond leaned on a nearby bulkhead. He covered his mike with his hand. 'Gianetti went overboard.'

The two men looked at him and Hammond shook his head in response to the unasked questions.

They took the *San Andres* in a wide circle out on the dark sea, listening to the frantic chatter on their headsets as Lorrie tried to coordinate McCann's rescue and coach Alvorsen's efforts to right the *Pontianak*. They'd had some success: Hammond saw that the ship now sat more or less upright, but Alvorsen was driving *Sturmkönig* hard enough that the two interlocked vessels moved in a slow circle.

'Hammond: Lorrie. We have McCann on deck. Carla and Big Jones are bolting down the lid. You're going to have to come alongside so we can lower McCann directly in a stretcher.'

'Lorrie: Hammond. Got you.' He paused. 'We lost Gianetti. Went down when the *Pontianak* listed.'

There was a long silence, and Alvorsen's voice asked, 'Did you search? Maybe he's—'

'He had his rad-suit on.'

Conversation on the headset became more subdued after that, limited to directions and commands.

One crippled and now one dead. Skittle steered the *San Andres* back towards the distant ships. For a moment, Hammond hated everyone. The fools in Washington who had held off again and again, always wanting a tighter case. Atwater and Richter and their crazy goals. Carla and Lorrie and their gung-ho leadership. The stupid, sorry Allens, playing soldier

327

with real lives at stake. And himself most of all – a lying, inde-
cisive yes-man who wanted it both ways.

He tried to remember who he had been before he went
undercover, what he'd lived for, what he'd planned on doing
with his life, and he came up empty.

His jaw clenched tighter and he felt a cracking in an upper
left molar. When he tongued the tooth, little fragments of
amalgam fell out and he spat them on the deck.

The *Pontianak* was now close to upright side-to-side, but as
Skittle guided the *San Andres* towards her, Hammond saw
that she had taken on a flood of water into the forward holds.
She'd tilted her nose down, and the whole deck slanted fore
at a good ten degrees, maybe more.

Everything had become an elaborate dance: Alvorsen continued to drive *Sturmkönig* into the *Pontianak*'s side to help
keep the ship upright, but the force, applied so far forward,
revolved the conjoined vessels in a long curve. *San Andres*
not only had to close with the *Pontianak*'s starboard side, but
had to keep steering both away and in an arc to maintain its
relative position.

Hammond let Skittle keep the helm – the man had shown
an unexpected talent at the wheel over the past weeks – while
he tossed over foam fenders and stationed himself at the
starboard rail as they closed. Skittle led them in from the
Pontianak's prow, the two ships aimed in opposite directions.

Hammond saw shadowy figures crowding the *Pontianak*'s starboard rail as they cruised in, and then the wide
overhang of her prow blocked his view of both ship and night
sky.

Skittle throttled her down and backed water, and the ship's towering hull kissed the fenders. The bottom end of a rope ladder slapped down on *San Andres*'s deck, and Hammond steadied it as Carla scrambled down.

The *Pontianak* had acquired a heavy wallow, and the midreach of her hull fetched the top of the smaller ship a sharp blow on each long roll. McCann's stretcher came down via one of the utility deck winches, and Carla and Hammond caught the handles and eased it to the deck. The big man's face was pale in the gloom.

Big Jones and Lorrie had already clambered down the rope ladder when Alvorsen's voice cried across the intercom, 'She's going! Christ, stand off! Stand off!'

The big ship tilted – and not away from the *San Andres*, but towards her. Dodge toppled from the rope ladder and crashed down on the deck, knocking Lorrie and Big Jones off their feet. The *Pontianak*'s hull smashed against the upper reaches of the little yacht.

Skittle had powered up and turned hard a-port when Alvorsen yelled, and at first the wave from the big ship's list carried the *San Andres* away from the looming hull. Yet they travelled no more than a dozen yards before the ship was jerked to a stop, as though a giant hand had yanked on a leash.

This time Hammond and Carla fell, too. Hammond scrambled to his knees and looked astern.

The arching starboard prow of the *Pontianak* had come down on the barge and cask. The weight of the bigger ship pushed down so hard that the barge's twin pontoons were submerged, and water sloshed around the base of the cask.

Hammond almost yelled for Skittle to give it full-ahead to try and pull the barge from underneath the cargo ship, but then he saw that the starboard anchor had clamped down on the cask – and not just the starboard anchor, but the fittings of the hawsepipe as well. The *Pontianak* had them pinned down.

'*San Andres*: Alvorsen. What's the score?'

'Alvorsen: Hammond. The barge is caught under the prow. You need to reverse and stand her up again.'

'Slim chance. Top part's ripped open. We've lost probably half our purchase.'

As if to emphasize Alvorsen's words, the *Pontianak* rolled, and her prow pushed the barge another foot deeper; when the barge rebounded, shedding water through the scuppers, she rode lower in the water.

Hammond stood, trying to keep his footing on the rocking deck. 'We have to cast her off.'

'No!' Lorrie's voice was almost a scream. She pushed past him towards the stern, clearly ready to run out the cable walk to the barge.

He grabbed her shoulders and spun her round. 'It's going to take us down!'

'No.' Lorrie forearmed his hands from her shoulders. 'No. We cut away the anchor, then get a lever underneath—'

'It won't work.' The body of a 'copter pilot knows everything about leverage, everything about pivot points, and Hammond felt the dynamics of the sinking ship as a quivering in his tailbone. 'It isn't just the anchor, it's the hawsepipe. The *Pontianak* goes down now, it'll take us to the bottom like bait on a sinkered line.'

She searched his face through narrowed eyes. 'You'd let it go? After all this?'

Hammond stepped round her towards the stern. 'Maybe it'll come up when the ship sinks. But we need to cast it off.' He opened the stern gate and knelt down.

'Wait.' Lorrie stood beside him, her voice calmer now. 'Let me get tools, get out on the barge first. Then cast off. But as long as it's floating, I want to work.'

'She's right,' Carla said from behind him. 'We have to try.'

He stood and sighed. 'Not like that.' An image had been forming in his mind as he considered the angles and the torque. He took a steadying breath. 'We can roll her – sink her astern, port side. Blow out her tail and lift her prow.'

He saw argument in Lorrie's eyes, but Carla said, 'What do we do?'

He swallowed, and wondered why the hell these words were coming from his mouth. '*I'll* do it . . . *if* you cast off and stand her out a hundred yards. Because if it works, this'll be the only ship afloat.'

The uninflated lifevest flapped at his back while he climbed the rope ladder. Hammond swung over the rail to the deck, and the *Pontianak* lurched beneath his feet.

A clench in his belly, and then a strange sense of comfort. It was fear. Good, clean, unambiguous fear pushed the ever-present clouds of anxiety and guilt from his mind.

The deck slanted both fore and to starboard, and he found himself running distinctly uphill as he headed for the bridge. He might not be doing the right thing, and he might not succeed, but he was past the turnaround point.

He yanked open the heavy door and clattered down the stairs towards the hold. The lights in the stairway flickered; already the ship was dying. At the landing, he stopped. The lower half of the stairwell was filled with black water.

No choice. He splashed down the stairs until he was chest deep and then began swimming breaststroke.

Beyond the stairwell the hold opened before him. The reflections of the overhead lights on the agitated water bewildered the eye, and all colour had been abolished.

The ship's list was now great enough that the water was deep to starboard, but to port the floor of the hold was exposed. He swam that way, pulled himself to his feet, and splashed his way forward towards the midline of the ship. Ahead he could see the first of the explosive packs wired to one of the *Pontianak*'s steel ribs.

He slipped and fell, clutching a beam on the ship's hull. A few steps further, and then he sat down beside the explosive pack. Far forward he made out the prow of *Sturmkönig* where it still thrust its steely beak into the hold, and the cries and creaks of the torn metal echoed across the slapping sounds of the water.

He had to retrieve both packs: they were synched to a single detonator, and if the one deep underwater to starboard blew in its present position, it would roll the ship right on top of the barge and probably break the *Pontianak* in two.

'Alvorsen: Hammond. Have you moved your explosives?'

'Check. Far aft.'

'Then start flooding your rear ballast tanks.'

'Can do. You're ready, then?'

'Don't have things planted yet.' Planted, hell. Still don't have the goods.

Hammond stared at the water that filled the starboard side of the ship. Shadows chased each other through the monochrome depths. Hell as animated by Goya. He pumped his lungs, hyperventilating, and then launched himself down the tilted floor and into the water.

He kept close to the floor of the hold, his chest grazing the bottom, and swam straight. Too dim to see, and the burn of the salt and the murky confusion of the shifting light made it hardly worthwhile opening his eyes. His ears popped: he was deeper than he'd expected.

His hands found the I-beam of the ship's great rib, right at the junction with the deck of the hold. Nothing. Nothing but steel.

Panic rising, he swam fore, feeling along the hull for the next beam. The fingers of his right hand hit the beam hard, and he grasped the angle of the steel and felt up and down, all the way to the deck flooring.

Feet planted, he pushed off and shot to the surface. The water was deep now. He gasped in air, clinging to the beam.

Above water, he swam back to the midline beam, and then to the next one further aft. He held his breath and dived straight down, pulling himself down the beam until his hands felt the decking. Steel, and nothing else.

Hammond's head broke water and he flicked the mike of his headset with his middle finger, scattering droplets. 'Kowinski: Hammond. I'm not finding the starboard package. You sure it's directly opposite?'

'Hammond: Kowinski. Affirmative. Same set-up both sides.'

One hand on the beam, he floated there breathing. His body told him to get out – get back on deck, dive into the water and float until it was over, because any minute now the *Pontianak* would take him down with her. And it might be best – he'd have tried hard enough to allay suspicion, and with any luck the barge would go straight to the seabed and trouble the world no more.

He paddled back to the midline beam, and glanced to port to ensure it was the right one. No doubt: the other pack sat there, still wired to the beam across the hold.

A long exhale, more like a sigh, an inhale and then he dived again, dragging himself down the beam hand-over-hand.

Something soft bumped his face. He groped at it with one hand, his other clutching the beam. It was the pack – floating up, buoyant, still tethered by the wire – but well above the decking where he'd been searching.

Why the hell hadn't anybody mentioned that the packs floated?

He pulled out the pliers, snipped the wire, and then swam for the surface, dragging the pack by its shoulder strap. No more than a minute later, a pack over either shoulder, he jogged aft. The water to port was up to his ankles.

It ought to be simple now. Plant the charges, head to the control room, flood the rear ballast tanks and then bail – onto the *San Andres* if time permitted, into the ocean if time ran short.

The water lessened as he passed the engine room, and the

aft of the ship was nearly dry. The slope towards the prow must have reached 15 per cent or more.

A small hatchway led down to a service bay to access the shafts of the giant propellers. At the bottom of those stairs, the water was over his knees – even along the port side.

A tool rack was mounted on the port hull. He clamped the shoulder straps of the packs onto a pair of hooks and hustled back up the stairs.

'This is Hammond. Alvorsen, you should get out of there, now.'

'Hammond: Alvorsen. I'm already in a lifeboat along-side.'

'Then go. *San Andres*: Ready to blow?'

'Boyce: Carla. Any time, ace.'

Hammond splashed his way past the engine room, past the understorey of the bridge. He rounded the corner to the port stairwell and shuffled his way into the deepening water.

The ship staggered as though she'd run aground, and then tipped forward. Hammond's feet were swept from under him and he floundered in the water that rushed towards the prow. His feet scrabbled for the bottom, only touching the decking for a moment. She was heading down, prow first. He had no chance of getting up to the bridge: the water was carrying him forward towards the middle hold.

'Blow 'em!' he shouted into his mike.

'Where are you?' Carla asked.

'Blow 'em, now!'

He jerked the inflate tabs on his lifejacket and the pressure of the vest embraced him, but now, more buoyant, he swirled round, a leaf in a storm gutter, whirling wherever the water took him.

Far aft there was a *whoomp* that he felt more than heard, like a hard punch in the gut. Moments later he heard an echo of the first sound, but more distant. *Sturmkönig*, no doubt.

The water spun him about so that he faced aft. From the tail of the ship a huge gusher of water rushed past the under-storey of the bridge, eight feet high and headed straight for him. In the seconds he had left he realized he must have failed: the stern had blown out, but the cataract of water would only serve to drive everything to the prow.

If you know you're going to drown, he'd been told, then take a big gulp of water into your lungs and get it over with. Don't fight. Give in to the sea.

To hell with that.

The sea found the electrical room at last and the lights went out.

In the darkness he took in a breath and held it.

The wall of water seized him. He gathered his knees up in his arms and let the churning liquid roll him until all sense of direction was lost. Eyes open, eyes shut – there was nothing but blackness and the tugging, dragging hands of the sea.

27

Rising water

After the charges blew, Carla pulled the mike close to her mouth and said, 'Hammond? . . . Hammond: Carla . . . Boyce, you there?'

Carla jumped over the rail of the *San Andres* into the Zodiac inflatable tied alongside. 'Who wants a ride?' she asked. 'Room for one more.'

'Hammond told us to stand off,' Skittle said.

'He told the *San Andres* to stand off – plus last time I checked, *I* was still in charge here.' She looked up at the faces on deck. 'Hammond's over there. The barge is over there.'

Kowinski nodded and climbed down into the Zodiac. Carla stood long enough to yank the starter cable on the outboard motor, and once it coughed into life she sat and steered them towards the sinking ships.

In the blackness Hammond's shoulders smashed against hard steel. It took a moment to realize his head was above water, though his whole body tossed on long, heaving waves. He sucked in a breath, but the sea dashed onto his face and he retched, breathed and retched again.

He called out to the *San Andres*, and then realized his headset was gone.

The water still tossed him from side to side, but as he blinked the droplets from his eyes he realized there was a dim grey light. The middle hatch, still open, letting in the night sky. He struggled in the water, turning his head to get his bearings. He was far forward – the open hatch was aft of where he floated – and he realized the wall he'd collided with was the prow of *Sturmkönig*. The upper deck was still many feet above him, and the open hatch too far aft, but he might be able to squeeze through the hole punched by *Sturmkönig* . . .

He flailed his arms in the water, turning himself to port. There was a ragged gap of grey light round the ship's intruding prow.

Hammond began to swim toward it, but he seemed to be swimming in place, and then he found himself dragged away. He winced at the sound of caterwauling metal as *Sturmkönig*'s prow moved. Its sharp beak lifted and then clanged against the top deck of the *Pontianak*, and then the slow suction of the water turned to a torrent as both ships lifted their prows from the sea.

On a river rushing towards the falls, Hammond saw the open light of the main hatchway flash above him as the water hauled him aft. Then he seemed to plummet over some edge. He grabbed one breath before he plunged into the water and tumbled with the currents.

When he surfaced he was in a maelstrom of rising water,

spinning round and round. The grey light was from above, as though through a high window, and he realized that the essence of his plan had succeeded. Both ships now stood tail-down in the water, *Sturmkönig* having helped lever the *Pontianak*'s prow free of the ocean. Both had only moments to live.

The water churning up from the stern spun in large, accelerating circles. With a flash of guilt, Hammond remembered a spider he'd flushed down the toilet as a child.

Cut the memory nonsense. He had one chance – to pull himself through the hatchway and get out into the sea. Once the hatchway was under water, there would be no way out: he'd be carried up into the prow and pinned there in the dark as the *Pontianak* headed for the sea floor.

He swam, trying to keep to the outer edge of water where it swirled in the hull. Too hard; the lifejacket kept him afloat, but it gave the water a handle to steer him by. Quick-release catch. His fingers fumbled, then cast it off, and he felt a new terror as his buoyancy vanished.

The hatchway stood almost vertical as the ship sank, like a 30-foot doorway to heaven's smoky light. The current carried him past it, its lower lip still three feet above the water, and he lunged upwards as he passed by. His fingernails rasped along the metal as he fought for purchase.

Once the eddy carried him back into the hold, he swam hard with the current and this time his desperate reach caught the edge of the hatchway. There was something there, some protuberance, probably a bolt smoothed by thirty years of overpainting, but he clung to it with both hands, nails piercing the paint. The current swept his legs out and round in an arc and pressed his body to the metal, but his grip held – and, as the ship sank further, his body was buoyed up, the angle lessened, and he clawed his way over the margin of the hatch and grasped the top of the coaming wall.

Hammond dragged himself to the starboard side of the hatchway, a matter of ten feet, but by the time he reached the corner of the coaming, the lip of the hatchway touched the top of the sea.

He understood what would come next. He braced his elbows over the corner of the coaming, hugging it to his chest. The lip of the hatch submerged and the sea began to flood in, clutching at his body, trying to drag him inside. He clung there, clung even as the water rose over his face, and after a moment the inward rush subsided.

There were cross-bracings on the outer side of the coaming, and he pulled himself up these as though they were rungs of a ladder. When his face hit the air he breathed, but didn't pause in his climb. When he reached the top of the coaming, still ten feet above the water, he clambered to his feet, took a long breath, and prepared to dive.

Metal crashed onto his back from above. Like a vast hand, it swatted him from his perch and out into the blackness.

The Zodiac bounded across the broken sea like a skipped stone. On the headset Alvorsen had announced that he was in his lifeboat, well clear of *Sturmkönig*, but Carla'd been unable to raise Hammond.

A hundred yards ahead the silhouette of the *Pontianak* lay low in the water, her hulk still angled downwards towards her prow. The superstitious part of Carla's mind swerved away from the thought, but it seemed that Hammond's plan had failed – had failed, and taken him down with it.

'Jesus Christ,' Kowinski said.

'What?' Carla throttled down the engine and stared. For the space of a breath, nothing – and then she saw the *Pontianak*'s beak begin to rise, levelling, and then lift from the water.

The wail of ripping steel cut through the sounds of the sea. Slowly, and then with increasing speed, the *Pontianak* and *Sturmkönig* lifted their interlocked prows, forming a black arch against the night horizon.

'The barge!' Kowinski shouted.

Carla's eyes followed his pointing finger, and she saw the silvery cask bouncing on the waves like a bathtub toy that had been submerged and then released.

There came a last shriek of protesting metal, and the two ships tore apart from one another and stood stern-down into the ocean, their prows pointing skywards, their profiles like two towers that had been planted in the sea.

Carla gave the motor full throttle and aimed the Zodiac's blunt nose at the *Pontianak*. Fifty yards, then forty, and she saw shapes falling from the deck. Was it only wishing that made one of them seem like a tumbling human form? She cinched her uninflated lifevest tighter. Her fists twisted the finger-long cylinder that dangled from the vest, and the blue strobe began its relentless flash.

Kowinski looked at her with his mouth open. 'Take the tiller,' she said. 'When I go over, steer aside and fetch the barge.'

He scooted back and grasped the tiller. 'But—'

The *Pontianak* was no more than thirty feet ahead and her hull loomed above them, but Carla saw that the ship was disappearing, rushing downwards. She crouched, slapped Kowinski on the shoulder. 'I trust you,' she shouted over the roar of the outboard, and then dived into the sea.

She swam hard in the direction of the vanishing ship, not bothering to look, burying her face in the water with each stroke like a competition swimmer, gasping in breath whenever her face turned to the side. A smooth, high wave lifted her, and she trod water and looked forward.

The *Pontianak* was gone, and a dozen feet ahead of her there seemed to be a hole in the water, black against black, pulling her towards it; but then the sea rebounded, and the resulting wave rolled her upside-down.

She came to the surface spluttering and trod water with frantic force, scanning the sea while she turned a full circle, her limbs working to raise her out of the water. The flash of the blue strobe illuminated the sea's surface, but also dazzled her eyes.

Off to her left, something bright – an orange lifejacket. She almost swam towards it, but then realized it was spread out on the waters, empty.

Then she saw him, a dozen yards away, floating face-up. 'Hammond?' she yelled. 'Hey, Boyce—!'

He didn't stir.

She swam a hard crawl, snagged his arm and pulled. Still no response. She pulled his chest against hers, pushed her shoulder under his chin to hold his head out of the water, and hugged him tight. 'Hammond . . . goddammit!' Her fists interlocked behind his back and she squeezed his chest with all her might, feeling his ribs bend and give, and water erupted from his mouth and he drew a long, wheezing breath.

The fingers of her right hand groped for the tabs on her lifevest and she jerked them. The vest puffed out around her. Hammond continued to convulse, spitting up water.

She floated on her back and he clung to her, coughing at first, and then relaxing into the motion of the sea like a dandled child. The drone of the Zodiac's motor came from far away, and beyond that she heard the murmur of *San Andres*'s engines; but where they drifted they seemed alone on the sea, and even the blue light strobing at her shoulder couldn't disturb the deep, comforting calm.

28

Unhitching

Two hours and many miles after the ships had gone to the bottom, Hammond heard the screech of a jet flying low above the sea. He stared back at their wake from the deck of the *San Andres*.

'Gotta be a search plane,' Carla said, standing beside him. 'Think it's one of ours?'

One of ours. Who exactly did Carla think 'us' might be? 'Probably American,' he said. 'Coast Guard had been standing by to escort the *Pontianak*. It's going to create some noise when they figure she sank. Navy'll put down subs.'

'And they'll find two broken ships and some intact casks. They'll bring 'em up whole, if they bring them up at all. But they might never open them.'

She was right, he realized. Navy, Coast Guard, DOE – they might never know the material was missing. 'They'll open them,' he said. 'There'll be an investigation.'

Carla laughed, a sound of genuine amusement. 'Maybe, maybe not. We're talking government plus military? Our job'll be long over before they even make a decision.'

He studied her out of the side of his eyes. She stood hands on hips, gazing out at the dark night, head tilted back. Like Peter Pan, he thought, cocky, happy Peter Pan with his shadow sewn back on. He'd never seen this side of her before; he'd seen her fierce and sullen, but fierce and joyful was in some ways more frightening to behold.

'Were the guys great,' she asked, 'or what? Did you ever think they'd shape up like this?'

'No,' he said, and he told the truth. All night he had been torn, wanting the plan to fail, but still rooting for it to succeed – rooting hard enough that he'd even sunk the *Pontianak* and rescued the barge. That ought to allay any suspicions about his commitment.

It'd been good, good to be on a team again, but now that team was dangerously close to carrying out a psychotic scheme. He couldn't wait any longer. At the first opportunity he'd blow the whistle – go public, call Homeland Security, call out the Marines. Whatever the hell Justice and the Bureau were thinking, it wasn't working.

'You were great, too,' she said.

'What's the schedule now?'

'Back to base camp; load the *Princess*; six hours' sack time, and then we sail for Panama.'

'We need to get McCann to a hospital. Maybe I can sail him down to Cabo . . .'

'No need. As soon as we get an all-clear from *Easy Angles*, I'm going to radio Richter that the goose has been plucked, and he'll meet us in Bahia San Andres with the chopper.'

'Richter? How come?'

'Mainly to bring us a captain – a real sailing master – to take us through Panama. Seems they're touchy about a bunch of nobodies bringing through big ships.' Carla smiled, and leaned towards him with a confiding tone. 'Second – and the guys don't know this yet – he's bringing a bonus. Fifteen grand for each of them, cash.'

'Cash? Where are they going to spend it?'

She shrugged. 'Probably aren't. But the smell of that much money, gratis, is something they deserve. Any case, Richter can fly McCann out first thing.'

He took a breath. This might be his last chance before Panama. 'I'd – I'd like to go along with him, if that's okay. Just to get him settled in.'

Carla stared at him. 'Why?' Then her expression softened. 'Oh. Right. They're your guys, really . . .'

'No.' He put his hand on her arm, and once again he felt as if there were two people living inside him, one who wanted to touch her to manipulate her, and one who just wanted to feel her skin under his fingertips. 'They're your men, Carla. Not mine.' He paused, and just as she opened her lips to speak, he added, 'Ray's got his weak points, but he's – well, he's practically my brother-in-law.'

She nodded, taking this in, and he watched her, because it could play all wrong, bringing up Earlene. 'See your point,' she said, and as far as he could tell there were no undercurrents – no resentment, no jealousy, just a reasonable assessment. 'Ride him up to LA or wherever, then. But make sure Richter choppers you back before we sail.'

It was what he wanted, but her reaction left him feeling oddly belittled. Didn't it mean anything to her? Didn't it hurt her a little that his heart belonged to another? Or that it seemed as if his heart belonged to another, or whatever the truth of the matter was?

Up until that night, he'd admired and pitied Carla Smukowski; but now it was as though she'd been promoted beyond any of his likes and dislikes, exalted above any judgement he could pass.

A little before noon the next day *Easy Angles* roused them on the radio. 'How's fishin'?' Madden asked.

Hammond picked up the mike, but passed it to Carla, and four of the men huddled round.

'Hey, *Easy*,' Carla said. 'Caught our limit and then some. We're heading home. Over.'

'Us, too. And about thirty shipwrecked sailors, if you can believe that. Dropped 'em off an hour ago with a northbound trawler, somebody in the Mexican Navy's looking for them, I guess.' Then, as an afterthought, he added, 'Over.'

'Must have been a real surprise. Where are you now? Over.'

'Few hours out of Cabo. Turn in our boat and then it's Margaritaville for us. Assume *San Andres* will pass through and pick us up before you go anywhere fun? Over.'

'You got that, *Angles*. And take it easy on the Margaritas, right? Drunks say stupid things, and all that crushed ice can give you a sinus headache.'

Madden signed off and the men surrounding Carla whooped, and it occurred to Hammond that they hadn't cheered the previous night; the night had been silent in respect for Gianetti and the two great ships that now sat on the floor of the Pacific.

'We should radio Simonsen and Slater, too,' Dodge said.

Carla stood and shook her head. 'Radio on the *Princess* doesn't work.' They stared at her in confusion. 'Loose lips sink ships. I trust all you guys – but not when you're so far away I can't listen in to your radio chatter.'

'No shit,' Kowinski said. 'Slater'd run up ten thousand bucks worth of phone-sex calls on the ship-to-shore.'

The men laughed, and someone else started in on Slater. Hammond listened while Carla donned a headset and called up a ship-to-shore operator somewhere in Baja. The number she rattled off had a 775 area code. When the call went through, she said, 'Champagne time', and then disconnected.

He raised his eyebrows. 'Richter?

Carla nodded, but was drawn out of the chair at the console by Lorrie tugging on her sleeve. Hammond slid after her through the circle of men.

'McCann's awake,' Lorrie said. 'Wants to see you guys.'

'How is he?' Hammond asked.

'I've straightened the leg, splinted it to death while he was asleep, but there's nothing to set.' Their expressions must have been uncomprehending. 'I got the swelling down enough to probe it an hour or two ago, and there's nothing there. Where his shinbone should be, it's like a bag of gravel. Crazy thing is, outside of that, it's not too bad. Blood flow seems okay . . . I'm no doctor, but I think he'll keep the leg.'

'How is he besides that?' Hammond asked.

'Had a real deep sleep. But doesn't want more morphine. Wants a heavy local instead.'

'So give it to him,' Carla said. 'C'mon, Boyce, let's go pay your almost-brother-in-law a visit.'

Lorrie stood the late watch with Kowinski and Skittle. They spelled each other at the helm; the sailing was all blue-water, and smooth enough, so the chief danger was monotony.

Kowinski had the wheel, and Lorrie stepped out onto the unlit deck to drink her coffee. Back by the stern, Skittle sat cross-legged, facing away from her. His posture seemed odd – his head was bowed, and his torso leaned forward.

Worried that he might be sick, Lorrie edged in his direction. From the side, she saw she'd been wrong. The man's eyes were closed, his lips moved silently, and his hands were clasped. He was praying.

She tried to back away, but her presence had somehow alerted him. He looked up, surprised, and then a little embarrassed.

'Sorry,' she said, and she was: praying, for her, was the most private of acts, and Christ himself had commanded that you should say your prayers in your closet, not making a spectacle of your piety.

'I was just—' He tossed his hand to the side. 'You know . . .'

Lorrie leaned her butt against the stern rail and looked down at him. 'Yeah, I do. I pray, too.' She offered him her coffee, and he reached up for it with both hands.

He drank, sighed and handed it back.

'Keep it,' she said.

He nodded his thanks.

'Something you want to talk about?' she asked.

349

A tired breath puffed out of his mouth. 'Nah. I'm just . . .'

She realized she was towering over him, and turned and sat down beside him on the deck. 'It's okay to talk.'

Skittle sipped the coffee, looking past the stern rail to the barge. 'I'm just not sure I'm cut out for this. And losing Gianetti like that . . .'

'Sure. Scary stuff.'

He sat silent for a long time. 'Not even that, not really. Everybody else here, I guess they're soldiers. I ain't.'

Pre-battle jitters? It seemed improbable – they were still ten thousand sea-miles from Mecca. 'Hey, Steve. We all get the heebie-jeebies when we know somebody might be shooting at us.'

'You don't get it, do you? Ain't that I'm scared of getting shot at. I just don't think I can kill anyone.' He paused. 'And look at that thing floating back there . . .'

'You probably won't have to kill anyone yourself.'

'Not sure I can stand by and let it happen, either.'

'You did okay with French,' she said.

'We didn't let him die, we—' He stopped short and she saw real fear rise in his eyes. 'I mean—'

'It's okay,' she said, 'you took him to a doctor. I know already.' She'd heard Hammond's story from Carla, back at Rancho Del Mar, when the two of them had made the decision to relocate to Baja.

'Not a doctor, really. A hospital or something, I guess. Hammond had me drop them off alongside the road.' Skittle's gaze darted all over her face, but refused to meet her eyes. 'How come you know? Hammond said none of the guys were supposed to know.'

'Carla and I both know, because he told us.' Skittle appeared to relax a bit. 'The hospital, though – how do you suppose he arranged that without the police coming in? Does he know some special place?'

Something in the man's face slammed shut. 'Something like that, I guess. I don't know.' He shook his head, and looked back to the barge towing behind them. 'Don't really know anything.'

Lorrie laid her hand on his arm, and he flinched. 'No big deal.' She left her hand there. 'Do you really want out of this?'

He nodded his head.

'No shame in that. We can send you back to the States before the *Princess* hits Panama. Of course, I doubt you'll get full pay . . .'

'I just want to go home.'

She patted his arm and clambered to her feet. 'That was the last of the pot Kowinski brewed. I'll go make some more coffee.'

In the narrow galley she started the coffee brewing, and leaned her head back against a cabinet. Something about Hammond wasn't right, and she kept coming back to that feeling. She'd often felt that he was trying to impede the operation; before French was unmasked, she even wondered if he might be the mole. But everything pointed to French – not an agent, just a low-level player who'd been roped into it by pressure from the ATF.

Why had Hammond let the guy live, and yet gone to all this trouble to keep it a big secret? Certainly not because Hammond was ATF; if he were, all he would have needed to do was drop French off with his handlers and then lead the cavalry in and arrest everybody. So Hammond wasn't some sort of cop . . .

Too many little things, too many inconsistencies. The ultralights, those were his idea; but back at Atwater's lodge, he tried to keep them from targeting the *Pontianak*, tried to steer their interest away from the Indonesian shipment. His on-again, off-again thing with Carla. Fiddling with the radio on the bridge of the *Princess Mishail*, having no more than the weak excuse of searching for a weather report.

And then the night they took the *Pontianak* – for a time she'd been sure he wanted the mission to fail, and then he saved it – saved it by risking his own life.

He didn't want the mission to fail, at least not the capture of the hot goods – he'd proved that. But she knew in her gut he wasn't on the same team she'd signed onto; the man had some other agenda.

The coffee-maker beeped, and she poured out two cups: Kowinski'd need an eye-opener after so long at the wheel. She wished she could talk to someone about Hammond, but he'd become a big blind spot with Carla. When they'd fished them out of the ocean on the night of the big raid, floating with their arms around one another, Carla's expression said she might as well have had a baby on her tit.

She clicked plastic sipping lids atop the cups and made her way out of the galley. As she passed, she glanced at the door to the cabin where Hammond slept.

I don't know what your game is, or why, Boyce Hammond. But my eye's on you now. Always on you.

29

Docking

Just before two in the afternoon they raised Bahia San Andres on the horizon. The *San Andres* was a luxurious boat, but she'd been planned to sleep six, not ten, and Hammond was thoroughly sick of it. The men, though in good humour, were starting to show signs of restlessness, too, and he assumed that was why Carla had set them half a dozen tasks: washing down the gear in fresh water from the desalinator, stripping and cleaning all the weapons and doing an inventory.

The cask in the barge behind them had been covered with netting and burlap, and now the rebreathers, wetsuits and rad-cloaks were spread on top of it, drying in the blaze of the Baja sun. It was as orderly as could be, but to Hammond's eye it looked as though they were towing a small garbage scow; there is no way for a wetsuit to look graceful.

He went into McCann's cabin, where the big man was edging off his bunk onto the stretcher they'd set up alongside. 'How you doing?' Hammond asked.

'Can't get to the head by myself, and when I'm in it I can't shut the door because of this splint. That's how I'm doing.'

'We'll have you in a top-class hospital by this evening. You need a hand?'

'No.' The legs of the stretcher left it four inches below the level of the mattress, and when McCann's butt hit the canvas, he winced. 'It's gonna take a while, getting the *Princess* all the way to Arabia or whatever, right? Weeks.'

'More like a month.'

'Right. So, I want to come.'

'Ray, you'll get paid your full end either way.'

'I want to come.'

He bent down and squeezed McCann's shoulder. 'I'll see what we can do.'

At the helm, Lorrie was bringing them into the bay, fighting the strong ebb current that set in right after high tide. As usual, the sharks were heading out of the bay as the tide turned, and their sleek shadows glided beneath the ship.

Hammond studied the camp through the front windows. Everything just as when they had left it. Well, what had he expected, that the lawn would be overgrown?

No, one feature was different. The big Sikorsky sat fifty yards inland from the pier. He smiled. His ride home had arrived.

Lorrie gave two tugs on the air-horn, paused and then repeated it.

Three huge groans echoed across the bay from the *Princess Mishail*, and the men cheered, but in the emptiness of Baja, Hammond thought their voices sounded thin and small.

*

'Hey, goddammit,' Carla shouted up to the men on deck, 'what is this, a Brownie troop? Gear and guns go with you when you land.'

Hammond waited for her to grab her end of the stretcher before hoisting his own. The *San Andres* gave one last lurch as the crew tied her up to the pier, and they both stumbled.

'Easy, there,' McCann said. 'You guys sure you can do this?'

'Fuck you, Ray,' Carla said, in the tone most people reserve for *how's it going?*

With the tide at this height, the deck of the San Andres sat four feet below the level of the pier. The men were all up on the pier now, and he and Carla lifted the stretcher onto the top of two chests that had been positioned in the middle of the deck.

Carla whistled. 'Jones, Dodge. C'mon, we're rusting away down here.'

She nodded at him, and Hammond mirrored her moves as she squatted down and situated her shoulders under the handles. 'Lift,' she said with a grunt, and they stood in unison.

They were docked at the north tip of the pier, with the *Princess Mishail* tied up along the top of the T, and the cargo ship's blunt prow towered over them. Big Jones and Dodge towered over them, too, where they hunched down on the edge of the pier to help hoist McCann's stretcher from the yacht.

He saw it before he heard it – a row of men at the railing of the *Princess*, a row of unkempt men, a row of unkempt men with guns. They were already firing before his ears registered the sound.

Carla jerked her head to port, away from the pier, and shouted something he couldn't hear over the roar of the gunfire, but her intention was clear, and he ran for the opposite rail. Dodge flew off the pier, over the stretcher, and Hammond stumbled across his body and crashed into the rail. McCann's stretcher catapulted off his shoulders and into the sea, and Hammond hurled himself after it.

Hammond fought to the surface. The bursts of fire from automatic weapons still rained down on the pier. McCann had a grip on the little port-side haul-out ladder, and Carla trod water beside him. 'Arabs,' she said, panting for breath.

The firing slowed and stopped, and he heard a moan from far away. It was silenced by another burst of fire. Hammond felt as though he were fighting to stay afloat, as though something were dragging him under.

'Get your boots off,' she said. He struggled to get at them, and Carla pushed his shoulder to get his attention and held out her knife. 'Cut the laces.' He sawed through one set, and the moment he kicked off that boot his panic subsided.

Carla edged up beside McCann. 'Scoot,' she ordered, and he floated off to the side of the ladder, keeping a one-handed grip on the lowest rung. She grabbed a rung level with the deck and pulled herself up, popping her head above the deck for just a moment to peer under the rail. 'Dodge bought it,' she said.

This wasn't news. 'Carla, we need to start swimming—' Hammond began.

'They'll kill us in the water,' she said. 'Now shut up and

help. When I get hold of his body, you drag on my legs, got it?'

She didn't wait for confirmation. She vaulted up the ladder and under the lowest rail, bending at the waist so that her hips and legs draped down the yacht's hull.

'Hammond!'

He lunged up, hugged her legs in his arms and dropped down, dragging her with all his weight until she came free and they sank into the water together. Under the water he heard more gunfire, muted and transformed, a far-off roar coupled with thuds when the rounds punched into the boat beside him.

Carla kicked free of his arms and he surfaced beside her. Dodge's body had been dragged under the rails so that his arms and torso, and what was left of his head, draped down the side of the boat. Carla hoisted herself up the short ladder, crouching, and undid his holster-snap, working out his Colt automatic.

She eased herself back into the water, keeping the pistol above her head. 'Think he dropped his weapon baggie on the pier.' She looked at Hammond. 'Listen. They're going to come down here after us. You've got to get a set of the rebreathers off the barge. Three if you can. Get back there and wait until I make my move. I'll give 'em something to think about.' She looked at McCann. 'You okay? Can you hold on here?'

'Jesus, Smukowski. I broke my leg, not my hands.'

'Then let's move.'

She swam aft in a strong sidestroke, around *San Andres*'s stern, keeping her gun hand clear of the water. Hammond followed until she reached the cable that towed the barge. It was taut, dripping. She hung from it with her free hand and nodded back towards the barge. Hammond slipped off in that direction, stirring the water as little as possible, and he saw Carla head under the pier.

When the *San Andres* kissed the pier, Lorrie was the first out of the yacht. A small, manual cargo derrick sat at the end of the pier; her first order of business would be to lower its cable and hook the handle of the cask-lid on the barge below. She wouldn't lift the cask – the derrick wasn't big enough – but it would serve as an anchor for the barge until they could deploy the main cargo winch on the *Princess Mishail*.

Behind her she heard the men piling onto the planks of the pier. Where the hell was the Bahia crowd, anyway? She'd seen the Sikorsky, and she'd expected Richter to be down there to welcome them home. And Simonsen and Slater – well, orders had them staying aboard the *Princess*, but she'd expected them to be lining the rails, cheering.

A glance up at the prow of the *Princess*. No one.

When she reached the cargo winch, she dropped her gear and edged round to the seaward side. Piss-poor mounting job – barely enough room to walk round the outside perimeter.

Lorrie hunkered down by the big bell-mount that bolted the winch to the pier and began undoing the hook from where it was stowed on its holdfast.

A thunderstorm of gunfire broke out from above.

She dropped to her knees and took cover behind the winch.

Down the pier she saw Big Jones take a solid dozen and

go down, while Dodge was blasted over the edge and down into the *San Andres*. Further towards shore, Alvorsen and Skittle went into the water, probably hit.

There were men lining the prow of the *Princess* – Arabs, from the look of them – raking the pier with automatic weapons.

She groped one arm past the bell-mount, trying to reach her gear bag. Bullets chewed up the planking and whined off the steel of the winch. Lorrie found she'd snatched her arm back without realizing it.

Her fingers felt for her sidearm, undid the holster and pulled it out. They shook as she clicked the safety, and she tried to even out her breath and think. What had gone wrong, and how?

Easing her head to the side, she stole a glance at the prow of the *Princess*, and another burst of gunfire rained down.

Richter. It had to be. These guys must have been ferried in on the Sikorsky.

She'd kill him. She'd kill all of them if she lived long enough, if she had enough ammo; but she promised herself she'd find Richter.

There was silence. After she finished undoing the hook from the holdfast, she started feeding out cable, letting it dangle off the pier behind her. At least this way she might have a chance of keeping her weapon dry. Then she'd swim to the *San Andres*, grab an MP5. With luck, she might even be able to unmoor her, and make a run for the ocean, with the barge still in tow . . .

She glanced down to make sure the cable reached the surface of the water, and she saw motion.

Hammond, swimming up alongside the barge, moving as silently as he could.

That was his secret, that explained it all. Richter and Hammond, together on this from the start.

And conveniently enough he'd put himself between her and the *San Andres*.

Her fingers twisted the ratchet, locking the winch. She spun on her butt, wrapped her legs round the cable and started climbing down toward the water.

Hammond hesitated at the corner of the barge. Where the hell were the rebreathers? Lined up along the front, if he recalled. If he hoisted himself up there, was the cask high enough to shield him from the gunmen on the prow of the *Princess*?

No way to tell. The gunwale of the barge rode about three feet above the water. He edged around until the barge was between him and the *Princess*, then pulled himself up until he could peer over. The rebreathers were all in front, too far to reach without exposing himself.

A burst of gunfire rang out from the ship and he dropped back into the water as chips of wood flew from the corner of the gunwale. The cask itself gave off a low ringing sound as a few rounds hit it. He heard angry voices and the gunfire stopped.

Were they afraid of injuring the cask? Preposterous. It was designed to withstand collisions with a locomotive. But maybe they didn't know that.

He heard footsteps running on the pier, and he edged back to the corner of the barge and peered through the wide gap between the front of the barge and the stern of the *San Andres*. He didn't see Carla, but he saw Big Jones crumpled at the edge of the pier decking, and beyond the man's body, four men in fatigues hustled in his direction, each cradling something squat and nasty.

Uzis? Arabs with Israeli machine guns? In another situation, it might have been funny.

The man on point stopped five feet short of the edge of the pier and held up his hand to halt his followers. He rattled off something in Arabic, pointing at the barge, and just as the men were moving to obey, Hammond heard the boom of Carla's Colt echoing from beneath the pier.

The point man clutched at his groin and fell to his knees. Hammond hoisted himself over the gunwale and hurled himself down behind the cask. There were more shots, and a burst of automatic fire from the pier, but he lunged round to the front of the barge on his knees, gathered up an armful of rebreathers, tanks and vests all jumbled together, and then threw himself flat on his back and pushed his way behind the cask just as bullets began to zing by. Any resistance they'd had to shooting near the cask had been overcome.

There was silence. How many had he grabbed? Including the one he had only by its strap, four. Three was plenty. Maybe more than plenty. Was Carla still alive? Or would it be just him and McCann?

He'd have to roll out of the barge into the water, one smooth move . . . wait. No wetsuit. With the weight of the tanks, he'd go straight to the bottom.

He remembered his first flight instructor telling him about crashes, in that Chuck Yeager drawl: There's always more time than you think. Yeah, you may well crash, but why be in a hell-fire hurry to do it?

Okay. Drop it all, roll on your side, pull one of them on. Find the buckle, find the damned buckle. Good. Open the feed valve and bleed out some gas. Now. Pump up the BCD, baby's own little lifejacket. Put the mouthpiece in. Can you breathe? Good . . .

Okay, hook two of them over your left arm by the shoulder straps. All the time in the world . . .

A dripping figure hoisted itself out of the water at the far end of the barge and rolled onto its knees in the shelter of the cask, about six feet away.

Lorrie. She'd made it. He waved for her to come over, jerked one thumb in the direction of the *San Andres*. Then he realized she had a pistol pointed at him. Her black Latina eyes glinted. She manoeuvred into a crouch and duckwalked towards him until the gun was only two feet from his face.

'Got you,' she said. 'You, and then your pal Richter.'

He spat out the mouthpiece. 'Lorrie, I don't know what crazy idea you've got—'

'Don't bother.' She lifted the pistol another two inches so that it pointed at his forehead.

A shot boomed out. Lorrie's arms flew up and she spun backwards and into the water. Hammond glanced over his shoulder. Carla supported herself in the water, with one hand on a fender at the stern of the *San Andres*. Her other hand still aimed the Colt.

Automatic fire raked down from the *Princess*. Hammond stuffed the mouthpiece between his teeth and squatted on his toes.

He rolled over the gunwale head-first into the water and instantly lost his orientation. The units on his left arm rolled him sideways and, with no mask, the underwater world was a blur. He concentrated on breathing while keeping his nostrils shut.

He was sinking. Slowly, but he was sinking. He began to fight his way back to the surface, and then mastered his instincts. Inflate the BCD a little. He gave the trigger a squeeze and his descent steadied and then stopped.

He saw what had to be the shadow of the *San Andres* and made for it. Carla and McCann were hanging from the haul-out ladder when he kicked hard and surfaced between them. He spat out his mouthpiece and gasped for breath as though he hadn't had a rebreather on.

Carla's face had the expressionless look he'd seen on trauma victims in the early stages of shock. 'What was that?' she asked.

'I don't know. She decided this is Richter's deal, and that I was his partner.' The way she studied his face made him add, 'She's probably right about Richter. She's wrong about me.'

Carla swallowed and stared at him. 'Don't make me sorry about the decision I made.'

Hammond wasn't sure he could guarantee that, but he nodded.

She exhaled. 'Killed three. Fourth one didn't like being shot at from beneath and took off – guess he wanted to arrive in Paradise with his balls intact.' She studied their faces in turn. 'McCann, you still keep your rifle in the adobes by the shooting range?'

'Wasn't gonna take it to *sea*,' he said, as though she'd trodden close to blasphemy.

'Okay. Listen up. No air in the BCDs. Go ahead and sink, but head towards shore while you do it – might be too deep here for pure oxygen. Try to find fifteen, twenty feet. Get on the bottom, walk on your fingers. When I catch up with you, follow me.'

'Where are you going?' Hammond asked.

'Unhitching the barge. Just to give them something to think about.'

There was a noise from the pier – footsteps? Hammond made sure McCann was buckled into his rebreather, and then did as Carla had ordered.

30

Faith and the sea

Lorrie had been hurt before, in training and combat both, but she'd never been shot, and she needed time to puzzle it out. There'd been a terrific force. She'd fallen into the water and floated on her back. There might have been some time where she wasn't fully conscious.

She tried to waggle her fingers. Her right hand felt nothing: it might as well have disappeared. The gun must be gone too, then.

All the parts of her body checked in except for her right arm. She turned her head in that direction and saw redness flooding out into the seawater.

Her left hand felt her right elbow, the biceps, up onto the triceps . . .

The pain came like a hammerfall. With teeth clenched, she reached for her upper arm and shoulder again. This time she was prepared for the agony. She probed and hefted. The triceps were torn, and something was wrong with the bone in the shoulder. Not good: shoulders were complicated.

Could be worse. Carla was good with sidearms; if she'd

wanted her dead, the wound would have been in the chest or head. The fact that Carla had shot her hurt more than her shoulder.

She tilted her feet down and trod water, her right arm useless and her left working double-time. Shore was distant. The current had already carried her well out into the bay.

Using her good hand to cut the water like a paddle, she turned to look back at the pier, and what she saw made her shake her head to clear it. The barge and rad-cask were drifting along behind her, not twenty yards away. She rolled to the left and began a hard sidestroke. There was no chance she'd make headway against the relentless ebb current; but if she could slow her motion, the barge would come to her.

With her back leaned against the cask, Lorrie used her teeth and left hand to tighten her belt round her right shoulder. After she cleaned the wound she pulled out her pocketknife and improvised a dressing from her blouse and a square carved from one of the wetsuits. The nerves in her shoulder cried out, but she found that her fingers still moved. Stunned, hurt, but not crippled.

The sound of a motor came from the direction of the pier. Lorrie scooted herself to the side and glanced round the cask. A launch from the *Princess* was pursuing the barge. Three men, from what she could see, and the posture of two of them showed that they cradled Uzis.

She scanned the barge for anything she might use as a weapon. Netting, dive gear . . . nothing lethal, not against three armed men, not with her arm out of commission.

Time for a tactical retreat. Lorrie struggled into a wetsuit, one thankfully several sizes too large, though she didn't even attempt to pull on the right sleeve. That would do for buoyancy. She pulled on swim fins and lowered herself into the water with the barge between her and the motor launch. Even with fins, the current was too strong to angle herself towards shore.

Faith, Michael whispered, *you can't fight the ocean*. Her own intuition, an angel or some manner of muse – whatever the source, it was sound advice.

Staying low in the water she flutter-kicked along with the current. Not far ahead, waves broke against the outer lip of the reef, and she knew that in a matter of minutes she'd be in the open ocean.

So be it. Perhaps she could come ashore down the coast.

As she rounded the tip of the reef, she saw shapes in the water below her. With sudden forceful writhes of their bodies, like salmon fighting their way upstream, the sharks were battling the current to swim back into the bay.

31

The firing range

They hauled themselves out of the water near the end of the Great Wall, where the long stone outcrop disappeared beneath the sand of the beach. Carla signalled them by example to ditch their gear in the shallows, in case they might need it again.

The buzz of a motor launch came from far behind her. The barge and cask were in the middle of the bay, riding out on the ebbing current, and one of the *Princess Mishail*'s lifeboats was in pursuit.

The pier stood nearly a thousand yards to their right, off to the south. She and Hammond helped McCann up onto his good leg, let him drape his arms over their shoulders and they half-ran, half-hobbled towards the shelter of the big stone dyke that ran across the north edge of the valley.

Maybe some of the others had escaped that initial shower of bullets, Carla told herself. Maybe. Big Jones and Dodge were gone, and she'd seen another body through the gaps in the planking of the pier before she'd begun shooting.

Simonson and Slater had probably been killed when the *Princess* was first taken. But still . . .

No. All dead. She had to assume they were all gone, that the two men beside her were the only survivors. Her eyes stung from the salt, and the sand burned her feet right through her socks. She still had Dodge's Colt stuffed into her back pocket, the weight tugging her wet pants down on the right. No ammo for it and scant chance of finding any, even if the pistol would still fire after that long swim.

Stop feeling sorry for yourself, stop feeling sorry for anybody. *Kill your enemies first*, Jill's voice said, *mourn your friends later*.

They had a dozen yards to go when gunfire broke out from the pier, and she and Hammond broke into a crouched run, dragging McCann along. They collapsed onto the sand behind the first rocks and then dragged themselves another ten feet. Carla and Hammond leaned back against the slope, gasping for breath, while McCann, wincing, rolled himself onto his back.

'What the hell's the hurry?' McCann asked. 'This distance? With an Uzi?'

Carla thought of telling him that there was always the chance of a lucky shot, sprayed high, of telling him that the gunmen might have rifles as well as Uzis, of telling him to shut the fuck up. Instead, she leaned forward and looked inland. A couple of hundred yards to where the path headed up to the cave. Fifty yards further to the old adobes beside the target range. She gathered her breath. 'Okay. We go together, as fast as we can, to the cave path. You guys get as close to the cave as you can while keeping out of sight. I'll get McCann's rifle, and cover you while you get in.'

'We should all head for the adobes,' Hammond said. 'We could—'

'Yeah, great, low ground, where they can encircle us and shoot down. This isn't a debate, flyboy.'

'What makes you so sure they'll come after us?' McCann asked.

'You guys think Richter will leave us here alive? Let's go.'

Instead of responding with the expected argument, Hammond gave a sharp nod and rolled into a crouch, ready to move.

McCann did what he could, hobbling and hopping and allowing himself to be dragged. The sweat burst from Carla's pores and immediately vanished into the dry air. If this were a siege, she thought, they could finish us in a day from lack of water.

But it wouldn't be that long. At any moment she half-expected gunmen to appear atop the long dyke. Would they demand surrender, or shoot first? The stones underfoot were cruel, and she blessed the fact she'd left her socks on. She reminded herself that Hammond and McCann must be in just as much pain – more, even, since they both outweighed her, and McCann was taking most of his punishment on just one foot.

They reached the bottom of the cave path where it switch-backed up into the boulders. They fell to their knees there and panted. Carla's tongue seemed to have wrinkled into leather, and she couldn't summon enough moisture to wet it again. She managed to gasp out the single word 'Go!' and then struggled to her feet.

Dehydrated and short of breath, but light now without McCann's bulk weighing on her shoulder – and she remembered the time Jill had them train on the obstacle course with ten-pound bags of sand on each calf, a whole week like that. She'd cursed the woman every night from her bunk, wished her every form of cancer known, but on the day they dropped the bags and ran, it was like flying, a feeling so good and so fine it almost hurt.

She slammed up against the wall of the first adobe, sucking air. She stumbled round to the doorway. This was it. What she thought of as McCann's personal stash was stacked against the back wall, atop what must have once been a crude oven, but now looked like an altar.

Ancient altars to Ares, the God of War, were always five-sided, Jill had told her once . . . and then, when Carla had nodded but shown no comprehension, Jill had added, *you know, like the Pentagon?*

Who'd designed the Pentagon, anyway, and why was it that shape? She'd always meant to look it up . . .

She staggered to McCann's altar and dropped to her knees. The rifle was wrapped in oilcloth, with chamois underneath that, and when she peeled both away she understood his love for it, because it was the most beautiful, most perfect thing she'd ever seen in her life.

No magazine in. Standard four-shot magazines, three of them stacked on the table. She grabbed a box of 30.06 shells, dumped it onto the altar. She needed to be calm. She needed to hurry.

She pulled the op handle back until it seated under the magazine followers, and then eased one long cartridge through the ejection port and into the chamber. She slapped the bolt forward to close the action, and felt better.

The first magazine she grabbed was full, thank God, and she slipped it into place and latched it down. The other two magazines were full, she could tell from their heft, and she stuffed them into her shirt pocket. She snagged an extra box of cartridges and worked it into the back pocket of her pants.

She ran the dozen feet to the base of the Great Wall and then started scrambling up the crumbly slope. Wouldn't it be funny, she thought, if they didn't bother to come after all?

When she got down on her belly and crawled the last few feet to peek over, she knew she didn't have to worry about that. There were six of them, spread well apart, and straggled forward and back. She nodded in appreciation – these guys at least had a little bit of training. A hundred feet away, easy work with a scope.

She moved the rifle up and thumbed off the safety. You're trembly, she told herself, what kind of shit is this? Catch your breath, pick your target. Like the men atop Breed's Hill, wait until you see the whites of their eyes.

The advancing men seemed damn near interchangeable, and once again Carla wondered why some Arab men grew beards at all if the best they could manage was that Yasser Arafat scrubble. But one, the third from the left, had a grenade launcher, and that, to Carla, was like volunteering to be shot.

She centred the crosshairs on his chest. Squeeze, don't pull.

A 30.06 is designed to stop grizzlies, so when the round punched his diaphragm he flew off his feet. Carla didn't wait to see him hit the ground, but instead whipped the rifle left. The next candidate in line had already hurled himself towards the ground, but the second was looking open-mouthed towards the man she'd just shot, and it was almost apologetically that Carla blasted him in the stomach.

She pulled her eye from the scope. Angry cries echoed from the *Princess*. Look out to the bay, she saw that the motor launch had retrieved the barge and was towing it back towards the pier.

She glanced over her shoulder, and saw Hammond and McCann belly-crawling into the cave.

The remaining four men on the plain before her had sought cover, and – as always – it showed that humans could find shelter anywhere, hollows in what seemed at first flat as a tabletop. Yet she could still see where they were, and she might be able to pick them off, especially the one on the far right, who sought to hide his whole body behind a ridge of sand no higher than his head.

She might be able to kill them all. But if she didn't, if they somehow got to her first, Hammond and McCann would be up in the cave with no weapon.

One more. One more shot. That would leave the rifle loaded with two rounds.

She almost felt sorry for the man, trying to flatten out where there was no real cover. But, if it had been her, she would never have tried something that pathetic, right? Maybe for a moment, but by now she would have made a move. Right?

She took him where his neck joined his shoulder, just as she'd intended. She didn't mean for him to suffer. She meant him to be dead.

She scooted back down the slope and ran behind the shelter of the Wall for the cave path. When she struck it she thumbed on the rifle's safety and crouched down to head uphill, scrambling on elbows and knees where the boulders shrank to scree. On the fourth switchback she reached the lip of the tailings that formed the landing. Must have scratched the hell out of McCann's rifle stock, she thought, crawling like that.

She couldn't see without raising her head, and she wondered what that would be like – to lift your head like a prairie dog and have a bullet smack into it. Would you remember? Would you know you'd died? *Keep your fantasies for when you climb into your bunks, girls*, Jill said. *Don't need no imaginations on the battlefield.*

Carla prepared herself to take a look, and then changed her mind. She already knew they were in the cave, somewhere.

And even in your bunks, Jill had added, *one hand for yourself, ladies, but your best hand on your weapon.*

She bobbed up and skidded the rifle across the landing, right between Hammond's and McCann's shocked faces where they lay prone on the floor of the cave. There was a cascade of Uzi fire and one long whine as she dropped into the rocks. Somebody down there had a real rifle.

'Carla?' It was McCann's voice.

'Yeah?'

'You got loaded magazines?'

'Yeah.'

'Toss me one. Come home on four.'

She dug into her shirt pocket and found a magazine, small yet weighty with its cargo of lead. She lobbed it up in an arc and heard it thud into the dirt, somewhere.

The air stood still enough that she heard him unlock the current magazine and latch in the one she'd thrown. 'Carla?' McCann asked.

'Uh-huh?'

'Wait for it . . .'

She did. Forever. The Baja sun pummelled her like a pair of big, padded fists, and even though she'd been underwater twenty minutes before, her clothes were already so dry that her panties seemed to be sucking moisture down out of her body, sealing her shut. Far off, she heard the sound of a motor down on the bay.

After church back home, she'd often climbed into the car before her parents were finished chatting with the pastor after the service. No one locked their cars in Burns, Oregon, in those days, and in the summer the heat had seemed intolerable with all the windows rolled up, yet an immense lassitude had always seized her – no, not seized her, but rather cradled her – and if Kevin hadn't always piled into the car a few minutes later and cranked down the windows, she might have gone on forever, let those goose-down, pillowy heat-laden arms carry her off to wherever they were bound; and she heard Kevin's voice crack out of the recoil of the 30.06 and all her muscles tightened, ready for action, and her body clenched with each crash: four, McCann had told her, and her body counted, sphincter to jaw, on every shot, *two, three,* a long pause, and then *four*, and she launched herself across the dusty tailings and dragged herself into the mouth of the cave.

She luxuriated in the caress of the shade, the cool, soothing shade, but something in her, some part of her poised and waiting, needed to count *five*, and *five* never came.

Someone lifted her into a seated position. God, it felt good to be held. 'Where's five?' she asked, but her voice came out as a croak that didn't even make sense in her own ears. She swallowed, wet her lips and asked, 'Where's five?'

Hammond. Oh, the weekends she could imagine with him.

One hand for yourself, ladies, but your best hand on your weapon.

Okay, okay. She spilled out of his arms and pulled herself forward on her elbows until she lay beside McCann. 'How we doin'?' she asked.

'Good, so far. But their boat already hauled the cask back to the pier, and now it's headed our way, packed with guys. Gonna land down there where we can't see it without crawling outdoors, sneak up under the Wall.' McCann laid his rifle down and patted it. 'I popped one good. Not much compared to the three you bagged.'

'I was closer than you are.'

'Whatever. I dropped the clip you came in with, fired four. That leaves two in the first clip, one in the chamber, so we've got three shots. 'Less you brought more, of course.'

She groped into her shirt pocket and slammed down two magazines between them. McCann grunted in surprise and exchanged magazines. Carla dug into her back pocket and struggled until she pulled out the full box of cartridges. 'This is all we got,' she said. 'Didn't have time to stop at the store.'

'Oh.' McCann's beefy hand wrapped over the box of cartridges. 'Oh, Jesus, Carla. Marry me.'

'Thought you had a wife, Ray.'

'Everybody makes mistakes.' She heard him pushing cartridges back into magazines, filling them out. 'Hell, this much ammo,' he said, 'we can kill 'em all.'

From the other side of McCann, she heard Hammond's voice. 'I make 'em fifteen, twenty.'

'Is that *with* the ones I nailed,' she asked, 'or after?'

'After. You got three on the pier, three down below. McCann popped one.'

'Hey,' McCann said, 'I ain't hardly had a chance.'

'Plus, there's Richter and whoever the pilot is. Chazz, maybe.'

'You've *seen* Richter?' Carla asked.

'Check it out. Down by the chopper.'

She squinted into the bright sunlight. Hard to be certain at this distance. Three figures alongside the big Sikorsky. One long-limbed and loose in a blazing white suit, fabric that might have been cream-coloured in any illumination less intense.

'I buy it,' she said.

'Probably in range,' McCann said, 'want me to nail him?'

'Blow his fucking head off,' Carla said.

'Wait!' Hammond said. 'We don't know what's happening here yet.'

'What the fuck do you need to know, Boyce? We're in a hole, he's walking around down there—'

'Carla. Don't be such a hothead.' She heard him making an effort not to say what came next. 'Why the hell do you think you got cashiered in the first place?'

That hit her like a physical blow. What did Boyce know about it? Was he one of Richter's pals after all?

'People sneaking up behind the Wall, I think,' McCann said.

Then there was an amplified voice, booming out across the valley of Bahia San Andres, and she knew that voice at once. He must have patched into a loudspeaker on the 'copter. '*Cah-lah*,' Richter said, 'there's no ill will. These boys here are going to be sailing off soon. We've already taken you down. We don't need any more fight. You can even share in the profits . . .'

'Kill the fucker,' Carla said.

McCann squeezed off a round, its report loud in the cave, and they heard it whine across the valley. Richter and the two men beside him flinched, and then backed up next to the body of the 'copter. 'Breeze is stronger than I thought,' McCann said.

'More than a thousand yards . . .' Carla said.

'A thousand I woulda had him. I make this twelve, thirteen hundred.'

'Watch the Wall,' she said.

A man stood, aiming a shoulder-launched grenade into the cave. Carla had barely opened her mouth before McCann said, 'Got him.' The boom followed in seconds, and the man hurtled downslope as though he'd jumped backwards with all his might. 'I make that eight,' McCann said, 'we're almost even.'

'We wouldn't be even,' Carla said, 'unless we killed a thousand of them.'

The grenade tip of the launcher came peeking over the edge of the Great Wall.

'Watch it,' Hammond said, 'somebody else adopted his theory.'

'He can't do squat from that angle,' McCann said. 'Let him poke up long enough to aim at us, and—'

The grenade swooshed through the air, its trajectory far above the cave, and McCann said, 'Oh, shit!'

The face of the mountain above them roared down and buried the mouth of the cave in dust and darkness and ruin.

32

Like princes

In the first few moments, when dirt and rock piled onto his prone body, Hammond thought the cave-in might never stop. His head and shoulders were buried under what felt like a thousand pounds of earth, but as he fought to extricate himself he discovered that most of his body was already free. By dragging his lower body up onto its haunches and wriggling and pushing with arms and shoulders, he hauled himself from the crumbly soil and sat back, coughing the dirt from his mouth and nostrils. He wiped his eyes, but still they saw only blackness.

The coughing did little good, since on every inhale he sucked in more of the dust that must have filled the cave, but between his own bouts of hacking he heard McCann and Carla doing the same.

'Everyone intact?' he asked.

'Alive,' Carla said.

McCann made a choking sound and then spat. 'We got two full magazines, rifle has one in the chamber and two in line. Think I lost the box of cartridges, though, so there'd better not be more than eleven bad guys.'

Hammond almost laughed. They were buried alive, and the man had a cartridge count.

'Okay,' Carla said. 'Dead air for a few minutes, in case someone comes to check.'

'Do you think they care that much, as long as we're out of the way?'

'I don't know. So be quiet.'

He tried to even his breathing and relax. The absolute darkness magnified every sound, and he could hear the rumble of McCann's inhales, and the tiny, involuntary movements each of their bodies made against the dirt floor. As the minutes passed, he felt a panicky disorientation, as though he had lost all memory of the shape of the cave, even of the shape of his own body. He felt, more than heard, a few tumbling rocks out on the hillside – possibly someone investigating, but just as likely rubble seeking repose.

At last he heard Carla clear her throat. 'Back away from this crap, McCann. Maybe ten, twelve feet.'

'Don't wait on me,' McCann said, 'with the leg it's slow.' Hammond heard the sounds of the man hitching his way back along the floor of the cave, belly down. 'And, Carla?'

'Yeah?'

'My apologies. I used to laugh at all those trench crawls you made us do. But, shit – crawling's all I've done today.'

The uneven, unpredictable sounds of earth falling in rivulets came, punctuated by Carla's grunts of effort. Hammond stretched his arms and legs, the friction against the rough floor restoring his sense of place and proportion. 'Carla,' he asked, 'shouldn't we have some sort of plan?'

'If you know what's going on out there –' Carla stopped, groaned with effort, and something large rolled away, '– I'd love to hear details.'

This frantic activity on Carla's part struck him as the action of a coyote gnawing at its own leg, but he was damned if he had a good alternative. 'We can't just randomly dig at this. We might make it collapse even more.'

'Uh-*huh*.' The effort of digging seemed to emphasize individual syllables of her speech, with little cascades of debris after each accent. 'You got a *plan*? Or maybe you can *just* . . . call 911. When you're done wringing your *fuck*ing hands, maybe you could find a minute to help.'

She was right. Death might be awaiting them outside, or death might appear in the collapse of a ton of dirt onto the three of them, or death might sidle in and cosy up, a companionable arm draped over their shoulders, as dehydration took them, but death's lipless smile grinned at them from every path he could imagine.

When in doubt, take orders. He crawled over towards the sounds of Carla's labours, patting his way along the rubble-strewn floor. He stood on his knees shoulder-to-shoulder with her, reached forward and began to dig.

It might have been fifteen minutes before they had their first hint of light; it might have been an hour. Hammond had been picturing it in his mind as they scrabbled and heaved, and he imagined a small ray of light, like a beam that might shine through a nailhole in a board; but when it came at last it was a tan glow, diffused through a thousand particles of soil.

Carla dug her hands into the centre of that glow and clawed away the soil, and then a ray of light did burst through, a big, fist-sized shaft of Baja sunlight, and Hammond saw Carla's bleeding fingers and broken nails.

They worked faster then, despite the crumbling ceiling of the tunnel they had dug, and at last Carla used her shoulders like a plough, burrowing them in to push the dirt away as Hammond crouched behind her, ready to pull her from the unstable soil. Her shoulders punched through the far side, and Hammond watched her keep on going, working her hips through the channel she'd made, until she slipped out entirely.

A pause, and then her face peered back at him. 'They're making ready to leave, I think. We have to hurry.'

She began to heave more dirt away, widening the tunnel and, without really being sure why, Hammond set to work again. It went fast now, and when it was wide enough Carla said, 'Help McCann. Get him into the tunnel with the rifle.'

McCann didn't need help, as it turned out, and Hammond scrambled out onto the landing ahead of him and knelt there.

The barge and cask were nowhere to be seen, and the deck of the *Princess Mishail* was busy. The Arabs seemed to have gathered up their own dead from the plain, but one body still lay sprawled on the pier. By the 'copter, Richter shook hands with a man and then turned to board the chopper's steps.

'You see him, Ray?' Carla asked.

'Yeah. No, shit, he's getting in already . . .'

'He flies in the co-pilot seat most of the time. Take him out anyway.'

'No!' Hammond said. 'Go for the pilot, before they take off.' When neither of his companions reacted, he said, 'We need the chopper. Richter can't fly it.'

'He's right,' Carla said. 'Do it.'

The props had already started whopping their way in circles, and dust rose from the ground. 'Glare from the windshield wasn't bad enough . . .' McCann said.

The Sikorsky lifted from the ground, its nose tilted, and McCann's rifle cracked.

The 'copter wobbled and then gained altitude, and Hammond thought he saw spiderwebbing on the Plexiglas on the pilot's side. Might be wishful thinking. Come on, Chazz, set it back down, get those feet back on the ground. He sensed Carla's impatience beside him, paralleling his own desire to urge McCann to shoot again, *shoot already* . . .

McCann squeezed off another round. The big Sikorsky kept lifting higher, rose to twenty feet and then pitched hard to the pilot's side, tilted down and slammed into the ground. Hammond groaned as the props cracked off and flew through the air like so much lumber.

The 'copter balanced there, on its side and nose, creaking, and then something gave way and it crumpled down further and came to rest, dust swirling away.

There were cries from the *Princess* as it cast off, but Hammond couldn't tell if they were anguish, excitement or some emotion foreign to him.

He slumped back against the mounded earth. 'It didn't blow up,' McCann said, in astonishment. 'It didn't blow up.'

The man had seen too many movies. 'Actually,' Hammond said, 'the guys who build them try to make sure they don't.'

The sound of an explosion echoed across the valley, but it wasn't the chopper. One of the pontoons had been blown from beneath the equipment workshop, and the floating building listed to the side, sinking.

'Oh, shit . . .' Carla said, and pointed.

Hammond's gaze followed her arm. The *Princess Mishail* was easing her bulk past the end of the pier, but for a long moment he missed what Carla had seen – a tiny figure bent over the rail, aiming an RPG at the *San Andres*.

The rocket swooshed down into the heart of the yacht. The boat exploded in orange flames, and then spewed black smoke as the fire found the diesel tanks. *San Andres* exploded once more, and her hull tilted away from the pier, tore from its moorings and then quenched the fires as it disappeared beneath the water.

Hammond and Carla cut off the calves of their pants, doubled them and bound them over their feet as makeshift shoes. Carla took McCann's rifle and urged him back into the relative coolness of the cave.

'Try not to get killed down there,' McCann said, 'leaving me up here with no gun.'

Hammond sucked at his dry teeth. Odd priorities. A lot of good a rifle would do without food or water.

They picked their way down the shallow ravine between the Great Wall and the mountainside. When they reached the sand, Carla broke into a trot. Hammond had little choice but to match her pace, and as he jogged along he considered his options. The *San Andres* sat at the bottom of the bay, and it was doubtful its radio had survived that explosion. The *Princess Mishail*'s stern was still visible to the north, taking that radio beyond reach – though, as he now recalled, Carla had left it disabled before they had set out days before. *Sturmkönig* was under thousands of feet of ocean, and *Easy Angles* was in her berth in Cabo, probably being leased out to some half-drunk Americans. No radios, and he'd just allowed a bunch of terrorists to sail off with hundreds of pounds of high-level nuclear materials.

No. He'd helped one group of terrorists steal them, and then sat by as another group confiscated them. His thirst-addled mind wondered what he'd really done, where his failures would appear around the world. New York? DC? There was enough hot stuff in that cask for twenty dirty bombs. Maybe it would show up everywhere – London, Paris, Rome, New York, Seattle, San Francisco, Chicago, Baltimore, Denver, Miami, Detroit, St Louis, Cleveland, Dayton, Boise, Tucson, Fargo . . . he stumbled, caught his balance and tried to resume his pace. He glanced at his watch. Even if its gears had been working after the long swim and the cave-in, it was useless now: the crystal had shattered away and the hands had been torn off.

From the sky and the heat he made it nearly 5 p.m. Happy hour. Maybe the radio in the chopper still worked. Why the hell had all the radios been on boats, anyway, why didn't they have one back in the main Quonset hut?

Because Carla knew something was hinky, even after French got himself shot.

How did you signal the world without a radio, without phones? Maybe set the pier on fire – they probably had enough gasoline to send up the whole thing. Torching off all the explosives down in the ammo dump might do it. Glancing out to the bay, he saw that the floating ammo dump was gone.

Even though the sun was sinking, it hammered the side of his face. No wonder the villagers had abandoned Bahia San Andres. The place hated life. Nothing but dust and sun.

He staggered on a few paces before he realized Carla had stopped jogging. They were almost at the pier. She looked as though she'd dampened herself and then rolled in the dust, her bloodshot blue eyes peering through a mask of dirt. 'You,' she began, and it turned into a dry cough. She swallowed. 'Check the 'copter. I'll do the pier.'

Hammond nodded. He wanted to say that they'd both be more clear-headed and more prepared if they took ten minutes to head up to the main dorm and rehydrate, but it was easier to obey orders than to make his dry mouth work. He'd check the 'copter.

The wreck of the Sikorsky was no more than a stone's toss away. He made his way there and sat down in the meagre shade under the nose. He tried to gather his breath and marshal what little moisture remained in his body. He was shaky and useless in this state. He looked up at the shattered Plexiglas windshield just above his head and saw it was covered with congealing blood. His hand patted about on the ground for a good fist-sized rock, and then he stood and hammered away the windshield.

Chazz was in the pilot's seat, still strapped in tight. The whole top of his skull had been blown away. Nice shooting,

Ray. Then Hammond saw that McCann's first bullet must have taken the man in the left shoulder, and he marvelled that he'd kept decent control of the chopper.

Nice flying, Chazz. Where the hell was Richter?

Hammond stood and pushed his torso through the open windshield. The console looked dead, not a gleam of light anywhere, but he flicked the switches. Nothing. He twisted the gain knob and the front of the radio crumbled into little PVC bits and the knob came free in his hand, carrying an assortment of wires and fuses.

'Boyce Hammond?' The voice came from the rear of the chopper, back in the VIP cabin – a voice in pain, but still an elegant Southern drawl. 'Now, keep your temper . . .'

Richter hadn't been belted in when the chopper crashed, and he'd been bounced around inside the cabin. His right arm seemed to have been shattered, and from the way the man clutched himself Hammond guessed there were other, internal injuries.

The fuselage sat at a 45-degree angle to the ground. Hammond had to clamber over the pilot's seat, trying to ignore Chazz's body. Richter lay cradled in what would once have been the curved join of the floor and the wall; now, it was simply the lowest place.

Before he even tried to move the man, Hammond stepped over him and fought his way across the angled chairs to the wet bar. He heaved open the door to the refrigerator and found cold, clear things: club soda, tonic and even one bottle of real, unadulterated, water.

*

He hadn't worried much about hurting Richter as he'd dragged him out. He hadn't gone out of his way to do so, either, but he hadn't been gentle; even with the renewed energy from the water in his belly, he hadn't owned the energy to be gentle.

Fractured pelvis, Hammond guessed. Broken ribs. Maybe something in the soft tissues. Even if you didn't fly MedEvac, chopper jocks got to see it all, sooner or later.

He'd patted the man down for weapons and left him there, leaning against the fuselage of the broken Sikorsky, and set off to find Carla, a bottle of tonic water in either hand, but before he'd gone twenty paces he saw her, so he waited.

She had boots on, and another pair slung over her shoulders by their tied laces. McCann's 30.06 dangled from one hand, and the other carried a heavy waterproof baggie. A plastic canteen jangled from her hip.

Already she was glancing around him as she arrived, and he put his bottles on the ground and reached out to hold her shoulders. 'Carla. Listen. Richter's still alive. We need—'

She pushed around him, shedding all she'd carried, and ran towards the wrecked chopper.

He dashed after her, but she got to Richter first and delivered a booted kick into his ribs. The man gasped in pain. Hammond grabbed her arms, spun her round and gut-punched her with everything he had.

Carla staggered a few steps and fell to her knees. She vomited clear water onto the sand, and then dry-retched a few more times, and Hammond dropped down beside her and wrapped his arms round her, saying, 'I'm sorry, I'm sorry, we *need* him, we still need him', and Carla nodded even as she choked.

He sat her up onto her heels and kissed her cracked lips. 'We need him,' Hammond said, 'do you see? We need to know what's happening.'

She nodded again, still trying to catch her breath. Hammond saw long tracks through the dust on her cheeks where earlier tears had run and then evaporated in the relentless heat.

'Tell me,' he said.

She swallowed. 'Alvorsen got hit, went into the water, swam under the pier. He'll be okay.' She took in a long breath and closed her eyes. 'Kowinski's dead on the pier. The rest . . .'

'Carla . . .'

'What?'

'Nothing. Just, whatever happens, whatever you hear, keep your head, okay? Let me handle it. Things aren't always what they seem.'

'The radio?'

'Dead and gone.'

'Any chance of fixing the 'copter?'

A shop, a week, a team of mechanics and about eighty thousand dollars, he thought, but only shook his head.

He helped her to her feet and then trudged over and picked up McCann's rifle where Carla had let it fall. Letting it dangle from one hand, he turned and walked back to where Richter lay propped against the tilted fuselage. Carla stepped up and stood a few feet to his left.

'Who are they?' Hammond asked. 'Where are they headed?'

A weak smile formed on Richter's lips. 'What do you plan to do with me?'

'Answer the question.'

Carla stirred, and Richter threw a worried glance in her direction. 'Now, Mr Hammond,' he said, 'if you're planning to kill me anyway, I hardly see any great reason for me to be cooperative. Give me an incentive, and I might see matters differently.' A drop of blood leaked from his nostril and onto his upper lip.

Hammond nodded. 'Fine. I *plan* to drag your ass back to the US to stand trial – and to testify against your pal Atwater. And I'm betting that Central Intelligence and Homeland Security will both want a piece of what you know, too.'

Richter's eyes opened in surprise, and then closed, and for a moment he looked serene, like some lanky Buddha. He chuckled and shook his head. 'Oh, that's good, Mr Hammond, that's very good.' His eyes opened. 'You, then. Not the ATF guy. Oh, the money we spent making sure you were the real thing . . . Seems you can't trust anybody these days, 'cept perhaps Cahlah, here.'

'Boyce . . . ?' Carla asked.

'The Bureau, then, I suppose,' Richter said. 'Why'd you string it out so long? You could have blown the whistle any time.'

'Immunity. They wanted to keep gathering evidence, keep me in place. They were going to let all my people walk. The Allens. Carla, Lorrie, all of them.'

'Hammond,' Carla said. 'What the hell's he talking about?'

Hammond glanced in her direction, but found he couldn't

meet her eyes. His gaze on the ground, he said, 'I'm with the FBI, Carla. Always have been.' He risked a quick look at her face and saw nothing there. He looked back at Richter, but continued speaking to her. 'I was going to get immunity for you.' Behind him, the sinking sun was still hot on his back. He half-expected Carla to lunge for his throat with her knife, and he half-believed he deserved it.

Richter laughed, and wiped his eyes with his left hand, his ruined right arm stretched on the ground beside him. 'My, that smarts . . . Seems everybody's been playing everybody. I been fooling both of you, and Gerry Graves, and Atwater; Boyce here has been fooling the Allens, fooling me, fooling you, too, Cahlah. How'd he manage it all that time? Been whispering sweet nothings in your ear? Same way he wormed his way towards the top of the Allens, by sleeping with McCann's sister?'

Hammond kept his gaze fixed on Richter, but he heard Carla's feet shifting on the ground. 'That's enough, Richter,' he said.

'And you, Boyce,' the man said, as though Hammond hadn't interrupted, 'your own people were fooling you.'

'What do you mean?' Carla asked. She took a step forward towards the man, and he flinched.

'I mean that this whole thing would never have come this far if people upstairs didn't want it to happen.' Richter looked at Hammond. 'Didn't you ever wonder? Right up to the top, my friend, right up to the top.'

Hammond felt dizzy. He didn't want to believe it, but it explained too much to deny. 'The Director knew?'

'Probably not him. A thin line of people in the Bureau,

probably – you boys are good at keeping undercover ops undercover, I'll give you that – a thin line, and then right up to the top of the Justice Department. Up to the kind of fellow who figured nuking Mecca would be God's will.'

'Hammond?' Carla asked. He glanced in her direction, but her gaze was focused on Richter, and her body balanced on the balls of her feet in that easy way that suggested she could spring at any moment. 'I'm getting *confused* . . .' She said this as if it were a warning that something might explode. 'Is he saying our guys wanted to nuke the Arabs, or give nukes to the Arabs, or . . . ?'

'Ah, Cahlah.' Richter looked at her with what seemed to Hammond like genuine affection. 'You're the only one who's worth a damn. No, honey. That last bit, I have to admit, was *my* little flourish.'

Her voice quavered. 'But *why?*'

Richter shut his eyes while he took a deep breath, like one steeling himself for a long explanation to children. 'Listen, both of you. There's crazies in the world, like the Arabs who just sailed off there, or like some of the folks in our government. Then there's the power people, the ones with money, the ones who run everything. And there's a few, like Atwater, who are both.' He paused. It might have been for dramatic effect, but Hammond suspected he was marshalling his internal forces for a sprint to the finish line, fighting for his life with his words while trying to appear reasonable.

Richter sighed. 'And then there's us, people like you and me. Oh, I know, Cahlah, you think I'm already rich, but you don't know money. It's always been this way, since people first settled down. Princes and serfs. Owners and slaves.' He licked the gathered blood off his upper lip. 'The President of the United States, the CEO of Exxon Mobil, Rex Atwater – they have more in common with the head of Red China, or the King of Saudi Arabia, than they do with other Americans.'

'Again, that's enough,' Hammond said. 'Where's the *Princess* headed?'

'Patience.' Richter held up an outward-thrust palm as if directing traffic, but he kept his face turned towards Carla. 'In the valise inside the helicopter here, I have some numbers and passwords that can make us all princes, the kind of money that can take us to a whole new level of life. Oh, I already had a couple of million, but I'm talking tens of millions each, and I've already got the down-payment on all this stashed away . . . Help me out of here. Just wash your hands and walk away – I know how to make us all dead on paper. And what's happening here, it was only a matter of time.' He licked his lip, tasting his own blood there. 'Anything you've ever imagined, anything. You can have your wish. All you have to do is—'

Faster than Hammond could assimilate it all, Carla skidded across the dirt on her knees, fetching up against Richter's side with the tip of her knife under his jaw.

Hammond raised the rifle and then lowered it. Who was he kidding?

'Who are they and where are they going?' she asked.

'Who? Arabs. Call themselves Allah's Martyrs, but that doesn't tell you anything.' He tilted his chin up away from the tip of her knife and she kept pushing the tip into the skin. Hammond saw that the blade was recurved, Middle-Eastern style; a damascened hilt showed between the fresh scabs on Carla's knuckles.

She poked, and Richter yelped. 'Who and where?' she asked.

'I don't *know* who. Money out of Saudi and the Emirates. But get two Arabs together and you have three political factions.' Hammond saw Richter's eyes dodge from side to side, as though seeking an exit. 'Where? Didn't tell me. Use your head. Somewhere nearby, somewhere big. San Diego? Maybe up to San Pedro, go for LA harbour.' He swallowed. 'Then kiss your so-called freedoms goodbye. You think Bush was sad to see the World Trade Center go down? It was a gift. You could—'

She pushed, and a trickle of blood ran down his neck. '*Where? When?*'

'Carla . . .' Hammond said.

'*I – don't – know!* Ease up, for Chrissakes, ease up for a second.' She must have backed off on the pressure, because Richter's body sagged in relief.

'Carla,' Hammond said, 'we need him if we want to put Atwater away . . .' It was all worse than he had thought – no, not worse, but far more immediate. He knew they'd unleashed something horrible, but he had somehow convinced himself that the threat was far away in time and distance. San Diego: just a short ride to the border.

'Give me names and places,' Carla said. 'If you met with government people, tell me who.'

'Not that simple. They don't get their hands dirty with things like this . . .' She poked the knife, and he gasped. 'Wainwright. Prescott Wainwright was the go-between; he knows everybody, he knows everything about the Washington side of this . . .'

Carla glanced back at Hammond, a question in her eyes. He nodded. Wainwright was one of Atwater's Known Associates. Wainwright was a Known Associate of everyone in DC.

She leaned her face back in to Richter's. 'What else?'

'Listen, Cahlah.' Richter's voice was smaller than Hammond had ever heard it, urgent, pleading. 'It's all politics, all of it's dirty. You can check out of it, today. Anything you want, every wish your little heart desires – anything. It can all be yours. We've got enough money here to buy a country . . .'

She removed the knife from his throat. 'It was all about money?' she asked.

'Cahlah – darlin' – I know you're better than us, I know you're better than most everyone who calls the shots. But, honey, no matter what they preach to you . . . money's power, and power's all it's *ever* about.'

'You know what I wish?' she asked.

'What?' Richter's voice was half-fearful, half-hopeful. 'Because it's all here now, all in front of you . . .'

'I wish,' Carla said, 'I had time to kill you slower.' She slid the blade up under his ribs. Her voice lowered to a whisper, and she leaned close to his ear as she twisted the knife. 'You sonofabitch.'

The bright aortal blood spilled out over her fist, and she urged the steel in with one final thrust. Richter stared down at his chest, amazed, as his heart pumped out two more scarlet gushes, and then his whole body slumped, more at ease than he deserved.

Carla stood and turned towards Hammond, fresh blood dripping from her knuckles and from the knife clutched in her fist. The droplets spattered in the dust and were eaten up by the hungry soil.

'Jesus, Carla,' he said, 'we needed him. Can't you look at the big picture for once?'

'*You* look at the big picture, Hammond. We have to go after the *Princess*. Tomorrow we'll probably be dead. You want him alive, slipping off to some hideaway?'

Hammond shook his head. Go after the *Princess*? How, swim?

'Is it true?' she asked. 'What he said?'

Richter had said so many things. Hammond felt his shoulders slump in defeat. He thumbed off the safety of the rifle. 'Probably.' He dropped it to the ground and waited, lacking the conviction to fight any longer, and unwilling to fight this woman.

He saw Carla studying him, but found nothing in her eyes. When she turned away from him and wiped her blade and hand on Richter's cream-coloured coat, he felt no sense of relief, only resignation, as though he'd been ordered from one line into another in some endless bureaucracy.

'Okay.' She faced him. 'We head to the dorm. You get some water up to McCann, I'll grab a first-aid kit and get Alvorsen pieced together. Meet me down at the pier and we'll decide what comes next.' Her eyes searched him, and he dropped his gaze. 'Are we in the same world here, Boyce?'

He nodded.

'Then let's go,' she said.

33

When you're in charge

The sun sat red on the horizon as Carla jogged towards the pier. The offshore breeze of the evening came in from the north-west, stiff enough to raise a few dust devils.

She saw Kowinski's body sprawled on the pier where it had fallen, and all the energy drained from her. She slowed to a walk, and all the voices gathered in her head, every voice that had ever told her she wasn't good enough, smart enough, pretty enough, that everything she ever touched went wrong.

And they were right. She'd failed the men who'd followed her. She'd failed all those she'd sought to avenge. And she'd failed her country – not only failed to defend it, but had given its enemies a devastating, horrific weapon. What was the use of running now? Stop for a minute and think.

She almost sat down on the ground and gave up. Then she saw Alvorsen limping up from the pier, supporting himself on a makeshift crutch that she suddenly recognized as a length of rail from the wreckage of the *San Andres*.

Ever since she'd been discharged from K-Force she'd been

running, but things were different now. You can't run away when you're in charge.

She called out to Alvorsen to stay where he was, and jogged down to meet him. 'Better sit down,' she said. 'I have some strange things to tell you.'

After she fetched one of the little electric carts and drove Kowinski's body to the dorm, Carla and Alvorsen sat at the edge of the pier, their legs dangling, and waited for Hammond, gazing off to the north.

The floating explosives dump was gone, which convinced her that Richter had been telling the truth. The *Princess Mishail* was now a seaborne bomb, destined for some US harbour.

Alvorsen had his sidearm and his MP5. The rest of the weapons had been stored in the explosives dump or on board the *Princess* . . . except that Lorrie always kept a spare kit in the shop.

She stood and looked south. When she shielded her eyes against the glare of the sun she could make out the shape of the floating workshop on the floor of the bay, tilted at a crazy angle by its single intact pontoon. The bridge that had led to it was still moored to the pier, but the tie-up to the workshop had ripped away, and now the walkway led nowhere.

'Oh, Christ,' Alvorsen said.

Carla turned and followed his gaze out to the middle of the bay.

There was turmoil in the water, and she realized it was a mob of sharks, rolling and tearing, worrying at a shape that must have been human.

Closer at hand, but deeper beneath the waters, another vortex of shapes struggled just above the wreck of the *San Andres*. Dodge, she suspected – Dodge, who had loathed the sharks so much.

'I can't watch this,' he said. He lifted his injured leg with both hands and set it down on the pier, and then scooched himself around until he stared inland at the barren hills.

'You were a Feeb the whole time I knew you?' Alvorsen asked. 'The whole time I thought you were my friend?'

Carla kept her mouth shut and watched Hammond flinch. 'Yeah,' he said. 'And I am your friend.'

'Like shit. People don't send their friends to prison.'

'If I'd wanted you to go to prison, I could have blown this sky-high ages ago. The only reason we're here is because I stupidly agreed to stay under in exchange for immunity for you.' He gave Carla a look. '*All* of you. Atwater and Richter were the ones going down.'

'We were after our country's enemies.' Alvorsen's pale complexion, already burned by the sun, reddened even more beneath his blond beard. 'Where the hell do you get off protecting them?'

'Fuck you!' Hammond jumped to his feet and Carla stared up at him. 'Fuck both of you. Most of the people in the world are just people, just trying to get by. Sure, the guys who took the *Princess* are enemies. They're terrorists.' He breathed, and then, seemingly against his will, added, 'Just like us.'

Alvorsen opened his mouth, but Carla said, 'He's right.' Both of them looked at her. 'I don't know what we were supposed to do about all the sickos in the Mideast. But it wasn't this.'

Alvorsen said, 'But—'

'Look what's happened.' She shook her head. 'That ought to be enough. The question now is how we stop them.'

Hammond was nodding even before she stopped speaking. 'There's a good chance that if we build a big enough fire, someone will come investigate. We have diesel, we have gasoline, we have the pier and the dorm—'

'No.' This was a council of war, not a debating club, and she needed to remind the others who was in charge. 'I said before, we need to go after them.'

'How?' Hammond asked. 'Flap our arms? We're wasting time here.'

'There were two Zodiacs folded up in the shop.'

Hammond made an exasperated sound that might have passed as a laugh. 'I'm sure there are. And four ultralights, too, and—'

'You don't think they took the planes?'

'Why the hell would they? They don't need 'em, they can just sail right into San Diego harbour. The shop is sunk to the bottom of the bay. Your Zodiacs and ultralights might as well be on the moon!'

'Would they run? If we got them out?' She felt excitement rising in her chest as she spoke. 'Wouldn't it take forever to assemble them? Aren't they ruined?'

'We didn't tear them into nuts and bolts, you know,' Alvorsen said. 'Just enough to pack them. And we can clean out the water with gasoline – God knows it evaporates fast enough around here. So, I don't know, thirty, forty-five minutes?' He winced as he stretched his injured leg.

'What does it matter?' Hammond asked. 'We can't get to them.'

'We can try.'

'There's more sharks in that bay than water,' Alvorsen said.

'So maybe an hour, hour and a half for two of them?' she asked.

'We don't need two of them,' Hammond said. 'Get me one and I'll fly to Ensenada, or whatever one-horse town I find first, and I'll call out the Bureau and the Coast Guard.'

'Do that if you want,' she said. 'I'm going after the *Princess*.'

'To do what?' Hammond jumped to his feet. 'Play Rambo? You think you can make up for all of this by committing suicide?'

'We have to try.'

'No. We have to *stop* them, not play hero.'

'Uh-huh.' Carla rose from her seat. 'And the people you call are really going to act? The same people who let it get this far?'

Hammond set his jaw. 'We'll call *everybody*.'

'I'll come with you, Carla,' Alvorsen said.

'We're wasting time,' she said. 'We need to get those planes.' She glanced at the sky. 'Maybe ninety minutes until dark? How long before the *Princess* gets to San Diego? Four hours? Five?'

'If they make twenty, twenty-two knots, sure,' Alvorsen said.

Hammond sighed. 'They can't.' The certainty in his voice made her stare, and she felt Alvorsen studying him as well. 'I sabotaged one of the engines. Just one. It'll die within a dozen miles. Not enough to put her out of commission entirely, but enough to make sensible people put into port for repair.' He glanced back and forth between them, his look defensive, though no one else had said a word. 'So, maybe fifteen knots, tops, if they don't mind wrecking their good engine, too. Twenty, twenty-two? No way.'

Carla looked at him for a long moment. 'If there's anything else you've neglected to tell us, now would be a good time. No? Okay.' She leaned forward, her hands on her cross-legged knees, and summoned up a confidence she didn't feel. 'We can get the stuff from the workshop. We can because we've got no other choice.'

The men's faces wore dubious expressions. 'Look,' she said, 'we're not going anywhere without the planes. So it's get 'em, or die trying.'

In the silence that followed, no one voiced the thought that there were better ways to die.

'My parents didn't let us watch much TV,' Alvorsen said, 'mostly Disney and nature shows.' She stared at him in alarm; this was such a non sequitur that it sounded like delirium. He grinned at the expression on her face. 'I learned one thing from Jacques Cousteau: if a shark can't get its mouth on you, it can't hurt you.'

She rubbed her face with both hands, feeling the day's grit drag between cheek and palm. Hammond began to say something, but she said, 'No, he's on to something. Let me think.' Her palms covered her eyes. She wished that Lorrie were there, and the memory of shooting her made Carla's whole body cringe.

No time for that right now. She dropped her hands from her face. 'Okay,' she said, 'let's review our resources.'

34

Shields

Hammond stood at the end of the floating walkway, Carla just behind him. Unmoored from the shop, the planks and floats had enough give that the whole thirty-foot walkway undulated like a lethargic serpent.

'Lights more to the right!' he shouted. Back on the pier, Alvorsen edged the big roller-mounted cargo lights away, and the glare off the surface of the water lessened. Crouching down, Hammond made out the shape of the equipment shop in the dark water. The intact landward pontoon tilted the whole shop about thirty degrees from level, while the shattered seaward pontoon rested on the bottom of the bay.

The shadows of sharks still glided through the water. 'Do you suppose they've calmed down yet?' Hammond asked.

'Don't count on it,' Carla said.

He stood and pulled on the steel cable that ran back to the pier's port-side cargo winch, gathering up some slack. 'Okay, here goes . . .' He twirled the hook in a circle and cast it two dozen feet, beyond what he judged was the rear of the shop roof.

The hook and cable splashed down. The water roiled as sharks mobbed the area, searching for the cause of the disturbance.

'Calm enough for you?' Carla asked.

Hammond shouted for Alvorsen to start winching. The cable slid past them, spraying droplets, and then jerked taut. 'Got something,' Hammond said. He crouched again, shielding his eyes. The hook seemed to have caught on the far side of the shop, perhaps behind the peak of the roof, and the submerged building rocked as the power of the winch began to drag it.

Something beneath the water screeched and the cable went limp. From the darting shapes, the noise agitated the sharks. Carla leaned beside him, squinting. 'We just peeled back a big section of the metal roof.'

Hammond signalled to Alvorsen as he saw the hook racing up through the water. A hammerhead, an eight-footer, dodged at the hook and bumped it with his nose.

Hammond gathered up slack onto the walkway beside him and let the hook dangle from a foot of cable. 'I'm going for the front of the barge this time.' His arm pendulumed back and forth from the elbow, as though he were working up an underhand pitch, and he let fly just a short distance ahead.

Again the sharks converged on the splash, arriving fast and silent as though shot from bows. This time Hammond drew the cable back in a delicate hand-over-hand, and then tugged hard when he met resistance, setting the hook. Arm upraised, he signalled Alvorsen to start the winch.

Judging by the angle of the cable, the hook had snagged

on the edge of the barge, just in front of the shop door. Water shot from the steel as the cable went taut, and Hammond held his breath as the silhouette of the building began to crawl forward and even rise a little, swaying from side to side with the buoyancy of the pontoon.

'Shit,' Carla said.

The cable reeled in, towing a section of wood. A shark, probably a tiger, shot through the water a few feet below the surface, rolled to the side, clamped its mouth down on the timber and thrashed its whole body, worrying the broken wood until it came free. It darted off into the depths carrying its prize.

He lifted the hook from the water, signalled to Alvorsen to cease and then sat down cross-legged, his face in his hands. Every minute they wasted here put the *Princess* a minute closer to the US. Stupid, stupid. There had to be something he was missing. Maybe he'd been right in the first place, maybe they should make the biggest damned fire they could . . .

Nonsense. The chances of being noticed were low; the chances that anyone would bother to investigate were infinitesimal.

'We need to get on the stick, Boyce.'

A weary nod of the head was the best he could manage. He clambered to his feet, the walkway swaying beneath him. 'I'll try for the side this time.'

Carla's hand lay down on his shoulder. 'Forget it. It's not going to work.'

He hefted the cable and hook. 'It's worth another try.'

'No, it isn't.' He heard the fatigue in her voice. 'We're

tearing the damned shop apart. If we keep it up, everything's going to end up scattered on the bottom of the bay, and then we're royally screwed.' She exhaled, and it sounded as if her whole body was deflating. 'The steel beams under the barge are the only things solid enough.'

Swallowing, he searched for words. 'I don't want you to do this.'

She chuckled, but her voice sounded thin. 'You just better hope I succeed. 'Cause if I don't come back, it all becomes your problem, ace.'

She'd known from the start that it would come to this, and despite the bitching from the boys, she'd made them set up the ersatz shark cage before they began the fruitless hook-tossing.

The first order of business had been rescuing the rebreathers they'd ditched in the shallow water near the Great Wall. The shark-mobbed pier stood about a half-mile away, but searching through the thigh-deep, inky waters had been unnerving despite the distance.

Then they'd torn the corrugated metal roof from the big outhouse, plus one of the panels between the stalls. With the few tools available in the dorm, ten minutes of bashing, bending and punching had done the job: a big inverted V of corrugated roofing taller than Carla, closed at one end. On either side, they incised a pair of U-shaped cuts at shoulder height and then curled the free edges inwards, making for primitive handholds. A dozen slits scattered near the apex of the metal shell ensured there was no danger that the device would hold air.

The panel of the outhouse stall was a gift. Bent and stomped to the right dimensions, it ended up almost Carla-high, with an industrial toilet-tissue rack as a hand grip; when she seized it and held it up, it resembled an oblong warrior's shield.

An over-high, corrugated pup tent, that's what the shark cage looked like to her where it sat at the end of the walk-way. She snapped the quick-release buckle on the rebreather and made sure the BCD was completely deflated.

Lorrie would have come up with something better. Lorrie would have come up with a totally different approach.

She had to assume Lorrie was shark-food by now.

She bent over to grab the cable and felt the excess burden of her gear: they'd cannibalized some weights from the other rebreathers and filled every belt and pocket on her BCD. When she found the hook, she jammed it down on one of the handhold slits inside the metal tent.

'Gimme my shield,' she said to Hammond.

He held the panel, but didn't hand it to her. 'There's got to be another way.'

'Sure, the wrong way.' She grinned. 'Look, this is going to be a breeze. I set the hook and then just take a walk up to the beach. It's you guys who are going to stay here and do the heavy lifting.'

He looked as though he was ready to say something emo-tional, maybe a little mushy, and she didn't need that right now. She glanced down, found the underwater pen-light dan-gling from her gear, switched it on, then pulled on the gloves. 'Once I set that hook, don't you boys blow it. 'Cause next time it's your turn to take this walk.' She put the mouthpiece between her lips and backed into the metal shell. Her right hand grabbed the handhold near her shoulder, and she gestured with her left hand for him to give her the shield.

Hammond stood the shield within reach and she grasped the handle and jerked it towards herself, wincing at the resulting stage thunder when the metal sheets met and reverberated around her. The shield was shorter than the apex of the metal tent, and not quite as wide as the tent's base. This left open two narrow – and, she hoped, inconsequential – triangles to either side, down at the level of her shins. More important, it left a triangular opening a handspan high just before her eyes.

Her shoulders flexed towards her ears to bear the weight of the metal up off the walkway, and she edged forward. The glow of the waterproof pen-light was a candle in a confessional.

Carla had imagined dying before. She'd taken bullets, blades and shrapnel, and could imagine any one of them carrying her off. But underwater, alone in the dark, being torn apart . . . she'd felt fear many times before, felt it until it no longer had power, but this was different: this was horror. Her hand abandoned the handle on the shell to open the regulator, and it trembled so she could hardly turn the knob.

You deserve it. The Army trusted you and you screwed it up. Then you took everything they taught you and became a terrorist. Your men trusted you and you let them die. A few hours ago you shot your friend, one of your only friends. Thanks to you, an American city is about to be engulfed in radiation. You deserve to die like this.

But you can't. Because staying alive is your only chance to repair any of what you've done . . .

Get your hand out of your panties and your mind out of the clouds, Smukowski, Jill's voice snapped, *and do your damned job.*

Her gloved hands clutched the metal handles and she took one giant step forward.

It might have been only a moment, but in Carla's view the damned contraption floated, floated with her only knee-deep in the water, and it was like a goddamned skirt, leaving you exposed to anything that came from beneath . . .

And then it sank, sank fast, and she exhaled in a steady stream, not wanting her lungs stuffed with oxygen, not at this depth; she ran a good chance of oxygen poisoning in any case.

Even as she plummeted, as the force of the water sought to tear her grip from the cage and the shield, her legs felt like bait, dangling, enticing. The sleek forms of the sharks must be gathering around her, and when the first bumps against the shell came, she knew she was surrounded.

Going under without a mask added to the terror. When the cage touched bottom and she felt mud beneath her feet, the stirred-up murk blossomed about her, fogging her already fuzzy vision. She blinked and shook her head, trying to see through the triangular opening above the shield.

Shadows swirled before her.

Her pulse pounded in her throat, and she felt dizzy. Wouldn't that be nice – a stroke? No, this was the oxygen and the depth talking, and she needed to slow her breathing, exhale twice as long for each inhale.

Had she turned when she came down? Which way was she facing? She couldn't be sure.

An unseen force slammed against the shell from the right, almost knocking her over. She braced her feet and leaned that way.

Move. If you stand here, they'll just keep coming.

Carla trudged forward, thankful for the extra weights. Muck swirled up at every step. Strong bodies swiped against the shell like huge fists, and even in the muffled world at the bottom of the bay, the force rang from the metal.

An unexpected jolt hit her straight-on, and she bit down on the mouthpiece and tried to forge ahead.

It was unmovable. She saw, through the murk, that she'd hit the barge that supported the shop; the underside of the decking blocked over half the triangle of vision she had above the shield.

She shuffled to the left, raising even more goop from the sea floor. Her temples throbbed. No question about it, oxygen poisoning was setting in.

A step forward, and now she was in the shadow of the barge. She let the cage sit on the bottom and groped her free hand out through the open triangle. A flattish surface up above, though already ridged with barnacles. C'mon, c'mon. She dragged the cage further and searched again through the opening.

A beam, a steel beam. Were these solid I-beams, or did they have holes? She'd seen them before, back when the shop sat in the hold of the *Princess*, and again on the day they lowered it down to float on the surface of the bay. Why hadn't she paid attention? She seemed to remember regular openings of some sort . . .

Yes. Oblong, capsule-shaped cut-outs, max strength for min weight. Carla pulled her hand inside and fumbled for the hook. She jerked it from the slit where she'd jammed it – some part of her brain registered that her movements were becoming a little spastic – and pulled it out through the opening, fit it to an aperture in the beam, then hauled down with everything her right arm still had.

Good. A nice, stiff grip.

Carla gathered up all the slack in the cable from pierside, and when she felt tension, tugged. Three tugs. Pause. Three more.

Three tugs in response. She backed away, held the shield away for a moment so that the cable could fall free, and then pulled the shield tight against the cage once more.

She needed to head for shore. Which was . . . where? To port. No, you're not on a boat. Left. Rotate this whole damned operation left and start hiking. Umbrellas and pina coladas on the beach, just a short ocean-floor stroll away.

A pointed snout forced its way through the triangle above the shield and struggled to drive its head into her shelter. Her fist tightened and she dropped the shield just enough to ram it upwards, again and again, punching towards the sky. *No – God – damn – you!* and she saw pointed teeth shatter and twinkle down like hail, and dark clouds bloomed where the shark's snout had been.

Blood. Not good.

She had only a moment before massy fists began to batter

at the thin metal shell of the cage. There was no way to brace herself sufficiently to stay in place; only the fact that she was assaulted from both sides served to keep her upright.

The light. The light wasn't smart. She loosed her right hand long enough to snap the pen-light from its lanyard and toss it through the open triangle.

For a second it glimmered outside the shell and then a shadow snatched it away.

Darkness. A probing, thrusting force tried to work its way under the shell, and she bore down as hard as she could, which was limited by her buoyancy, and felt the invader tear itself away.

Then the fists began to beat at the cage again, and she felt the metal deforming around her. Insensate, the sharks in their frenzy drove themselves against the thin steel. In time – a very short time – it would be wrapped around her like foil.

The truth dawned on her: she'd never make it to shore. Forty yards? It might as well be a hundred miles.

Where was the shop? Behind her, now. She needed to turn round and head back deeper. Though all her instincts fought to make her head for the shallows, she pivoted, coming round as ponderously as a laden tanker, and the movement seemed to baffle the invaders. There were no major blows until the front of the shell tolled against a resisting structure. Through the triangle her salt-raw eyes made out the blur of the shop's ruined pontoon, dim in the light from the pier. That meant she was towards the seaward side.

The shop was up, and to her left. She could clamber on somehow and ride it as Alvorsen and Hammond towed it. Or she could abandon the shark cage and head for the surface.

Or go for the door of the shop. Do something. Do something to get out of here.

She hesitated only a moment. I'm so sorry, so sorry.

What a pathetic last thought.

She braced a foot against the metal that protected her, gathered her shield against her shoulder and kicked free of the shark cage.

Hammond knelt at the end of the floating walkway. The winch had begun to drag the shop towards the pier, but now he saw that Carla had thrown off the shark cage. Through the miasma of troubled shadows, in painfully slow motion, he saw Carla hoist herself onto the deck of the barge and then spin about, her back to the wall of the shop, her makeshift shield between herself and the world.

As though challenged, a dark shape, a dozen feet long, hurtled through the water and slammed against her shield; deflected, it whipped about and shot off into deep water.

Carla was hidden by her upraised shield as she edged her way upwards on the deck of the barge, and then, halfway towards the intact pontoon, he saw the shield fall away and sink towards the bottom.

Hammond cupped his hands round his eyes and pressed his face to the water. Carla was gone. But then he saw the submerged shop door slide closed. She'd gone inside.

He reared up and shouted to Alvorsen, 'Faster! Get it up here *now*!'

The sharks were everywhere in the water, swirling round the rising shop like a flock of buzzards about to settle on a kill. The landward pontoon, still filled with air, lifted towards the surface, and for a moment Hammond feared the entire building would fall onto its side.

The shadow of the shop drew towards the pier, the building still rising. The winch pulled it seawards of the walkway, and it bumped the floats as it passed. Hammond dropped to his knees and clutched the planking to avoid being hurled into the water.

Part of the roof broke the surface to his right, and then the whole structure juddered to a halt, washing water over the walkway. The front peak of the roof stuck up through the water like the prow of a surfacing submarine, but the rest of the building remained submerged.

'The shop's still anchored!' Alvorsen shouted from the pier.

Hammond stood and backed away a few feet to where he could cling to one of the walkway's upright posts. Alvorsen was right: the anchor at the rear of the barge held the whole shop down. 'Drag it!' he shouted.

'She won't come! Put any more tension on it and the cable may give!'

If the cable broke, she'd go back to the bottom – not to mention that a snapped cable could cut a man in half as it whipped round.

He leaned out on the post, craning and squinting into the water at the roof of the shop. Though the front peak of the shop roof protruded a few feet above the water, the rear of that same peak was submerged a half-dozen feet. Near that rear peak he made out the hole they'd ripped in the corrugated metal when he'd tried to hook the shop earlier. The dark rip in the metal was large, maybe even large enough for Carla to swim through.

A long shadow cruised past that hole. Not a good exit.

A clanging, hammering sound came from the shop. Carla was banging on the peak of the roof from the air gap inside. Signalling?

No, she was trying to bash open the roof.

Hammond ran back to the pier, staggering as the walkway wobbled beneath him. He jerked his arms through the strap of a rebreather and snatched up the hammer they'd been using earlier to beat the shark cage into shape.

No sense in turning on the regulator; submerging would be a last resort. Back at the end of the walkway he paused, cinching the hammer into a strap on his BCD, and then jumped for the peak of the roof where the water sloshed round it. Water splashed and his chest slammed down on the corrugated roof. The oxygen tank crushed into his ribs, but he ignored the pain and hugged the roof peak with both arms.

The surface of the waters in a wide arc round him came alive with predatory shapes, circling. His body straddled the tilted crest of the roof. He lay in water from the waist down – only a foot or so of water down at his ankles, but it made his legs tingle with apprehension.

He clasped the roof peak with his left arm while he freed the hammer from his BCD. Once he had the claw in the gap between the roof metal and the truss, he prised and was rewarded with the squeal of nails leaving wood. He cranked up a corner of the metal and then bashed it away, tearing a ragged hole the width of a dinner plate.

Below the gap he saw Carla's face, her head up in the air gap. 'Light,' she said, panting.

'What?'

'A light, give me your light!'

He jammed the handle of the hammer into the vest of his BCD and then undid his pen-light. When he handed it to her, lanyard and all, he saw she had the mouthpiece of her rebreather between her lips again.

She looped the lanyard round her wrist, snapped on the light and her face sank from sight.

Leaving him to do what? He took the hammer and began to work at opening more of the roof, without any clear purpose other than to take his mind off those circling shapes. How much of a weapon would the hammer make if one came at his legs? He'd heard that a hard blow on the snout could often drive away even a huge shark. It wasn't a theory he wanted to test.

Carla's face surfaced again and she spit out the mouthpiece; he saw that at some point she'd bitten nearly through the rubber all the way round. 'No good. Thought maybe I could get through the back wall and unlatch the anchor. Tons of stuff in the way.' Her voice sounded shaky. 'Need to move fast. A three-footer came in here already through the hole in the roof. Not hungry, just lost. But . . .'

'I'm getting this hole wide enough. Maybe we can make it to the walkway—'

'Doesn't solve anything! Ideas?'

Nothing that didn't involve swimming down to the anchor hitch from the outside. 'Not unless you've got an extra pontoon. Or a hand grenade.'

'Shit, you're right! Give me that hammer.'

She took it and vanished without explanation. There weren't grenades in the workshop; there'd never been grenades in Bahia San Andres at all.

Six to ten feet of water to cross between the roof peak and the walkway, depending on how the walkway drifted from moment to moment. Logic told him they could make it, but imagination gave him a vivid picture of jaws snatching him from beneath, just as he tried to drag himself from the water.

Something bumped his foot and he jerked his legs up under himself and clung to the roof peak, curled into a ball. Where was Carla? He heard noises muffled by the water, but surely nothing violent . . .

She surfaced at last. 'You know how these work?' An impact fuse. He nodded and took it. 'Here.' She was offering him a dark rectangle, like an oversized packet of cigarettes, and it took him a moment to recognize it as one of the lead weights from her dive gear. 'Tie the fuse onto this, and blow the damned anchor loose.'

Tie the fuse to the weight? Tough to do with his arms clutched round the roof peak. And tie it on with what? After a long minute of one-handed fumbling, he managed to detach a Velcro strap from one of the rings on his BCD. Then, fearing every moment that he would drop the weight or the fuse into the water, he freed both hands by clamping onto either side of the roof with the pressure of his elbows. His left hand held the fuse snug against the weight, while he cinched the strap tight round them. 'Won't this blow when it hits the water?'

'Be delicate.' Her breath came in short gasps. She must be

oxygen-sick from her time on the bottom, maybe too deep for a rebreather. 'Be delicate, but hurry up about it, too.'

It would take turning round; he couldn't throw it gently or accurately back over his shoulder. Trembling with the need to make every movement precise, he edged himself round until the crest of the roof pressed against his spine, one arm still draped over the peak. He worked his heels up under his rump and then used the leverage of his arm to pull himself into a squat.

He flipped open the little lid of the impact fuse and clicked off the safety to arm it. The angle of the roof gave him a good idea where the anchor sat, since he and the shop were hung between the anchor chain and the winch cable like so much laundry.

A gentle toss. A toss where the weight, not the fuse itself, hit the surface of the water.

What the hell. He stood up, teetering, hefted it twice and then tossed it underhand. It disappeared with a plop. His hand groped behind him for the peak, to help him lower himself back to the roof.

A dull thud of a sound from beneath the water, and then a boiling at the surface. Nothing else. It didn't work. Or he'd missed.

Then the anchor let loose and the sudden motion of the shop threw him backwards and into the water between the shop and the pier. He came to the surface sputtering, and the shop, riding forward on the winch cable, bumped against him and carried him before it.

A huge shape moved beside him, and he clawed at the roof, trying to drag himself from the water. A shark, a twelve-footer, came to the surface and rolled onto its side and then thrashed along, its pale belly exposed.

When he hoisted himself onto the roof, now higher out of the water, he saw a dozen more out in the bay: sharks, wounded, concussed, struggling. By the time they'd got the winch cable hooked to the back of the electric cart to drag the building shorewards, the sharks had begun to feed on one another.

35

The Midas touch

She'd only meant to close her eyes for a minute, to rest and let the sting of the salt subside.

A horrible screech woke her where she lay on the sand, and she struggled her way upright, blinking her salt-reddened eyes. Hammond and Alvorsen had one of the ultralight crates up on the beach, and the sound came again as Alvorsen prised the lid off.

'How long was I down? You shoulda woke me.'

'Only twenty minutes,' Hammond said, 'and you needed it. Why were the impact fuses in the workshop?'

'One of Lorrie's little rules. Kept a crate there, a crate on the ship. Didn't believe in storing them in the ammo dump, didn't trust 'em.' She watched him flop the lid onto the sand and then study the disassembled plane with his flashlight. 'Looks okay to me.'

'Told you it would be,' Alvorsen said.

Beside her they had laid a waterproof bag, and Carla made out the unmistakable silhouette of the MP5 inside it.

Lorrie's spare. Good. With Alvorsen's kit, that made Toys for Two.

She climbed to her feet and rubbed the sand from her palms. 'Okay . . . let's drag the next one up here.'

'One's enough,' Hammond said.

She stared at him. 'The hell it is.'

Hammond threw his hands in the air. 'We need to move. Get the picture, Carla. We can't count on storming a boat, two or three of us, getting past maybe twenty, twenty-five people—'

'More like fifteen left, by your own count. And if we can't take them, maybe we can at least get to the explosives. Take the whole damned thing to the bottom.'

'They'll shoot us out of the air.' Hammond spread his hands, beseeching. 'Carla, thousands of people could die, hundreds of thousands – I'm not going to bet all that on a frontal assault.'

'You're right.' She saw relief spread across his face. 'And too risky to stake it all on some phone calls, too. We need to do both.' She turned to Alvorsen. 'Can you fly? With the leg, I mean?'

He gave her a grin. 'It hurts, but it works.'

'Good. Boyce here can head for a city and raise the hue and cry. You fly me to the *Princess* and I'll board her.'

'I'm coming aboard with you,' Alvorsen said.

'Not with that leg.'

'With a climbing belt and a little help—'

The pressure of time bore down on her back like an eighty-pound field pack, and she tried not to let her emotions stampede her into an unconsidered decision.

'Carla,' Hammond said, 'let's get going . . .'

She sat down on the edge of the crate and chewed her lip. Alvorsen's spunk was admirable, but she'd rather board the ship alone than with someone who'd have to be hoisted up. 'Did you ever get trained on the remote-pilot gear?'

'No.' Alvorsen gave a sheepish smile. 'Made me queasy the one time I tried.'

'What the hell's that got to do with anything?' Hammond asked.

'I have an idea that will give me a better chance. And we'll need three planes.' She considered him. 'Let Alvorsen go make your calls. I need you to help me.' He started to respond, and she raised a hand. 'You don't have to fly along. You just have to help me get there properly.' She stepped towards him and looked up into his face, remembering what it was like to touch him. 'I need your help, Boyce,' she said. 'Please.'

He looked down, avoiding her gaze, but nodded. 'I'll help.' He froze and stared at her chest. 'What's the story with your badge?'

She held up her radiation badge. The slightest mist of yellow showed against the blue. 'Lorrie noticed it, too. Took a little dusting when I went in after McCann, I guess. No big deal. About like the UV from a tropical vacation.' She lifted his, still dark as space. 'Looks like you're okay.'

'Makes me glad I stayed on the other ship,' Alvorsen said.

While the men started assembling the ultralights, she drove the electric cart north across the plain. She'd decided not to think, not until her job was done, but with nothing but the headlights for company her mind grew disobedient. There wasn't a single instance she could cite where the world was a better place for having had Carla Smukowski in it. Her path through life was littered with pain, wreckage and corpses. She had that Midas touch, all right. She ruined them all, enemies and friends alike.

If I'm still alive tomorrow, I'll be different. I'll do something good with my life.

Right. Wake up in the morning and suddenly you're Mother-fucking-Teresa.

Moot point, because there's not going to be a tomorrow, not for you. If you're lucky, you'll get a chance to clean up some of the mess you've caused. If you're lucky.

She fetched McCann down from the Cave, helped him hobble across the Great Wall – a formidable undertaking in the dark – and then drove him to the dorm. There was food and water aplenty, and the air conditioning still worked; she figured he had a better chance of being alive a week hence than anyone else in Bahia San Andres.

By the time she got back to the pier, one of the ultralights was fully assembled, and two others had everything bolted and guy-wired but their wings. Gasoline fumes still drifted from the motors where they'd dunked parts to get the moisture out. 'Remotes still work?'

'Sure,' Alvorsen said. 'Takes a longer swim than that.'

Hammond had primed Alvorsen with written lists: phone numbers, passwords and names of people to call. The man frowned through it all, but asked no questions. The three of them rolled the ultralight up to the smooth ground just beyond the high-tide mark on the beach.

Alvorsen belted himself in and looked at Carla. 'Kill 'em all,' he said, and started the engine.

Carla stood beside Hammond and watched the frail craft lift off and move into the night. With its low-decibel motor, dark paint and lack of running lights, it was only a matter of seconds before it vanished.

They waited silent for a moment after the hum of the motor could no longer be heard. 'Okay,' Hammond asked, 'what do we need to do next?'

'Remote-piloting gear and extra gasoline tanks for the one. Pontoons for the other. And a trainer seat – if you're really riding along.' She looked up at his face in the dark, wishing she could read what was there. 'You don't need to come, you know.' You *shouldn't* come, she thought, you've still got so much. The knowledge that you did the right thing. Someone who loves you. People waiting to hear from you. 'You can pilot it from here. You don't need to come.'

'Yes, I do,' he said. 'I'm boarding the ship with you.'

36

San Diego

His body rolled with the rhythm of the waves, but his vision bounced in the increasing wind. Hammond's virtual self had lifted off from solid ground ten minutes before, and was now miles gone, flying through the night; but his corporeal self, including his queasy stomach, was strapped into the seat behind Carla, their ultralight still rocking on its pontoons alongside the pier.

The remote-piloting gear had been bolted down on the strut between his legs. They'd put up the windshield in front of Carla's pilot seat, an extra twenty pounds. With the batteries, the servos, the weapons they'd gathered and the weight of their bodies, they were close to the carrying capacity of the aircraft.

Through the goggles, his virtual plane swerved in the breeze, and he steered her back on course. They'd attached two extra gas tanks where the seats had been, three impact fuses clamped onto each tank like limpets. The weight of the tanks showed in the drone's performance – sluggish, heavy and unwilling. Hammond tilted his mike down in front of his mouth. 'There's a hell of a headwind out there,' he said, 'and it gets worse as you go higher.'

'Not sure we can go very high anyway,' Carla said. He heard her both through the earpiece, and, since she sat only two feet ahead of him, through the air as well, a disconcerting effect of two stereo voices that weren't in perfect sync. The hum of the engine came alive, and the muted sound of the prop cutting air echoed off the water. 'I'm casting off.'

He hadn't liked the remote piloting he'd done from the ground over the past months, and he liked it even less now that he was in motion himself. There were moments when the sway of the two planes were coordinated, where what he saw and what he felt matched; but there were other times when the plane he was piloting was buffeted up at the same instant that the craft he was riding on lurched downwards, and he felt as though he were a new recruit back in his first rough-weather training flights.

He concentrated on coaxing the most out of the drone. He took it higher so that he could survey more sea, and weaved it from side to side so his fixed field of vision could scan from east to west. There was no point, not yet – the *Princess Mishail* had to be at least two hours ahead of them – but it was touchy business with that sloshing cargo of gasoline, and challenging his skills helped him ignore the conflicting signals coming in through the seat beneath him.

'It's my fault, isn't it?' Carla's voice asked. 'Getting hooked up with Richter in the first place, thinking I could decide what's right and wrong . . .'

He thought about it and half-wanted to laugh. Islam, free-dom, oil politics, Zionism, terrorism, money, the whole of history since Moses led the Jews out of Egypt, and Carla wanted to take the blame for all of it. His eyes looked out on the sea thirty miles ahead, but he spoke to the woman he knew was sitting just in front of him. 'I don't know whose fault it is.' He paused. 'Unless you're God, though, I can tell you that it sure isn't yours.'

Carla fell silent, and he wished he could see her face.

He'd been called in on quite a few long MedEvac missions, and this reminded him of flying in on one of those: an urgent hurry coupled with prolonged boredom, ticking off mile after mile, the uncertainty and fear growing about what he would find when he reached his destination. Disher, one of his old co-pilots, had a name for it: *fear hypnosis*, low-level anxiety plus unspeakable tedium combining to create some state that was neither awake nor asleep, the body poised, but the mind suspended in some blank space.

It might have been an hour, it might have been more, before she spoke again. 'Did she know about it?'

He shook his head, coming out of emptiness. 'About what? Who?'

'Earlene. Does she know you were undercover?'

He shook his head and then felt foolish; no one in the world could see him now. 'No. No, she doesn't.'

'Did you ever want to tell her?'

Only every day. 'Yeah.' Then, without understanding why, he said, 'Carla? When we made love those two times? I meant it.'

She laughed, but there was little mirth in the sound. 'When we *fucked*.'

'I meant it.'

He waited. Then he felt her hand atop his right knuckles where they clutched the wheel, and he let go and held her hand for a moment until she gave a squeeze and released him.

'Boyce? You don't need to come. Bring the drone in, then get me alongside and go.' She paused, waiting for him to speak. 'They're going to need you, to take down Atwater. There's people waiting for you.'

Back in Desert Storm he'd been riding along in a prop plane, buckled up in a back seat, when they'd hit a flock of seagulls, hit them hard. The windshield had shattered, the engine had died and, as it turned out, they'd even lost a wing-strut. All his piloting reactions had leaped up, his nerves jangling for action, his hands groping for controls that weren't there . . . and then, when he realized he was in the slot and going down, that it wasn't his plane, wasn't his crash, there was a sense of peace and confidence he'd never known before.

'I want to come,' he said, and in an instant all the nausea and tension sublimed right out of him.

Over the course of the flight, the drone had passed two container ships, a trawler and a good half-dozen fishing boats and yachts, but nothing shaped like the *Princess*. Off to the north-east Hammond now saw brightness, and he steered the drone's nose in that direction.

City lights, the profusion and extravagance of illumination that marked an American city. Skyscrapers, and one vaulting arch of a bridge reaching high into the night.

'Jesus,' he said. 'I think I'm in San Diego already . . . Where are we, Carla?'

'Not sure. Bright lights onshore a while back, now bright lights inland. Maybe level with Tijuana?'

He brought the drone through a long curve to the south. He hadn't been paying proper attention, hadn't realized how far north they'd come. But he couldn't have missed something as large and distinctive as the *Princess Mishail* if she'd been in sight.

He turned west and then urged the drone higher into the sky. 'We must have passed her somehow,' he said. 'I'm sweeping wide. Maybe she went far out from the coast.'

And maybe Richter had been wrong. Maybe the hijackers had sailed off to Mindinao, or Cuba, or Pakistan, to use the goods to fabricate devices. Perhaps he could glide in to San Diego International and issue an alert, let the US Navy pick up the ship before it made landfall anywhere overseas.

Then he saw her. In this part of the world, where tramp steamers had been pushed aside by containerization, her outline was unmistakable. 'Found her,' he said. 'She's running almost due east towards San Diego. Maybe fifteen miles offshore. She went wide.'

'Gotcha.' He felt the plane tilt as Carla took her further out to sea. 'How far away are you from her?'

'Half-mile at most.'

'Back off then, circle back. We need to arrive about the same time.'

'Done.' He pulled into a wide circle, not stressing the drone: now he had time to waste. San Diego glowed, and he could even make out the two 'screwdriver' buildings of downtown, the ones the locals called the Phillips and the

431

Flathead. Where the hell was the Coast Guard, the Navy? Did that mean Alvorsen hadn't made it?

'I see her,' Carla said. 'I'm going to run out and come up from behind. You still sure you want to climb on board?'

'Yeah.'

'Okay.' The plane wobbled, and he felt something being stuffed into his shirt pocket. 'The fuses for the radio. You'll want to put them somewhere safer.'

'Understood.'

'I thought you should take the drone right into the bridge, but if you're coming on board, you'll need the radio. So pick your own target.'

'Okay.'

'Boyce . . . listen. I'm going to get on deck and raise hell, then head down into the hold. That should be your signal to head for the bridge. If you clear things out, signal by turning hard to port, then overcorrect.' She paused. 'But if I get to the explosives before I get your signal, I'm going to blow the bottom out of the ship. That case, look for me in the water.'

Look for your remains in the water, you mean. 'Check. And what if they've already got the nukes piled on top of the explosives?'

'Then we improvise.'

'I'm still two minutes away,' Carla said.

'I'll buzz 'em.' He came in low over the prow of the *Princess* and saw two figures patrolling the deck, back by the bridge and the quarters. One pointed, and then both swung up their Uzis. He swerved aside and lifted, heading into a big circle.

'I hear automatics,' she said.

'They saw me. I hope you're ready, because this is my last pass . . .'

'I'm right on her tail, coming in low, starboard side. Do it.'

Hammond brought the drone round and sailed her in, twenty feet above the deck, just far enough to port to avoid the cargo derrick. A cluster of men had gathered there, weapons raised, and he tilted the nose down and dived right for them. Most of them scattered but two stood their ground, and he had the illusion that they were firing straight into his face.

For the first time in his life, he deliberately crashed, and everything went blank.

He tore off his helmet. Carla had them low to the water, coming in along the ship's starboard side, and the pontoons probed the water and then skipped across the waves.

Far forward and high above, the gasoline-laden drone exploded on deck.

'You okay?' Carla asked.

'Yeah. Just . . .'

'Then get ready to hit the water.' She cut the engine and the ship began to slide past them.

The sky and water were illuminated in flickering orange light. Hammond patted at his body, trying to reorient himself. He inflated his belly-float. He tugged on the shoulder strap of his baggie.

'C'mon,' Carla said. 'Stay a few feet behind me.'

He tried to bail out and couldn't. Seat belt, seat belt. He

unbuckled himself and then jumped into the water right behind her.

They bobbed in the water together. 'Here comes,' she said. He raised his firing tube. The bridge passed and he had an image of missing his shot, of being left floating alone at sea ten miles from land. 'Now,' she said, and the pop of her pneumatic launcher made him fire his own.

The fire still raged forward. They hooked on and set their ratchets, and then dragged themselves up to the ship's hull, a hard job with the ship underway. Carla planted her dive booties on the steel and began to run up the side, and he followed, five feet below her.

Halfway to the rail she paused and signalled him to halt. There were the sounds of cries and shouts forward. Up on the deck, right above them, he saw a man running towards the stern. The man darted a glance over the sea behind them and then turned forward, cradling an Uzi in his arms.

Carla hung on the side, braced on both feet, and took one hand off the cable to twist the ratchet on her belt. She fed out six feet of cable that dangled down from her waist in a loop.

Using both hands she ran up the side of the ship to the rail and then whipped the loop over the man's neck and let herself fall. Hammond saw her twist the ratchet. The loop took the man by the throat and launched him up and over the rail and then cinched taut. Carla landed on her toes beside Hammond, and the man's body smacked into the hull a few feet above them, suspended by his head.

She climbed up, her feet straddling the body, until she could reach the cable above his head. She braced there in a tripod and used her free hand to undo the loop round his neck, and the body splashed into the water and disappeared behind them.

Carla ran up the side, peered under the rail and then gestured for Hammond to come along.

He rolled under the rail and onto the deck. They were on the walkway beside the living quarters. The bridge stood two storeys above them.

He unbagged the MP5 and his sidearm, and stuffed two of the long, curved MP5 clips into his pants pockets. Carla had done the same. Now she motioned him to follow.

They passed the outside stairway to the bridge – usually only an emergency stair – and Carla pointed to it, and then gestured with one upraised finger, tap-tap, like a conductor cueing an orchestra. Wait . . .

There were still flickers of the fire forward, and Carla headed that way, crouched, her MP5 at the ready.

She disappeared round the corner.

He heard the MP5's throaty roar, and he turned and ran up the stairs towards the bridge.

37

Shoot the moon

The mistake most people make with an MP5, or any compact submachine gun, is sweeping too fast. A slow pivot required self-control – after all, it gave the opposition time to take aim – but it let the Room Broom do its job, which was to lay down a round every six inches, carving a circle a dozen feet from the barrel.

Carla didn't wait long enough to take in the full picture. The gasoline from the crashed drone had burned down to blue flames on the deck, and two men were directing fire extinguishers on the wreckage. Two more stood by with Uzis.

She spun on the ball of her foot, slow, deliberate, and laid out a half-moon of lead at waist height. The last man was raising his weapon when she finally finished her slow arc and he doubled over.

The second he fell she ducked down the gangway at her back. Bullets rained down on the deck where she had stood. Gunmen up on the walkway that fronted the bridge. A good move for them – guard the perimeter of your C&C – and a signal to Hammond, she hoped, since he was running their way.

She edged down two more steps and glanced out across the deck, now at eye height. There was at least one burned body in the wreckage, but she plunged down the gangway towards the hold before she could make sure if that was the only casualty of the crash.

She threw down the clip and it clanged on the stairway. So. Five down, maybe six. Ten left, maybe fifteen. She pulled another clip from the baggie slung on her shoulder and snapped it into place.

The landing. She stepped to the side, did an about-face and dropped to her knee. She peered down the next set of stairs into the aft cargo hold. There was no sign of life there, only a few scattered dummy crates.

She heard a noise behind her, at the top of the stairs, and twisted and fired up at the gangway, a single round. The shadow that had appeared there jerked out of sight. Still, it might make him a little more cautious about heading down the steps.

Her ears rang from the echo. As they cleared, she heard someone shouting instructions from the main cargo hold, forward of the big bulkhead.

She turned on the landing and stole down the stairs.

The bulkhead doorway between the aft hold and the main hold was as wide as a two-car garage. Carla stayed well to the right as she made her way across the aft hold. She edged round the doorway and then kept to starboard as she slithered into the narrow corridors between the empty plywood crates.

When she neared the middle of the hold, she peered down one of the lateral corridors. The big crates and plywood dummies blocked most of her view, but she saw the gleaming edge of the transport cask in the centre of the space.

'Get back in there! Break it now!' a voice shouted in Arabic. Break it? Or crack it, open it, expose it? Deflower it, even, in some dialects. The accent was so thick – Moroccan? – she couldn't be sure of the words that followed. They seemed to come from the opposite side of the hold, from the doorway leading on from the main hold into the foremost hold, up in the ship's prow.

She crept towards the cask, avoiding the main corridors between the boxes, working her way through the alleyways of dummy cases that towered above her head. She eased down onto her belly and crawled the last dozen feet.

The cask lid was gone. She balanced on the balls of her feet and then rose into a crouch and peered forward down the main corridor of crates. Perhaps thirty feet away, in the doorway to the forehold, six men stood.

She darted a glance into the cask. The two insulated cavities that had held the capsules were empty.

There were shouts and the booming of gunfire, and she ducked. Several rounds ricocheted from the cask and screamed away to clang against the ship's hull. She backed into the corridors of crates on the starboard side.

'He's over there!' a voice shouted in Arabic.

He, she thought. Good thing for you guys that *he* doesn't speak Arabic, isn't it?

'Hurry up in there!' the Moroccan voice said in its thick

Arabic. 'Farid – circle left, make noise. You all come with me.'

Left. The way they were facing, that would mean starboard. The others must be circling to port. Carla pushed over a crate so that it tumbled against the cask. A burst of gunfire came, and she tipped another one. She heard shouting – the leader telling them to hold fire, no doubt – and she backed between two other crates and kicked one of the plywood panels with her foot. Nails screeched as the panel inched apart from the cross-braces. She bent down and hit it with her shoulder. It gave at the top. One more firm kick at the base and it fell into the empty crate.

Forward there were a few shots. Farid raising a commotion, no doubt. She ran a dozen steps in that direction and toppled over a few more small crates.

Then she slipped back, edged round the detached panel into the empty crate, and stood the panel back up to cover the hole.

It was shadowed inside the crate, but light streamed round the edge of the panel; the nails acted as spacers, holding it a good inch inside the big cube. Better to kneel, she decided. If they saw what she had done, then the crate she was in would have a giant target on it, right about chest level.

Far off to starboard, Farid was kicking things and firing off an occasional shot. Good thing this duel was with Uzis and MP5s. A powerful gun would make the lead ricochet in here like the steelie in a pinball machine.

Even if Farid's commotion didn't serve to draw her in that direction so she could be taken from behind, it provided cover for the other men in the form of noise. She tried to ignore his sounds and listen for the muffled steps of the men stalking her.

Waiting felt wrong. How close were they to San Diego now? How close would they need to be? Everything might end here with her still waiting. And how different was their plan from the one she'd been pursuing for months? Were these men nothing more than her mirror images, on the other side?

No. What she'd been doing might have been wrong, but she'd been trying to destroy an idol, not kill civilians. And yet the men out there would consider her actions blasphemy, and their actions blessed – a building and a rock valued above the lives of millions. She might be wrong, but she wasn't the same.

She ached for something to happen, for action to silence the chatter in her head. Don't second-guess, don't think, not in the middle of things. She closed her eyes and tightened all the muscles in her body. One long squeeze, and then relaxation.

Farid popped off two more shots in the distance, but she heard footsteps approaching the cask. They seemed to gather there. A whispered quarrel in Arabic. That's good, she thought, all lean in close now, form a huddle, help me out here, boys . . .

She aimed at the wall of the crate and pulled the trigger, sweeping back and forth in a short arc until the clip was exhausted. Her fingers dropped the clip and then snapped in her last one. Light blazed through the plywood before her. The MP5 had chewed a rough sidelong slot, as though someone had assaulted the crate with a chainsaw.

Carla pulled the panel aside and leaned her head out, glancing both ways. Four men sprawled by the cask.

The sounds of running feet echoed from forward. Farid, perhaps, heading for the forward hold. She stepped out of the crate and jogged to starboard, and then set off after the footsteps, her dive booties nearly silent on the deck.

She reached the forward bulkhead and turned left. At the edge of the doorway she glanced back towards the cask. Nothing.

She peeked into the forehold. There it was, in the centre of the hold, all of the explosives from their dump, stacked six feet high like the logs for a funeral pyre. One RF detonator – at least she assumed it was radio-frequency – near the floor, jammed onto a long roll of plastique. And something shining at the top of the pile . . .

She straightened and craned her neck. One of the capsules. The lines that crazed across its surface told her it had been scored and prepared to burst apart.

The makeshift workshop at the prow of the ship came alive with blue stabs of light. Acetylene. Christ. They must have decided the way to score the capsules was with a welding torch. A millimetre too deep and everything would pour out.

She felt that tingling in her tailbone that told her someone was watching, but it was too late. Carla hurled herself sideways, back the way she'd come, but the spray of bullets from behind her had already begun. A savage blow to the chest spun her as she fell. Another took her in the left arm, and when she hit the floor her MP5 went skidding from her grip.

*

The second Hammond heard Carla open fire beside the wreckage of the ultralight, he began his run up the emergency stairway towards the bridge. Halfway up, he could tell she'd exhausted her clip, and there was only a breath-long silence before gunfire erupted above him, from the walkway outside the bridge. A trio of Uzis, maybe more.

He snapped his head up and saw a gunman leaning over the rail, firing. At that same moment the man saw him.

The gunman swept the barrel of his weapon round, still firing on automatic, and Hammond tried to do too many things at once – to squeeze against the wall below the man, to aim his MP5 up, to brace his feet on two stairs and to obey the primal instinct to duck. It might have been the sum of all those motions, or it might have been the wisdom of his body, but he fell. He fell, tumbling back onto his shoulders. Years of training took over. His finger jerked away from the trigger and clutched the body of the MP5 instead. He let himself go limp, and his body rolled and somersaulted back down the stairs and onto the deck.

He ended on his knees, and he lunged onto his belly and crawled astern, beneath the stairwell. All was silent. As the echoes in his ears cleared, he heard the innumerable sounds of a ship working its way through the sea. He rolled into a seated position, and inched back on his butt until his spine pressed against the cold steel wall of the mess hall.

Had that falling fire from the bridge taken Carla? For a moment he thought he should check. Then he shook his head. She'd given him a job, and that job wasn't to babysit her. He braced his feet and leveraged himself up the wall until he stood.

There was no chance that a frontal assault would get him to the bridge. With gunmen above, the command centre of the ship was a crenellated tower, secure behind its battlements.

Hammond edged down the wall, towards the broad stern of the ship, but kept his gaze fixed on the top landing of the stairway. A shadow forward. He fired a burst from his MP5 and felt a grim satisfaction as the figure jumped back. Not smart, though. If he'd waited, he might have hit the man.

Still, it was nice they knew he had teeth.

He crept back into the deeper shadows at the rear of the ship. Somewhere miles behind them, in the ship's wake, their ultralight floated on its pontoons. He pictured some fisherman finding it in the morning light, a fragile aeroplane abandoned on the surface of the Pacific, and tried to imagine the stories the man would invent to explain it to himself . . .

. . . If anyone in San Diego was still fishing tomorrow morning. He knew what his mind was doing, for he was a master at it – dodging about, looking away from the real problem, hoping things would sort themselves out. If Carla were alive, she needed his help. If Carla were dead, then he was the only person left to prevent what was coming. He ought to muster up his courage and charge the bridge . . . but that would be suicide. Suicide might solve all his personal problems, but it wouldn't solve anything else.

His shoulder bumped against one of the big pipes that ran up the side of the main tower. Exhaust, a standpipe, ventilation? He should have learned the ship better. He should have done a thousand things better. He stepped out and round the pipe, and then relaxed back behind it, grateful to have something solid between his body and the stairs.

Their climbing packs lay beneath the railing across from him, the grappling hooks still hanging on the top rail. Their ladder, their gateway, the elevator that had brought them to this. At any moment a cloud of radioactive dust could erupt from the ship. At any moment Carla could be successful, and the hull of the ship could burst in an explosion that would send them straight to the bottom. The easiest thing might be to grab one of the cables and lower himself into the Pacific. Leave it up to God to sort out.

As he saw it, there were two things that could happen now. They might come after him, circling round from both sides. Or they might just wait. What difference did he make, hiding here at the rear of the ship? Why even bother to track him down?

He heard the distant, hollow sound of gunfire down in the hold.

Carla must still be alive.

He poked his head out past the shelter of the pipe and peered back the way he'd come.

A burst of automatic fire came down the deck from beyond the stairs.

Hammond jerked the barrel of his MP5 round the pipe and answered in short bursts. As he did, he stepped out into the walkway and scuttled to the rail. With his left hand, he grabbed one of the grappling hooks from the top rail. Firing with one hand, his shots were going wild, but these rounds were all for show anyway. He used the hook and cable to drag the whole belt along after him as he slid behind the cover of the pipe.

He dropped the clip and snapped in another before buckling on the climbing belt. He released the ratchet and let the cable feed back into the reel. He snapped the three-pronged hook back and stuffed the sabot back into the tube. When he released it, the firing tube dangled down between his legs like some obscene joke.

He found the pneumatic lever on his left hip, cocked it and began to pump air into the chamber. Each stroke gave more resistance, until at last he had to grit his teeth and lean against the wall to lock the lever down.

Down at the stern corner of the living quarters he peeked round to the port side. Night, sky and sea.

He backed up against the stern rail. The wake of the big prop churned the waters behind him. He aimed his firing tube up and then squeezed the release. The satisfying *pop* reverberated in his pelvis as the sabot launched, and the hook flew in a long, high arc, up above the roof of the bridge.

Be ready, don't get preoccupied. He hefted the MP5 in his arms and looked right and left, ready for someone to come round the corners.

Nothing. He set the ratchet, and felt the flywheel start to reel in the slack.

Far forward, disguised by yards of steel and buried beneath the thrum of the big diesel engines, he heard more gunfire from deep within the ship.

The cable stopped feeding. It had latched onto something. He let the MP5 hang from his shoulder. A tug on the line. It felt firm, but who could tell? One of Carla's first lessons had been to make sure you had hooked something that could support your weight . . .

Under the circumstances, that was like pausing to look both ways before crossing the street when you were already dodging bullets.

Hammond yanked hard, leaned back and decided to trust it. He ran across the short stern deck and started up the two-storey wall, keeping up his momentum. Twenty feet up the wall, ten feet from the top, he hesitated, and wondered why.

Then Carla's words – quoting someone, he supposed – came back to him: *Going in, decide first if you're the hunter or the hunted.*

It was a hell of a place to take a stand: years late, and with no firm ground beneath his feet. But Hammond stopped climbing, set his ratchet and then walked himself in a series of stump-footed pirouettes, wrapping the cable in three turns round his waist. When he was done, he was suspended out at right angles to the wall, his feet planted on steel, his face and his MP5 facing the rolling deck of the ship's stern. There. In the blind, waiting for the morning mists to rise. A hunter.

The whole ship might go up in a radioactive cloud – big joke on him, hanging here waiting; or Carla might blast the bottom out – big joke on his Arab buddies below, halfway around the world and tens of millions of dollars to the wind, just to gurgle down into the drink.

But he'd wait now. He'd wait because it was his decision.

A minute more might settle the fate of millions. Too bad. He'd spend his minute as he pleased. The citizens of San Diego, they were making choices, too, like all of us did every minute of our lives. Spending time. Microwaving that burrito, flipping on the TV, saying something cutting to a spouse, placing a comforting touch on a child's arm, casting a seductive glance over a shoulder, calling back to the office, yelling at the dog. Decisions, every one.

Humans make bad targets from directly above. Maybe, Hammond thought, that's why God seems to hit the wrong person so damn often.

One of the Arabs rounded from the port side, and two from starboard. As targets, they were nothing more than heads atop shoulders. He waited until they converged to confer, and then he gave them everything that was in the clip, hurling death from above, a murder as dispassionate as a shower of meteors.

Not even one shot came in reply.

He unwound himself, reversing his ungainly pirouettes, and reset the ratchet to resume his climb. Once he breasted the roof of the bridge, he saw what he'd been suspended from: a small dish antenna had been bent flat to the roof by his cable.

Hammond undid the hooks from the aluminium channel of the antenna. His fingers fumbled at the MP5's clip, dropped it and pulled out the remaining one: snap it in place, flip off the safety and stand erect. Crazed, drunken, half-dead: he stood on the roof of the bridge, all of the Southern California coast visible before him in a golden, pixellated miasma that hovered over the black sea.

A new sound, the sound of hydraulics. He ran towards the front of the bridge. Far forward, the forehatch was grinding open.

From the opening hold came the thick, palpable boom of an explosion, and he knew things were at an end.

He hadn't thought it would be like this – that his only thoughts would be of vengeance. Yet he hooked his three-pronged grapple to an exhaust pipe, yanked out some slack, set his ratchet and hurled himself forward over the roof.

38

Seeing stars

Carla sat up, groping at the holster for Alvorsen's Walther P99, and she tried to push up onto her feet, but her left arm collapsed under her. Broken. Not just a flesh wound, but a broken arm. Shit.

But still, an amateur. If he'd had any patience, he would have cut her in half.

From the main hold, where the gunman had been, she heard footsteps and a voice shouting in Arabic, 'Now! Now! Don't wait!'

Carla lay onto her back and spun in a circle. She brought her heels up by her buttocks and then kicked, sliding herself head-first across the deck and into the doorway.

The man who'd shot her was about ten paces away, running towards her, and she pumped four rounds into him.

She heard the whine and roar of hydraulics and chain-drives, and the forehatch began opening to the night sky.

Carla rolled onto her knees and braced on her right hand to help herself to her feet, crushing her fingertips between the pistol and the deck. Only then did she feel a gurgle from her chest. She looked down and saw red foam bubbling just below her right breast. Not good. She might not have long.

She staggered into the forehold. At first she saw no one, but then, over on the starboard hull, she saw a scraggly man working the switchbox. One hand sat on the hatch control, but in the other he held an RF controller, its antenna dangling from his fingers. His Uzi hung from his shoulder.

Stupid, stupid. One hand for yourself, ladies, but your best hand on your weapon.

Pistols weren't her strong point, not at this distance, but she aimed and squeezed, flexing her wrist just a bit to get some spread. A twelve-round magazine, standard on the new Walther, and she gave him the remaining eight.

She might have hit him with the very first shot – she couldn't be sure – but his arms flew up and the RF controller did a long dive through the air as the spent brass rained down round her wrist. He slammed up against the hull, and it seemed as though he had been held upright by her gunfire, because when the last empty cartridge chimed on the floor he slumped, dragging his back down the wall.

Christ in a Kotex, her arm hurt. One of the bullets must have gone right through the bone. She tried to remember – did that mean that she was more likely, or less likely, to bleed to death? She needed to bind it up, either way, and get this chest wound to stop sucking . . . but first she should get the RF transmitter. No. The detonator. No, no, no, she needed to get the capsule the hell off the top of the explosives – then, if they wanted to blow a hole in the ship they were welcome . . .

Right. Right. Get the capsule.

She stumbled towards the stack of explosives, and was only a few steps away when she heard something.

Running. Stealthy little steps, but running.

She looked back. A man, darting towards where the other man had fallen. He still wore his welding gloves.

The detonator.

She hurled herself across the floor, skidding on her knees, and ripped the fist-sized boomer from the plastique. She turned. The man had the RF controller in one gloved hand and groped at it with the other, trying to flip up the switch-guard. He cried out in fury and shook the glove from his hand and flipped the switch, but as the glove fell, Carla spun and hurled the detonator.

It was a good, hard pitch. They hadn't let girls in Little League, not back then, but her brother Kevin had taught her everything he learned, every weekend evening in the season, coaching her. This was easy, really. It wasn't like the man had a bat or anything, he had no time to prepare, no time to rub his nose or spit or tug up his pants or waggle his butt.

And almost was good enough.

The force of the detonator's explosion knocked her back against the pile of plastique and gasogens. She waited. Plastique slumped to conform to pressure, but only slowly, like putty, and the longer she lay there, the more comfortable it became. Explosives were touchy, unpredictable – more so, in some ways, than people. It could all go up now.

Nothing happened.

Over against the hull, by the switchbox, her rival had been splattered into a mess that reminded her of the Driver's Ed films she'd watched in high school.

Damn, her arm hurt. Her arm hurt, and the vague ache in her chest threatened to blossom into something huge. She wished she had a first-aid kit, even something rudimentary. Jesus, at this point even an aspirin would have been welcome; but no, aspirin slowed down clotting, did something to fibrinogen and platelets or something, so she sure couldn't have any, which didn't matter because there weren't any aspirin here in the first place.

It was still up there, at the top of the pyramid. She rolled onto her knees and began dragging herself up to the top of the pile. Not so hard, really; they'd stacked them in nice, set-back rows, like the rice terraces she'd seen in South-East Asia.

There it was. So much trouble over something so small. When they'd taken it from the *Pontianak*, it had been flawless, smooth, as close to silken as metal can be. Now the surface was rough and uneven where acetylene torches had eaten into it, the cuts edged with alternating pits and lumps.

She fell back on the bagged explosives at the top of the pyramid, and then shifted her hips to get some leverage. She pressed her heels against the cylinder. How much had Lorrie said these would weigh? Maybe three hundred pounds? Or did she mean three hundred kilos? If it were three hundred kilos, she couldn't move it, could she?

She pushed, and lifted her hips, and put everything into it, from her pelvis up to her jaw, her good hand clutching at the bags of gasogens beneath her, and at last it moved. It moved, and it rocked, and then finally it rolled away, and her legs pushed out flat and she heard the bong as the cylinder clanged onto the deck, and then a long, hushed grumble as it ran away from the explosives and sought the wall.

The hatchway above her was a black square cut in the upper deck, but as she let herself relax, she thought she could see stars in the sky.

Her arm needed binding up. Plastic wrap around her chest to slow the bleeding and keep her lung from collapsing. Her duty. She knew it was her duty – she was getting stupid. But she wanted to take just a few more moments to gaze at the stars. Hard to believe they were always up there, even in the day. Hard to believe.

The force of the belt around his waist drove all the breath from Hammond's body, but he could still squeeze a trigger, and he did, firing through the windows of the bridge. The motion of the sea used him as a pendulum, and revolved him until he swung upside-down, yet he contorted himself with every motion to keep the gun aimed through the shattering windows, and kept the trigger depressed long after he'd swept the bridge clear of life, long after his store of bullets was depleted.

Then all was quiet except for the sounds of the ship working its way through the waves. Still swinging from side to side on his back, suspended from his waist, he rolled his head to look forward at the open cargo hatch near the prow. No cloud of radioactive dust glittering in the darkness. No sign the ship was taking on water.

He did what she'd asked – hard a-port, then starboard – before he inserted the fuse into the radio. He didn't bother with the Coast Guard or even the Bureau; he called the First Marine Expeditionary Force near Del Mar, where he knew people he'd trust at his back. *No Beach Too Far*, their motto ran. Try me, boys. This beach was only five miles from San Diego harbour.

He cut the engines and let the *Princess* drift with the swells.

Down the stairs, four landings and into the stern hold. No more ammo for his MP5; he carried someone's thirty-eight in his hand. Who had elected the thirty-eight as their sidearm? Someone, someone in the Allens, but already the men he'd lived with for more than three years were becoming insubstantial, ghostly, as was the whole ship. It might be that he was the only one alive.

His eyes caught a motion in the room, and he pointed the pistol. It was Carla.

She sat with her back against a crate, an Uzi against her shoulder. When she sensed him there, she whipped the barrel in his direction, holding it in one arm. A strip of blue tarp had been wound round her chest. Dark liquid stained the waist of her shirt.

Her eyes focused on him and she tried to struggle to her feet. Her left arm hung useless at her side, and Hammond saw that it had been bandaged with uneven strips of cloth. 'They coming?' she asked. 'Our guys?'

'Yeah,' he said. He thumbed the safety and fit the pistol into his belt. 'Come on. We need to get you on deck for MedEvac.'

She shook her head and gazed down. 'I'm hot,' she said, and he heard a wheeze in her breath. On her chest, her rad-badge showed bright yellow. 'You have to tell them. It cracked. In the forehold. Keep everybody out of here unless they have rad-suits.'

'Carla.' He stepped down onto the deck of the cargo hold and walked towards her, one hand out to help her up. 'Come on, Carla, let's go upstairs.'

She braced the Uzi in her good arm. 'I was there when it broke. *I think maybe it got on me.* Don't you get it?'

He shook his head and kept walking. Damned if he was going to let her sit down here and die. 'Carla. The badge is still yellow. Come up on deck. We won . . .'

A drop of bubbly red spit dribbled over her lower lip. 'Nobody won.' She gestured at him with the barrel of the gun. 'Now get out of here or I'll shoot you.'

He shook his head. 'You're not going to shoot me.' He was no more than a dozen feet away from her. He put his hands up but kept advancing. 'Just let me help you up the stairs—'

She had it on single shot, and the bullet took him in the left calf.

He cried out, as much in shock as in pain, and fell to the floor. His hands clutched at his leg, but his face looked up. 'Carla—'

The barrel of the gun wobbled. 'I won't kill you, Hammond,' she said, the gurgle from her lungs loud now, 'but, swear to God, if you don't get the fuck out of here, I *will* cripple you.'

Blood welled under his fingers. It doesn't have to be like this, he wanted to say, but what did he know about it? What did he know about anything?

He pushed himself back to the gangway, skidding on his

butt. His leg left a long smear of blood. Now this is madness, he thought. You survive everything you've come through, and take your first wound from someone trying to help you?

He clawed at the balustrade of the gangway and pulled himself to his feet, though his left leg wouldn't support any weight. He hopped round to face her. If he couldn't help her, he at least needed to persuade her to crawl out into the open air.

She sat cross-legged, bent over the Uzi on her lap like a tailor over his cloth.

He had only opened his mouth before she looked up at him. She gave him a sad smile and blew a kiss. 'Don't think I won't shoot you again, Boyce,' she said. 'I will.'

He dragged himself up the gangway, his face burning with pain and humiliation, and pulled himself out onto the deck to wait for the Marines.

39

Badges

On the crowded Metro, a young black man in a floppy beret rose from his seat and offered it to Hammond. Hammond stood there like a fool until he realized that he'd been transformed from a healthy member of the public into a man with a cane.

What the hell, his leg hurt. 'Thanks,' he said, and sat.

Several of the standing passengers were reading the paper. The normally staid *Post* shouted: 'FBI, HOMELAND SECURITY FOIL NUCLEAR ATTACK ON U.S.' from its banner, and Hammond found himself staring. He'd read the article that morning – no mention of the Allens, no details of any involvement from inside America. A band of Arabs had hijacked an Indonesian nuclear shipment, and only quick action by the government had avoided disaster.

The kid in the beret noticed Hammond's scrutiny of the paper. 'Government earning their pay for a change, huh?'

'Yeah,' Hammond said, 'I feel safer already.' The train slowed for the Dupont Circle stop, and he climbed to his feet.

He took a back booth in the Portobello Grille, sat facing

457

the door and ordered a meal he didn't want. It had been strange being back at the Bureau, and in the few days since he'd arrived he'd used his hero status shamelessly – twisting arms and cashing in favours, even making unkeepable promises and vague threats.

Prescott Wainwright pushed through the front door and stretched his portly frame upwards, surveying the restaurant. Peering about, he looked like a marmot searching for danger, and Hammond imagined that at any moment the man might give a whistle of alarm and bolt for his burrow.

Hammond half-stood and waved two fingers. Wainwright huffed his bulk through the dining tables and stopped at the booth. 'You told me this concerned my son,' he said, and drew a long, trembling breath. 'You had details that seemed authentic, but—'

'Sit down, Mr Wainwright.'

'. . . but, but I'm warning you, if this is some sort of a blackmail attempt, I'm going straight to the police.'

Hammond reached inside his jacket and pulled out the folder that held his badge and ID. He flipped them open and slapped them down on the tabletop. 'I am the goddamn police. Now sit down.'

Wainwright slid into the booth, shaking. 'My son—' he began.

'Is an average Ivy League white-collar crook. Using your money to do most of it, I might add. SEC and the Bureau have both been watching him and his pals for a while. Let's see, what else? He's banging two of the secretaries in his office, which is a pretty good average since there's only five in the place. I'm sure that one of them would be happy to launch a

458

fat sexual-harassment lawsuit with a little encouragement. So we could be talking divorce, and a huge cash settlement, on top of the prison term he's got coming. Furthermore—'

'What is it you want?' A pulse throbbed at the man's perspiring temple, and Hammond worried that he might have a stroke.

'. . . when it comes to your daughter, I don't care who she screws, or how many of them, but she's going to be in the wrong house at the wrong time some day soon, and then she'll be up on big-time drug charges.'

'I don't have as much money as you think!' The man wiped his forehead. 'I'm willing to deal with you, but I'm not a billionaire.'

'I'm not after your money.' Hammond waited for that to sink in. 'I want to talk about Atwater and Richter.'

'Well.' Emotions battled for control of Wainwright's expression: confusion, surprise, alarm and just a touch of growing relief. 'Rex I know, of course – everybody knows Rex. Lamont Richter I've only met briefly . . .'

'Richter's dead. And so are most of the people involved in the whole Mecca scheme.' He watched the shock reverberate across the man's jowly face. 'I'm not asking for much. Just the truth about the government side.'

Wainwright took a deep breath. 'It's a complicated situation, but I can—'

'Not here, not now. I need a real statement.'

The man nodded. 'And, in return . . . ?'

'I can back off some of the dogs. But as to your kids' chosen lifestyles, that's your problem. I think the fruit of your loins need a long talking-to.' Hammond pulled a folded sheet of paper from his shirt pocket and pushed it across the table. 'Another thing. Atwater needs to set up some big trust funds. Widows, orphans, cripples. Girlfriends of murdered men. Sisters. Mothers.' He leaned his forearms onto the table. 'If he's smart, the generosity he shows will be legendary.'

He needed to collect three temporary badges to be admitted to the special basement ward of Walter Reed Army Hospital, but when he limped off the elevator on the bottom floor, there was no one there – no nurses' desk, no receptionist, only long linoleum corridors that smelled of pine-scented disinfectant.

The first office down the left side of the hallway wasn't an office at all, but some sort of lab. An abandoned lab, for all he could tell – amidst the glassware, a half-eaten sandwich lay on a napkin as though the site had been evacuated by some emergency.

He wandered further down the hall until he came to a window that looked into a large room. Three figures in white rad-suits clustered round a bed. When the one near the head of the bed stepped aside, he saw there was a patient in the bed.

It took longer to recognize the patient as Carla. She looked like the poster girl for a battered women's shelter: her eyes sunken in a bruised face, her left arm in a cast, her chest bound in bandages, her right arm a mass of tubes and surgical tape. Always pale, she now looked as though they had drained all her blood. Only a week since they'd taken the *Princess Mishail*, and the strongest woman he'd ever known was a ruin.

He blinked hard and dropped his gaze to the floor, but

then forced himself to look again. One of the technicians noticed him then, waved an angry hand as though warding him off and jerked the curtains closed.

Down the hall he heard hurrying footsteps. 'Mr Hammond?' He turned.

The doctor – probably forty-five, and tennis-player fit – smiled in relief and jogged the remaining distance, white coat flapping, a clipboard in one hand. 'I'm so sorry, Mr Hammond. I'd left word upstairs they were to contact me the moment you checked in, but we were on Grand Rounds and – well, I apologize.' He held out his hand. 'McCloskey. I'm lead consultant on your sister's case.'

Hammond shook the man's hand. 'My sister?'

'You aren't . . .?' The man peered at his clipboard and read. 'Next of kin: Boyce Hammond. Relationship: Brother.' The man stared at the badge clipped to Hammond's pocket. 'That's what she said on admittance . . .'

'It's true,' Hammond said. 'But it's . . . not widely known.'

'Ah.' McCloskey nodded. 'We gathered there was something special about this patient.'

'Can I see her? What's her – her outlook?'

'You can't see her, not yet. We're hitting her with every chelating agent known, trying to pull out any heavy stuff she might have taken in. We've changed 100 per cent of her blood already, and by tomorrow we'll have changed it again . . .' The man shook his head. 'Do you know much about these things, Mr Hammond?'

'Not much. Cancer. Hair falling out. All that.'

'Sure. But she didn't get dosed that high, and we're cleaning her up. It's . . . a combination of things here. The radiation

461

won't kill her now. But it suppresses her immune responses, and it slows healing, and this woman was terribly hurt irrespective of the radiation exposure. The gunshot wounds themselves . . .' His eyes darted round Hammond's face as the man wondered how much to say. 'I'm going to be frank. I've seen people die from far less. But I've seen people far worse off get up and walk away.' He put a hand on Hammond's shoulder. 'I talked to her when she first came in. She seems tough.'

Hammond ran the back of his hand across his eyes. 'She's tough, all right.'

'Then there's plenty of room for hope. And if she makes it through the next few days, there's no reason she shouldn't make a full recovery. But—' The doctor paused, uncomfortable. 'She's designated you as the person to make decisions about . . . protocols and procedures.'

'Meaning?'

'There's times, in the course of something like this, when the patient may end up on life-support for some time. In some cases, for a very long time indeed. Ms Smukowski designated you to decide – *if* it should come up, I'm not saying it will – whether we should terminate life-support or take heroic measures to preserve life.'

The thought of Carla lingering on, with some machine breathing for her, was almost more than his heart could take. Yet the doctor's words echoed in his ears, and at last he smiled. 'Keep her alive,' he said. 'For her, yeah. Heroic measures.'

A corner window office, filled with custom furniture instead of government-issued junk. A carpet on the floor. Hammond knew that in DC these trappings meant something specific about rank, like the number of guns employed in a salute, but protocol had never been his strong subject.

A couch and two armchairs faced off over a coffee table on the other side of the room, but Hammond and Troy had been ushered towards two chairs that faced the desk. Richard Moffatt, the young, bespectacled Deputy Assistant Under-secretary for Something-or-Another, had bustled in late, shaken their hands and then assumed his seat behind the desk with a gravity that suggested he was taking the helm of a ship.

Moffatt rubbed his palms together. 'To begin, let me express on behalf of the Attorney-General, and the whole Department, our gratitude for an extraordinary job. We understand the sacrifices you've—'

'What happens now?' Hammond asked.

The man frowned. 'Hmm? If you'd let me—'

'What happens now? To Atwater, to the bullshit story you're putting out . . .'

Moffatt's chuckle suggested that they had shared an inside joke. 'Under the circumstances, we can't really prose-cute Rex Atwater without having *everything* come out . . . I'm sure *you* don't want that, and neither does the Adminis-tration. Atwater's not in a position to do any damage, and we feel the general effect on the country of this little nuclear contretemps has been entirely salutary, raising awareness of a problem that—'

'That the fucking AG helped create. Give me one good reason why I shouldn't march out of here over to the *Washington Post*.'

Moffatt listened to this while bringing his fingertips

together, then moving his palms wide apart and then bringing them together, as though playing a concertina. 'Very well. I'll give you four reasons: Ray McCann, dozens of weapons charges plus all manner of conspiracy; Jack Alvorsen, the same list; Earlene McCann, obstruction of justice; and Carla Smukowski – well, everything from obstruction to conspiracy to piracy on the high seas.' He made a throwaway gesture with one hand. 'I should also remind you that you're still an employee of the FBI, and that much of the information about the operation you've been engaged in is classified. With the provisions of the Patriot Act, well . . .'

'I'm not an FBI employee any more. I resign.'

Moffatt laughed, an easy, false, we're-all-friends-here laugh. 'No. Because I've placed you on administrative leave. Six months, full pay. You've been under all kinds of stress. Now isn't the time to make decisions. Take a vacation. Spend some time with your girlfriend, give that leg some time to heal. And when you come back . . . well, a promotion seems in line. You're a hero here, Boyce. Rest on your laurels a while.'

'That's not how it's going to come down. I want a little justice here.'

Moffatt folded his hands on the table. 'Mr Hammond, I think we've already been more than generous. Carla Smukowski is getting the best care Uncle Sam can provide. If it weren't for the extraordinary steps we've taken, she could be dying in some third-rate prison hospital right now.'

The man smiled, and in his mind Hammond slapped Moffatt's face with such force that the man spilled out of his chair and onto the carpet. The image was so vivid and tempting that for a moment he thought he might have done it in reality. 'No. It's not even close to enough. People died. Whole cities could have died – San Diego, Mecca, at this point I don't give a shit which.' Moffatt opened his mouth, but Hammond cut him off with a pointed finger. 'As far as I'm concerned, the people at the top who let this happen are war criminals, and they're going down.'

A condescending smile from Moffatt. 'People at the top had nothing to do with this.'

'The hell they didn't.'

'Oh? Where's your evidence? You've got nothing more than he-said she-said.' The smile faded from Moffatt's face. 'If we wanted to, we could even come after you, Mr Hammond. There isn't a shred of evidence that the Bureau, or DOJ, encouraged you to participate in this crazy scheme.' The smile returned, but now it was malicious. 'And once Federal prosecutors go after you, the truth doesn't matter much, now does it?'

Troy leaned sideways in his seat and put his hand on Hammond's arm. 'He's right, Boyce. Back off.'

Hammond jerked his arm away and stared at Troy. 'And you won't tell them the truth?'

'Where's the point? You aren't going to win.'

Hammond watched Troy until the man looked away, out the window.

He turned back to Moffatt. 'Where's my evidence? Alvorsen, Smukowski, McCann. Atwater.' Moffatt shrugged. 'Plus a tape of Troy instructing me to continue pushing ahead with the scheme—'

'You taped me?' Troy asked. '*Me?*'

'At the hospital after French got shot.' Hammond glanced at Troy. 'That's right, search your memory, try and remember what the hell you said.'

'Rogue agent,' Moffatt said, though the way his shoulders hunched up showed the man didn't care for surprises. 'Doesn't prove anything.'

'I also have a long Q&A video with Prescott Wainwright, Senior, where he names the AG and Jake Landau, his Special Legal Counsel. Names, dates, times. I have Richter on tape.' He prepared himself to sound casual, the best way of selling a lie. 'I have Atwater on tape, I—'

'*You have tape on Atwater?*' Troy asked, his voice three keys higher than usual.

'. . . have things you can't even imagine. If I open this can, they're going to smell it all the way out in Fargo, North Dakota.'

Hammond studied Moffatt's wrinkled brow.

'I know what you're thinking,' Hammond said, 'and you can forget about it. Duplicate, triplicate, septiplicate. I have copies of the evidence stashed everywhere, and not just in the US. Anything happens to me, it all comes out, and you shouldn't doubt it for a second – I was trained by the best.'

Moffatt drew in a breath and exhaled heavily. 'What is it you want?'

'Landau. The AG. Anybody else in Justice who knew.'

'And?'

'An investigation. One that goes wherever the facts lead. Right up to the President, if necessary.'

Moffatt took this in, and then laughed – not a nice laugh, but one that bespoke genuine amusement. 'It doesn't work like that any more. This isn't the Watergate era. We're post Iran-Contra. Nothing sticks and nobody cares.' He clasped his hands, elbows on the desktop, and released his index fingers and bobbed them at Hammond like a wobbly cannon. 'It all comes out at the end? This isn't Hollywood.'

'I wasn't thinking of Hollywood,' Hammond said, 'I was thinking of junior-high civics class.'

'You probably were,' Moffatt said, 'that's about your speed. News bulletin, Boyce – I can call you Boyce, can't I? If it saved them three cents on toilet paper, the citizens of this country would be happy to wipe their asses with the Bill of Rights.'

Hammond sat and stared until Moffatt looked down at his leather desk blotter.

After a long pause, Moffatt rose from his chair and paced back and forth in front of the window, drumming his fingertips together just below his chin. 'The AG is on his way out anyhow . . . Jake Landau, he doesn't matter – shoot him, for all I care. Resignations. A few others trashed in Justice, and maybe a couple in the FBI . . . Would that satisfy you?'

'Resignations? I want them prosecuted.'

The laugh that came from Moffatt was like a bark. 'You're living in a fantasy. Resignation is a big deal these days. Nobody even resigned after 9/11.'

'People need to know the truth.'

'The people who count will. The AG will do the "mission accomplished" speech you give when you've fucked up, and everybody'll know he's taking off with his tail between his legs.' Moffatt leaned his palms down on the desktop. 'As for the "People" with a capital "P", fuck 'em. Jefferson nailed it two hundred years ago: in a democracy, "the people" get the kind of government they deserve.' Moffatt dropped into his chair as though the subject was closed.

Hammond closed his eyes. Moffatt's position was half-bluff and half the reality of politics after the turn of the century.

He stood, limped round the desk and leaned on his cane, staring down at the man. 'I want those resignations right away. No more of this dick-waving about how we foiled the terrorists. Not by those guys.'

Moffatt nodded, short, curt and unambiguous.

'Another thing. I disappear or go out of commission – everything goes public, big time. And the same thing if Carla Smukowski dies. Everything.'

'Oh, be reasonable,' Moffatt said. 'We're doing everything we can for the woman, and the doctors say her prognosis isn't bad. But we can't perform miracles.'

'And as I understand it, this Administration is filled with born-again Christians. Maybe they should get together and have a prayer breakfast.'

He turned and headed for the door. 'Take some time and think about it,' Moffatt called after him. 'Going public – I assure you, you don't want to do it.'

Hammond braced his cane and looked back. 'I'm divorced, no kids. Parents long dead. Been somebody else for more than three years. No friends, no family. But you're too eloquent for your own good, Moffatt. You just convinced me my country's gone, too. So if Carla dies . . .' The word made his throat constrict, and he waited for a moment. 'Don't fuck with somebody who's lost it all.'

He trudged out into the hallway, letting the pain in his calf make him grit his teeth at every step. Behind him, he heard lowered contentious voices, Troy conversing with Moffatt, but he strode on down to the elevator.

Troy caught up with him before a car had arrived. 'Suits,' Troy said. 'The whole DOJ. Politicians.' He laid a hand on Hammond's shoulder. 'This wasn't our show. Don't blame the Bureau.'

The elevator's bell rang and the doors slid open. 'I don't blame the Bureau,' Hammond said. 'But I sure as hell blame you.' He stepped into the empty elevator and pointed back at Troy with his cane, as though fending him off. 'From now on, you stay the hell away from me, you understand?'

The doors closed. He rode down to the ground floor and tossed his badges across the table of the security desk.

Outside the Dupont Café he studied Earlene through the window. She was engrossed in a fat paperback fantasy novel with a glass of white wine at her elbow. The index finger of her free hand coiled and uncoiled a strand of hair. Sensing his gaze from beyond the windowpane, she looked up and smiled.

She stood to kiss him when he came to the table. 'How's Carla?'

He nudged out a chair with his good leg and they both sat. 'I don't know. Not good.'

'Ray called,' she said. 'His leg's gonna be okay, some day . . . but they have to put in some kind of rod or something for the bones to regrow around.'

'Earlene . . . I've got something to tell you. A really long story.'

'Is it about us?'

'Yes and no. It's about me.' He sighed. 'Suppose I started by telling you that my name isn't my real name.'

'You're not named Boyce?'

It started as a chuckle and then turned into a laugh, and then a hard belly laugh that had tears running from his eyes, and he knew that in a moment it would turn to sobs, and now wasn't the time for that.

Earlene touched his arm, and he swallowed the saliva that had gathered in his mouth as though he were choking down a fistful of vitamins. Through watery eyes he saw her peering into his face. 'Hon,' she asked, 'you okay?'

He sniffled and calmed himself. 'I'm named Boyce. Just not Hammond. But everybody still calls me that. Try Harrison. Boyce Harrison.'

'That's not a very long story.' She leaned over and kissed his cheek. 'I've known for ages that there was plenty you didn't tell me. I don't need to know everything.'

'I want you to know it all.'

'Then let's go get dinner. A nice dinner with a nice bottle of wine, and you can tell me everything.' She gave him a worried frown. 'Is your leg okay? I mean, are you good to walk for a while? Because I wouldn't mind walking around the Lincoln Memorial, and the pools, and the park and all that before we eat, and you said you wanted to get more exercise, work the leg a little . . .'

'I'd love it.'

They paid her bill and stepped out onto the sidewalk.

'You know,' Earlene said, 'I'm not so sure you know me, either.' He glanced at her, unsure of her meaning. 'What you've seen isn't all of me, not by a long shot. I got things I want to do, and I'm a lot more than you think . . . Boyce whatever-the-hell-your-name-is. I been sitting around a couple of years now, hoping you'd grow out of this whole Allens thing . . . Hadn't been for you, I'd have headed off for college somewhere.'

Earlene, college? It had never occurred to him. He laughed. 'You don't know me. I guess I don't know you, either. Suppose we get to know each other and don't like what we find? Suppose we figure out we'd be happier with somebody else?'

She shrugged. 'This book I'm reading, one of the characters quotes the Buddha, or somebody, and he says that all suffering comes from wanting things to be something other than what they really are.'

The fall weather was fine, one of those deceptive days that suggested to visitors that Washington had a livable climate. He asked, 'You ever think about moving somewhere else?'

She hugged up against his arm. 'And leave Stockton? Oh, boo-hoo.'

'Where would you go? If you could pick some place, where would it be?'

'I've never been much of any place.' She glanced up at the sky. 'I could live here, I guess.'

'Not *here*,' he said, and then laughed at his own overreaction. 'Sorry. But, Christ, anywhere but here.'

'Well, wherever, then. Every place is new to me.'

That must feel good, he thought, but he said nothing,

settling instead for squeezing her hand where it held his arm. He thought of Carla in her hospital bed, her valiant little body fighting for life; of McCann, with his leg being pieced back together by a team of surgeons; of Gianetti, wearing a lead cloak at the bottom of the sea; of poor Lorrie, who'd been both right about him and yet wrong; and of all the other wounded and dead and deceived, wherever they might be. And for just the remainder of one day, just for this one evening, he decided to be a Buddhist, and let things be what they were.

Together Boyce and Earlene stepped onto the ribbed steel stairs of the Metro escalator, and some trick breeze blew the first leaves of fall round their ankles as they descended from the street.